The Sonoma Project

A Dodson Novel
Book 1

VERNON JESSUP

ISBN-13 978-0-9914413-1-0

LR 150422

To see a description of my other books go to:

www.vernonjessup.com

DEDICATION

This book is dedicated to Marsha, my wife of over 36 years.

ACKNOWLEDGMENTS

I would like to thank Marsha Jessup, my wife and editor, for her support during this project. Also I want to thank Kerry Fleet for taking the time to be my copy editor.

The unique aircraft featured in my book and book cover is a Rutan Long-EZ. It is a home-built aircraft with a canard layout designed by Burt Rutan's Rutan Aircraft Factory.

I would like to give a special thanks to Ken Miller. He is the proud owner and builder of the aircraft you see on the book cover. His patience and hard work in building this aircraft from scratch really shows.

The photo of the motorcycle is from:
www.canstockphoto.com/Stevemc

I would also like to give a shout out to the following:

Dale Martin of Owl Eagle Aerial Composites for introducing me to Ken Miller.
www.Long-ez.com

Matthew Tait, President and Chief Engineer TERF Inc. for taking time to talk to me.
www.dragonaero.com

Erlend Moen for taking time to talk to me.
www.cozy.ljosnes.no/calendar.html

Chapter 1

Las Vegas, Nevada

"Beep, Beep."

Kate jerked and opened one eye. The fog in her mind pulled her eyelid down again.

"Beep, Beep."

She forced both eyes open and sat up on the side of the bed. As the fog slowly evaporated, she turned her head and scanned the darkened room. Her eyes stopped on the chest of drawers across the room as she remembered that her purse was on top of it.

"Beep, Beep."

She stood up and started toward it. "Oh, man, I'm sore!" she mumbled, glancing at Randy and smiling at the memory of their night together.

"Beep, Beep."

Still drowsy, she focused on her purse as she started across the dark room. She didn't see Randy's straw hat in the middle of the floor with her panties draped across it and she stepped in the center of it, putting her foot through one of the panties's leg holes. Startled by the sudden crunch of the straw and feeling something around her ankle, she jumped forward, turning as she did, and lost her balance.

"Beep, Beep."

She fell backwards into the chest of drawers, causing it to bounce against the wall. Her purse fell off and hit her on the shoulder as she landed sitting on the floor with her back against the drawers and her panties dangling from her foot.

Randy jerked awake, sat up and said, "What the hell!"

Awake now, but dazed, she stared up at his dumbfounded expression.

"Are you OK?" he asked.

She yanked the panties from her foot and threw them at Randy, hitting him in the face. He picked them up and threw them back, but they landed on top of the floor lamp.

"Beep, Beep."

She reached into her purse, yanked her smart phone out, and turned off the alarm clock app. She said, "You better get up, Libby will be here soon."

Sore, exhausted, his mind barely functional, he mumbled, "Yeah," as he laid his head back down and fell asleep again.

Kate took her purse to the bathroom, turned on the light, washed her face, and brushed her long black hair. She walked back into the bedroom and started looking for her clothes. She found everything except her panties. After searching the floor, twice, she gave up and told herself that she did not have time for hide and seek. She had to go home and get ready to go to work at the bank. So she just stepped into her denim shorts and sandals and went back into the bathroom. She looked in the full length mirror as she stuffed her large breasts into her bra and leveled them up. She finished with a tank top and large hoop earrings. She liked the young, trim, tan body that she saw in the mirror, but her brown eyes were bloodshot, which just made her think of Randy again and she grinned at her reflection.

Libby, a shy, slim, plain looking girl of 24, was about to reach Randy's front door when she realized it was opening.

Kate and Libby's eyes met as Kate walked out of the apartment. "Hi," each said to the other.

"I tried to get him up. Lord, I made enough noise, but," Kate paused, "he went back to sleep."

"I'll get him up," sighed Libby, as she walked into the apartment, and shut the door behind her.

The apartment was a one bedroom, one bath, with eat-in kitchen, and a small living room with a two person sofa where Libby dropped her backpack. A small computer desk was located in one corner of the living room with a large tower computer underneath.

Libby opened the bedroom door, walked in, grabbed the sheets, and pulled them off the bed. She raised her voice and said, "Randy, get up, it's Lib."

She walked back to the door, flipped on the light switch and froze when she saw Kate's panties hanging from the lamp shade just a few feet from her face. She knew that Randy just thought of her as a friend and work partner, but she had a little crush on him and was suddenly unnerved by her visions of Randy and Kate together the night before. After a few seconds, she turned to see Randy, naked, sitting on the side of the bed.

"It's time to get up," she said in a soft voice as she turned, walked to the kitchen and started the coffee. Libby heard the shower running as she opened her backpack, took out her laptop, and turned it on.

When the coffee was ready, she poured two cups, left one on the kitchen counter, and took the other with her to the sofa.

Randy, his long blond hair still wet and wearing just a robe, walked out of the bedroom to the kitchen and grabbed the coffee. Slowly sipping the brew, he made his way to the living room.

"Morning, Lib."

She pushed her long blond hair behind her shoulder, looked up at him, then reached into her backpack and pulled out a sack that contained two large fresh blueberry muffins. She took one and handed the bag to him. He sat down beside her and pulled the other one from the bag and they ate their breakfast in silence.

The apartment complex that Randy lived in was small, only 8 units, four down and four up, and was well maintained. The upper and lower apartments opened into corridors that ran through the center of the building, much like a hotel. The corridors were always well lit and had small CCTV security cameras in each one that fed a VCR tape recorder that reused the same tape every 24 hours. The 60 something year old owner-manager lived in unit number one, on the lower floor. Randy lived above the manager in unit number 5.

A black Suburban pulled into the apartment parking lot and backed into one of the empty spaces that had a straight shot to the street. Two men, wearing dark glasses, blue jeans, and dark sport coats, got out leaving the driver to watch the street and parking lot. Carlos, a slim, black haired man, carried a small bag, and walked with an air of authority into the building. Marcos was a big man with huge hands and a muscular body of 6 feet 5 inches and 250 pounds. They scanned each area as they walked into the complex, up the stairs, and down the upper corridor. They stopped outside of unit number 5 and knocked on the door.

Randy went to the door and called, "Who is it?"

"Police, there has been an accident."

Randy cracked open the door. "Let me see some ID."

Marcos stood out of Randy's field of view as Carlos reached into his jacket and pulled out a badge to show him. Carlos stood back far enough that Randy couldn't see that it wasn't real, but as soon as Randy started to open the door, the big man, Marcos, ran up and pushed the door open like a linebacker breaking through a scrimmage line to get to the quarterback.

Randy froze when he heard the man hit the door, and could only watch as its edge smacked him in the face and chest and knocked him, unconscious, to the floor.

The big man continued into the room, eyes searching for other threats with each step he took. He saw Libby, considered her as no immediate threat, and ran by her checking out the other rooms in the apartment.

Libby's eyes darted from Randy on the floor, to the door, and then to the man that ran past her, as she unknowingly climbed backwards up the back of the sofa. Just as she reached the top, the large man ran back into the room, picked her up, put her against the wall, and grabbed her neck with his hand. He put his face inches from hers, enjoying the fear in her eyes. Then he raised his other hand, put a finger to his lips, and whispered, "Shh.."

She didn't blink an eye, just stood there, shaking. Carlos walked in then, his hand inside his jacket, lying on the holstered pistol. He closed the door, locked it, then opened his bag and took out some duct tape. He looked down at Randy and covered his mouth with a piece of tape, bound his hands in front of him, and then bound his feet. Next he walked over to Marcos and Libby. She was trembling, and still staring, not blinking, into the eyes of the man holding her by the neck. Carlos put tape on her mouth, bound her feet, and then asked her to put her hands together. She nodded her head and closed her eyes as she put her hands together and held them out to be restrained.

"Take her to the bedroom, throw her on the floor, then come back and put him in the bed."

The large man bent down, put her over his shoulder, and with no effort picked her up, carried her into the bedroom, and laid her on the floor in the corner of the room. He noticed a tear running down her cheek. With one finger he reached out and wiped it from her face. He put the finger into his mouth, paused, then smiled and winked at her. She curled up, pulling her legs against her chest, and cried.

He went back to the living room, grabbed Randy by his hands and dragged him to the bedroom. With one hand around Randy's arm, and the other hand around Randy's thigh, the big man picked him up and threw him on the bed.

Carlos followed them into the bedroom. He got some rope out of the bag and handed it to Marcos. "Tie his hands to the headboard, then his feet to the footboard." Then he reached into his coat pocket, pulled out a cell phone, punched the speed dial button, waited a second, and reported, "We have secured the apartment and restrained a man and a woman. I'm in the process of talking to them now."

Carlos placed his bag on the bed next to Randy. He took an ammonia capsule out, broke it, and held it under Randy's nose. Randy's head suddenly jerked and his eyes slowly started to open, and Carlos pushed the capsule under his nose again.

Randy jerked his head back and tried to say, "Ahhh, damn!" but, with duct tape over his mouth, only a muffled noise came out. Then he tried to move his arms and legs, and realized his head was all that could move. When he heard a voice say, "Good morning, Mr. Hunter," he turned his head to look in the direction of the voice, and he stared at the man sitting on the side of the bed looking down at him.

"Good morning, Mr. Hunter," the man repeated. He paused, then said, "My boss believes you have taken something from him and he wants it back. Do you understand me, Mr. Hunter?"

Randy studied the man's face, then nodded his head yes.

"We have your girlfriend tied up and laying on the floor. We would like to resolve this very quickly without anyone being hurt. But I assure you, if you play any games, I will hurt you and your girlfriend."

Randy nodded his head yes.

"OK, let's resume. I am after the files you took from the bank, all of them. Will you please tell me where they're located?"

Randy nodded his head yes.

"Good, now that was not so hard. Thank you. Now I will take the tape from your mouth and you can tell me where everything is."

Randy nodded his head yes and the man pulled the tape enough that Randy could talk but left it stuck to his face. "There is a data CD in the living room, a working copy on my server in the living room, and last night's files are on an Internet server that we download from."

"Is that everything?" asked Carlos.

"Yes."

Carlos smiled, nodded his head and said, "Thank you. Now I am going to cut your feet free so you can walk and collect everything for me." He pulled out a knife and showed it to Randy. Carlos put the point of the knife against Randy's leg and slowly moved it up to the bottom of the robe. He twisted the knife where the point caught the bottom of the robe and flipped one side of the robe open, exposing Randy. He did the same thing to the other side. Randy's body tensed as Carlos gently slid the knife under his penis, pressing it against him. He looked back at Randy's face and smirked, "Oh, one thing, if you fail to do what I ask, the first thing I will cut off is your little man."

Randy looked into the man's eyes, and saw black ice, and he knew this man would have no trouble doing exactly what he said.

Randy nodded his head. "OK," he said.

Marcos was standing at the foot of the bed watching. He saw Carlos look at him and nod. He reached down and untied Randy's feet, then he cut the duct tape and removed it. Carlos was doing the same to Randy's hands. Then he pulled Randy out of the bed.

Randy closed his robe and tied the belt, studying the men as he did. He was about the same height as the man who was doing all the talking, but the man was in better condition. The other one was larger, about seven inches taller and had about 75 more pounds.

Carlos walked to the bedroom door, stopped, pulled out his pistol, a 9mm Glock, and said, "Mr. Hunter, if you please," motioning him to come.

Randy went to the door, but Carlos blocked it. "Turn around," he said. They stood there while Marcos grabbed Libby, put her on the bed, and tied her hands to the headboard. He sat down beside her and slowly started to unbutton her blouse. She started to squirm and kick, and he grabbed her by the neck, looked down at her and shook his head no. Randy saw the tears in her eyes as they looked at each other from across the room.

Randy turned to the man beside him. "Please don't hurt her," he begged, "I said I will give you everything."

"I suggest you get started."

Randy's free-and-easy attitude was missing now. He just wanted to get Libby and himself out of this mess. He walked across the living room to the computer desk, pulled a data CD from the desktop, and held it out. Carlos, standing next to the sofa, reached out to take the CD, when suddenly the front door opened.

The apartment manager was standing in the door holding a 12 gauge Remington 870 shotgun pointed at the floor. Carlos quickly turned and pointed his gun at the man who was interfering with his job and he fired just as the manager started to raise his gun. The bullet struck the manager in the right shoulder causing him to jerk back and pull his trigger as the shotgun was rising. The buckshot tore a hole in the side of the sofa, several pellets going into and through Carlos's leg, causing him to fall and hit his head on the coffee table. The pistol fell at Randy's feet and he picked it up.

Randy looked at the manager lying on the floor, he was conscious, but in pain. Randy thought about grabbing the shotgun, but was afraid the other man would come in before he could. So he just stood there waiting. Soon enough the big man stuck his head around the corner and quickly pulled it back. Randy pulled the trigger. The bullet lost a lot of momentum when it went through the door frame, but it hit the big man in the head, knocking him out, even though it didn't penetrate his skull.

"I saw those two come into the building on the security camera," said the manager. "I didn't like their looks. Then I saw the way they came into your room and I knew you were in trouble. I called the police, then came up."

Randy saw blood coming from the manager's shoulder, and he ran to the kitchen and got a towel. He ran back. "Put pressure on the wound with this." As he helped the manager with the towel he said, "Thanks, man."

He then ran to the bedroom, picked up the big man's gun from the floor, and ran to Libby. She was lying on the bed wearing only her pants and shoes. Her blouse and bra had been cut off and tossed on the floor. The bag was still lying on the bed. Randy put both guns on the bed, then grabbed the bag and pulled out the knife that Carlos had introduced to his little man.

When Randy finished cutting all the duct tape, he grabbed Libby and held her tight in his arms. "Lib, I am so sorry."

With tears still running down her face, she pulled away and looked in his eyes. "Someone at the bank knows what we did."

"The police are on the way, it will be OK," stated Randy.

"No, Randy, we can't tell the police anything because we hacked the bank's servers. They'll put us in jail with these two guys." She pointed to the man lying on the floor. "He might be your cellmate."

His expression quickly changed from relieved to frightened as he asked, "What are we going to do?"

"We need to destroy everything except our backup drive and then find some place to hide until we can figure out what to do."

He touched her face and nodded, realizing she was right.

She reached up and took his hand. "We need to go now!"

Randy ran to the living room, grabbed all his data CDs and DVDs, ran to the kitchen, put them into the microwave, pressed the one minute button, and waited until he saw little lightning arcs jumping around each disk.

Libby went to the Linux server, typed in *shutdown now -h*. As the computer started to shutdown, she grabbed her backpack from the sofa and stuffed her laptop in it, then went back to the server, disconnected the backup external hard drive and placed it in her backpack. She grabbed another CD, put it in the server and rebooted the computer. She then started the *wipe* program and began destroying the contents of the hard drive.

Randy ran back to the bedroom and collected the pistols. He then ran back to the kitchen and dropped them into the garbage can. He ran back and forth a few more times. Then he stopped moving and searching and looked at Libby. "I can't find my car keys."

"Then you will ride with me." She started toward the door, but suddenly stopped. "Wait. I have something I need to do." She ran over to the big man lying on the floor. Her eyes went down to his crotch, and her right leg swung back, then forward, giving a kick that would have put a soccer ball through the hands of a professional goalie.

"Now," she said, picking up her backpack.

Marcos moaned as he started to wake up, his eyes barely opening in time to see Randy and Libby run out the front door.

As they ran down the corridor, Randy saw a neighbor crack open her front door. He paused as he yelled, "Call an ambulance, the manager's been shot." Not waiting for a reply, he took off running again and caught up to Libby as she was going down the stairs.

"Lib, you're not wearing a top," Randy said as they reached the bottom of the stairs.

She looked down. "Damn! We don't have time to go back and get anything."

The driver of the black Suburban was reaching for his cell phone when Randy and Libby ran out of the building. Surprised by the sight of Randy in a robe and Libby holding her backpack in front of her, he watched them run around the corner. Then he pushed the speed dial button and waited. No answer. He got out and started to the complex, then stopped when he saw Marcos carrying Carlos out of the building. He opened the rear door and helped put Carlos into the back seat.

"What happened in there?" asked the driver.

"I don't know," said Marcos. "I woke up on the floor with a splitting headache and my balls feel like they went twelve rounds with Joe Frazier. Did you see them leave?"

"Yeah, they came out and went around the building."

Just then Randy and Libby shot out of the apartment complex, with a topless Libby driving her new Vespa GTV 300 scooter, her backpack tied to the chrome-plated front carrier, and Randy holding on to her with his robe flapping behind.

Hearing sirens getting closer, the driver ordered, "Get in, we need to go."

"We need to follow them," said Marcos.

The driver pulled out of the parking lot, turned in the other direction, and said, "Carlos is bleeding. We need to get him some help."

Randy noticed that they were heading downtown. He put his head close to Libby's and asked, "Where are we going?"

"To a friend's place. I have some clothes there."

"We can go to your place and get some clothes."

"No, they may be watching it."

Randy glanced quickly back to see if he could tell if they were being followed. As he turned back to the front, he noticed something on Libby's lower back. He lowered his head to see a small tattoo of a gecko sticking his head above Libby's pants, staring back at him, with a cartoon caption saying "What are you looking at, Mate?"

He was grinning at the gecko when they stopped at a red light beside a Toyota Tundra pickup pulling a seventeen foot Casita RV travel trailer. The older man driving the truck noticed them pull up out of the corner of his eye and gave them a quick glance. Then he turned his head back and stared.

Libby felt somebody's eyes on her and she looked around and saw the man in the truck staring at her. She reached down and pulled Randy's hands up to cover her breasts. Surprised, Randy turned his head in the direction Libby was looking. The man smiled, nodded his head and gave him a thumbs up.

The light turned green and as Randy and Libby took off, the wind caught Randy's robe, blowing it around, so it seemed to be waving goodbye to the couple in the truck.

"Are we in Vegas yet?" asked the woman in the passenger seat.

Still watching the Vespa, the man said, "I think so, don't believe we would see that in Memphis."

~ ~ ~

Libby drove to an older apartment complex. There were two buildings, each two stories, one on each side of the driveway and parking area. Each apartment building had four units, two top floor and two bottom. There was a utility and storage building located at the far end of the driveway. They looked abandoned to Randy. Most of them were boarded up and had not seen paint in twenty years. At the back of the complex, Libby turned and drove straight at one of the apartment doors, pushing a button on a remote dangling from her keychain. The door opened and she drove in and parked in the living room.

They got off the scooter and Randy looked around. The front door was wider than normal, making it handicap accessible, and it was connected to a remote controlled motorized opener. The carpet had been removed, and several tire tracks were visible on the concrete floor.

"Hi," said a voice from behind them.

Randy turned and saw a black haired, middle-aged man in a wheelchair looking at Libby with concern all over his face.

"Lib, I know this is Vegas," he said, "and I like your new look, but I know it's not like you. You're in trouble, aren't you?"

"Yes, I need to get my things, then we'll get out of here."

"Lib, I watched you drive in, no one was following you. You're safe here. Did you disable your cell phone?"

Libby shook her head. "God, no, I forgot." A tear started down her face.

"Lib, it's OK, just give me your bag."

He took the bag, found the phone, pulled it out and stopped. He looked at them, and held up the phone for them to look at, then in a very calm voice said, "Lib, there's a bullet hole going through your bag and your phone. What's going on?"

Libby's voice cracked when she began speaking, "Two men broke into..." Then she started sobbing, and after that neither Randy nor the man could understand what she was saying.

The man took her hands, pulled her to him and said, "Lib, sit down, let it out, and let it go."

She sat on his lap for several minutes and cried while he held her. When she could compose herself, she whispered, "I'm sorry." Then she wiped the tears away with her hands, looked up at him, and said again, "I'm sorry."

"Lib, you know that you never have to say that to me." A few seconds passed, he smiled and said, "It's been a long time since I have had a beautiful girl sitting on my lap."

She bowed her head, started to blush, and then looked back at him with a half smile.

"Why don't you go take a long shower?" he said. "I'll bring you some fresh towels, and we can talk later. No buts."

She nodded her head. Then he asked, "Is this Randy?" She nodded her head again. "You go get a shower, Randy can fill me in after I get the towels."

She got up and started down the hall. When they heard the bathroom door shut, the man turned to Randy and stuck out a hand. "Hi. I'm Joe Morgan, Lib has talked a lot about you."

Randy grabbed his hand and they shook.

Joe turned and started down the hall. "Come on back."

Randy followed Joe to one of the bedrooms. He saw Joe push some buttons on an electronic panel attached to his chair. The bedroom door opened and they went through. Randy stopped and stared at the darkened room. The windows had been boarded up and all he could see were the fifteen computer monitors mounted to a u-shaped metal frame above a u-shaped wooden desk located in a corner of the room. Most of the monitors were about twenty inches, but there were two larger monitors in the center of the frame. He saw two racks of computers, one on each side of the monitor frame.

Joe turned to Randy and asked, "How do you like my office?"

Randy, standing in the middle of the room with his mouth open, could only say, "Wow!"

"Pull up a chair and watch those three monitors, and let me know if you see anything, OK? They're the security cameras surrounding the apartment complex."

"Yeah, sure."

"I'll get some towels for her and be right back."

"OK."

Randy pulled up a chair and studied each screen.

Joe rolled into the hall, opened the linen closet and got some fresh towels. Then he went to his bedroom, got a clean robe, and continued to the bathroom. He knocked, then opened the bathroom door and said, "Lib, I have some fresh towels and a clean robe. Are you OK?"

"Yeah, I am now."

"Take your time. I'm going to talk to Randy now."

She pulled the shower curtain back and poked her head out. She looked at him for a second then said, "Thanks, Joe."

He smiled back, laid everything on the counter, and left the room.

"See anything?" Joe asked when he entered his office.

"No."

"OK. Tell me what happened."

Randy told him everything that happened, then said, "Obviously, these men were not police."

"You're right, it doesn't sound like it."

Joe pulled up to the center of the u-shaped desk and stared at the monitors for a second. "OK, I need to call some people. I have a retired friend that sits and listens to police and fire scanners all day. Let me find out what he has heard."

He reached over to his track ball, looked at one of the large monitors, and started scrolling down the screen until a list of phone numbers appeared. He then reached for a headset, put it over his head, and adjusted the microphone.

Randy watched and listened as Joe punched in a number on the desk phone, waited a second, and started talking. "Hey, what have you heard about a shooting about an hour ago, around midtown?" Joe paused, "Is the manager OK?" He listened again. "Call me if you hear anything else, OK? Thanks."

"Randy, the manager is at the hospital, the report from the ambulance said it was a through and through and does not seem to be life threatening. The police are still trying to put it all together and they have not taken a statement from the manager yet. The two men must have got out before the police arrived. The only person the police found in the apartment was the manager."

Randy watched Joe spin the ball on the track ball. The mouse cursor flew across the screen and stopped on top of an icon named News RSS Filter. With a click, a window appeared and Joe started typing.

"OK, now we will be alerted to anything from the local news outlets."

Libby walked in wearing Joe's robe and asked, "What have you found out?"

Joe looked at her and smiled. "It doesn't look like the police know what is going on yet."

"How's the manager?" she asked.

"He's at the hospital and is going to be OK. The two men got out before the police arrived."

Joe hesitated, watching for Libby and Randy's reaction to his next question. "Obviously, someone at the bank knows that you two have been poking around in the bank's computers. Do you think Kate may have found out and told someone?"

Randy and Libby looked at each other, then Libby responded, "No, she had just left a short time before they broke in and they referred to me as Randy's girlfriend. I got the feeling that they thought I was Kate."

"I put the worm on Kate's office laptop computer," said Randy, "she doesn't even know it's there. Besides, how do you know about Kate?"

Libby turned to Randy. "Joe is the person that gave me the code to create the worm. We planned this before I talked to you about it."

Joe waited for a few seconds, then said, "If someone at the bank knows that Randy has been getting files from the bank's computers, and Libby, if they thought that you were Kate, then she's in danger too."

"I have to call her," said Randy.

"I have someone that can talk to her, and get her to safety without anyone tracing it back here," said Joe. "Let me make a call. Randy do you have something that only you and Kate know? Something that would convince her that my person is telling her the truth?"

Randy thought for a second. "Ask her why she was sitting in the floor, naked, throwing her panties at me this morning."

~ ~ ~

"Good morning, Miss Dodson," said the security guard, as Kate entered the bank and headed to the elevator. JP Bank of Nevada was the newest bank in Las Vegas. It occupied a five story building near downtown and had a large parking lot. Two older women were already in the elevator as Kate entered and pressed the button to take her to the fifth floor. No one talked, the only sound was the bell on the elevator control panel, announcing each floor as the elevator slowly rose. The elevator stopped at the fifth floor and the women started walking toward their respective offices. Kate was getting used to the fact that most women in the office did not talk to her, it was like they resented her for becoming the newest rising star in the office. Kate had little use for office politics, and resented the innuendos about her using sex to become a manager so fast. She knew that her looks carried her a long way, and given her age, most people were very surprised by her knowledge of corporate banking. She was proud of the number of new corporate accounts she had created for this bank and she was lucky that the executives took notice of her achievements and made her a manager. Walking though the hall, a smile grew on Kate's face as she thought about how she had used her looks and limber body to dance at men's clubs to put herself through college. Yes, Kate knew that Mother Nature had been good to her, but she also knew her future would depend on all of her abilities.

Kate's cell phone began to ring as she walked into her office. She put her purse on her desk, pulled out the phone and said, "Hello."

"Hello, I have a message for Kate Dodson," the voice on the phone said.

"I'm Kate Dodson."

"Miss Dodson, Randy and Libby are OK, they're safe."

"Who is this, what do you mean they're safe?" Kate asked.

"Miss Dodson, two men broke into Randy's apartment this morning, the apartment manager was shot, and you may be in danger."

"Are you the police?"

"No. I'm a friend."

"How do I know you're a friend?"

"I have a question for you, Randy wants to know why you were naked, on the floor, and throwing your panties at him this morning?"

Kate did not say anything.

"Miss Dodson," the voice said, "Randy and Libby were almost killed this morning and they think the same people may come after you. Ma'am you may be in danger. And it may be someone from the bank that's responsible."

"OK, what do I need to do?" Kate asked, the tension making the words stick in her throat.

"Memorize the phone number that I am calling you from. Turn off your phone and take out the battery. Then go to a nearby drugstore, and tell them that you are having car trouble and you need to call your husband. Dial the number, and act like you're talking to your husband." There was a pause, then the voice continued, "Are you at the bank now?"

"Yes."

"Then get out of there as fast as you can without drawing any attention to yourself."

"OK."

"Good luck," said the voice.

Kate turned off her phone, took out the battery, and put it into her purse. She left her office and headed to the elevator. She looked around and saw the bank president, Jerry Powell, talking to a security guard and pointing at her. The guard started walking toward her, reaching for his gun. She reached the elevators, but instead of pushing the button she pulled the fire alarm and ran to the stairs. When she reached the next floor three people opened the door to the stairway and began to follow her down. Several people were already in the stairway when she reached the next floor. By the time she reached the ground floor the lobby was full and she walked out with everyone else.

She drove to a nearby drugstore and told the sales clerk about having car trouble and asked to use the phone. Kate was shaking as she dialed the number.

"Hi, Honey, it's me. I'm having car trouble again," Kate said as the sales clerk stood nearby.

"Did you disable your phone?"

"Yes, I already tried that," Kate said.

"You are doing good. Did you get out of the building without being noticed?"

"No. I haven't tried that."

"OK. I need to see if you are being followed. I need you to drive to the corner of East Stewart Avenue and North 8th Street. I'll be at the bus stop just past the corner. Do not stop. Just drive by to the next street and turn right. Keep turning right until you get back to the bus stop. If it is safe, I will stick out my hand, like I am hitchhiking. Stop and pick me up. Randy said you drive a green 2009 Dodge Charger. Is that correct?"

"Yes," Kate said.

"OK, I will see you in a few minutes."

Kate thanked the clerk, got back into her car, and started driving. She slowed down as she reached the street corner. She checked the mirror after each right turn. Just before she reached the bus stop again she saw a man stand up and stick out his thumb. He was carrying a bag, wearing a dark jacket and a baseball cap with the jacket hood pulled up over the hat. She stopped and unlocked her door. The man opened the door and looked into the back before saying anything.

"Are you Kate Dodson?"

"Yes," Kate answered, as she noticed that the man had short blond hair and a small nose stud and that he spoke in a low soft voice.

He got into the front seat, placed the bag on the back seat and said, "Please drive to the next light and turn right."

She made the turn and waited for the next command. The man said, "I need to check your car to see if there are any tracking devices. Pull into the next parking lot, stay in the vehicle, while I get out and check it."

She pulled into a small shopping center and stopped. As he got out of the car he said, "Pop your hood," then he started walking around the car. She saw the man bend down, and he disappeared for a while. When he stood back up, he raised the hood, and looked for anything that did not look like factory work.

After he closed the hood, he reached in the pocket of his jacket, pulled out the cell phone that he had called Kate on, and put it in the bed of a nearby pickup truck.

He got back in the car and said, "I need to examine your purse." He took a quick look inside. From his jacket, he pulled out a box with a small antenna on top and red LED lights on the front. He held her purse up with one hand then moved the box all around the purse with the other hand. The LED lights did not flash.

"OK, your purse is good. Now I need to check you." The man waved the box around Kate as best he could while sitting in a car. "You're good, too," he said. "We need to go. Drive back to the street and turn right. I will give you directions as we go."

"What were you checking for in my purse?" Kate asked.

"Anything that transmits RF energy. It could be used to track you."

They were driving down the street when the man pulled from his jacket a small box with a short wire attached to it.

Kate saw the man examining the device and asked, "What is that?"

"It's a GPS tracking device. It was under your car."

She looked at the man and asked, "Who put it there?"

"Good question."

"Are they tracking us now?"

"Yes, but this doesn't have a transmitter. It only collects data and stores it. Someone has to retrieve it, read the data, reset the device, and then put it back."

"Is it a good idea to keep it?" Kate asked.

"Well, I need to try and read the data from it. I hope they turned it on at their house or business and recorded their location before they put it on your car. If they did that, we can figure out who they are from their location."

The man looked up and said, "Turn into the next parking lot. It should be a twenty-four hour hospital parking lot. Drive into the parking structure and back into one of the parking slots that is furthest away from the elevators and stairs, and get very close to the wall behind you. We will be leaving your car there."

Kate did what the man said to do, then asked, "Why back into the parking slot?"

"The police have a camera on top of their cars that will automatically read license plates as they drive through a parking lot. Each license plate is sent to a computer to see if the vehicle is stolen or if it has an APB or a BOLO on it. Most police will not stop and get out to look at a car that's turned around."

He reached over and got the bag from the back seat. "OK, Miss Dodson, we need to change our looks. This is a busy parking lot so we need to hurry. So, let me go first, then I'll help you."

He pulled the hood back and took off the hat, putting it on the dash. Next he pulled the blond wig off to expose long black hair. The jacket came off next, revealing a hairless body with medical tape around the chest. Then pulling surgical scissors out of the bag, she cut the tape off, freeing her breasts. She slipped on a tube top, traded her baggy pants for some short shorts and slipped on a pair of open-toed three inch heels.

"You weren't kidding when you said change our looks," said Kate in a voice that expressed her astonishment at the young woman's transformation.

Then as she pulled a mirror out of the bag and started applying her makeup, she glanced at Kate and asked, "Can I call you Kate?"

Kate laughed nervously, "After what I have been through today, you can call me anything."

"OK, Kate, everyone calls me Candy. Now we will have to change your looks. You need to take everything off except your panties. We need to hurry." She helped Kate out of her clothes. "Hold up your arms as I tape down your breasts."

Kate watched as Candy worked. "Candy, you look like you have done this a lot."

"If you mean with the tape, my mother was a nurse for a sports doctor. She showed me how to wrap people up. OK, now put these baggy pants on and the hoodie. Then tie your hair back and put it through the baseball cap."

Candy got three pairs of socks from the bag and handed them to Kate. "Put these on, we need to make your feet bigger so you can walk in these men's tennis shoes." She waited for Kate to get the shoes on, then said, "OK, Kate, I need you to pull your hood up over the baseball cap. Hide your hair in the jacket." She helped her tuck all her hair in. "That looks good. And when you walk point your feet just a little to the sides. That will change the way you walk."

"Candy, you're dressed like a hooker, won't that draw attention to us?"

Candy smiled. "I want all the attention on me, not you. We won't be walking together. I'll walk about a hundred feet in front of you. You just follow behind me. We only have to walk a few blocks. We're almost there. You ready?"

Kate nodded her head.

"OK, good," said Candy, and then she grinned. "And since a

manly man like you wouldn't carry a purse, just put your wallet in your pocket and drop your purse in the bag, and carry the bag."

Kate waited while Candy got out of the car and walked toward the street. When she thought the distance was right she followed. They turned north out of the parking structure. Halfway down the block a police car stopped next to Candy. She pulled her top down a little more as she walked over to the car and leaned onto the open window. Kate saw the man reach out the window and put his hands on Candy's hips and legs. As she walked past them, she heard Candy laugh and say, "Now, you know I'm a good girl."

Kate continued walking down the street but jumped when the police siren came to life. She turned and watched as the police car drove by and turned left at the next corner. She saw Candy walking a little faster and she had caught up by the time they reached the next light.

"That was too close," said Kate.

"Yeah, to be on duty, they seemed a little too interested in a good time. I'm glad they got that call."

"You look like you held your own with them."

"Yeah, they asked for my phone number. I gave them my work number."

"Where's that?"

"I work downtown at a phone sex business."

Kate laughed. "I put myself through school working as a bartender and dancer at the Fremont Experience. I know what appendage most men think with."

"Yeah!" Candy said, laughing.

The light changed and they walked the last block side by side.

Chapter 2
Las Vegas, Nevada

Jerry Powell stood outside of the bank, waiting like all the other bank employees. Jerry was an average looking man with a slim build, dark brown hair, and a narrow face with oval shaped glasses. He stood shaking his head, arms crossed, watching the firemen entering and leaving the building, wondering how much longer this was going to take.

Finally, the fire chief at the scene gave Jerry the OK to allow everyone back into the bank. When the vice president of the bank, Angelo Diego, found Jerry in the hallway on the executive floor, he was talking to the accounting manager. "I'm sure there is nothing to be concerned about," said Jerry, "send me the files so I can look at them."

"I'm sorry to interrupt," said Angelo, "I need to talk to you." At 6 feet tall, Angelo Diego stood over Jerry by four inches. His slim build, light tan skin, straight black hair, charming manners, and tailored suits made him popular with the women in the bank. Most days he enjoyed the attention, but today, things weren't going as planned.

The accounting manager nodded and left. Jerry and Angelo went into Jerry's office and closed the door. Jerry exploded, "Damn it! Now accounting has found some of our bogus accounts. This morning just gets better and better. What the hell happened this morning? What kind of people did you hire? I thought you said that your men had them at the apartment this morning?"

"My men said that they had a couple tied up at Mr. Hunter's apartment."

"Well, I don't know who they have. As I was walking to my office, I found Kate Dodson at her desk. I called security to hold her, and she ran before they could catch her. Hell, she's the one that pulled the damn fire alarm."

"What! Dammit! I came to tell you that I haven't talked to my men in over an hour. I don't know what the hell is going on."

Angelo's cell phone rang. He answered, "Yes," listened, then said, "Find them now! Get everyone looking, private investigators, bounty hunters, even the dealers! And above all, do not let the police find them first. I'll call our computer people at OCS and see if they can help."

He looked at Jerry and said, "Mr. Hunter and the woman escaped, the apartment manager was shot, one of my men was shot, and the other beaten up."

Angelo could see the anger building in Jerry's face as Jerry said, "I thought you said that these men were professionals."

"They are! I don't know what could have happened, but at least they didn't get caught."

Jerry turned back to his desk, picked up a paperweight, and threw it through the glass door of his liquor cabinet.

Angelo grabbed Jerry by the arm. "Stop! You're going to draw attention to us. You handle the bank, I'll fix this."

Angelo moved quickly to his office and shut the door. He reached for his cell phone and dialed. He pictured the guard sitting at the security desk in the lobby when he answered in his intimidating voice, "OCS, Inc. Can I help you?"

"This is Angelo Diego, I need to talk to Claudette Godard."

"Yes, sir."

As he listened to the soft instrumental version of Leon Russell's *This Masquerade*, he thought about the woman he was waiting to talk to and he slowly relaxed.

"This is Claudette Godard," she answered softly in her heavy French accent.

He smiled as he said, "Hello, Claudette, this is Angelo."

"Hello, Angelo, what can I do for you?" She picked up a pen off her desk and started playing with it.

"I have a problem that I hope you and your team can help me with."

"What's wrong?"

"One of our bank employees, and her boyfriend, introduced a malware program into the bank's network system and it has spread to all the office computers, including mine. Somehow it has managed to get past all the network security and anti-virus software."

"Have your IT people determined what it is doing?"

"It appears that it's getting files from all the office computers and sending them to a server on the Internet."

"Have your IT people blocked that server's address to keep any more files from getting out?"

"Yes, I think they took care of that this morning."

"Good, it sounds like your IT department is getting a handle on it."

"Yes," Angelo confirmed. "The problem is that the couple knows that we are onto them and they're on the run. What I need from you is help finding them."

"And you don't want the police involved in this, correct?"

"That's correct. I'm afraid they may have discovered some files that we don't want the police to see."

"I understand. What are their names?"

"The bank employee is Kate Dodson, her boyfriend is Randy Hunter. I'll email you all the information from human resources that I have about Kate Dodson."

"I'll get my team started right away," she said, as she jotted down the names.

"Thank you, Claudette." he said, then he listened until the phone disconnected.

Angelo's anxiety flooded back as he stared at the phone for several moments, waiting, hesitating, not wanting to make the next call. He took a deep breath, forced his hand to dial the number and said, "The men that we sent to do the job this morning screwed up." He listened to the explosion of profanity. "I don't know all the details yet," he said, when he could slip the words in, "but I'll keep you posted."

He put his elbow on the desk and laid the phone down. Bringing that hand back up, he dropped his head into it, hiding his face. He took another deep breath, ignoring the sweat on his palm, and said to himself, "Dammit, Cortez is going to kill me."

~ ~ ~

As Kate and Candy turned into the apartment parking lot, Kate saw the condition of the apartments and asked, "Randy is here?"

"Randy and Lib are at Joe's apartment. He owns the complex." She looked at Kate's expression and said, "Joe bought this place after he was discharged from the army. He was in Iraq when an IED exploded near him. It killed some of his buddies, and left him with very little use of his legs. He bought this place to try and fix it up and give disabled vets a low rent place to live."

"It doesn't look like anyone lives here," said Kate.

"He had a few people renting, but they had to leave."

"Why?"

"He only had a couple of apartments fixed up, and the government bureaucracy said that the complex didn't meet their housing standards. It's turned into a real money pit for him. He runs a computer business out of his apartment and what he makes from that can cover the bills. The problem is, there isn't enough to fix up the other apartments and he's not able to sell because of the economy."

Using a remote control, Joe opened the front door as Kate and Candy arrived at the apartment. Randy and Libby met them as they entered the living room.

Randy squeezed Kate's hand and said, "Kate, I'm so sorry I got you into this."

She bit her lip as she looked at Randy's worried face. "Randy, what am I into?"

Joe rolled in a moment later and stopped next to Kate. "Hello, Kate, glad you made it here safe. I'm Joe Morgan."

She looked at Joe and said, "Someone needs to tell me what's going on."

"I'm the one that got you into this mess, and for that I am deeply sorry," Joe said.

Kate stared at Joe. "Would... Somebody... Tell... Me... What... Kind... Of... Trouble... I'm... In!?" she demanded.

"Yes, of course. You deserve to know." He glanced at Libby, then turned his attention back to Kate. "JP Bank of Nevada has the largest foreclosure rate of any bank in this area. I wanted to find documents that would show if the bank was doing something illegal. There was a computer worm installed on your laptop computer. When you connected your laptop to the bank's network the worm traveled to the other computers and started collecting documents and emails. At night the worm would send the information to a server that I control. The next day I would download the information and scan through it and try to find something. Obviously, the bank's IT department thought the information was going to Randy's apartment. I don't see how that happened, and I don't understand why the bank sent a couple of goons to Randy's apartment to get the information back. In a situation like this they would normally call the local police and the Feds. Believe me Kate, I did not think I would be putting anyone in danger by doing this. Again, I am sorry."

Candy asked, "Could the IT people trace the worm to Kate's laptop?"

Joe thought for a second, "I didn't think they would be able to do that, but it's possible. What are you thinking?"

"I found a tracking device on Kate's car. Someone may have put it there to see who she was meeting. That may be how they found Randy."

Joe said, "I bet they checked out everyone in Randy's apartment complex and discovered that he was the only person there with the computer skills to do this. Damn!"

"Joe, how did you get the worm on my computer?" asked Kate.

Still holding Kate's hand, Randy said, "I'll tell you."

Joe looked up at the two and said, "You two stay here and talk; everyone else come with me to my office. We have a lot of work to do."

Joe, Libby, and Candy made their way into Joe's office. Joe said, "You two grab some laptops from the cabinet, and set up some workstations. Candy, please monitor the RSS news feeds on server number five. I have already set it up. Libby, would you copy the backup files from the external hard drive that you got from Randy's server to my server number eight? Then I need you to watch the local chat room to see what's going on there. I'll touch base with some of my contacts to see what they have heard, then start looking at those files to see what is so important."

"Joe," said Libby, "Randy and I were the ones getting the information from the bank. Why did you tell Kate that the information was being sent to you?"

"If we get arrested, I wanted Kate to think I was the one that put this together, I want to take the heat on this, not you, Randy or Kate."

"But Joe, I'm the one that came up with this plan. I'm the one that talked you and Randy into helping me. I'm not going to let you go to jail for what I did."

"Let's hope that it doesn't go that far," said Joe. "For now, it might be best to let Kate think I'm the one. Until this is over, you, Randy, and Kate will need to stick together and try to stay friends."

Suddenly they heard Kate yell, "Do you know what I had to do to get that job, how many years it took me to get through college, and now it's all gone? Hell, I should be the one to cut your dick off!"

"Should I get between them?" Joe asked. He looked at Libby and Candy but they just shrugged.

Then something on his computer caught his attention and he shook his head, looked at the floor, and said, "Shit, this is bad. Libby, would you go and get those two? I need to talk to all of you."

They came back into the office. Randy in front, then Libby, and finally Kate.

"Everyone, please pull up a chair," Joe said. When everyone was settled he continued, "Sometimes I work for a couple of private investigators. I just got an email from each of them and they want me to build profiles on Kate and Randy. They have a very good description of Libby but they do not know who she is. They have Randy's name with a full description. Kate, they have everything on you, even a photo, probably from the personnel file at the bank." Joe paused for a second to let everyone think about what he said. He continued, "There are a lot of hackers out there that know Libby and Randy work together. A few of them know that Libby works with me too. It may take awhile, but eventually, they may figure out that I'm the one hiding you. Also there is a bounty of $50,000 on each of you."

A quietness fell over the room when Joe stopped talking. Kate looked at Randy, then turned her stare to Joe. As he looked back at Kate, he saw slow smoldering anger building up in her face and nervous energy in her body, as she thought about the situation she was now faced with.

She stood up and started pacing the room, then she said, "A bounty. I don't understand. If the bank thinks we're stealing something, why don't they just call the police?"

Trying to keep Kate from getting too enraged, Joe said calmly, "Please remember Kate, the only reason they would not call the police is that they are hiding something and they think we found it."

"Then why don't we go to the police and explain what happened," said Kate.

Joe thought for a few seconds then said, "Because we haven't found out what they're hiding. If we go to the police now, with nothing, the bank will deny everything and say that we are part of a gang that hacked into the bank computers to steal credit card and personal information from their clients. They will say that the attack on Libby and Randy was some sort of gang hit that went bad. I will be arrested and go to jail and be killed, then they will still come after Libby, Randy and you. They will kill all of you and make it look like a gang ordered hit to keep everyone quiet. Kate, we have to find out what they're hiding first. Then we can make a decision about going to the police."

Kate stopped pacing and turned her dark brown eyes to Joe. He dropped his gaze from her stare and said, "You will be safe here. If there's trouble, you can hide in the safe room next door."

"You have a safe room?" asked Kate.

"Yes, when I had this building remodeled, I took over the entire bottom floor. The safe room has reinforced walls and ceiling, and it's fully stocked. We can survive there for about a month if we need to." He looked at Candy and said, "Candy, will you show them how to get to it? Libby, will you stay? I need to talk to you alone."

"Sure," said Candy.

Joe turned to Libby and said, "I need to make these PIs think that I am working for them. I need to give them your name before anyone else does. That way they may not realize that I'm the one protecting you, but I won't do it if you say no. I'm sorry Lib, but it's your call."

"Like you said, it won't take them long to find out it's me, so go ahead."

"How's Kate taking this?" asked Joe.

"She just had everything taken away from her. She's mad as hell but I don't think she will do anything stupid. Randy will have to stay out of her way for a while, though."

"She seems to be a very smart girl, she could be a big help looking at the files we got from the bank. What do you think?"

"She would be a big help," said Libby, "but those files are the reason her life was just turned upside down. It may be difficult for her to look at them."

"Yeah, you're right. Right now may not be the best time to ask."

As Libby and Joe turned back to their workstations and started reading the information on the screens, Candy and Randy came back up to the office.

Libby noticed that Kate was not with them and asked, "Did Kate stay in there?"

"Yeah," said Randy, "she crawled into one of the bunks and crashed. Maybe I should stay with her."

"Randy, just give her some space. I'm sure she just wants to be left alone for now. She'll be OK."

"Yeah, maybe."

"Randy, I could use some more eyes looking at the files from the bank," said Joe, "Grab a laptop from that cabinet and set up a workstation. Libby can show you what server they're on."

"OK."

~ ~ ~

Kate saw herself running past the elevator to the stairs in the bank. The blanket wrapped around her restrained her quick, jerky movements and made her feel like hands were grabbing her, stopping her. Her eyes flew open, and the nightmarish images vanished, but not the fear, she didn't know where she was. She was in a different bed with unfamiliar noises surrounding her. Moments passed as she shook beneath the blanket that now felt like a protective shield against an unknown world. She heard someone's soft snoring coming from somewhere in the room and she slowly looked around. Reality wormed it's way in and her heart rate slowly dropped as she heard Candy roll over in her bunk and she identified the snoring as Libby's. She quietly slipped out of her bunk and walked to the office where Randy was asleep with his head on the desk next to a laptop. The large LED clock on the wall showed 3:40 AM. "How long has he been asleep?" she asked Joe.

Joe smiled and said, "Not long."

"Do I smell fresh coffee?"

"Yes, I just made it. Help yourself."

She pointed to Joe's cup and asked, "Can I pour you a fresh cup?"

"Sure, thank you."

"What do you like in it?"

"Just a little milk, no sugar. I'm sweet enough."

She gave him a half smile and walked into the kitchen with his cup.

She came back in with two cups and as she handed Joe his coffee, she asked, "What do you do here?"

Before he could answer, they heard Randy mumbling, and saw him shaking when they turned to look.

"I bet he's dreaming about what happened yesterday," Joe said.

"Yeah, poor thing," said Kate, "let me wake him up so he can go to bed."

She picked up a large C/C++ language reference book and walked over to Randy. She held the book as high as she could, then slammed it on the desk next to his head. Randy jumped straight up and tried to step away, but tripped over his chair and landed on his back. He frantically waved his hands in the air, then grabbed his crotch and yelled, "No, no, not my little man!" Then his eyes focused and he looked up at Kate standing over him.

She looked down at him with a vengeful smile and said, "Honey, it's time you went to bed."

Joe was laughing as he watched a very confused Randy get up and leave the room.

Kate moved the chair next to Joe, sat down and asked, "Now, where were we? Oh yeah, I was asking what you do here."

"Well, I try to use technology to help people."

"Like me?"

"Sometimes it backfires on me, but never like this! Most of the time I work for lawyers, private investigators, and bounty hunters. I look for people who have skipped bail, or are not paying alimony or child support. Sometimes it's getting information on a cheating spouse. And I do background checks."

"And you do this using computers?"

"Yes, I wrote a program that looks for a digital pattern of a person's life. It looks at their search engines use, chat rooms, information from financial institutes, what shops they use, even what coffee shops they like. I build a digital profile of a person and it predicts where that person might hide or at least shop."

Kate asked, "Why so many computers?"

"I have one master computer that I enter the basic information into, like the person's name, social security number, things like that. The master computer starts processes on the other computers. Each computer then searches its own unique area, like server 2 may search the web, server 3 may search blogs, server 4 financial. It divides the work load over several computers and gives me a faster result. Each computer reports back to the master computer by putting its results into a database. The master computer then sends the database to a different group of computers to analyze and create a document that I can send back to my client. And that is the simple explanation of my system."

"Have you built a profile on me?"

"Yes, and I sent it to the private investigators."

Kate looked at Joe without saying a word.

"I had to, Kate," said Joe, "they would have suspected something if I didn't."

"Can I read it?"

"Sure, let me pull it up on my screen."

Joe watched her as she read through the document.

"That's very accurate, about the only thing you don't have is my bra and panty size."

"I would not be surprised if it's in the database. I don't put that in the client's document unless they ask for it."

"And the files from the bank, you use them in this system?"

"No, that's for a personal project. It seems the bank you work at has three times as many foreclosures as any other bank in the city. Like I said before, I was looking for documents that would show some criminal activity that would explain this."

Kate peered at Joe suspiciously and asked, "How do you make money with that? Blackmail?"

"No, Kate, I never make money on something like this. Most of the time I will send what I find to the news media, but sometimes I will send it straight to the attorney general, anonymously."

Joe studied Kate's face as she glanced up at the computer monitors. After a few seconds he said, "Kate, I know I have no right to ask for your help. But there has to be something in these files that's making people at the bank very nervous."

Kate did not respond, she just kept looking at the monitors.

Joe turned back to his desk and started looking at the files again.

Kate sipped her coffee and watched as he worked.

"Joe, can you sort or search by a person's name?"

Joe replied, "Not their full names, I only recorded the person's user name, which most of the time is a form of the person's full name. In most office networks people like to keep their user names short, like my user name would be something like jmorgan and yours would be kdodson. But I'm sure you knew that already, didn't you? Sorry. But back to your question, searching for a person's name, what are you thinking?"

"The day before yesterday I saw something that was unusual. At the time, I didn't think much about it, but now it may be something. I needed to ask the vice president of the bank, Angelo Diego, something, so I knocked on his door, and it must not have been closed, because it came open. When he noticed me standing there he seemed to be nervous. He pulled a memory stick out of his laptop, and put it in his pocket."

"Why is that unusual?" Joe asked.

"No one is supposed to have a memory stick at the bank, it's against policy. I heard two of the accountants were fired for it."

Joe said, "I don't have the files for that day, but I can download them, it will just take a little time. Will you get another laptop out of the cabinet for me?"

"Thanks," he said as he took the laptop.

She watched as he hooked everything up. "Why are you using that computer instead of one of these from your system?"

"That is a very good question. If I use my hardwired Internet connection someone can trace it here. What I am going to use is a wireless long range WIFI antenna that's mounted on top of this building. It's designed to be used on a boat that is docked at a marina, or an RV at an RV Park."

"You said it's long range, how far are you talking about?"

"I will be connecting to one of three casino hotels that are about one mile away."

"A mile, I have trouble getting my wireless to work on my patio."

Joe got a connection, and then started the download.

Kate asked, "Why can't the IT people from the bank just delete the files that were uploaded?"

"Another good question. The web server that I have the information uploaded to belongs to a business that used to be one of my clients. I was their administrator. I did all the server updates, and things like that. After about a year the owner fired me and turned it over to his nephew. They never changed the administration passwords, so I still have administration rights to it. That lets me have full control of it. I wrote the program that is used to upload the files, and it has full administrator rights, it renames the files to look like system files, then stores them in a system library folder. That makes it very difficult for someone to find them, even with administrator rights. I use the same program to download the files. After the files are downloaded, I send the program a command to delete the files from the server."

When the download completed, Joe disconnected the WIFI connection. He copied the files to his main workstation using a memory stick. Kate and Joe watched the big monitor as he pulled up a list of folder names.

Kate pointed to a folder that was displayed on the monitor and said, "I think that is his."

Joe moved the mouse cursor over the folder and clicked. Another list of folders appeared. Joe pointed to a folder named F_DRIVE and clicked. This time a list of files appeared; three files with the extension name MOV and one with DOC. Joe moved the cursor over the file named COMPLET.MOV and clicked. Joe said, "Well Mr. Angelo, let's see what kind of home movies you have." A second later a window appeared on the monitor and the video file started to play. Kate and Joe watched as a tall black man about thirty five years old entered a motel room with a young white girl who looked like a prostitute.

The young girl slowly undressed down to her panties as the man watched. Then she helped him get out of his clothes. He reached down, picked her up and put her in the bed, and climbed in with her. Then he reached down, grabbed her panties and ripped them off.

Kate said, "I guess all Mr. Diego was doing was downloading porn." She looked at Joe and said, "I'm going to get some more coffee. Do you want some?"

"No, thanks."

Joe was still watching the monitor when Kate returned and sat down beside him.

"Yes, oh yes," said the young girl in the video.

Kate said, "Well, it looks like this didn't help us any."

Joe looked at Kate and said, "This was shot at one angle, and without a studio light system. This looks more like a home movie than a professional porn film. I would think a vice president could afford better quality video than this."

They quickly looked back at the monitor when they heard the girl's voice change. "No! Stop! Stop it!" The man was on top of her with his hands around her throat. They watched as she tried to push against a man twice her weight. Seconds seemed like minutes as he pushed down on her throat and she struggled to break free of his grip. Soon she stopped. Her hands fell to her chest, then slid down to rest next to her body. The video stopped, just like the young girl's life.

"Oh, my God!" exclaimed Kate. "Was that real, did that really happen?" She got up and started pacing the room. "What kind of people would do that? We need to take this to the police!"

Joe turned toward Kate. "Kate, I don't know if this was real or not. I need to watch the other video files and do some research to see if a body was found on or around the date this was filmed. I have never seen a snuff film before, but this is what I would think one would look like. Why don't you go and lay down. I'll let you know when I'm through. OK?"

She nodded and he turned back to the monitors, slipped on a pair of headphones, cut the speakers off, and started the file RAW1.MOV.

Kate went back to the safe room and lay down. She was unable to get the young girl's image out of her head and soon her deep depression was replaced by anger. She sat up on the side of the bed, then walked back into Joe's office and sat down beside him.

Joe paused the video and turned to Kate. "Are you OK?"

"Yeah, no, I don't know!" She turned to look at him and said, "I need to do something. What can I do to help?"

"You can look at the other files and see if there is anything that doesn't look right. Use the laptop that Randy was using."

Kate moved her chair near the laptop, sat down, and started opening a file.

Joe watched her for a few moments then said, "Thanks, Kate."

She turned to him and nodded.

~ ~ ~

Candy walked into the office around 6:30 AM. "Good morning," she said. "How are you doing, Kate?"

"I think I'll be OK."

Candy looked at Joe and then asked Kate, "Why is he wearing a headset? I have never seen him do that before."

"He's watching a video and he doesn't want me to hear it."

"A video? What kind of a video?" Just then she noticed the images on the monitor.

Out of the corner of his eye, Joe saw Candy standing next to Kate. He turned to them and saw Libby coming into the room. "Good, you're both up. We got something, and it is big. Kate found some files this morning." He looked at Kate and said, "The video that we saw is being used to blackmail an Air Force Officer. Kate, this could even be a national security problem."

Kate shook her head. "Wow, it just keeps getting better and better. Did he kill that girl?"

Candy said, "Kill a girl, what girl, what did you find?"

"Hold on," said Joe. "Kate is not aware of everything I have found, so let me bring all of you up to speed. First, the video that Kate and I saw was edited from the other two video files. The person that we saw at the beginning of the video was not the person that killed her. The second video file showed him leaving the motel room and she was still alive. The third video file showed another man entering the room and killing her. The two men have a similar build and with the poor lighting, I really couldn't tell the difference between the two. But there was enough light to tell them apart when they entered the room."

"So there was a girl murdered?" asked Kate.

"Yes, I did a search on the local news web sites and found one article about a young prostitute that was killed in a motel on the date that the movie was created. So yes, it is real."

Candy and Libby looked at each other and then back to Joe.

"Also, the document that we downloaded talked about using the video to blackmail the officer into cooperating with them."

Kate asked, "Cooperate with who? Angelo Diego?"

"I don't know. I can only assume so. Kate, what makes this officer important is that he is in charge of the drones. The ones used in Afghanistan and Iraq."

Everyone just looked at each other. Then Libby spoke up. "It looks like we need to build a profile on Mr. Angelo Diego and the Air Force officer, and we need to do it fast. Joe, it may be terrorists looking for us. We may not even be safe here."

"You're right. Why don't you girls get started while I fix everyone some breakfast. I have been up all night, I'm tired, my butt hurts, and I need to get some sleep soon."

Kate said, "I need to get away from this computer monitor for a while, and I doubt that I would be any help to Libby and Candy. So, why don't I help you make breakfast?"

"Sure."

Candy looked at Libby, smiled, and said, "Wow, we might get

something other than cereal."

Libby returned her smile and said, "Hallelujah!"

Joe turned his chair around and started to the kitchen. Then he said, "I heard that."

~ ~ ~

Tennessee whiskey, or straight bourbon whiskey, as some call it, was Jerry Powell's drink of choice. He sipped his whiskey breakfast in his office, grateful he hadn't broken his last bottle when he damaged his liquor cabinet. As he relaxed, a rare thing most days, he reviewed the previous day's events and wondered if it had been a mistake to let Angelo talk him into getting involved with his drug business. He was doing well with his other not so legal activities where he had the control. The drug money had looked too good to pass up, but he liked being in control, and he wasn't the boss in this mess. And now, thanks to Kate Dodson, things were even more complicated. He was glad Angelo was handling that problem; that left him free to think about a couple of loose ends that he needed to take care of. He called his secretary and said, "Ask Miss Walters to come into my office." He finished his whiskey as he waited.

Moments later, Miss Walters, a tall, thin woman in her late forties, knocked on the door and came into the office. "Good morning, Mr. Powell," she said as she sat down across the desk from him.

He put his glass down on the desk. "It's good to have you back," he said. "How are you doing now that you're through with the surgery and chemo?"

"Not too bad. I'm getting stronger every day. Thanks for asking."

"If there is anything I can do to help you and your son, let me know."

"I appreciate that. Thank you."

"How is your son doing?"

"The doctors are saying that his condition will never change. He will always need constant care."

"He has cerebral palsy, right?"

"Yes, motorcycle accident. He had been drinking and decided to ride without a helmet."

Jerry took a moment then said, "That's tough, I'm sorry."

She just nodded her head.

Jerry picked up his empty glass and said, "I think I could use another, would you like one?"

"No, but thanks. If I weren't still taking medicine, I would take you up on that."

Jerry just smiled and walked to the liquor cabinet. He started to fill the glass and said, "I understand you and Angelo straightened out the special accounts that I tried to create. Thanks, I kind of made a mess of things while you were out on sick leave."

She smiled and said, "Don't worry about that, everything looks legit now. I just hate that Lara Manning found them and almost exposed us."

"Yes, she just wouldn't let it go. I hate that I had to fire her."

Miss Walters fell silent for a moment, then looked down at her feet and softly said, "She's young, healthy, smart, and attractive. She'll bounce back. I wouldn't worry about her."

Jerry sat back down behind his desk. He opened a drawer, pulled out an envelope, and handed it to Miss Walters. "I just called you in to say I appreciate your help with the special accounts. I think this will help with some of your medical bills."

She looked in the envelope. "It will, thank you." She stood up and said, "I better get back to my office. I still have a lot of catching up to do."

Jerry watched her leave, then picked up the phone, dialed, and said, "I have a job for you. Her name is Lara Manning."

Chapter 3

Cortez villa, north of Puerto Vallarta, Mexico

A young Mexican couple lay face down, bound and gagged, at the feet of Cortez and his men. The couple's eyes were fixed on each other as Cortez pulled the girl's skirt up. He laughed and said, "Look at that boys, I think we may have to take that for a little ride."

Her boyfriend, lying next to her, started twisting and jerking, but soon realized that he could not free himself.

Cortez said, "Oh, look at that, he wants to protect her."

They all looked down at the young man, and they laughed at his concern for her honor, knowing that he hadn't realized yet that tonight would be their last night alive.

Hernando Cortez, a tall, slim man of 34 years, with light tan skin, and brown hair, pushed his rectangular glasses toward his face, turned to his lieutenant, Raul, and said, "Take them to the guest room and make them comfortable. Make sure her boyfriend has a front row seat. I want him to watch his girlfriend entertain us tonight."

Raul was about six feet tall, heavy, with medium tan skin and short, black, curly hair. He didn't say anything, just pointed to the couple, then to the door. The other men grabbed the couple by their arms and legs and carried them to the guest room upstairs.

Cortez asked, "Do you have someone looking for their friends?"

"Yes," said Raul, "my brother, Fernando, is going through their cell phones looking for anyone else that has been blogging about cartel business. He is better with computers and cell phones than I am."

"Good, Fernando is a good man and very smart."

"What do you want to do with the couple after tonight's entertainment?"

"I don't know. It should be very public."

"One of the men suggested that in the morning, we should hang them upside down from a busy bridge. That way, everyone driving under the bridge will see them as they go to work."

Cortez thought for several seconds. "That's a horrible way to start a work day," he said, "do it, and gut them too."

Raul smiled. "Yes, sir."

Raul and Cortez were the same age, and Raul felt close to him, more like a friend than an employee, and he liked the fact that

Cortez made decisions very quickly. Cortez's men respected him too; he was tough, but fair, and paid them very well in a country with very high unemployment. For their pay, Cortez demanded two things: loyalty, and for his men to follow his commands without question.

Cortez walked to the cabinet behind his desk, opened the humidor and pulled out two hand rolled Cuban cigars. He clipped the ends off each, handed one to Raul and asked, "Has anyone heard from Angelo?"

Raul held it under his nose for a moment, then said, "Not that I know of. Should I call him?"

"No, not yet."

Raul put his cigar in his mouth, pulled a lighter from his pocket and lit Cortez's cigar first, then his. For several moments both men smiled and stared at the thin waves of smoke slowly rising from the highly prized roll of tobacco leaves, then Raul said, "Angelo is a good man. I bet that he will find the people that got into his computer."

"He better. I have several million invested in this project and I don't like it when things go wrong."

"We have been able to move our products a lot easier now that we are able to keep track of the American surveillance drones that are flying over our fields. I would hate to lose that ability."

Cortez threw his hands in the air and bellowed, "I cannot believe I'm having so much trouble with a bunch of computer freaks. Look at the two you just brought me. What did Fernando call them, bloggers? They are Mexicans. They should know better than to talk about me and my business. And those cocky ass Americans, I can hardly wait until I get my hands on those damn people that got into Angelo's computer."

Raul waited silently until Cortez calmed down, then said, "The last time I talked to Angelo, he said that the people that were hired to make the drone tracking system have been a real asset in tracking the people that stole the files from his computer. He also said they gave the tracking system a name. Gringo Reconnaissance Avoidance Support System, GRASS for short."

Cortez started laughing, "GRASS, I love that. We need to keep those young boys happy. Be sure to get them some girls." He turned, started walking to the door and said, "Well, we have some entertainment for tonight. Let's not keep them waiting any longer."

~ ~ ~

Las Vegas, Nevada

Angelo pulled his car into the parking lot of the small single story office building marked by the sign out front as OSC, Inc. He opened the front door of the building, entered, and walked past the guards at the security desk to a door with an RFID reader mounted next to the door. He pulled a blank white card out of his pocket and waved it near the reader and the LED on the RFID reader turned from red to green. Angelo opened the steel door, but turned back to the guard before he walked through and asked, "Is Claudette Godard in her office?"

The guard stared at the computer monitor for a moment then said, "We still have her in the building sir. I assume she is in her office."

Angelo nodded, then walked down a hallway to the first door on the left, where he stopped. He stood outside the open door and watched Claudette working at her computer. She was an attractive 25 year old brunette wearing blue jeans, sandals, and a tan Henley shirt that was left unbuttoned, exposing a black choker holding a silver cross against her tan skin.

"Hello, Claudette," he said as he entered the room. "It looks like your brother has the security system working."

She looked up. "Yes," she said in her sexy French accent, "Antoine has been very busy getting this place ready. Do you wish to talk to him?"

"Later. First I need to know if you have any leads on the people that stole the files from us?"

"No, but I have all my programmers looking at chat rooms and social media sites." She paused for a second, and then added, "It shouldn't be much longer. They can't stay underground very long, and web searches will go much faster when Antoine gets the server cluster completed. We will find them."

"Antoine mentioned something about a server cluster." He sat down in the chair opposite her. "I still can't say I understand what that is."

Claudette smiled and said, "It's where several computers are tied together in a network to make a single computer system. It has the ability to distribute the work load over several computers. Most of today's supercomputers use a system like this."

Angelo smiled. "When I hired you and your brother to put together a computerized transportation and distribution system, I never realized it would take a supercomputer."

Claudette laughed. "This is only 20 servers, by today's standards it's far from a supercomputer."

"Is GRASS completed?" asked Angelo.

"Antoine said this morning that the people that are installing the mobile data systems into the trucks in Mexico told him that only a few trucks are left and they should be done this afternoon. They're the ones used in the marijuana and opium fields during harvest season so they are the hardest to reach."

"Good. Any problems with the GRASS network system at the Air Force base?"

"No, everything is working, from the network tap at Creech AFB, to the host server in Dallas, and then to the servers and the mobile data radio system in the trucks in Mexico. It's a very simple system and as long as the network tap at the Air Force base isn't discovered, everything should be fine."

He leaned toward her, keeping his eyes on her face, and put his arms on her desk. "How is the online gambling system coming?"

"Since I have all my programmers looking for the people that stole the files from the bank, it's very slow. I am the only one writing any code for it."

"When you called yesterday, you said that you and Antoine want to make some changes to the distribution system."

"Yes," she looked down at her desk and picked up a pen. "The way we distribute the product will be more like an online store with its own delivery network." She tapped the pen on the desk. "Customers purchase products from the online gambling website. That information is sent to the warehouse computers where people package the products with the route and package numbers attached to the box." She noticed him watching the tapping pen and she stopped. "Then the boxes are placed into backpacks marked with their route number and loaded onto a truck. The trucks leave the warehouse to drive to a location near their customers. About thirty minutes before pickup the customers will be sent a text message saying to get ready to pick up their products. At the same time, our delivery boys on bicycles will get a text message on their smart phones. The message will be the GPS location to meet the truck."

She put the pen down and looked in his eyes. "Then the customers will be given a time and GPS location to pick up their products." She absentmindedly reached up and played with the cross around her neck. "And when the truck is at the drop off location, the boys on bicycles will each get a backpack. The truck driver signals to turn on a long range WiFi network, located on a tall building nearby. The signal should reach several miles around the building. The truck then drives off to its next location."

He smiled as her hand moved up and twisted a strand of hair around her finger. "The boys will then log into the local long range WiFi network with their smart phones and start an app that I have created. The app will download a map that has a route, a delivery point, a time and a package number. As a package is delivered, they will click on the package delivered button on the screen, then a new map pops up just like before with a new route, delivery point, time, and package number. About the time the boys have completed their deliveries, another truck pulls up at the end of their route. The truck driver takes back the backpacks and any packages that were not delivered. He pays the boys $50.00 each and signals to turn off the long range WiFi network. And everyone leaves."

"That sounds very complicated," he said, still smiling, his eyes caressing her face.

She dropped her hand from her hair, and glanced down at her desk. "The software, that we write, handles 95% of the work. The workers just have to follow the instructions on their computer monitors or smart phones."

"What does it add to the cost?"

"We calculate about 5% increase to start with but as we grow we expect the higher volume will cut that cost down. Since we are dealing with upper middle-class clients, who can afford the extra cost, we think they will appreciate the extra layer of security that we provide. And if they get their order in before 4:00 PM they can expect delivery that night."

"What extra security are you talking about?"

She looked back at him and saw a twinkle in his eyes. "First the client has to join the online gambling website." She paused. "Then he will be given an account number and user name, and he can make up a password." She paused again, watching his eyes. "Then he gives us credit card information that will be used for the purchases. That way, if someone looks very hard at a customer's credit card statement it will look like gambling losses. And since it looks like gambling losses, it's a very efficient way for OCS and your bank to launder the money." Another pause. "We can also do a quick electronic background check on the customer."

She reached for her hair again, and then continued. "The next security layer is, if at any time one of the delivery boys misses a delivery time, a text message is sent to the rest of the clients in his route. The message will say something like, 'The delivery system has been compromised, please leave now. We will reschedule for the next day.' Also the routes and delivery locations change every day."

"Sounds like you have thought of everything." His eyes moved down to her breasts.

She let go of her hair and waited until he noticed her silence and looked back up at her eyes.

He smiled. "I can hardly wait to see your system in action."

She looked directly into his eyes and said, "We still have a lot of code to write." Then she paused, still staring into his eyes, the corners of her mouth turning slightly up. "But once we install your hardware, you'll see plenty of action in my system."

He smiled. "Will there be any more changes to the computerized inventory control system for shipping from Mexico to the warehouse here in Vegas?"

"No, that's up and running. We have it here on a couple of servers in the back room. We can even track the locations of the shipments on a map. That way if one shipment is taking too long, and we think it might be compromised, we can take whatever actions we think necessary."

"Wow," he said softly, his eyes caressing her again, "I'm impressed."

Angelo's phone rang. "Hello, Jerry." Claudette watched his face change as he listened. "Just calm down," he said, a serious tone in his voice now, "I can be back in thirty minutes." He hung up and smiled at Claudette. "I need to leave, Jerry seems to be in panic mode lately. But I would love to talk some more. Would you have dinner with me tonight? I could pick you up about 7:00. And if it's OK with you, I would love to cook for you at my place."

She smiled, started playing with her necklace, and said, "Yes."

"Where do you live?" Angelo asked.

"Pick me up here, I still have a lot of work to do."

"Don't you ever leave, it seems like you're always here."

"Antoine and I haven't had time to find a place yet. We have converted a couple of offices in the back into small bedrooms. That works out well for us because we like to stay close to our work, besides we're not used to having a lot of stuff."

Angelo, trying to hide his surprise, smiled and said, "OK, then I will see you here at 7:00."

~ ~ ~

Angelo carefully pulled his new red Mercedes, SLS AMG Coupe, into the parking lot of OSC, Inc. He pulled the door latch and smiled as he watched the gull-wing door lift up. An unseasonable light cool wind passed over him as he confidently walked to the front of the building, and then entered into the small lobby.

"Good evening, sir," the guard behind the counter said, "I already informed Miss Godard that you've arrived. She said she would be right out."

"Thank you."

The door opened a few seconds later, and Claudette entered the lobby wearing the same clothes she had on earlier.

Angelo smiled and said, "Hello," as she drew near him.

"I hope you don't mind what I'm wearing, I lost track of the time and was unable to change."

"You're perfect. This is just a casual dinner at home, and I haven't had a chance to change either."

She smiled at him and said, "Thank you for that, you are a gentleman."

He laughed as he held the door for her. "I don't think anyone has ever called me that before."

As they walked across the parking lot, a cool gust of wind caused her to wrap her arms around her slim body. Angelo took off his jacket and draped it around her shoulders. "Here," he said, "you may need this tonight."

When Claudette saw the car they were walking toward, she said, "Is that yours?"

"Yes," he said, grinning from ear to ear. "I just got it this afternoon. You'll be my first passenger."

He pulled the door latch, stepped back and watched a big smile appear on her face as the door lifted itself up.

"Oh, wow! I know I'm under dressed to ride in this car."

Still grinning, he looked her up and down and said, "Claudette Godard, I think you would look good in anything you wear."

"Merci beaucoup," she said, grinning back, as she got into the car.

Laughing, he said, "I don't think anyone has ever said that to me either."

She watched him as he shut the door and walked around the car to get in.

"If you don't mind, let's drive down The Strip before we head home, the little boy in me wants to show off the car."

She laughed at him and nodded her head.

Evening traffic was heavy as gamblers and tourists converged on one of the most illuminated streets in the world, Las Vegas Boulevard South, also known as The Strip. Claudette studied Angelo as he carefully weaved the car through the limos, the mobile billboard trucks with their vivid ads, the buses, cars, trucks, and the sprinkle of other sport cars, all of them trying to avoid hitting each other, and the thousands of pedestrians crossing the street. Claudette jumped when Angelo suddenly hit the brakes, barely stopping in time as some young men squeezed their car in front of his so they could make a turn into a casino-hotel driveway. Angelo said nothing, just patiently waited, as they slowly pulled out of the way.

"That was close," said Claudette.

"Yes, this may not have been a good idea."

Claudette sat back and tried to relax by people watching. Then she realized that some of the people she was watching were watching back. She saw them pointing and she wondered what they were saying, not sure she was comfortable with the attention. *Well, I guess that's what you get when you're in this kind of car*, she thought. She felt Angelo look at her and she looked at him. He smiled, and she smiled back, as she watched him steer through the heavy traffic with a steady hand.

"Look, Elvis," Angelo said, as he pointed to a group of celebrity impersonators on the sidewalk having their photos taken with tourists.

Claudette started laughing and pointed at an older man getting his photo taken with Marilyn Monroe. She said, "As they were taking the photo, the wind blew her skirt up."

Angelo laughed. "I hope he paid her extra for that shot."

As they stopped at the next light, they noticed a woman wrapped in an aluminum foil looking survival blanket.

"That wind must be getting colder," said Claudette.

Angelo smiled. "That, or she just doesn't want the aliens from Area 51 to read her mind."

Claudette paused and gave him a questioning look, then asked, "Aliens?"

With a straight face, he said, "Sure, the government built Area 51 just north of Las Vegas so the little green men would have a place to land when they come here to visit." Then he looked at her and grinned. "It must be true, I read it in a tabloid magazine at a grocery checkout."

Claudette laughed. "Yes, it must be true then."

They continued south, turning west at Tropicana, then headed to the Summerlin area. When they arrived at Angelo's house, he pulled into his gated, circular driveway and stopped at the front door. He got out, opened the door for Claudette, and held out his hand to help her out of her seat. As she slid out of the car, he pulled her close, kissed her on the cheek, and said, "Thank you."

"For what?"

"For letting me show off tonight. I'm sure you have heard about boys and their toys."

She laughed. "Yes. I didn't mind at all."

After they entered the house, Angelo asked, "Can I get you something to drink, wine, or maybe a cocktail?"

"White wine would be nice."

He handed her a glass of wine. "You will have to pardon me, I feel like I need a shower. I won't be long. Feel free to explore my house."

She peered through the family room windows and noticed a mural of mountains, trees, a river, and a small village painted on the tall walls surrounding a large patio. At the back of the patio were pots with short palm trees surrounding a hot tub and a lap pool. Then she walked around the house looking at each room. She heard the shower turn off as she reached the master bedroom. The door was not completely closed and she pushed it open a little more to peek in. A large full length mirror was mounted next to the king size bed giving her a view into the bathroom, and in it she could see Angelo as he stepped out of the shower, took a towel, and started drying his hair. Claudette smiled as she watched the water sparkle against Angelo's tan skin.

She turned and walked back down the hall, and in a soft voice said, "Nice."

Claudette was sitting on the sofa sipping her wine when Angelo returned to the family room wearing a black guayabera linen shirt with light khaki pants. The sounds of a Spanish guitar softly poured into the room from hidden speakers.

"Good, I see you found the sound system. I can change the music if you like."

"No, leave that playing, it's very relaxing, and different from the heavy metal that the boys play at work."

"Don't you get to listen to what you like?"

"Only if I have my mp3 player and noise canceling headphones."

"I'm starving," said Angelo, "how about you?"

"Yes."

"An omelet would be quick. Would that be OK?"

"Yes, can I help?"

"Sure, you can break some eggs while I chop."

"That sounds good," said Claudette, "and I definitely know how to break eggs."

Angelo poured more wine, put on an apron, and started chopping the peppers.

Claudette watched him as he quickly sliced and chopped the ingredients. "Where did you learn to cook?" she asked.

"My grandmother was the cook for a wealthy family in Mexico. She taught me. She also raised me."

"Where were your parents?"

He stopped chopping and took a sip of his wine. "I never knew my father, and my mother was murdered when I was young."

Claudette leaned over and kissed him. "I'm so sorry," she said. "I did not mean to stir up bad memories."

"No, don't be sorry, I have very fond memories of my mother. She would often play with me down by the river near our village. And I try not to think about how she died; just how she lived."

Angelo reached up to a hanging pot rack and grabbed a large frying pan. "I think it's time we start cooking."

Claudette watched as he cooked the potato, pepper, onion and then ham. He put that aside and started cooking the eggs. When they were ready, he layered the other ingredients on top and added a little cheese. He folded the omelet, then cut it in half and placed the omelet on two plates with fresh salsa spread on top.

"That not only smells good, but looks delicious, too," said Claudette.

Angelo pulled some forks out of a drawer and handed her one. "Try it."

He watched her take a bite as he refilled their wine glasses. "How is it?" he asked.

She had taken three more bites before she realized he was standing next to her grinning, and watching her every move. She looked up at him, smiled, and just gave him a thumbs up.

He started laughing.

She said, "I'm sorry, but this is good."

"Don't be sorry for enjoying something you like. You want to sit at the table or just stay here?"

"Here's fine." She smiled and said, "I'm almost finished anyway."

They stood at the kitchen counter, not saying a word, just occasionally glancing at each other as they finished their meal.

"Why don't you go sit down while I put everything in the dishwasher and do a quick clean up," he said.

"Your patio looks interesting, can we sit out there?"

"Sure, go ahead, I'll be out soon."

She was looking closely at the mural on the walls when he joined her on the patio. "What do you think of it?" he asked.

"This is beautiful. The detail makes it look very real. I almost feel like I'm there."

He pointed to a small building, and said, "That's where I grew up as a young child." He then pointed to the village and the river. "That's the village and river I was telling you about earlier, where I used to play."

"This is just beautiful."

"Thank you. I had a local artist do this from an old photograph my grandmother had. It took her about nine months to finish it."

Claudette said, "I really like how the lap pool looks like it's part of the river."

"Yes, the artist was very good." He paused then said, "I haven't been back to that village since I was 9 years old. That was when my grandmother and I left." He looked at her and said, "This is where I go to get away from everyone and relax."

She took his hand and held it. "That sounds nice."

As they walked around the patio, Angelo told her about his early childhood in the village with his mother and grandmother. He told her about his time with a very young Cortez. But he never mentioned his mother's death again and she wondered if it was too painful to remember, or if he even knew the details.

They stopped next to the lap pool and stood quietly for a few moments. Then she said, "I haven't been swimming in ages. Can I try it out?"

"Sure, but I don't have a swimsuit for you."

"That's OK, I've seen you naked, it's only fair." She put her hand on his chest, lifted her foot up and pulled one shoe off, then the next.

"When did you see me?"

She unzipped her pants, pulled them off, and placed them in a chair nearby. "When you got out of the shower." She smiled. "You said I could look around." She raised her arms above her head and said, "Help me with my top."

He laughed. "I hope you weren't disappointed." He reached down, pulled her top off, and placed it on the chair.

Still smiling, she looked up at him and said, "No! Not at all." Then she turned around, pulled her hair up, and said, "This, too."

He unhooked her bra and helped her out of it.

She turned back around, put one hand on his chest again, reached down, pulled her panties off and said, "You're going to join me, aren't you?"

~ ~ ~

Angelo opened his eyes when he heard Claudette roll over in the king size bed. He stared at the clock until his eyes could focus and make out the time. It was 8:30 on Saturday morning. His normal weekend day consisted of reading the Journal and Investment Daily newspapers and updating his investment portfolio. Today he just wanted to entertain his guest. He slipped carefully out of bed and picked up his robe, watching the gentle movement of Claudette's breath as he put it on. He walked into the kitchen and started the coffee, then cut up some strawberries and sprinkled them with powdered sugar. He put some bagels into the toaster and squeezed some fresh orange juice. He put everything on a tray and headed back to the bedroom.

Claudette jumped when she heard the tray bump the bedroom door. Her eyes widened in surprise as Angelo entered the room and put the tray beside her in the middle of the bed.

He climbed back into bed and said, "Good morning."

She sat up, adjusting her pillows behind her back. "Wow! Breakfast in bed! I could really get used to this." Then she caught a glimpse of the clock and said, "Oh, no! I hate to eat and run, but I need to get to work."

"You really need to go in today?"

"Yes, I'm afraid so," she said. "Right now I'm the only programmer who's writing any code." She smiled. "Well, I could be a little late today. Can you keep a secret?" She leaned closer and whispered in his ear, "I am sleeping with the boss."

Angelo smiled and said, "Is that right?"

Claudette thought for a second then said, "Well, there really wasn't much sleeping was there?"

When their laughter subsided, they finished their breakfasts quickly. "If I'm going to drive you back to work," said Angelo after he finished his coffee, "I need to get a shower and get ready."

She watched him as he took his robe off and turned on the water. She finished her coffee, got up, and walked into the shower. They stood looking at each other as the warm water ran over their bodies. She put her arms around his neck and he placed his hands on her waist and pulled her close.

~ ~ ~

Libby called to Joe, "The profile on Angelo Diego is done."

"Go ahead and read it to us," said Joe.

"Angelo immigrated to America from Mexico with his grandmother when he was 9 years old. He graduated high school at 18. He went five years to a business college. To help put himself through college, he worked fulltime as a teller at a bank. He did have some financial help. He had a grant from an unknown benefactor. When he got his degree, the bank made him a manager of one of their small branches. A few years ago he started working at JP Bank of Nevada as vice-president. At thirty years old, he is one of the youngest vice-presidents in the country. Never been married. No children. Can't find anything about any relationships. His grandmother died a few years ago. He has a very nice house with no mortgage. And he just bought a new Mercedes SLS AMG coupe."

"That's a nice car," said Kate.

Libby continued, "I have been looking for more information about where Angelo lived as a child but can't find anything. I also cannot find anything about the college grant he got."

Joe said, "Mexico is not noted for keeping good records so we may not ever find anything about that part of his life."

"The computers are still working on Jerry Powell. We should have something soon," said Libby.

"Anyone got any ideas about what we can do next?" asked Joe. "Kate, I'm sure you have talked to Mr. Diego a few times, can you think of anything?"

Kate just shook her head.

Candy said, "The tracking device that I got from Kate's car, I can delete the data in it now, then put it on Angelo's car, leave it a few days and see where he goes. That might tell us something."

"That's good," said Joe. "Anyone see a problem with that?"

"The only place we can get to his car is at the bank," said Kate. "There are security cameras in the parking lot. How are we going to get to it without being seen?"

Joe looked at Kate and asked, "What part of the parking lot does he park in?"

"He has assigned parking next to the building."

"I assume there is handicapped parking near the building too?"

"Yes."

"Let me pull up Google maps and get a satellite view of the building and parking lot."

Everyone watched as the satellite image came up on the large monitor.

"Kate, please sit next to me and point out everything you can remember about the parking lot. I need to know where Angelo parks, where the handicapped parking is, the security cameras locations, the exits, and anything else you can think of."

~ ~ ~

Randy pulled Joe's van to the curb around the corner of the bank, away from their security cameras, to let Candy get out. She was wearing a very short pleated skirt, heels, and a red bra that was clearly visible through her thin white shirt. She watched the van drive away, admiring Libby's work on the magnetic signs on the sides that read, Golden Years Assisted Living of Las Vegas.

Then Randy drove around to the bank's parking lot and pulled the van into a handicapped parking spot. He got out, opened the side door, and pressed a button to activate the automated ramp. While Joe's wheelchair lowered, he pulled his baseball cap down and tucked in some stray hairs as he casually looked around, making sure Angelo's new car was there.

Joe was dressed to look much older. He was wearing dress pants, a white tee shirt, a navy sport jacket, and a white Panama straw hat with the brim turned down.

Randy handed Joe a 36 inch grab tool. Joe placed it on his lap and when Randy started to push his chair, he made his voice sound old and cranky and he loudly said, "I don't need your help! I can do it myself! You just stay there and leave me alone!"

Randy turned around, walked back to the van, and stood there, waiting. The security guard opened the door for Joe and he entered the bank and rolled to a counter where he started picking up papers from the top. He picked up several at once and dropped them all on the floor.

An employee noticed Joe trying to pick them back up with his grab tool and she hurried over to his side. "Can I help you?" she asked.

Joe said, "Yes, thank you, I was looking for information on your CD rates."

"Here you go. Is there anything else I can help you with?" she said as she handed him one of the papers from the counter.

"No, this is what I came in for." He then smiled and said, "Thank you so much young lady."

"You're welcome."

Joe turned and rolled back to the door.

Candy had joined Randy while Joe was inside and the guard's attention was on her. Joe tapped on the glass and the guard opened the door, while still keeping his eyes on Candy.

Randy and Candy seemed to be so focused on each other that they didn't notice when Joe rolled up, but the guard saw Joe take his grab tool and lift Candy's skirt up, and he started laughing when he saw Candy slap the tool away and grab Joe's hat. Then she walked away and threw the hat under Angelo's car. She continued on around the bank building and down the street to where Randy and Joe had dropped her off.

The guard watched her until she was out of sight around the corner, then he shouted to Joe and Randy, "Do you need any help?"

"No, thanks," yelled Randy, "I'll get his hat."

As Randy was lying down, reaching under the car, he pulled the GPS tracker that Candy had reset out of his pocket. He found some steel that the magnets could hold to and placed the tracker there. Then he grabbed Joe's hat, stood up, waved it at the guard, and shouted, "Got it!" Then he walked back to the van.

Randy helped Joe into the van and closed the door. As he started walking around the van, he waved at the guard again. When Randy got inside he said to Joe, "That seemed to go like clockwork."

"Yes, it's best to just keep it simple."

As the van pulled off, another guard came to the door and asked, "Is everything OK?"

The first guard laughed and said, "Yeah, some old fart in a wheelchair just got a peep show from a hooker. They're gone now."

~ ~ ~

As Antoine walked down the hall he pulled his long brown hair back into a ponytail. At 5 feet 9 and 155 pounds, he was slim and not very muscular. He always dressed casually, in blue jeans, button down shirt with the tail out, and a comfortable pair of Crocs.

He entered Claudette's office and sat down in a chair in front of her desk. He leaned forward, put his elbows on her desk, put his head in his hands and just smiled and stared at her.

Claudette turned her head from the monitor, put her elbows on the desk, her head in her hands, and smiled as she stared at Antoine and said, "What?"

He just grinned and stared.

"I'm working, what?" she said.

"Oh, I'm sure you were working it last night."

She smiled at her brother and said, "I like him."

Antoine's expression became serious, and he said, "Claudette, I love you, and I am glad you found someone you like, but I don't want to see you hurt. Angelo is a major player in the drug world. This man will have us killed if he ever thinks we screwed him."

"I know."

"OK, I will not say anything else about him."

"Thanks."

Antoine said, "Remember the web server that Kate Dodson and Randy Hunter used when stealing the files from the bank. We noticed that someone downloaded files from it early this morning."

"When?"

"About 4:00 AM."

"Where?"

"Downtown at the Fremont Hotel."

"Did you contact Angelo's men?"

"Yes. And they walked all around the hotel, and nothing."

Claudette said, "They could have been anywhere; lobby, restaurant, gambling, even outside at the Fremont Experience."

"Yeah. A dead end."

Claudette sat looking at Antoine for a moment, then said, "They may live or work near the downtown area. They could walk to the Fremont, download the files, then go back home. I think we should concentrate our search in the downtown area."

"Yeah. I think that's a good idea. Right now that is all we have. I'll call Angelo's men and have them do that."

Antoine gazed at Claudette, his love and concern for her evident in his face. "Claudette, remember to call me if you get into trouble."

Claudette came around the desk and kissed his cheek and whispered, "You, too."

"OK," he said, as he stood up and gave her a quick hug. Then he turned toward the door. "I'll let you get back to work."

~ ~ ~

Kate greeted them at the apartment door and asked, "Well, how did it go?"

Randy smiled. "Everything seemed to go fine. Candy put on quite a show."

Kate looked at Joe then and said, "Libby has the other profiles ready."

"Good, let's change clothes," Joe said, "then I'll put on a pot of coffee, and we can join you in the office."

"You go change. I'll start the coffee," Kate said.

"Thanks."

Everyone soon met back in the office, sat down, and started sipping their coffee.

"OK, Libby," said Joe, "what did you find?"

"I'll start with Jerry Powell. I could not find anything unusual about him. He's married with two children, nice home. And the only thing Powell and Angelo have in common is that they work at the bank. I'm hopeful the files that we downloaded from the bank might tell us more."

"Next is the Air Force officer. His name is Commander Nathan Conner, 39 years old, joined the Air Force at 18. A commander at Creech AFB for two years. He is married and has one son. He owns a house in a middle-class neighborhood just outside of the city of Vegas. His wife works as a bookkeeper at a hospital. His son is 11 years old and going to public school. I see nothing unusual about his finances: mortgage, owes a little on some cards, owns two cars, and a motorcycle. I'll keep looking deeper at him but it is going to take more time."

"Well, while Libby is digging into Nathan Conner, the rest of us can be looking at the files from the bank," said Joe. "I don't think we have found everything, there has to be more here. Look for anything suspicious or out of the ordinary. If you find something, show it to Kate. Then in a few days we can get the tracker back and see where Mr. Angelo Diego has been."

"How are we going to do that?" Randy asked. "I don't think we can do the same thing that we did today, can we?"

"We have a couple of days to come up with something," Joe said.

"I don't see why we can't do the same thing," said Candy. "But next time I'll drive and Randy can wear the short skirt and heels."

As everyone started laughing, Joe looked around the room, enjoying the moment. Right now they were still able to laugh, but he knew this wouldn't last long, a group of confined and stressed out people will soon get on each other's nerves. Already he could see

Kate's smile vanishing. He knew this would be hard on her, she seemed to be an outgoing person who wouldn't like being confined, and she hadn't decided to do this, she had been forced into this.

He watched as they turned back to their computers, knowing they were hoping, praying, to find the one thing that would get them back to the life they knew before, knowing that if they didn't find something soon, that some of them would fall into a deep depression. And he knew that some people have a lot of trouble pulling themselves out of the lows. He had seen it when he was stationed in Iraq.

He also knew that even with weeks of searching, they might not ever find anything else. He put his coffee cup to his lips, then realized the brew had already turned cold. He put the cup down, turned to his computer monitor and started to read another document, hoping, praying, that this would be the one.

~ ~ ~

Kate leaned back from the laptop computer and started rubbing her eyes. "I need to get away from this for a while. Wish we could go outside, I could use some sunlight."

"If you girls want to chance it," said Joe, "you can go out back and sit on the patio and Randy and I will watch the surveillance monitors."

The girls looked at each other and Kate said, "Yes, that sounds good."

"Stay close, OK?" said Joe, as the girls were leaving the office.

They grabbed some colas from the fridge and carried them outside. Just outside the door, Kate stopped and stood with her face to the sun. "That feels good," she said, "it seems like we've been inside for months."

They sat down at the table and enjoyed the sunshine and fresh air and sipped on their colas. Candy looked at Kate and said, "You said that you used to dance at the Fremont Experience. Did you like that?"

"Well, it wasn't a bad job, most of the time I made very good money, and it paid for school," Kate said.

"I couldn't do that," said Libby.

"Why not?" asked Candy.

"To start with," said Libby, "I don't have the boobs."

Kate and Candy smiled.

"When I started dancing," said Kate, "I noticed most of the other girls were making a lot more money than I was. And they were smaller than me. What they had was a better attitude, and confidence. They were friendlier. At first I was just plain scared and it showed, but once I got a little confidence I started making some money, too."

"What about you, Candy?" asked Kate. "How did you and Joe meet up?"

"It's a long story, but basically Joe picked me up off the street and saved my life," said Candy.

"What happened?"

"Well," she continued, "two years ago, I ran away from home with my boyfriend. We were from Oklahoma City. He had this idea that he could come to Vegas and make a living playing poker. All I wanted was to be with him. It turned out he was not that good at playing poker and most of the time he would lose, sometimes he would break even. What little money we had was soon gone and I had to get a job waiting tables to pay the bills. He started taking pills and one night he talked me into taking some of his pills. I got so messed up. That night two men came to the apartment wanting their money back from my boyfriend. I didn't know he was borrowing money to get into the games. They started hitting and kicking him and I tried to stop them. One man grabbed me and said that if I wanted them to stop, then I would have to pay them. I was so messed up and scared I didn't know what to do. They took me to the bedroom and said, 'You know what to do.' Those two men did things to me all night. When they left the next morning, my boyfriend was gone and there was a note on the table. All it said was, 'Sorry.' I lay on the floor and cried. I was alone, my boyfriend took what little money I had, and I knew that I couldn't go home."

Candy stopped for a second and took a sip of her drink. "Later that day those two men came back. They brought me some groceries and fixed me something to eat. They explained to me that they still needed to get their money back. I told them that I would get a second job and pay them a little each week. They laughed and said that they had a better idea, that I would work it off by working for them. They said that I would be set up in this apartment with what I needed. The next two nights they showed me what was expected. One of the men said that he would be the one to manage me."

She paused and looked at Kate. "A nice way to say he was going to be my pimp," she said. "Soon guys started showing up at my apartment. My pimp would give me a little money, and some groceries, and all I had to do was entertain the guys that they would send over."

Candy looked away from the girls and stared blankly across the back fence. Then with a voice that radiated the pain of her memories, she said, "After several months, I started taking pills and the johns started complaining that I wasn't worth what they were paying. I tried to clean myself up. I would stop taking the pills, then I would get depressed and start again, then I would stop again. After about a year, I just didn't care anymore. I was so messed up that I started a fight with one of the johns. He finished the fight by beating me up. My pimp found me, and I guess he thought I was dead. He drove me here and threw me out at the corner. Joe had just had the surveillance cameras installed and he saw him dump me. He came out in his wheelchair and somehow picked me up and got me back to his apartment. Libby wanted to call for an ambulance to take me to the emergency room, but Joe said that whoever dumped me here probably thought I was dead, and if he found out I wasn't, he might try to finish the job. So, Libby and Joe fixed me up and they took turns watching me until I woke up a couple of days later. Then for the next month, I went through withdrawals. They stayed with me even when I gave them hell."

Candy looked at Libby and said, "Joe and Libby keep saying that I don't owe them anything, but I feel like I do. They saved my life and Joe has been letting me stay here for free, until I can get a better job."

"Wow, it sounds like you were very lucky to land here," Kate said softly.

The sounds of the city surrounded the girls as they quietly reflected on the twists and turns of life that had brought them together.

After a moment Kate turned to Libby. "What about you, Libby? I've known you for several months, but I really don't know much about you."

"There's not that much to tell," said Libby. "I finished high school and was getting ready to go to college and major in IT system administration and programming. Then my father died, and I stayed at home to help my mother. Then about three years ago my mother found a live-in boyfriend. Well, he started getting too friendly. I complained to my mother one day and she just blew up at me. A couple of days later while mom was at work, he came into the bathroom as I was taking a shower. He said that he wanted to be friends, and he handed me a towel. I wrapped the towel around me and got out of the shower. He came close and put his arms around me. I put my knee right between his legs and he fell to the floor. The only thing he got was the view of me stepping over his head as he was looking up and holding himself."

Kate laughed. "Well, that served him right."

"So, I packed a backpack with my laptop and some clothes, hopped on my scooter and left. I stopped at a library that had WIFI, logged into a chat room where some of my hacker friends stayed. They told me about someone looking for a C/C++ programmer and gave me Joe's email address. I sent him an email and in about a minute, he responded. He wanted to see me as soon as possible. I drove over here, stopped and looked at this place and thought, what have I gotten into. He opened the front door of the apartment and I was scared. I almost didn't come in. But I did, and we sat and talked about everything that had to do with computers. After we talked about two hours I asked him about the job. He said, 'Oh, I'm sorry, I forgot to tell you, I hired you an hour ago.'"

Everyone started laughing.

"He asked me when I could start," said Libby, "and I said, right now. He said he could only pay me in cash, and I said that was fine, that I wanted to stay hidden for a while, and I explained the problems at home. Then he asked if I had a place to stay that night and I said, no, but that I could find a motel. And I'll never forget what he said then; he said, 'I know this place looks like it's out of a slasher movie, but I'm trying to fix it up.' Then he told me about his safe room and he said I could stay as long as I needed to, rent free. He showed me the room and said, 'Not as bad as it sounded, is it? But if you're uncomfortable with the area, keep this on you.' And he handed me a can of pepper spray."

Kate laughed, "Really?"

"Yeah, and he said that he wouldn't mind having the company and I ended up staying here a year helping him put this system together."

"Joe sounds like a hell of a guy," said Kate.

Libby and Candy both said, "Yeah, he is."

Kate took another swallow of her cola. "I know Joe was in Iraq when an IED exploded near him," she said. "What else do you know about him?"

Just then Randy opened the door, startling the girls, and he motioned for them to come inside. "Hurry," he said as they came toward him, "get in, someone is riding around the parking lot."

They quickly made their way back to the office. They looked at the monitors and saw a young boy on a bicycle riding around looking into each apartment window.

"Do you think he is looking for us?" asked Kate.

"I don't know," answered Joe, "but before he came into the parking lot he made a call on a smart phone, and he's taking a more than casual ride around the complex. He's looking for something!"

Libby said, "Joe, do you think that someone has hired kids to search for us?"

"Well, I know drug dealers hire kids to watch the streets that they deal on. So yeah, it could be."

Everyone watched the monitors as the young boy rode up to their door. He got off his bike and looked around. The office seemed to get hotter as they watched. It was like a submarine, everyone silent, barely breathing, waiting, listening, not wanting to give away their position. Then the boy raised his arm, one finger pointed. Ding Dong! Everyone jumped as if a depth charge had exploded nearby.

Joe put his finger to his lips, then he pushed the intercom button and said, "Can I help you?"

The boy said, "I'm looking for work. Do you have anything I could do?"

"No, not at this time. I may have something in a few weeks. If you can, check back then."

"OK, thank you."

As they watched, the boy tried to look through the front window, then he stood back and studied the door for a second. He walked back to his bicycle, hopped on, and stared straight into the security camera, then he typed something on his smart phone before he rode off.

Kate asked, "Do you think that was really why he was here?"

"No, I don't think so," said Joe. "We need to have someone watch the security cameras all the time now to see if someone is watching us."

"Just how secure is that safe room?" Kate asked.

"Well, it's designed to keep normal burglars out long enough for me to call the police. If someone really wanted to, and had the resources, they could get through that door."

Concern was evident on Kate's face and in her voice when moments later she said, "Joe, I do appreciate everything you have done, but it may be time for Libby, Randy, and me to find somewhere else to hide. We can't be found here, that would get you in trouble, too."

"Where else can you hide?"

"I need to make a phone call," she said. "I know someone who can help, my Uncle David."

Chapter 4
Sturgis, South Dakota

It was the last day of the annual Sturgis motorcycle rally when bikers from around the world descended for the first full week of August, and turned Sturgis into the largest city in South Dakota. A heavy thunderstorm was forecast for the area around the Black Hills and the bikers wanted to get in one last ride before going home, when they would start making plans for the next rally.

David Dodson was standing at the end of the bar with some of the other members of his club finishing his beer. He smiled as he watched his men joking and laughing with each other and any other biker that wanted to join in. It had been a long two weeks and everyone was tired. The club members always arrived a week before a motorcycle rally started to make their deliveries. This rally was always their biggest and their most profitable.

Betty, a 40 year old redhead, wearing hot pants and a bikini top barely covering her large breasts, leaned over the bar, placed her hand on David's arm, and said, "Honey, can I get you something else?"

David turned his head and smiled at her. "No, Betty, I'm good. We're going to be heading back soon."

Just then a big hand grabbed David by the shirt collar and pulled him back. Then a voice from behind said, "What the hell do you think you're doing, talking to my wife?"

David turned his head and had to look up to see the face of the 245 pound, six foot four inch, former pro football player. Then he said, "I was explaining to the attractive young lady that I was looking for a meaningful overnight relationship and was just wondering if she might be interested."

The other club members started laughing.

The big man wrapped his arms around David, picked him up, then dropped him on his feet. He picked him up again.

"Mac, stop that, you're going to hurt him," Betty said, laughing.

Mac put David down gently, holding him as he got his feet back on the ground. Then he stuck his hand out and said, "This is the first time that I have seen you since you made your deliveries last week. Where have you been?"

David raked his long salt and pepper hair back from his face, grabbed Mac's hand, looked up and said, "Hell, this place has been so busy we couldn't get in until now."

"Yeah, this has been a very good week, I think this will help us out this year. You know what, I want to double our order next year. We sold out of your stuff in the first two days."

"OK, Mac, next year I'll remind you," David said.

"Where's that pretty niece of yours?" asked Betty. "You know she was a big hit when she worked here serving drinks and dancing on the bar. Mac took some photos of her. We have them hanging on the back wall."

"She doesn't dance anymore," said David. "She's a manager at a bank in Vegas."

"Ain't that something," said Betty. "Well, you tell her if she ever gets tired of that, she will always have a job here. OK?"

"I'll tell her that, Betty."

David looked at the boys and said, "Well, we better ride back and start packing the RV before the weather gets bad."

Mac shook David's hand. "You better stop the next time you're out this way."

Betty winked at David and said, "Yeah, especially if you want that meaningful relationship."

Mac pulled a bar towel from his shoulder and popped Betty on the butt. "You better get back to work, girl."

She grinned at Mac, walked off, and said, "I'm working it."

"Goodbye, you two." David waved as he followed the other club members out the door.

A few drops of rain landed on David's glasses as he walked to his bike. He looked up and noticed how dark the clouds were on the western horizon. Everyone knew this would be the last ride for them at this year's rally and because of the weather it would just be to the RV. They put on their leathers, cranked their motors and waited for David to signal with a nod of his head. He signaled and slowly pulled away. Each member pulled in behind him and revved the engines of their Harleys while following him to the street, and then they carefully merged into the heavy traffic.

~ ~ ~

Jeffery Hodges, a slim young man with short brown hair, stood outside the trailer, waiting, as the other club members rode their bikes back to the RV park. He had the 20 foot enclosed trailer already hooked up to the Ford pickup and parked next to the 30 foot RV that they used for a home base. He let the tailgate down on the trailer as the club members pulled up.

The rain was light, but the wind was picking up and everyone could sense that it was going to get much worse. The fast moving storm front had caught many off guard and people were outside trying to secure their belongings while they still could. As David pulled his bike to a stop behind the trailer, a quick gust of wind blew a neighbor's lawn chair over, and it barely missed him as it tumbled by.

David looked at Jeffery, the newest member of the club, and asked, "You already have everything secured and ready for travel?"

"Yes sir. I saw the storm coming and went ahead and took care of it. I even put on a pot of coffee."

David smiled and said, "Good. Thank you. Let's go in and have a cup while we wait for the rest of them."

Max Henderson took his commemorative Sturgis doo-rag off, and raked his hands through his sleek black hair that fell just below his chin. He grinned at Brad and said, "Let's get these bikes in the trailer before this rain makes me melt."

Brad Jarell laughed at Max then said, "You won't melt, but a shower would do you some good. Especially if I have to ride back with you in the truck." He then started pushing one of the bikes into the trailer.

Dennis, the clubs VP, walked around the RV checking to be sure everything looked OK. Dennis Lawford stood at 5 foot 10 inches, 210 pounds, a slightly heavy build, with very short black hair. He came into the RV and asked in a no bull, commanding voice, "Jeffery, did you take care of everything?"

"Yes, sir."

"Emptied both the gray and black tanks?"

"Yes, sir."

"Flushed them both?"

"Yes, sir."

"And he made coffee," said David.

Dennis smiled at Jeffery, then said to David, "Not bad for a college boy. We may have to keep him."

A loud clap of thunder exploded nearby as the RV door opened and Brad and Max entered.

"Damn, that was close!" said Max.

Brad looked at David and said, "Boss, it doesn't look like anyone is moving on the road. We may have to wait out the storm."

Everyone looked out a window at the rain when another flash of lightning and clap of thunder exploded. Suddenly there was a flash from the electrical transformer that fed the power to the RV park. Everything went dark. The RV started shaking even more as the wind became heavier.

Jeffery jumped when David's phone started singing, *Who let the dogs out, Woof, Woof, Woof, Woof.*

David reached over to a switch and turned on an overhead light. He smiled at Jeffery and said, "Down boy, everything will be OK."

Everyone started laughing.

David glanced at the number and didn't recognize it. "Hello," he answered.

"Is this David Dodson?"

"Yes, can I help you?"

"David, it's me, Kate."

"Hi, Kitten. Listen, I'm in the RV with a thunderstorm outside, so I am having trouble hearing you."

"OK, David, I'm in ... I ... people looking for me," Kate said as the phone started breaking up.

"Kate, Kate, are you there?" He looked at the phone and stared at the display that read 'No Signal'.

"That was Kate?" asked Dennis. "What did she say?"

"I'm not sure, the phone had a bad connection, then I lost signal. I think she may be in some trouble," he said as he turned to look at Dennis.

~ ~ ~

The sky turned red as the late afternoon sun peeped under the lingering clouds. The downpour was over, now only a very light rain was falling, but the people that had been caught in the deluge were now stuck in a miles-long traffic jam. Two hours had passed and the phone still displayed 'no signal'. David sat helplessly in the passenger seat and stared at the windshield, calmly watching the beads of water race each other as they slowly zigzagged down the glass.

Jeffery asked, "Can I get you anything, Boss?"

David didn't say anything.

Dennis touched Jeffery on the shoulder.

Jeffery looked around at Dennis and saw him shake his head. He nodded once, then said quietly to Dennis, "I'm going to the back and try to get some sleep. I think it's going to be a long night when we do get started."

"OK," Dennis said.

Jeffery walked to the back of the RV, closed the door to the bedroom, and climbed into one of the six large bunks that were custom made for this RV.

Dennis sat behind David and read a motorcycle magazine. Brad picked up his guitar, sat down on the sofa next to Max, and began softly playing one of his old songs.

Max would usually try to sing along when Brad played, even though everyone complained, but not now. Now was not the time for singing, good or bad. Now they needed soft, relaxing sounds. Now he listened, and the music took him back to when he met Brad. The first time Brad had come by the clubhouse was the day after he got out of drug rehab. He was looking for work and David gave him a job taking care of the farm. He had been there about a month when Max heard him singing a song while changing the oil in the tractor, and he had admitted to Max that he was once in a band, and that he and a close friend wrote and recorded the song that he was singing.

Brad soon became a member of the club and he and Max became good friends. There was just a few years difference in age and as they teased each other and stood up for each other, they became brothers.

Brad had recently started writing songs again, and Max smiled as he remembered Brad's announcement that he would make all of them get on stage with him and perform someday. Then he had promised to teach Max to lip synch first.

The street lights came on and Brad stopped playing when David's phone beeped to indicate that it was receiving a cell signal.

David called the last number received and waited.

"Hello," said a man's voice.

Surprised to hear a man's voice, David waited a moment, then said, "Can I speak to Kate?"

"Yes, just a second."

Joe handed the phone to Kate, "For you."

"Hello."

"Kitten, is that you, are you OK?"

"David, yes it's me. I'm fine right now, but I need a place to hide."

"What's wrong, girl?"

"I'm in some trouble. I don't want to talk too long on the phone."

"Are you safe right now?"

"Yes, I'm staying with some friends here in Vegas, but I don't know how long we can stay here."

David said, "You said 'we'. How many people are with you?"

"There are three of us hiding, two more are helping us."

"Do you have transportation?"

"I have a car, but I don't know if they have found it yet."

Joe waved his hand at Kate and said, "Put the phone on speaker."

"OK."

"Mr. Dodson, I'm Joe, a friend of Kate's. We hid her car the other day and I don't know if it's safe for her to drive it. I have a van that they can use to get out of town, they just need a place to drive to and stay until we can figure out what we can do. Can you help with that?"

"Yes," said David. "I can make something work. I just need to make a few phone calls. I can call you back at this number, right?"

"Yes," answered Joe.

"I will call right back as soon as I have made some arrangements. OK?"

"We will be waiting."

"Joe, thank you for taking care of my little girl, I owe you."

"Mr. Dodson, that's no problem, besides we have enjoyed her company."

"Thank you, David." said Kate. "Bye."

"Bye, Kitten."

David ended the call, placed the phone on the dash console, then reached over to the laptop mounted next to the passenger seat. He typed in a name then studied the display. He grabbed his cell phone and dialed.

~ ~ ~

Several minutes passed before Joe's phone rang again.

"Hello," Kate said. "Let me put you on speaker."

"Hello, Kate. I have someone that can help. He's about 120 miles north of Vegas on Highway 95 in a small town called Beatty. He owns a bar named Ray's. That's also his name. He owns an RV in a mutual friend's RV park nearby. And all of you can stay as long as you need to."

Joe said, "That sounds like a plan. I will get them out tomorrow afternoon around rush hour."

"Kate, all of you stay at the RV park until I can get to you," said David. "I'm in Sturgis with the boys and it will take us a couple of days to get to you. OK?"

"OK," Kate said.

"One other thing, I want you to call before you leave and after you get there."

"OK," Kate said. "And thanks."

"Kitten, you watch yourself, OK?"

"Yeah, I will."

Chapter 5
Las Vegas, Nevada

After supper, Kate started loading the dishwasher. Libby walked into the kitchen with a couple of coffee cups from the office.

Kate said, "I don't understand why we're not able to find more in the files from the bank."

"Yeah, it's a shame we don't know someone else who works at the bank. Maybe they could find something."

Kate stood up straight and looked at Libby.

"Kate, what are you thinking?"

"There were two people fired in the past six months. I wonder if they found something or were close to finding something and that was the real reason they were fired."

Libby said, "Maybe. If we could look at what they were working on at the time it might help."

After Kate started the dishwasher, they went back to the office.

Joe was explaining to Randy the search algorithm that he decided to use in his computer system when Libby said, "Kate has an idea that sounds promising."

Kate explained about the people who were fired and suggested that they look at all the documents from the weeks they were dismissed. "If they found something, we need to see it."

"Do you remember the dates they were fired?" Joe asked.

"No, but I did see the dismissal documents in Jerry Powell's folder."

Joe grabbed his mouse, clicked on Jerry Powell's folder and got the dates from the documents. "Kate, this is a good idea, but we have only been collecting data from the bank for about two weeks. These people were gone before we started. Mr. Powell probably had their computers wiped clean after they left."

"So you don't have anything from their computers?"

"That's right," said Joe. "But they may have sent a copy to someone else. We may be able to find something that way. All the documents and emails that were on everyone's computers in the last two weeks have been entered into a database."

Joe focused on the computer monitor, opened a terminal window, and said as he quickly typed, "Let me create an SQL Statement that will search for that person's name in the Send Field."

After the first search, Joe said, "Did not find anything on the first person that was fired. Let me do the same search on the second person."

"Bingo!" Joe yelled. "I found an email to a person named Walters."

Kate said, "Miss Walters was sick for several months, she just came back last week."

Joe opened the email and started reading it out loud.

Miss Walters, just to let you know, I found a new account that Jerry Powell created. He forgot to include all the federal tax information with this account. I will contact Mr. Powell and see what he wants me to do.
Company Name: Vegas Holding LLC
Account No: 476239

Kate said, "I don't understand why Jerry Powell would create an account. He has employees that do that."

"Unless he is hiding something," said Joe. "Let me do some research on that company."

"Joe, I need to talk to her," said Kate.

"Who? Miss Walters?"

"No, Lara Manning, the person who was fired. She may be able to tell us if this was why she was fired."

~ ~ ~

The morning skies were clear with a promise of another hot day in Vegas. Lara Manning was putting boxes in a small U-haul trailer with the help of her elderly father. Her son, Mike, was playing in the yard with a neighbor's child when Candy drove up in Joe's van.

Kate and Candy got out and said, "Hi," to the kids playing in the yard.

Candy saw Lara walk around the trailer as she headed back to the house for another box.

"Hello, Miss Manning. My name's Kate. May I have a word with you?"

"What about?"

Kate said, "I need to know why you were fired from the bank."

"Who the hell are you?"

"I worked at the bank, too."

Lara snapped back at Kate, "You tell that son of a bitch I have not told anyone, and I'm not going to, so get out and leave my family alone."

Lara's father, a frail looking man, stepped up to them and asked, "Lara, is there something wrong?"

"No, Dad, I have this. You go sit down in the house and rest, OK?"

"I'm sorry," said Kate, "but I no longer work at the bank. All we are trying to do is find out why you were fired and if it had anything to do with the email you sent to Miss Walters about a company called Vegas Holding, LLC?"

"Why?"

"Let's just say that some people are looking for me and some of my friends."

"Those same people are probably watching me," said Lara.

"Why?"

"I can't tell you. They said that they would kill me and my family."

"They threatened you?"

"Yeah. The day I was fired my son came home from school in a big black SUV. The men that gave him a ride home also gave him a photo to give to me. The photo was of him at school with a note on the back that said, 'Life can be short.'"

Kate and Candy looked at each other.

"It looks like you're moving," said Candy.

"Yeah, I can't find a job, can't pay my mortgage, so the bank, that I worked for, just foreclosed."

"Lara, I hope things get better for you," Kate said.

"Yeah, you too."

Candy and Kate turned and started walking to the van. "What do you think?" asked Candy.

"Well, all I know for sure is that she was fired for knowing something that she should not have known."

~ ~ ~

Joe rolled his wheelchair outside to the van and said, "You people need to finish packing up and get out of here. Be sure to secure Libby's scooter. And Libby, get the cash out of the safe."

"Joe, you can come too," said Kate. "There will be plenty of room."

"I know. But I can do more here. Besides, they're not looking for me. If they try to break in here, I'll hide in the safe room and call the police. Something I can't do if you're here."

"I'm sorry we have to steal Candy away from you," said Kate.

"It's the best way," said Joe taking Candy's hand, "you all need to stay out of sight, Candy can drive and run errands."

"I hope you both know how much we appreciate your help," Kate said.

Joe looked up at Candy. "Maybe after Kate's uncle picks them up you can come back, if it's safe."

"OK," said Candy.

Randy walked out of the apartment and said, "I'm glad we're not trying to go to California using Interstate 15 right now."

"Why?" asked Joe.

"The southbound lanes are closed. A car pulling a U-Haul trailer just blew up, killed everyone in the car."

Kate turned to Randy. "How many people were in the car?" she asked.

Randy could see the alarm in Kate's face. "I think they said two adults and a child. Why?"

Kate looked at Candy and said, "Lara Manning."

"Oh no!" said Candy. "Do you think someone saw us talking to her."

"Lara?" questioned Joe. "The woman from the bank? The woman you saw this morning?"

"Yeah, this morning she was packing up a U-Haul to leave town. There were three of them, her, her father, and her son."

They stared at each other until Joe said, "Candy, did you see anyone around the van this morning?"

"No, and it was never out of our sight either."

"You need to go over it just to be sure it's safe. Randy, help her out, will you?" Then Joe turned his attention to Kate and Libby. "Try not to call me on the phone anymore. I don't know if it's safe. Libby, use those email accounts through the anonymous server to communicate with me, OK? Kate, don't use the cell phone to call your uncle until you're away from this area. These people might be watching for cell phone activity in the area and might be able to track you even using these burn phones. Be sure you turn them off after you use them."

"The van looks OK," said Candy, as she and Randy joined the others.

"All of you need to look out for each other, OK?"

"We'll do that, Joe. Thanks," said Randy.

"You be careful too, Joe," said Candy, giving him a hug. "I'll be back soon."

Libby leaned down for her hug. "Be safe," she said.

"Thank you, Joe," said Kate, as she hugged him too.

"Randy, would you go check the security monitors one more time?" said Joe.

"All clear," he said as he came out of the office.

Joe gave the group a quick look and said gruffly, "Now all of you get out of here." He watched as they left, and for several minutes he listened to the sounds of the city during rush hour. Then he rolled back into his apartment, looked around the office, and said to himself, "It's sure going to be quiet around here now."

~ ~ ~

The small, quiet, unincorporated township of Beatty, Nevada, the home of 1000 people, sits between Death Valley National Park on the west and the Nevada Test site and Area 51 on the east. On the drive up from Vegas everyone sat quietly, staring out the windows, thinking about Lara Manning and her family. The sun was going down behind the Black Mountains as Candy drove the van into town, turned right on Main Street and started looking for Ray's bar.

When Candy found the bar she parked in front, got out of the van and went inside. She felt like she had traveled back 100 years as she examined the old mining gear and other antiques decorating much of the wall space. A tall balding man in his late 60's was standing behind the bar handing a cold beer to a customer.

He saw Candy, smiled and said, "I don't get many beautiful ladies in here. What can I get for you?"

"I need to talk to Ray."

He leaned over the bar, studied her and said, "I'm Ray."

Candy said, "I'm with the Dodson party."

Ray motioned her to follow him to the other end of the bar.

"You don't look like the girl that was described to me."

"Kate Dodson is in the van," said Candy. "No one is looking for me so we thought it best that I come in and talk to you."

He studied her again, then said, "My RV is located in the first RV park on the left, up 95, about a quarter mile. The manager has the spare keys so she can let you in. I stocked it with supplies today. Let me make a phone call to let her know that you are here."

"Thank you."

Ray called the manager, then looked at Candy and said, "OK, she's ready for you." He grabbed a napkin and wrote his cell phone number on it and handed it to her. "That's my cell number, call me if you need anything."

"Thanks again."

Chapter 6
Las Vegas, Nevada

There was a low rumble in the server room at the back of the OSC, Inc. building. The AC was trying to keep the room at 68 degrees; when the Las Vegas desert temperature reached over 100 degrees, the AC unit ran constantly. In the center of the room were four racks of rack mount computers, four uninterrupted power supplies, and two routers. A cable ladder mounted to the ceiling ran above the racks and ended next to the wall where the business broadband Internet connected and where the network cables were distributed throughout the building.

Claudette found Antoine bent down plugging a network cable into one of the new servers that he had just received. The scene reminded her of their home in France, when she would watch her father working on the family car. It was an old car and always needed repair, but their father always managed to keep it going. Often Antoine would try to help, and their father patiently let him, even though he made the job take longer. She smiled. "For a second I thought you were father."

Antoine stopped and looked up at her. "I wonder what he would think of what we're doing?"

"I believe he would be very proud of us. Maybe a little disappointed about who we work for, but still proud that we went to the university and that we work together in the United States."

They had seldom discussed their work, the fact that it was illegal, or the fact that the appeal of making their fortunes quickly was too great to resist.

Antoine became quiet and Claudette knew he was thinking about their parents. First, cancer had taken their mother and then an automobile accident took their father. The only good thing was that they had grown so close they could almost read each other's minds as they had helped each other through their grief and faced life's challenges together.

After a moment of silence, she said, "It looks like your system is coming together."

"Yes, this is the last server to install. I'll start installing the Linux operating system and the cluster software after lunch. I hope I can have this up tomorrow morning. Then you can have your programmers back and you can complete your programs."

"Great. It would be nice to tell Angelo something positive for a change," she said.

"Are you two OK?"

"Yes." She smiled at Antoine and said, "I like being with him, he's very different from the other men I have dated."

"Well, the sex must be great," he said.

"And how would you know?"

He laughed. "Because, Claudette, you're wearing dresses, more makeup, and you're smiling a lot more."

She smiled and hit him on the shoulder. "You better get back to work."

As she walked back to her office, more childhood memories surfaced. They were poor, and they had to move around a lot so her father could look for work. He had done construction work and factory work and whatever else he could find. But the one thing she remembered most was that he loved American movies. Every weekend he would rent at least one and the family would sit and watch it, sometimes more than once. She could remember her mother fussing that it was an unnecessary expense, but she enjoyed them too. She enjoyed seeing her family having fun together.

Claudette was halfway down the hall when she saw Angelo looking into her office. "Hi. What brings you here?" she asked, as she walked up to him and kissed him.

"I came by to give you something."

She smiled. "You can't wait until tonight, so you're going to start coming here for nooners."

Angelo started laughing. "I wish. No, I have something else." He reached into his coat pocket and pulled out a small box and handed it to her.

Claudette's eyes scanned the box before she took it and asked, "What are you doing?"

"Open it," he said.

Without being aware of it, she started playing with her hair. "Angelo, I can't take this."

He smiled. "Well, it will make it a lot easier for you to get into my house."

She paused for a second, then looked up to him and said, "What are you talking about?"

"Just open the box," he said softly.

She carefully raised the lid and saw two keys tied together with a bow. She took them out and looked at each key and said, "These are for your house?"

"One is for the car, so you can drive me to the airport, and the other is so you can house sit for a few days. But I'm hoping that when I get back, you might stay with me. So, I do want you to keep them."

She put her arms around him. "Are you asking me to live with you, are you sure?"

"Yes, I'm sure." Then he grinned and said, "Besides, as your boss I feel a need to keep a close eye on you, and I think you need a place to relax at night so you can get more work done the next day."

"Oh, so this is just to help me be more productive?"

He kissed her. "Of course, what else would you think it meant?"

"You know I'll have to bring some clothes over and keep them there."

"There's room in the closet, and several drawers are empty."

"Just how long have you been planning this?" she asked.

"Since the first time I saw you eat my omelet."

They started laughing. Then she looked at him and asked, "What's this about me driving you to the airport?"

"Cortez called me, he wants to talk."

"What about?"

"I have to go and see him two or three times a year. We drink, talk, and I just reassure him that everything is OK."

"When do you need to go?"

"Right now, so grab your keys."

She looked up at him. "If you drive," she said, "I can sit on your lap, and you might get that nooner."

He smiled. "I know this is Vegas, and everything is supposed to stay here, but I'm afraid that might show up on YouTube."

~ ~ ~

Puerto Vallarta, Mexico

The sudden afternoon monsoon-like rain started to dissipate above the city of Puerto Vallarta, a resort city of 250,000 people located on the Pacific coast of Mexico. As Angelo's flight flew into Puerto Vallarta International Airport, he could see the resort hotels that stood beside the white sandy beaches of Banderas Bay. Angelo's trip took about 7 hours total, including a 3 hour layover in Phoenix. He was tired, and still had a 45 minute drive to get to Cortez's villa after he cleared customs. All passengers arriving on an international flight had to clear customs, which used a traffic light system to randomly select people to have their luggage searched. Angelo watched as two passengers in front of him caught the red light and had to leave the line and go to a room to have their luggage searched.

After he cleared customs he proceeded outside and looked for the car. He saw Cortez's driver waiting beside a black Chevy Tahoe SUV. Angelo got in the back seat as the driver put his suitcase in the trunk. He tried to relax as the driver left the airport and started the drive north past the shops, resort hotels and plush golf courses. The road narrowed into the two lane Federal Highway 200 and Angelo asked, "How has the tourist season been this year?"

The driver just shrugged his shoulders. Angelo didn't expect any reply, this man never replied, but he made the attempt, and then quietly stared out the window. The poor rural setting that they were passing now was a stark contrast with the resort hotels. They passed tiny communities separated by dead trees and overgrown vines. Trash littered the side of the road. Each community they passed had small businesses in rundown buildings made of tin, or broken brick, or crumbling concrete. The homes were old and in need of repair. He saw small fruit and vegetable stands and an occasional small church, a small ray of hope. Angelo pulled back his sleeve and checked his Seiko watch. They still had twenty minutes to get to their destination, just north of San Francisco and south of Lo De Marcos.

At last the driver turned into the driveway and passed the guarded gate. Moments later Angelo could see Cortez's villa, which stood on top of a hill that formed a peninsula along the Pacific coastline. The six bedroom villa was of a Spanish architectural design and had a splendid view of the ocean coastline on the west side of the property and a view of the large protected cove on the east side.

The housekeeper, a middle aged woman whose long black braid hung halfway down her back, greeted Angelo with a big smile. "Good afternoon, Mr. Diego, it's good to see you again. I hope you had a nice flight."

He smiled back and said, "It's always a good flight when I can come here and see you again. How is your family?"

"They are good, thank you," she said. "Mr. Cortez has not arrived yet, but he should be here soon. If you would like to freshen up, you can follow the driver to your room. Then if you would like to wait on the patio, I'll be happy to bring you a drink."

After changing clothes, he walked down the stairs, out the French doors on the south side of the villa, and then up the short set of steps to the patio. He leaned on the patio railing and looked over at the panoramic view of the cove on one side and the Pacific Ocean on the other. He absorbed the view and let the waves breaking against the rocks along the beach wash away his problems at the bank, and for a little while, he relaxed. Then he heard an airplane fly over and head out to sea. The plane banked right, then banked left to turn around and head back to land. He watched the seaplane descend and bounce a few times as it landed in the cove. The seaplane's motors revved up as the plane turned around and pushed itself back to the villa. On the beach was a flat concrete pad connected to a boat ramp, with a small jetty as an aid to the pilot as he maneuvered the plane into position to push itself up the ramp to the concrete pad.

A large golf cart traveled down a path to the parked airplane. Cortez came out of the plane first, followed by three young women. He got in the front seat of the cart, next to the driver, and the women got in the back seats. About three minutes passed before they reached the front door.

Cortez greeted Angelo with a big hug. "How are you, my friend?"

"I'm good."

Cortez released him but reached behind Angelo and grabbed the back of his neck and said, "Look at you, Las Vegas has been good to you. Tell me how you stay fit sitting behind a desk all day?"

"It's all that work making money for you," said Angelo, smiling.

Cortez laughed. "That is a good answer," he said.

The three women walked onto the patio as Angelo said, "You're in good shape, yourself. What's your secret?"

He laughed and pointed to the women. "I make love to two of these beautiful women each night. It keeps me young."

"I have enough trouble keeping up with one woman. How do you keep up with so many?"

Cortez put his arm around Angelo, pulled him close and

whispered into his ear, "I must admit, sometimes I have to take that little blue pill."

They both started laughing.

Cortez said, "Come, supper is almost ready, let's eat. Then tonight we can party and tomorrow, we must talk business."

~ ~ ~

After supper, Cortez dismissed the staff for the night. Cortez and Angelo walked out to the patio as the girls went upstairs and changed. When the girls came back they fixed Cortez and Angelo a straight Tequila while they had margaritas. Two of the girls handed Cortez his drink, then sat down beside him. The third gave Angelo his, then sat down close beside him, put her hand around the back of his neck, and started to gently massage. As Angelo sipped the drink, he noticed that the young girl next to him was wearing nothing under her sheer tunic. His eyes followed her long dark brown hair up to the soft curves of her face, to her beautiful dark eyes and full lips creating a soft smile. Angelo could not help but smile back.

An hour passed as Cortez and Angelo talked about Las Vegas, and then about the small village where they both lived as small children. Then Cortez stood up, winked at Angelo and said, "Come on girls, it's time for me to do my exercises." He turned his eyes to the young girl beside Angelo and said, "This girl is here to entertain you. Please accept my hospitality."

Cortez put his arms around the two girls beside him and led them upstairs.

The young girl sitting beside Angelo smiled, reached down and put her hand on Angelo's leg and said, "I'm Mayra, can I get you anything?"

Angelo took her by the hand and smiled. "Mayra, you are a very attractive girl, and I would love to spend the night in your arms, but I just started a relationship with someone that I like very much."

After a few seconds she gave Angelo an uneasy smile, and asked, "What's her name?"

He hesitated, then said, "Claudette."

She looked down at their joined hands. "Is she as pretty as her name?"

"Yes, and she is as enchanting as you are."

She looked back at him with a radiant smile. "You think I'm enchanting?"

He laughed and gave her hand a gentle squeeze. "Very."

They sat silently for several minutes, then Mayra said softly, "Cortez made it clear to me that he expects me to please you tonight." She squeezed his hand. "He only keeps a few girls around at a time, and he goes through them very fast. One of the other girls told me that as soon as he's tired of a girl, he gives her to his men."

He saw a tear roll down her cheek as she said, "They can be very mean, and when they get tired of a girl, she works as a whore in the city."

Angelo wiped the tear from her face. "Why do you do it?"

She hesitated, but continued, "Cortez is paying my mother's doctors bills, and I wouldn't be able to pay them if I did anything else, I have no other skills."

Angelo could see the nervous tension in her body as she turned and looked at him. "Please, don't say anything to Cortez. He would get very mad if he knew I told you any of this. And I didn't mean to make you uncomfortable. I'm sorry. Please, just forget everything I said. OK?"

He stared at her. "No."

She bit her lip, then pleaded, "Please, don't say anything to him, please!"

In a very soft voice he said,"Mayra, I'm not going to say anything to him, but I'm not going to forget." They sat silently, holding hands, and sipping their drinks. Then Angelo smiled at her and touched her soft cheek. "Let's go up to my room," he said. He helped her up and put his arm around her as they started up the stairs.

She looked up at him. "Thank you," she said. "You won't regret it."

After they entered the bedroom, Angelo pulled off his shoes and socks. "It's been a long day," he said. "I think I'll take a shower."

She stepped close to him and said, "Let me help you." She unbuttoned his shirt and slid it off his shoulders. Then she unfastened his pants and helped him out of them. Finally, she slid his shorts slowly down his legs.

He looked at her young face as she stood back up, then he put his hands on her waist and slid them up her body, pulling off her tunic. He reached down, picked her up, and carried her to the shower. When the cold water splashed against their bodies, Mayra shrieked and stepped around Angelo so that he was shielding her from it, and he took her in his arms and held her close. When the water warmed, she looked up and smiled as she took the soap in her hands and started lathering him. When she had done every inch, he took the soap. His right hand started gently on her shoulder, then slowly slid down to her breasts, and then all the way to her toes and back. As the warm water flowed over them washing away the soap, he raised his hand and wiped the water from her face. Then he placed his hand on the back of her head and lowered his lips to hers, and he entered her.

While they dried each other she looked up at him with a playful, mischievous grin and asked, "What kind of games do you like?"

"What kind of games do you mean?"

"I think there are some sex toys in the night stand, even some pills. I'll even dress up like a little girl if you like."

"Well, what do you recommend?"

"Sometimes I like to be tied to the bed post and spanked. Just don't hit me too hard."

Mayra lay on the bed, face down and watched as Angelo went to the night stand and looked at each item. After she explained what each item was for, he asked, "How do you know so much about these things."

She answered saying, "Cortez likes to play a lot. He likes to role play. I often dress up like a little school girl for him."

Angelo smiled at her, then put the toys back in the night stand. She rolled onto her back as he got in bed and gently got on top of her and said, "Let's just keep it simple tonight, OK."

She wrapped her legs around him and answered the way she had been taught, "As you wish, Master."

~ ~ ~

An intermittent cool ocean breeze blowing in the open window caused Angelo to reach for the covers. He slowly opened his eyes when he couldn't find them, and as the mid-morning light that filled the room brought him further out of his deep sleep, he realized that they were still on the floor where he had thrown them the night before. Then he looked at Mayra, still asleep beside him, and smiled as he thought about the night and how their hot, sweaty bodies had moved together until they were both exhausted.

He quietly got out of bed and picked the covers up and gently laid them over Mayra. Then he showered, put some clothes on, and made his way downstairs, where the housekeeper directed him to the patio for a buffet style brunch.

Cortez was sipping coffee with one of his girls. "Good morning," he greeted Angelo.

Angelo waved, grabbed some coffee and a bagel, then walked over to the table and sat down.

Cortez smiled and said, "I hope you enjoyed your entertainment last night. I know that I enjoy her company."

"Yes, she is very entertaining."

Cortez asked, "How did you sleep?"

"What sleep I got was fine."

Cortez laughed. "Good. I am sorry, but I have to leave this afternoon for an unexpected meeting. So tonight you can have the villa, and Mayra, all to yourself. I will have a driver take you back to the airport tomorrow and I will send my plane back for her."

Angelo smiled and said, "OK. I think we can tough it out here for one more night. Thanks."

"No, Angelo, I would like to thank you for all that you have done for me. We wouldn't have come so far without your vision and ability to find people to put together such a system as this. So please enjoy."

Cortez saw his lieutenant, Raul, standing by the door. He got up, made his apologies, and walked to the door where the man was standing. "Was everything recorded last night?" he asked in a low voice.

"Yes, sir."

"Good. I want to record tonight too. I want to be sure I have leverage on him. He doesn't know he is sleeping with an underage girl."

"Yes, sir, I understand and will set everything up for tonight."

~ ~ ~

Angelo and Cortez finished their business meeting about noon and it went much better than Angelo expected. Angelo explained what they were doing to find the people who stole the files from his laptop and Cortez seemed to understand the problems of finding people who don't want to be found. A little too understanding,

Angelo thought.

Angelo remembered that as a child, he had seen Cortez blow up over little things. He had learned to hide his rage as an adult, but Angelo never felt 100 percent comfortable around him. He always felt something was wrong, like Cortez resented him. *He must have inherited that from his mother*, thought Angelo, *since I always sensed anger and hatred from her, too. Cortez's father was completely opposite, I felt friendship, even love from him, especially when his wife and Cortez weren't around, and he would play with me.*

After the meeting they made their way back to the patio where the girls were lying around in their bikinis drinking margaritas.

"Go change," Cortez ordered the girls. "Be ready to leave."

Mayra smiled as Angelo sat down in the chair next to her and took the drink the housekeeper handed him.

"Please, enjoy my home tonight," Cortez said after Raul announced that the plane was ready. "I will be in touch soon." He left the patio with Raul, and the girls came hurrying down the stairs right behind them.

Angelo and Mayra walked to the edge of the patio and watched the seaplane descend the boat ramp into the water, then float to the far side of the cove, turn around and skip across the water as it ascended into the air, heading west over the Pacific Ocean. They kept watching the plane as it turned around, came back, and flew over the villa, heading east.

Angelo looked at Mayra, breathed a sigh of relief, and asked, "What would you like to do the rest of the day?"

"How about a walk along the beach? I don't get to do that very often."

They hopped onto one of the golf carts and Mayra drove them down a path to the ocean. She looked up and down the beach. "We seldom get many people on this part of the beach," she said as she took off her top and dropped it in the cart.

Angelo pulled the tail of his white shirt out and unbuttoned it. He bent over, pulled off his shoes and socks, and as he was rolling up the pants legs, he noticed a surveillance camera at the end of the cart path and asked, "Does Cortez have a lot of cameras around the property?"

"I don't know, I have never paid much attention to that. But he is paranoid about security, so I wouldn't be surprised."

A good security system would have cameras in the house, he thought, *maybe in the bedrooms*. He suddenly realized that Cortez had probably recorded his night with Mayra. The thought of that made him shake his head, but he also realized that there was no way he could have avoided this situation. And he couldn't see a way out of it either, he was in too deep, and people who say no to Cortez don't live very long.

He looked at Mayra, walking topless beside him. She was a naturally seductive young girl with an innocent looking smile. *I wonder if she knows that she's being used to create a blackmail video*, he thought. Mayra felt his gaze and smiled at him, her innocent smile, and he thought, *no, she probably doesn't know*. He smiled back, put his arm around her, and asked, "Where are you from?"

"I'm from a small village in the mountains southwest of Durango."

"How did you meet Cortez?"

"My father worked in some of his marijuana and poppy fields during harvest season. My father was murdered when a group from a rival cartel attacked the field workers. Cortez's men fought them off, but several men from the village were killed. Soon after that, my mother became sick, and couldn't take care of three children. I was the oldest of the three, so I tried to find work to pay the bills. Cortez helped the families of those that were killed, but Mom's bills were very high. I asked him if I could work in the fields like my father, but he said no. He told me that I could work in other ways, and here I am. I have money to give my mother. And mostly, I don't mind the work." She paused and smiled up at him again. "Now I want to hear about you. Why do you work for Cortez?"

The warm afternoon sun was bright, causing the waves to sparkle as they splashed against the sand and the rocks on the beach. Angelo looked down and watched the water sweep over their feet as they walked. The ocean was calm today with a light wind that kept blowing Mayra's hair into her face. She looked up at the man now holding her hand, and wondered why he hesitated to answer her question.

"The reason I work for Cortez is that I became impatient and greedy." He looked at Mayra's young face and continued, "I made good money working as a bank manager. But when I saw what many of my customers had, the nice homes, the nice cars, the beautiful wives and girlfriends, I wanted that, too. I heard that Cortez was building a drug organization and looking for a banker, and I approached him with an idea to make a more efficient drug trafficking network. He gave me the money to start it, and now here I am."

"I guess we all sell ourselves for money," said Mayra.

Angelo looked back at the beach and said, "Yes, and sometimes the price of someone's soul is very low."

They quietly walked along the beach, avoiding eye contact, as they thought about the decisions that brought them together today.

Mayra broke the silence when she reached down and cupped a handful of water and threw it at Angelo. She ran deeper into the water and splashed him several more times. He walked closer and began splashing her. She went farther out, and continued to splash him. Suddenly a larger wave appeared behind her. Angelo tried to warn her, but the sounds of the surf drowned out his voice and the wave swept her off her feet. Angelo could not help but smile as he struggled through the water to help her.

After they walked back onto the beach, Angelo started laughing and said, "I guess I won that battle."

The sun hid behind a cloud and the wind suddenly picked up. Shivering, Mayra said, "I'm cold," as she wrapped her arms around herself.

Angelo took her hand and guided her behind one of the large boulders on the beach to shield her from the wind. He took off his shirt and wrapped it around her shoulders. Then he gently put his arms around her and held her close.

She laid her head against his chest. When she stopped shivering, she looked up at him, smiled and said, "Thank you." Then she stood on her toes and gently brushed her lips against his.

He bent down and kissed her, holding her tight. "You're welcome," he softly said.

They held each other until the sun broke through the clouds and the wind died down. Then they walked over to a shorter boulder and climbed on top where they sat letting the Mexican sun shower over their bodies, warming them and drying their clothes.

"What would you like to do if you could get away from here?" asked Angelo.

She pointed to a 40 foot sailboat sailing by several hundred yards from the beach and said, "Sometimes I watch these boats go by and wonder where they have been and where they're going. Someday I would like to sail away on one."

He watched the boat sailing by. "If that's what you want, I hope you get to do that."

She shook her head. "The only way I will ever get away from Cortez is when I'm too old and of no use to anyone."

He watched her, not knowing what to say. She seemed to be in a daze, staring at the boat as it moved out of view, and he wondered if she was imagining herself on it, traveling to an unknown location, escaping her life here. He put his hand on her shoulder, bent down, and kissed the top of her head.

She suddenly asked, "Can I ask you a personal question?"

"Sure, anything you want to know."

"Are you in love with Claudette? Are you going to marry her?"

Taken aback by the questions, and unsure what to say, he took her hand and said, "I think I could see myself sharing my life with her."

Mayra kept looking out to sea. "She's a lucky girl," she said.

Angelo put her hand to his lips and kissed it. "I hope you can find someone to share your life with, too."

She smiled. "For today, and tonight, I have."

They walked along the beach until sunset, then Mayra drove them back to the villa. After supper they waited on the patio for the staff to finish their duties and leave for the night.

Mayra looked at Angelo and said, "I'll be right back. I'm going to change."

Angelo thought she might put the tunic back on, which was fine, she looked good in it.

"How do I look?" she said as she spun around wearing a school uniform.

He watched her for a second. "You look like a 12 year old school girl."

"Do you like it?"

"Yes, you make that look good."

"I want to play. You be the teacher. And I'm the naughty school girl."

Angelo started laughing. "Yeah, OK. Are you sure about this?"

She had a small paddle and she popped Angelo on the shoulder.

He cried out, "Damn, girl, that hurt!"

She stuck her tongue out and tried to pop him again. He moved and just got a glancing blow, but his momentum caused the chair to tip over and he landed on his back.

He looked up at her as she laughed, bent over, and stuck out her tongue again. "OK, I'll play this game," he said as he was getting up. "And you're going to get a spanking."

"You have to catch me first!" she said. Then she turned around and ran into the house.

He ran after her and watched as she ran up the stairs. He caught up just as she reached the bedroom door, and he took the paddle from her hand, scooped her up and over his shoulder, and carried her in. He sat on the side of the bed and put her across his knee. "You have been a very bad little girl and I am going to have to teach you a lesson," he said. Then he raised her skirt and paddled her bare bottom.

When he stopped, he said, "Now, are you going to be a good little girl?"

Mayra raised up and twisted around to straddle him face to face. She unbuttoned her shirt, pressed his head to her breasts and said, "Do you want me to be a good little girl, or bad for a while longer?"

~ ~ ~

Sunlight poured into the bedroom as Angelo woke up to the sound of the housekeeper knocking at the door.

"Mr. Diego, your flight is scheduled to leave in a few hours. Would you like some breakfast?"

He walked to the door and said, "Some coffee and toast. I'll be down in about 30 minutes. Thanks."

"That's not going to give us very long for a proper goodbye," Mayra said.

He got back in bed, looked at her and said, "What kind of goodbye did you have in mind?"

She rolled on top of him and smiled. As he cupped her breast in his hand and looked into her eyes, she bent down, kissed him, and said, "A long one."

Chapter 7
Beatty, Nevada

While on the road, David liked to keep up on hometown news and weather forecasts. Today's high in Bodega Bay, California, was 57 degrees. The RV's temperature gauge told him that it was 101 degrees here in Beatty, Nevada.

Jeffery pulled the RV next to the park office. David stepped out of the side door into the dry desert heat, with Dennis following. Max pulled the pickup behind the RV and got out. He lit a cigarette and waited beside the truck with Brad.

Not knowing what kind of trouble Kate and her friends were in made them uneasy. Dennis looked back at Max, put his hand on his side and nodded his head. Max repeated the signal. They were armed and ready.

Dennis looked at David and said, "Ready, Boss."

They entered the RV office. David stopped at the counter and Dennis stood with his back near a wall scanning the doors to the room.

A middle-aged woman dressed in shorts and tank top opened the door behind the counter, walked in and said, "Can I help..." She stopped when she recognized David, then continued, saying, "You old dog, look at you." She came around the counter and gave David a big hug.

"Hi, Ruth, it's been a long time," he said, hugging her back.

She saw Dennis and said, "Dennis, are you still riding with this old dog?"

Dennis laughed, "Yes, ma'am."

"Have you had any trouble?" asked David.

"No, you boys can relax, nothing has happened. The kids have been good and staying in the RV out of sight. Ray stocked the RV so they wouldn't have to go out for anything. And I haven't heard a peep out of them."

"Ruth, I'm sorry we couldn't make it here for Glen's funeral," said David. "We didn't hear about it for a few weeks afterwards."

"Hey, that's OK. I know you boys stay on the road a lot. You know I miss the old fart, but all of us told him he needed to stop smoking, and then it finally caught up to him." She shook her head. "Come on, I'll show you where the kids are. I left a slot open next to Ray's RV so you can park yours next door."

"We have a pickup with a utility trailer, too. Where can we park that?" asked Dennis.

"You can park it on the other side of Ray's RV. I left it open too."

The boys followed Ruth to Ray's RV. She knocked on the door.

Randy pulled the curtain back, looked out and said, "Kate, the manager is outside with a couple of bikers."

Kate ran to the door and looked out, then pulled the door open and exclaimed, "Come in! Come in!"

As David walked through the door, Kate wrapped her arms around him and said, "God, I'm so glad you're here." Dennis came in and she gave him a hug. "Dennis, it's good to see you. How are you holding up?"

"I'm OK. I'm just worried about you right now."

After Kate introduced everyone, Dennis looked at David and said, "Boss, it's getting late, I'll get the boys to park and set everything up."

"If you boys need anything just call the office," said Ruth, as she followed Dennis outside.

"Thanks, Ruth."

Dennis pulled a small hand held radio out of his pocket and said, "Whiskey 2 to base."

Jeffery picked up the microphone to the mobile radio in the RV and said, "This is base."

"I need all of you to drive around to the back. I'll be standing outside waiting for you."

"Roger that."

They drove around and stopped, and Dennis motioned for them to get out of the vehicles. When they were all gathered around he ordered, "Park the RV here and the pickup and trailer on the other side of Ray's RV. Drain the gray and black water tanks, and fill the fresh water tank. In case we need to leave in a hurry, the only thing I want hooked up tonight is electricity. Jeffery, I need you to set up surveillance cameras and motion sensors around the RVs and pickup. I want eyes on everything surrounding us tonight. OK. That's it boys." As they got to work, he went back into Ray's RV to hear Kate's story.

While David and Dennis listened, the men outside worked efficiently and in silence and had everything done in fifteen minutes.

After Kate and the others had told all they knew, David looked at Dennis and said, "Everyone would be more comfortable at the clubhouse. The warehouse in town might be more secure but not that comfortable. The next option would be to have someone drive them around in the RV."

"Yeah," said Dennis, "the clubhouse would be the most comfortable. That's where I would take them."

"OK, decision made, we're going to take you to our clubhouse," said David. "It's an old farmhouse that we use for a clubhouse; it was my grandfather's farm and it's where Kate grew up. But first, I would like to talk to Commander Nathan Conner and get my take on him."

"How are you going to do that?" asked Dennis. "We wouldn't get 10 feet inside that base."

Libby said, "I think I have his home phone number. You might start there."

David and Dennis looked at each other and smiled.

David called the number that Libby gave him. "Hello, can I speak to Commander Nathan Connor."

"Speaking."

"Commander, I need to talk to you privately about a mutual problem that we have."

"What kind of problem."

"I don't want to talk on the phone, sir. Can we meet somewhere tonight."

"I'm sorry, I don't think I can help you."

David raised his voice. "Sir, I have seen the video."

There was a long pause, then the commander said, "OK, I can meet you at 21:00 hours. There's a bar, 40 miles north of the base near Highway 95 and SR 373. It's called Star Base 51, you can't miss it, there's a wrecked flying saucer in a field next door."

"A wrecked flying saucer?"

"Yes, I understand it's been good advertisement for the bar. The place is new so it's not listed in any phone books or Internet search engines yet, but you can look up directions on the place across the street. It was called Nevada Joe's, but it has been changed to Area 51 Travel Center. Think you can find it?"

"Yes, sir. Thank you." David hung up, then turned to Libby and said, "Now I need directions to Area 51 Travel Center."

She clicked on Google Maps and pulled it up for him to look at.

"Thanks, Libby."

David looked at Dennis and said, "Let's take everyone next door and introduce them. It might be best to keep them over there until I get back."

"You mean until we get back. I'm not going to let you go alone."

"I want you to stay here this time. I can take Max tonight."

Dennis knew not to argue when David had made up his mind, so he said, "OK." Then he grabbed his radio. "Whiskey 2 to base," he said.

"Base."

"We're going to bring everyone over so you can meet them. Is the area clear?"

"Yes, there is no movement around us."

Everyone walked over to David's RV and introduced themselves. Libby noticed the three surveillance LCD monitors mounted on the dash and walked over to study the setup. Jeffery was sitting in the driver's seat wearing a communication headset and watching the monitors. "Can I sit down?" she asked, pointing to the passenger seat.

He took the headset off, smiled, and said, "Sure, go ahead."

She scanned the dash. "What do you have here?"

"We have wireless surveillance cameras and motion sensors surrounding both RVs and the pickup truck. If a sensor detects something, a red dot will flash on the monitor with the corresponding camera image," he explained with pride. "As you can see, there is a small laptop that we can do Internet searches on and this is our communication radio."

"Nice setup," said Libby. "Did you build this?"

"Dennis and I did the design and the wiring. He designed the mounting; he's very good with machine work. He also came up with a way that the security system can be mounted and unmounted quickly for travel. I can have the security system up and running in just a few minutes."

"Nice job. I'm Libby Harrison. And you are Jeffery?"

"Yes, Jeffery Hodges. And thanks."

A few minutes later, Kate heard Libby laugh, something she had never heard before. She turned and smiled as she saw Libby and Jeffery talking and she tapped Randy on the arm and pointed to them.

"Looks like she's found a new friend," said Randy.

~ ~ ~

Creech Air Force Base, north of Las Vegas, Nevada

The four-stroke, 1,043cc, inline-four cylinder Kawasaki motor came to life with the push of the start button on the Ninja 1000 motorcycle, or crotch rocket as some people like to refer to them. Commander Nathan Connor let the motor idle as he secured his helmet and put on his gloves for tonight's ride. The afternoon had been especially stressful with the increasing number of missions in Afghanistan, Pakistan, and Mexico. And added to that, the phone call requesting a face-to-face meeting tonight about the video that could ruin his career, his marriage, his life.

He raced the motor a few times before stepping on the gear shifter and shifting the transmission into first gear. The slight increase in throttle and the slow release of the clutch set the bike in motion as Nathan guided it to the front gate. The guards at the gate knew who he was, but protocol dictated that all personnel be checked and cleared before entering and leaving the base. After he was stopped, checked, and then cleared, the guards saluted as Nathan slowly passed by them, and made his way to the street. He rolled onto Highway 95, then as soon as he was straight with the highway, he increased the throttle enough to bring the front tire off the pavement. The street lights along the front of the base became a blur as he reached over 120 MPH well before he reached the north end of the base. The guards stepped away from the guard house to watch the taillight from the bike quickly disappear into the night.

There were no streetlights past the base on the two lane road making driving a bike much more dangerous. Mule deer and other animals became even more of a driving hazard at night as they searched for food. He dropped his speed soon after he passed the base. He was comfortable at 80 MPH, still higher than the posted speed limit, but he had a meeting to get to, one that he was not sure he wanted to attend.

~ ~ ~

Highway 95 and SR 373, Nevada

David and Max didn't have any trouble finding the bar. It had a bright neon sign with stars surrounding the words, Star Base 51, and the wrecked flying saucer next to it was so brightly lit it couldn't possibly be missed. There was a blue 1960 style London Police Box in the parking lot next to the building. They backed their bikes next to it, turned the motors off, and stared at the Police Box, then looked at each other and shrugged. They hopped off their bikes, took a few steps into the half full parking lot and took a closer look at the flying saucer. There was a little gray alien sitting on the ground next to it, his hand holding the side of his head. He had a shocked expression on his face that said, "What Happened!?" Standing over the alien were two humans dressed in black suits. One was writing in something that looked like a traffic cop's ticket book. Beside them was a sign that read, "Don't fly drunk! Always have a designated pilot."

Max said, "You know, we could sell some of our stuff here." He grinned at David, "Could call it 'Rocket Fuel.'"

David laughed. "Let's go inside, I could use a beer."

The old, recently remodeled building had once been a general store. It had a front porch with benches lined up against the walls. There were old style tin signs nailed up haphazardly and they read the ones near the door as they walked up the steps: 'Fly High at the Saucer,' 'Last Bar before Mars,' 'Try our Martian Zombie.' The one on the door said, 'Please check your ray guns and light sabers at the bar.' Inside science fiction memorabilia was scattered around on the walls and ceiling.

Sounds of laughing, talking, TV volume on high, assaulted their ears when they opened the door and stepped inside. A group of young adults, all dressed like they had just stepped off the set of a science fiction show, had several of the tables pushed together, and they were watching an episode of *Doctor Who* on a large TV that was mounted to the wall across from the bar.

Wiping down the bar was a middle aged man dressed in a uniform with 'Star Base 51' printed across his heart. He watched the two bikers walk toward him and said, "Hi, I'm Scottie, can I beam you up a couple of beers?"

"Sure, Scottie, beam us up a couple," said David.

There was an empty one foot square box, made of clear glass, sitting on top of the bar. The bartender pressed a button on top of it. The futuristic transporter hummed and colored light pulsed throughout it and a bottle of beer appeared inside. He opened the box, reached in, took out the cold beer and handed it to David. Scottie pushed the button again, repeating the light and sound show, as David and Max stared.

"I may have to get a second just to see that again," said Max as he took the beer.

Scottie laughed. "That box has paid for itself many times over."

"I bet you reverse engineered it from that space ship that crashed outside," laughed David.

"Hey, I like that. I'm going to start telling people that."

"Where did you get it?" asked Max.

"I have a friend who creates equipment for several of the illusionists that work in Vegas."

Max took a long sip of his beer and said, "I'm impressed."

Suddenly, from across the room, loud yells and laughter came from the group watching TV. David paid for the drinks and said, "We're waiting for someone, so we'll drink these outside."

As they walked to the door, Max said in a spoiled, childlike voice, "I want to see the magic box work again."

Scottie laughed when he heard David say, "Be a big boy now, or I'll put training wheels back on your motorcycle."

~ ~ ~

Nathan slowly pulled into the half full gravel parking lot of Star Base 51 where he spotted two bikers sipping beers on the front porch, one sitting on a bench against the wall, and the other sitting on the porch rail. He parked his bike near the porch steps, took off his helmet and gloves, and unzipped the jacket of his riding suit. He walked onto the porch carrying his helmet by his side with his right hand. The two bikers watched and sensed the tension building in the air.

"Nice night for a ride," said David, "where did you ride in from?"

"I'm from the base."

"Are you Commander Nathan Connor?"

"Yes."

David paused for a second then said, "Commander, you can relax, I'm hoping we can be friends, and maybe I can help you get out of this problem concerning the video." David looked at Max and said, "Give us some space."

"Yes, sir."

Nathan watched Max walk to the end of the porch. He gave David a curious look and said, "Sir?" He paused for a moment then said, "I wouldn't have expected that much respect between a couple of bikers."

David laughed. "I'm his boss and club leader, but the respect, that comes from our military background as Army Rangers."

"Did you see action?"

"Yes, Max was in the first Gulf War. I was in Vietnam."

"I was in the first Gulf War, too."

"Yes, I know," said David, "you flew an F-15."

"You seem to have good intel on me."

"I have good people," said David. "Commander, can I buy you a beer?"

"No, but thanks, I still have to get back to the base tonight. It's been a very busy place lately."

"I'll try not to keep you long. I know the work you and your men have been doing is important, probably saving the lives of thousands of our boys. I just wanted to tell you that I have seen all the raw footage and I know you didn't kill that young girl. But I do need to know what they wanted from you."

Nathan sat down beside David. "They gave me a piece of equipment, with instructions on how to tap one of the network cables that goes to a computer used in the drone monitoring system."

"What does that equipment do?" asked David.

"It's not part of the control system. It has something to do with the command room where all the drones are monitored on several large LCD monitors."

"You're saying that they are not trying to control them."

"That's correct."

"Then what are they doing?"

"The best I can tell, they are only monitoring where the drones are and their direction at a given time. That information can give them the ability to hide before we fly over and detect them. I'm sure they know that if they were to try to control the drones that we would shut everything down and find out how it was done. So it's in their interest not to control them."

"That's interesting," said David. "Do you have any idea who is doing this?"

"I suspect it's a drug cartel."

"Why?"

"They would have the money to buy the information, plus the equipment to put a system together like this, and since the equipment was installed, nothing has changed in Afghanistan or Pakistan. But, in Mexico, in the mountains west of the city of Durango, suddenly the drug related activity in several areas has dropped off significantly."

"What kind of drug related activity?"

"They obviously know when we're in the area because we don't see anyone harvesting in the fields now. We can't find any movement of the trucks used in the harvesting. And that's the biggest problem because one of the main things we do is find a group of trucks leaving the fields, and follow them to their destination. That way the Mexican police can arrest the entire group."

David took a sip of his beer as he looked out over the parking lot. "Damn. That is very interesting. What drug cartel runs that area?"

"I don't know. I'm afraid to start asking too many questions, because I don't know what they will do to my family."

"I can understand that." David said as he looked out over the gravel parking lot at a truck rumbling by on the highway. "This just doesn't sound like a typical drug cartel, this group is very smart. Their creating and using the video of you to gain access to the government drone system proves that they have some balls. And killing that girl shows that they're ruthless."

"I wish I could go down there and talk to the people in that area and find out who is responsible for this mess."

David looked at Nathan and said, "I don't think that anyone would talk to you or me. I'm sure that everyone in that area has been bought, or scared off. They're just poor farmers who just scrape by. This drug cartel probably offers them a lot more money than they can get selling produce in a city. It gives them the ability to provide a better living for their families."

"It sounds like you have sympathy for them."

David smiled. "My grandfather was a farmer during the depression. He found that he could get more money by turning his corn into moonshine than by selling the corn at the market."

Nathan paused, studying David for a moment. Then he said, "My family depends on me to provide and protect them. That's why I need to do something to eliminate this threat."

David nodded his head in agreement, "That video has put a member of my family in trouble, too."

"How?"

"Friends of hers stole a copy of it off a computer where she works. There are people that think she had something to do with stealing it, and they have been trying to find her and her friends for a week now."

"Where did she work?"

"JP Bank of Nevada."

"That bank must be connected to the drug cartel."

"Probably," said David, "drug cartels use U.S. banks to launder their money."

Nathan looked out over the parking lot, shook his head, and said, "I can't believe that I have put my family in danger, and compromised the Air Force Drone system, just because I couldn't keep my dick in my pants." He turned to David, then said, "You realize that this drug cartel could sell the drone positions to terrorists?"

"I think this group is too smart to harm their cash cow. It's more likely that they will just use the information to protect themselves. That way they can keep selling drugs in the U.S."

"I hope you're right." Nathan put his hand out to David. "I need to get back to the base. Let me know if there is anything I can do."

David smiled. "Keep your dick in your pants, and keep a close watch on your family, OK?"

"Roger that, and please, keep me informed of what you find."

Nathan stood up to go, but turned around. "When we find out who is doing this, I would like to fly down there and drop a bomb on his ass."

David laughed. "Partner, that sounds pretty good. In the meantime, get a throw away phone and call me on it. We can keep in touch that way."

"Sure, I can do that, but do you really think you can get me out of this?"

"I have to. I have family in trouble, too. The problem is we both need to be patient while we gather as much intel as we can."

David looked up the road when he heard the sound of a large group of motorcycles getting closer. "Commander, I think you better leave now. I hope these guys aren't trouble, but if they are, you don't need to be here."

Nathan zipped up his jacket and put on his gloves and helmet as he ran to his bike. The bikers started entering the parking lot just as he reached the road. He stopped and waited as they pulled in, passing him on both sides.

David walked to the edge of the porch where Max was standing and watched the Commander leave and the bikers park their bikes in a row in front of the building.

"How's it hanging, grandpa?" asked one of the young bikers.

David took a sip of his beer, smiled, and said, "It still works, just not as long as it did when I was your age."

Everyone started laughing.

David asked, "Where you boys from?"

"We have a club in southern California."

"What brings you here?"

"We were trying to camp in Death Valley tonight, but the rangers just kicked us out. I think we scared the other campers. Where are you from?"

"North California."

Two of the bikers walked up to David and Max and just stood there and looked at them. Then one said, "I never liked northern California."

David looked at the man and said, "Why don't you let me buy you boys a beer. Go on inside and tell them to put it on my tab."

The biker stared at David for a few seconds then said, "Yeah." He turned to the door, and as he walked inside he said, "Come on boys, grandpa's going to buy us a round."

As soon as the last biker went inside, David closed the door while Max pulled the bench up and wedged it between the door and the front porch rail.

"Let's get the fuck out of here!" said David.

David and Max started their bikes and spun the tires throwing gravel everywhere as they made their way to the road. David looked back to see something crash through one of the windows but didn't take the time to see what it was. They just hauled ass as fast as they could.

~ ~ ~

Beatty, Nevada

It was a warm, clear night, 83 degrees, but inside the RV the stress of confinement put everyone on edge and made it feel much hotter, so Dennis broke out the beer. "I think we can go outside for a while, if you'll all stay between the RVs and don't turn on any lights," he said. He stood guard at the front of the RVs and Brad took a radio and stood at the rear.

The radio was tuned to a classic rock station, playing 70's, 80's, and 90's music. They started to relax as the combination of fresh night air, good music, and beer lessened the stress.

Brad started singing along with the radio and Kate was tapping her toes. "You have a really good voice," she said. "Have you ever been in a band?"

"Yes," he said, "I was lead singer in a small band for a few years."

"What happened?"

"Drugs, booze, and women."

A new song started on the radio and Kate said, "Turn that up, I used to dance to this on stage. It was one of my best songs." She grabbed Randy's arm and said, "Stand up and play your air guitar."

A soft voice on the radio sang, "I want my MTV."

The organ started to play, then the drum and finally a guitar played the beginning of Dire Straights, "Money for Nothing."

Randy played the air guitar and Brad started to sing the first verse as Kate danced in front of them.

An older couple parked in a space nearby woke up to the music. They looked out the back window of their Casita travel trailer and watched Kate and the boys pretending to be a rock band. The woman turned to look at her husband as he started to sing the chorus. She turned back to look at the band and wondered if her husband was just enjoying the music or wishing he could be over there dancing with Kate. She laid her head back on the pillow, and smiled as she watched her husband move his head in time to the music as he sang the rest of the song.

When he looked back at his wife, she was laughing at him.

"You old rocker," she said, "I guess you want me to be one of your groupies."

David and Max arrived back just in time to hear the last chorus of the song. They leaned over their handlebars and David said, "Yeah, that sure ain't working."

Everyone started laughing.

"OK, that's enough playing for tonight," said David. "Let's go inside, I need to tell you what we have learned." David waited while everyone piled back into the RV. As he was walking up the steps he heard a slight squeaking noise. He stopped, squeak, turned around, squeak, looked around, squeak, squeak, then saw the Casita rocking back and forth. He grinned as he turned to go back up the steps of the RV. Squeak, squeak, squeak, squeak.

~ ~ ~

David was scanning the headlines of several online news services when he heard the local news announcer on the radio talking about a disturbance at a business north of Vegas the night before. "A gang of bikers entered the building and tore the place up. The police are looking for two bikers who managed to leave the scene."

Dennis spoke up from the seat behind David, "It sounds like we need to keep off the bikes until we get out of Nevada."

"Yeah, that means we're going to have to use the truck for running point this morning."

"If we go west through Death Valley, we can be in California in a few minutes," Dennis said.

"That will work."

Libby checked her email while the men were working and saw that she had one from Joe, saying, "Everything has been quiet here. The boy on the bicycle still comes by and looks around, but nothing has happened." She called to Candy to come see the email.

"That's good," Candy said. "I've been worried about Joe being by himself. I would bet that he's not getting any sleep." She was silent a moment. "I'm going to miss you all, but I think I should go back. I think I can be of more help there, with Joe, now that Kate's uncle is here."

Candy quickly gathered her things while Brad and Max took Libby's scooter out of Joe's van and put it into the club's trailer and Jeffery finished getting everything ready for today's drive to the farmhouse in Bodega Bay, California.

"Please, be careful," Candy said, "and stay in touch with me and Joe. We'll do whatever we can to help from there." She shared tearful hugs with Kate, Randy, and Libby, got into Joe's van and drove away.

Brad, Max, and Dennis drove off in the pickup, towing the trailer. They took point. Jeffery drove the RV with David in the passenger seat. Kate, Randy, and Libby stayed out of view in the back seats.

David usually wanted one man riding a bike to take point as they traveled. The point man's job was to scout the road ahead and report back by radio anything that might jeopardize the cargo in the RV, and today's cargo was three people who were wanted by the Vegas Police Department and by people who wanted to kill them.

The plan was to drive into Death Valley National Park and stop at the Mesquite Flat Sand Dunes to unload one of the motorcycles. Then Brad would take point on the motorcycle and the truck would drive behind the RV and watch the rear.

As the truck and RV pulled into the parking lot of Mesquite Flat Sand Dunes, an older couple driving a Toyota pickup and pulling a Casita travel trailer was pulling out, heading west. David thought about the squeaking trailer from the night before and wondered if it could be the same one.

Brad and Dennis pulled the Harley out of the trailer and got it ready for today's ride. Brad hopped on the bike and started it up. He plugged in his helmet with the built in microphone and speaker to a connector that went to the Kenwood VHF mobile radio mounted on the back of the bike.

He pressed the PTT, push-to-talk, button and said, "Point to base, radio check?"

David, wearing a communication headset, pushed his PTT button and replied, "This is base, you're loud and clear."

Brad replied, "Roger that."

Dennis closed up the trailer, got back into the passenger side of the truck and got his radio check. Brad took off as everyone else waited a few minutes. Then the RV started with the truck following.

The RV caught up with the older couple pulling the travel trailer as they were passing the top of one of the mountains on the west side of Death Valley.

~ ~ ~

"Look at that," the old man said to his wife as he pointed to the valley that had opened up on the right side of the road. She turned to look and saw a military plane flying through the valley at their eye level. Several seconds later the jet turned and headed straight at them with a loud roar and passed a few hundred feet over their heads.

The old man laughed. "I did not expect to get buzzed today," he said.

~ ~ ~

A few seconds later, another jet plane followed the same path as the first.

"What was that?" were the cries inside the RV from everyone behind David.

David turned and said, "Military jets practicing maneuvers. Most of the airspace over Death Valley is used for military training."

~ ~ ~

"Did you get a picture of them?" the older man asked his wife.

"I tried," she said, frustrated, "but the camera auto focused on the bugs on the windshield instead of the plane."

Chapter 8
Las Vegas, Nevada

The dark unmarked Ford Crown Victoria police car pulled into the parking lot. Detective Hector Rodriguez slowly drove past the mostly empty apartments as he searched for Joe's unit number. After stopping in front of Joe's apartment, he called the dispatcher and gave his location. He sat in the car as he studied the apartment complex making mental notes of the condition of the buildings. Then he opened the car door and walked to the front door and pressed the door bell.

Joe pressed the intercom button and said, "Can I help you?"

"Yes, I'm Detective Hector Rodriguez of the Vegas Police Department. I'm looking for Joe Morgan."

Joe was sitting in his wheelchair on the other side of the door. He pressed a button on the chair's control console and the front door slid open.

For a few seconds the two men looked at each other, then Joe said, "Hello, Detective. I'm Joe Morgan. What can I do for you?"

"I'm trying to locate a Libby Harrison. Do you know her?"

"Yes, is she in some sort of trouble?"

"Her cell phone records show that she called you the night before she disappeared. Do you know where she is?"

"She disappeared?! What do you mean, she disappeared?! I haven't heard anything."

The detective waited a few seconds then said, "Mr. Morgan, I think Libby Harrison and Randy Hunter may be in some kind of danger and all I'm trying to do is help." He paused again then continued, "May I come in so we can talk?"

"Yes, of course, come in. Follow me to the back room."

As Rodriguez walked into the apartment, Joe pressed another button and the front door closed. Rodriguez followed Joe to the back room, stopping briefly at each door that they passed and looking in. He stood at the door of Joe's office taking in all the computer equipment against the walls, then as he continued into the room he said, "Mr. Morgan, what do you do here?"

"Research."

"What kind of research?"

"Companies hire me to run background checks on people, and sometimes it's for people wanting to know if their spouse is cheating."

"You seem to have a lot of security equipment here."

"Yes, my clients like to know that the information I collect is not going to be compromised."

Joe watched Rodriguez as he studied everything in the room then he said, "Please, tell me what's going on."

Rodriguez sat down next to Joe and asked, "What kind of relationship do you have with Miss Harrison?"

"A few years ago I hired her to help me put this system together. We finished it about a year ago and she has been working with Randy Hunter since."

"What were they working on?"

"I have no idea," Joe said.

"What kind of work did she do for you?"

"Mostly it was writing programs. We wrote about 100 programs."

Rodriguez asked, "Did she ever do any research for you?"

"Sure, if I had a lot of work she would come in and help me out."

"Can any of this research be traced back to you or her?"

"I don't see how. Everything we look for is on the web."

"Has anyone ever threatened you or Miss Harrison?"

"No," said Joe.

"Can you think of any reason someone would want to hurt Miss Harrison?"

"No! Please, what's going on?"

Rodriguez paused for a few seconds then asked, "Can I get a copy of your client list?"

"I can only give that to you if you have a warrant. You understand that I have to keep my clients' information private."

Rodriguez opened a notepad, flipped several pages, and asked, "Do you know a woman named Kate Dodson?"

"No, who is she?"

"Randy Hunter's apartment manager said that Miss Dodson was Mr. Hunter's girlfriend, and that she had just left before the men attacked Mr. Hunter and Miss Harrison."

"They were attacked!? What the fuck is going on!?"

Rodriguez closed the notepad, reached into his jacket and handed Joe a card, "That's all I know right now, but if you hear from Miss

Harrison, please tell her that we need to talk to her and Randy Hunter."

"Sure, I'll let her know if I talk to her, but please, let me know if you find out anything."

Rodriguez stood up and walked to the front door. Joe opened the door.

Rodriguez turned back to Joe and said, "I think those three are in danger. When you talk to them, tell them that we can protect them." He turned and walked out of the apartment.

Joe closed the door and sat there thinking about what he should do next. Then he returned to his office and composed an email of what Rodriguez had said.

After he sent the email to Libby he started backing up and then deleting client files from the servers. He locked the backups in a fire proof safe in the safe room.

Joe did not like lying to the police. He knew that most of them were trying to do a good job, but he could not afford to take any chances. He started a background check on Detective Hector Rodriguez of the Vegas Police Department.

~ ~ ~

Bodega Bay, California

It was late at night when Jeffery steered the RV onto Hwy. 1, just east of Bodega Bay. They were driving through thin, spotty fog, but everyone was starting to relax knowing they were getting near the clubhouse. Then Jeffery rounded a curve and ran right into a wall of thick fog. The mood in the RV suddenly became anxious as everyone strained to look out the windows to find some points of reference. Jeffery was familiar with the road, but still slowed the vehicle to a crawl. David was in the passenger seat, not saying a word, just staring out the front window. What should have been the final ten minutes of the trip stretched into thirty and Jeffery's knuckles were turning white on the wheel.

Jeffery turned onto the road that led up the hill to their driveway, and David said, "Jeffery, you did fine. You can relax now."

As they approached the house they saw the lights that Brad had turned on welcoming them home. Jeffery parked next to the house and they all stood up and stretched their legs and stepped out of the

RV. As Kate and Randy got out the fog horn at the end of Doran Beach called a welcome back to her.

Kate stopped and looked toward the bay and smiled. "I haven't heard that in a long time." Randy turned his head to look, but the fog was thick and moved slowly, hiding everything. The fog horn blew again, and the cool moist air softly touched Randy's face reminding him of Kate's gentle caress.

~ ~ ~

Las Vegas, Nevada

Detective Hector Rodriguez arrived early at the squad room at the Vegas Police Department. He entered the large room, flipped the light switch, and walked quickly to his desk in the center of the room as the recessed florescent lights flickered to life. He sat down, turned on his desk computer, and sipped his first coffee of the day as he watched the computer slowly boot up, wishing there was some way to speed it up. Several seconds later the old computer paused to ask for a user name and password. He entered the information then waited again as it finished loading. Finally, he opened a program to search the FBI NCIC database system. He entered a name and as he waited for the search result, he watched as other detectives entered the squad room. Frustration grew with each name he entered, and the message '0 records found' displayed back at him. "Come on," he said to himself, "someone has to be in the system." Suddenly he stopped, he got a hit, the program found someone.

He leaned forward to read the display and heard a voice say, "You look like you just found something."

Hector looked up at the person standing beside him and said, "Hi, Captain, yeah I just found something on one of the relatives on the case I'm working. It seems that this one is wanted by the FBI for murder and drug related crimes."

"Who is it?"

"Charles Dodson. He's Kate Dodson's father."

"OK, remind me, what does she have to do with your case?"

"She's the girlfriend of Randy Hunter, she was the woman that left the apartment just before the attack."

"Do you think this has something to do with her father? Maybe the men were after her. It could have something to do with drugs."

Hector shrugged and said, "I don't know yet, I just discovered this. Something else, her father has a brother named David Dodson, I thought I would start looking for him next. He might be able to tell me something about his niece."

Captain Coleman looked over Hector's shoulder at the display then asked, "How did you find out about her father and uncle?"

"From a genealogy website." Hector smiled at the Captain's expression and said, "I joined a genealogy website to help my mother trace her family tree. Last night, after I was through working on my mother's, I decided to build a family tree on Kate Dodson, Libby Harrison, and Randy Hunter. I came in early this morning and started running the list of names, and so far Kate Dodson's father is the only one that I got a hit on in the NCIC database."

"Good work, Detective. I'm sure I don't need to remind you to update the department's computers with everything you find."

"Doing it now, Captain," said Hector as he watched him walk to his office.

Suddenly, the phone rang on a desk across the squad room. One of the new detectives answered it, and motioned for his partner to follow him. Hector watched the two men walk into the Captain's office. He had an uneasy feeling about those two, something was off with them. Most new detectives try to fit in and socialize with the other detectives in the squad, but these two stayed by themselves and seldom had more than a few words to say to the others. Hector started typing his notes, but occasionally glanced at the Captain's office door, wondering what they were talking about.

~ ~ ~

Las Vegas, Nevada

Angelo gently slipped out of the bed, trying not to wake Claudette. He froze in place as she rolled over and pulled the sheet up. When she didn't open her eyes, he slipped on a robe and left the room. As he reached the kitchen the phone rang.

"Hello."

He grabbed a pad and pencil and started making some notes as he listened. Claudette walked naked into the kitchen as he hung up the phone.

She put her arms around him and said, "You have to let me get to sleep earlier, these all nighters are killing me."

"If that's what you want," he said as he put his arms around her.

She looked up to him. "You better not."

He pushed her hair out of her face and kissed her, and when he felt her shiver, he took his robe off and put it around her.

"Now you're going to get cold," she said.

"No. I'm good."

"If you're going to play the naked chef," she said, "then put on an apron. I wouldn't want anything to get burned." She laughed as he put on an apron, turned his back to her, and started the coffee.

He heard her run to the bedroom and come back a few seconds later. He didn't notice her as she walked around the counter, but the flash from the camera in her phone did get his attention. "You didn't just take a picture, did you?" he asked.

"I couldn't help it, it's a Kodak moment."

He started toward her and she turned to run, but he was too fast. He grabbed her wrists and pushed her up against the wall, and holding her arms above her head with one hand, he untied the robe and pushed it open with the other. Then he took the phone from her hand, held it in front of her and said, "Smile," as he pressed the button. Then he let her go, but he kept her phone.

She said, "Don't delete your photo, I want to keep it."

He looked at her, then pushed several buttons on her phone before he handed it back to her.

She looked at the phone and noticed the photos were still there. "What did you do?" she asked.

"I emailed the photos to my phone."

She put her hand over her mouth, looked at him and said, "Oh, no."

"What?"

"You sent the photos to everyone in my address book!"

He just stood there trying to think of a way to explain this. Then she started laughing.

"Do you think this is funny?"

She just kept laughing.

"What's wrong with you?"

She finally stopped laughing. "You didn't send it to everyone," she said. Then she laughed again. "You should have seen your face."

He stood there watching her laugh. Then he took the phone from her and placed it on the counter. He grabbed her waist and picked her up, placing her over his shoulder, and he carried her outside.

She started yelling, "What are you doing?"

He walked over to the pool and threw her in.

When her head appeared above the water she yelled, "Damn, it's cold! Get me out of here!"

He reached down and helped her out.

She said, "Dammit! I'm freezing!"

He took the robe off of her, then he took off his apron and put it on her. He grinned as he looked at her, and he put his arms around her and said, "It looks better on you."

~ ~ ~

Claudette found her brother in the break room pouring some coffee into a large mug. She sat down at a table and said, "Angelo got a lead on Libby Harrison, and Kate Dodson."

"OK, what did he get?"

"Libby Harrison has a friend and former employer, a Joe Morgan." She took the paper out of her purse and handed it to him, "Here's some more information. Kate Dodson has an uncle his name is on the paper."

"How did he get this?"

"He got a call this morning from someone inside the police department. It seems Joe Morgan was the last person Miss Harrison called."

"Good, we haven't had a lead in several days. I'll get started on Mr. Morgan first thing."

Antoine poured her a cup of coffee, placed it in front of her, then sat down beside her. "You look tired. Angelo keeping you up too late?"

She smiled at him, leaned over and put her head on his shoulder and said, "Yes, I think I have met someone that is as big a sex addict as I am."

Antoine laughed and kissed her on the top of her head, "Why don't you go to your bedroom, close the door, and get a nap. I'll wake you in a few hours. Go."

She raised her head and looked at him, "I think I will."

Chapter 9
Bodega Bay, California

David found Kate, Randy, and Libby eating breakfast in the kitchen. "Good morning," he said, "I'm glad to see you have made yourselves at home." He sat down at the table. "You've been hiding out for over a week, so I thought you might like to get out today and enjoy yourselves while I take care of some club business. I don't think anyone will find you here, but just to be sure there are some rules that I must insist you follow. Stay out of town. We'll do any major shopping for you. If you want to buy something while you're out, use cash. Don't use your phones, turn them off, take the batteries out. In a few days I will try to get you some cheap phones to use while you're here. Never leave without one of my people with you. They're trained bodyguards. If they suddenly give you an order, don't ask questions, do what they say immediately, it's for your safety, so you'll be alive to ask about it later."

David looked around the table. "Kate knows the area so I will let her show everyone around. Jeffery and Max will be your escorts today. This afternoon I would like to put our heads together and look at all the information you have collected. If we are going to find a way out of this, then I need to know all the players."

~ ~ ~

A small patch of fog floated by as Kate and Randy took seats inside the black GMC Yukon. Jeffery was sitting in the driver's seat checking out the instrument panel and getting a radio check as Max helped Libby get into the SUV.

Max sat in the front passenger seat, then turned around to Kate and asked, "Where to first, Kate?"

She thought for a second then asked, "How far can we go?"

Jeffery said, "We could drive up the Coastal Highway to Sonoma Coast State Beach, then work our way back."

"That would be good."

Jeffery took his time as they drove up the Coastal Hwy., letting everyone take in the sharp bluffs of the coastline. He turned onto

Goat Rock Road, then took a left at State Park Road, which took them to the bottom of the bluff to a parking lot by the beach.

Max got out of the van and opened the side door. The cool, gusty wind caught their hair and pitched it around as Kate, Randy, and Libby stepped out. Libby was following Kate and Randy to the beach when she noticed a white bird, hovering at eye level, 10 feet away. She grabbed her hair, pulled it out of her face, and watched the bird float backwards, then land on one of the boulders that circled the parking lot. She looked around to see if the others had seen the bird and she noticed that Jeffery was not with the group. She waited for Max to catch up to her and asked, "Is Jeffery not coming?"

"No, someone has to stay with the van all the time. That's one of our rules when we're doing protection duty."

"Oh, OK," she said. "What's his story, anyway? He just seems different from the rest of you."

Max smiled and said, "Yeah, Jeffery is not like the rest of us. He has a formal education. He has a degree in chemistry from MIT."

Libby looked at Max and said, "You're kidding."

"Except for him and Brad, everyone else has a military background, and we like that kind of structure. It's very orderly and that helps to keep us out of trouble."

"How did he end up here?"

"After he graduated, he was hired by a pharmaceutical company that was working on cancer drugs. He was pulling down six figures, was married to his high school love, and they had one son. Everything was good until one day he discovered that some of the research data was being manipulated."

"I think I see where this is headed," said Libby.

"Yeah," said Max, "he fought with them for a while and when one of the drugs was about to be approved, he wrote a letter to the FDA about what was going on. Long story short, Jeffery lost his job, his wife divorced him, and he has not seen his son in two years."

"That's a shame."

"Yeah, his life had reached bottom. Then one day David was visiting one of our clients, a bar owner, when he noticed Jeffery sitting at the bar sipping a whiskey. David started talking to him and saw that he was very drunk. David was about to leave him to his drink, when Jeffery suddenly held a glass of whiskey up in front of his face, and started rambling about how easy it is to make. That got

David's attention, and he started questioning Jeffery about what he knew about making whiskey. Jeffery wasn't normally a big drinker, so he soon felt sick. David helped him to the men's room where Jeffery promptly vomited all over both of them."

Libby laughed and said, "Oh, no."

"David cleaned them up as best as he could in a men's room. Then he got some bottled water and some coffee and took Jeffery out behind the bar to sober him up. When David thought he had done all he could and was ready to leave, he wanted to get Jeffery to his car. But there was no car, just broken glass. That was too much for Jeffery, he had a breakdown. He had been living in his car for the past two months and everything he owned - photos of his son, his books, everything - was in that car."

Libby stared at Max, shook her head and said, "That poor man."

"Yeah, that was the last straw for him. The only thing he had left was two dollars in his pocket and the clothes on his back. David offered him some work and a place to live until he got back on his feet. Jeffery said no at first, he can be stubborn, but he finally agreed. And David brought him, hanging on the back of his bike, to the RV. Well, we all thought David had lost his mind. I mean, Jeffery was starting to look like a bum, and he smelled like... well, he had just been sick all over himself, you can imagine what he smelled like. And while Jeffery was in the shower, David gave me two hundred dollars and asked me to run to the store and get Jeffery some clothes. I tried to argue about hiring him; I thought he would just be dead weight. But David's the boss, I did what I was told, and that, as it turned out, was a good thing."

"What happened?"

"We took Jeffery back to the clubhouse and let him work around there. It was nice having someone else around to do most of the shit jobs for us, and he worked his butt off. Soon everyone started to accept him and got to know him a little. I noticed that, at night, David would bring Jeffery into his office and they would spend hours talking. Then one weekend the club rode to Vegas to a motorcycle rally, and we left Jeffery at the clubhouse. When we got back Jeffery had written up a plan to make our entire operation more efficient and he presented it to David. The next night David had a club meeting and told us that Jeffery had a degree in chemistry from MIT and that he also knew a lot about industrial control systems. At first all the club members thought David was joking. Then Jeffery got up and presented his plan and everyone just sat there in silence, completely stunned."

Libby smiled, then said, "And..."

"Last year we started using Jeffery's system and made almost twice as much money as the year before. The club made him a full member and two months ago I sold him a used motorcycle and started teaching him to ride."

"I just realized that I don't know what your club does to produce an income. It's not illegal, is it?"

Max paused for a few seconds, looked at Libby and said, "I thought you knew. I'm sorry, I probably said too much already. I'm sorry, I need to call David."

Libby stared at him as he reached for his phone, dialed, and walked away.

When Max walked back to where Libby was standing he waved to Kate and Randy, motioning them to come back. He said nothing else as they walked back to the SUV.

After everyone was seated, Jeffery turned around and said, "David called and told me that when we get back to the clubhouse, I can show you around my lab."

Kate, Randy, and Libby looked puzzled and Randy said, "Lab? I hope it's not a meth lab."

"What's David up to now?" asked Kate.

Jeffery and Max looked at each other and started laughing.

Jeffery said, "No. No. It's not a meth lab." He turned to face the front of the SUV and looked in the rear view mirror at Randy, then laughed and said, "But it is illegal."

Kate, Randy, and Libby gave each other a quick glance but said nothing.

Jeffery drove them back, making a few more stops so their guests could get more views of the California coastline. When they got back to the farmhouse they all went in and freshened up.

Kate found David in his office and asked, "What's this about the club having an illegal lab?"

"You'll find out when everybody else does," said David, grinning at her. "And if everyone's ready, we can go to Jeffery's lab and he can explain everything."

They walked out the back door to a huge garage area, housing two

SUVs, several motorcycles, and three John Deere Utility Vehicles. Libby followed Jeffery and sat beside him in one of the utility vehicles. David, Kate, and Randy got into one of the others.

David looked at Jeffery and Libby talking to each other, then turned to Kate and said, "I don't think I have ever seen Jeffery smile that much."

Randy said, "I have never seen Libby act like that either."

Jeffery took the lead as they rode up the driveway to a new concrete block building north of the farm house. He held open the front door for Libby as she entered, then he waited for David, Kate, and Randy to enter. He pushed the curtains open to let in the sunlight. "Welcome," he said. "We tell everyone that this is just a maintenance building, but as you can tell, the front part of the building is my living area. The back is where David has let me set up a small lab. We also have a basement for storage of equipment and supplies, and there's a safe room and a shooting range." He opened the door to the lab. "Come on in."

Kate, Libby, and Randy entered the lab and stopped, amazed. "This 'small lab' is as big as a house!" said Libby.

Jeffery said, "Yes, this room is 2400 sq. feet with a very high ceiling so I can house the processing equipment. It's not only a lab but a production area."

"OK, I'm impressed," said Randy, "but I still want to know what you make here."

Jeffery motioned with his hand. "Follow me."

They walked to the back of the building where they saw copper columns coming out of the top of two large 300 gallon stainless steel tanks and rising almost to the ceiling.

They stood there for a minute, then Randy asked, "OK, what is it?"

Jeffery smiled and said, "It's two 300 gallon reflux stills."

"OK. And what is a reflux still?"

Kate started to laugh. "Are you using my great-grandfather's moonshine recipe?"

Libby and Randy looked at Kate and said together, "Moonshine?"

Jeffery smiled. "Yes."

Kate turned to David and said, "You told Jeffery the recipe, but you won't tell me."

"Need to know, Kitten."

"How long have you been doing this?"

"The boys and I started making small amounts right after you left for college. It wasn't long before we started making larger amounts and selling it. We didn't get into it in a big way until Jeffery joined us."

"I didn't think anyone still made moonshine," said Randy.

"Especially in California wine country," Libby said.

"It's making a comeback," said David, "especially the specialty whiskeys that we are starting to make."

Randy looked at Kate. "So your great-grandfather was a moonshiner?" he asked.

"Yes," said Kate, "during prohibition he was one of the biggest moonshiners in this area, and he never got caught."

David said, "During that time he supplied a lot of the speakeasys in San Francisco."

"Do you make it all here?" asked Libby.

"Yes," said Jeffery, "I have an automated computer control system here."

"How long does it take?"

"It can take a lot of time depending on how much we have to make. It takes sixty days to make enough for a big motorcycle rally like Sturgis." Jeffery paused, then said, "Most of the time is in the fermentation process. When it's time to start distilling, the procedure becomes mostly automated using the computer control system."

Kate said, "I didn't realize it took that long."

"It only takes about 10 to 15 days to make one batch of plain corn whiskey like your grandfather made," said Jeffery, "but we make a lot of it so we have to repeat the process several times. David also wanted to experiment making specialty whiskeys, like our apple pie moonshine. It looks like it's going to be a big hit, and a lot more profitable."

Randy started laughing. "I'm sorry," he said. "I just can't see bikers sitting around a table drinking something called apple pie moonshine."

"Why not?" said David. "We're bikers. And 99 percent of bikers are just regular people, like us. Most have 9 to 5 jobs and families. It's the 1 percent that the movie industry and news people show everyone." He grinned. "And I bet they would like it, too."

"OK, I'm sold," Randy said. "When do I get to try it?"

"How about tonight?"

Randy gave a thumbs up as Libby asked, "How do you transport it?"

"It depends on where we're going." said David. "Most of the time we carry it in the RV in large tanks, then bottle it when we get there. Some police departments will pull over an RV and search it for drugs, so when we know that we're going to drive near those areas we carry it in the trailer. So far we have been very lucky and haven't been caught. It also helps to have someone riding ahead who can look for the police and call on the radio or cell phone to let us know where they're located."

"Don't your neighbors know what you're doing?" asked Libby.

"Some of the local farmers know what we do, but they love us because we buy their corn at top dollar to make the mash and then we give them the waste products for free. They feed it to their livestock and that cuts down on their overhead. But I don't think most of them have a clue as to what we are doing. We try to keep very quiet here, and not do anything to draw attention to ourselves. But if someone needs help with something, we try to do what we can, so they don't mind having us around."

"What about local police?"

"The county sheriff and I are good friends. We even do some work for him from time to time. And we sell very little in this county, most of what we sell is at bike rallies located out of town. Most of these rallies bring in big money to their local economy, so the local police tend to turn a blind eye during these events."

"Doing everything, the manufacturing, bottling, and distribution, sounds like a lot of work," said Libby.

Jeffery said, "The fermentation process and distilling procedure we do here, that takes the most time. But with the automated computer control system, I can do that by myself. The hectic time is the week right before the rally. That's when we drive up to do the bottling and distribution. After that the boys help me clean up and put the bottling equipment back onto the truck. Then they go to the rally and party. I join them later after I crash for a few days."

"Don't you like to party?" asked Kate.

"I drink a little. I just don't like getting so drunk that I can't function. I do like to hear the bands, watch the people, and take a lot of photographs."

The group, led by Jeffery, with Libby at his side, had made a loop around the lab as they talked and were now headed back to Jeffery's living space.

"What kind of computer control system do you use?" asked Libby.

"It's homemade. I put the system together myself. I did have to hire someone to create the software. What they created works but it's not very easy to use. It's a command line program that requires me to enter setup data each time I run it."

"I've done some controller programming before," said Libby. "If you want, I can look at it and help you with that."

Randy spoke up, "Libby is the best programmer that I know. She can help you with that."

Jeffery said, "If David doesn't mind I would be glad to show it to you."

"How about now?" asked Libby.

David said, "I would like to see all the information that everyone has collected from the bank."

"Randy has the portable hard drive with everything on it," said Libby. "He and Kate can show you how to get to it. And if you need me you can call me."

David looked at Libby. "OK. Jeffery, you lock this building down and don't go out."

"OK."

As Kate, Randy, and David got back into their utility vehicle Kate said, "I bet we won't see those two anymore tonight."

"That's OK," said David. "Jeffery knows how to use a gun, and that building is better fortified than the farmhouse. They'll be safe there and I think they do like each other."

Chapter 10
Miami, Florida

"Good afternoon, Captain," said Frank, as he entered the large, tobacco scented, corner office of Jack Roberts, President of CJ Global Securities.

Captain Jack sat in his overstuffed executive chair and looked over his pipe at Frank. "What's so important that you couldn't tell me over the phone?"

Frank Warwick, Director of Intelligence of the DEA Miami Field Division, walked to the wall of windows and stared out at the panoramic view of the Miami coast line. Frank loved the view, a stark contrast to the view from his office at the federal building. "Our old friend, Charles Dodson, has popped up on a search of the FBI NCIC database."

"Why is someone searching for him?"

"It seems his daughter, Kate Dodson, went missing after a couple of men broke into her boyfriend's apartment and assaulted him and a friend. There is a Las Vegas detective investigating the incident, and he wants to talk to her, so he started running names of family members through the system." He glanced at Jack then looked back out the window.

Jack pulled his pipe out of his mouth, "You must have a notification flag on Charles Dodson's NCIC file." he said.

Frank turned to face the captain and said, "Yes, and the FBI gave me a call when the detective ran his search."

Captain Jack leaned back in his chair, put his pipe back into his mouth, intertwined his fingers and placed his hands in his lap. He started puffing on his pipe again and for several long seconds they quietly watched the smoke slowly floating between them. Jack broke the silence when he pulled his pipe out of his mouth and asked, "Should I send some men to Las Vegas to look for him?"

"No. I think it's too early to get the company involved; besides this may be nothing. I'll just keep monitoring it, and see if anything breaks. If it does, I'll ask the FBI to get involved."

"OK, but keep me updated."

"You know I will, Captain. I want that SOB, too."

~ ~ ~

Bodega Bay, California

Libby and Jeffery worked late into the evening before Jeffery noticed it was dark outside.

"Libby, I'm sorry," said Jeffery, "I didn't realize it was dark already. I can still drive you to the house."

"That's OK. I saw that it was getting dark. I would rather not go back to the house anyway."

"Why? David is a very good cook."

"Kate and Randy are a couple and sometimes I feel like I'm in the way. Besides, I like to stay busy, and I like the company here."

Jeffery smiled at her. "Thanks, I like your company, too. Would you like something to eat?"

"Sure."

They walked into the small kitchen and Jeffery started describing the contents of his pantry to her.

She said, "It's been a long day, something like a frozen dinner would be fine with me."

"OK. I can do that. What would you like to drink?"

She thought for a second. "I have never tried moonshine. What's it like?"

"It's very strong, and you may need to be extra careful."

"Why?"

He smiled and said, "The guys tell me that it will put hair on your chest."

She started laughing. "I'll take that chance."

"Are you sure? It is very strong."

"Yeah, I would like to try it."

"OK, I'll have to go downstairs and get a bottle."

Libby put the two dinners into a toaster oven, and waited for Jeffery to return.

Jeffery took two glasses out of the cabinet and poured a small amount in each glass. He handed her a glass and said, "This is the apple pie, sip a little at a time and see if you like it."

She took a sip. "Wow! That burns a little."

"Yes, go very slow with it. Remember I can cut it with some soda or water."

"No, that's OK."

They sat at the kitchen table and talked as the dinners finished cooking. When they were done, Jeffery took them out, put them on plates, and brought them to the table. Then he got some ketchup out of the refrigerator and set it on the table. "I don't have any sauces to go on the meat, but I do have this."

Libby shook the container, turned it upside down and squeezed. Nothing came out. She tried again and squeezed harder. Suddenly ketchup shot out all over the table, her dinner, and her.

Stunned, Libby sat motionless for a few seconds, staring at the mess. "I don't know why I even try. Everything I have done the past few weeks seems to screw up, and always comes back on me," she said in a defeated tone.

Jeffery grabbed some paper towels and tried to help her clean up.

Dejected, she stood up, looked at her clothes and said, "I really can make a good first impression, can't I?"

"Libby, look at me."

She lifted her head to face him and he saw a glimmer of light from the moisture in the corners of her eyes.

He reached up and held her by her shoulders. "You don't need to try to impress me. I already like you."

They looked at each other for a few seconds, then Libby tried to smile.

"You need to get out of those clothes and let me wash them," Jeffery said.

"I don't have anything here. What few clothes I have are at the house."

"I can offer you a shirt or robe while I wash them."

"OK."

He said, "Just grab anything you like out of my closet and I'll clean this up."

She went into his bedroom and took everything off. After examining everything in the closet, she found a black button down shirt and put it on. It looked like a very short dress and it highlighted her blond hair and fair skin. After a few moments in front of the mirror, she decided to leave several of the top buttons unfastened.

Jeffery stopped cleaning, and stared at her when she came walking back into the kitchen.

Libby said, "I'm sorry I made such a mess."

Jeffery smiled. "That's OK. It's worth it to see you in that shirt."

They took her clothes to the washing machine and got the first load started. After dinner Jeffery poured another drink as Libby looked at his music collection. "If you see something you want to listen to, go ahead and start it," he said.

She started a Leon Russell CD and sat down on the loveseat. He sat down beside her and handed her a glass, and she slid over and put her hand on his leg as the song titled, "A Song for You," started.

"I like this CD," he said as he put his arm around her.

She leaned her head onto his shoulder and he kissed the top of her head.

She looked up at him, turned toward him, reached up, pulled his head down and kissed him.

He touched her cheek as they kissed, then let his hand slide down her neck to her breast and back again. He pulled slightly away and when she opened her eyes and looked at him again, he said, "Libby, it's been a very long time since I was with anyone. I may be a little out of practice."

She laughed. "Well, you didn't have any trouble getting me to take my clothes off with that ketchup bottle that I know you rigged, but if you think you need it, I'm sure we can find some instructional videos on a porn site."

He laughed. "No, I bet with your help, I can figure it out." He bent over and kissed her gently on the lips just as the washing machine buzzer went off.

~ ~ ~

Las Vegas, Nevada

As the night gave way to dawn the security cameras showed more detail of the street and parking lot around Joe's apartment. With only the glow of the monitors as a light source, Joe's dark office seemed small and cramped. There were desk lamps on the u-shaped computer desk, but they were never turned on at night because it made seeing detail difficult on the security monitors. The nights seemed extra long when the only thing to do was stare at a dark security monitor and watch time slip by on the large LED clock mounted on a wall nearby. Candy's thoughts were about Kate, Randy, and Libby, wondering what they were doing, and hoping they were safe. It had only been a few days, but she missed having them around. It was nice having someone to talk to who was close to her own age. She snapped out of her daydream when she heard a noise nearby. She stood up to stretch as Joe rolled into the office.

Joe looked at the security monitors and asked, "Did our friend come back?"

Candy yawned, and shook her head to wake up. "Yeah, twice, but he never came into the parking lot. He just rode his bicycle up and down the street for a while, then stopped at the driveway and looked around."

"Go get some sleep," said Joe. "I know you're tired."

"You haven't had much sleep either. And you need it more than I do."

"Has anyone ever told you that you're stubborn?"

Candy laughed and said, "Joe, when you have a problem to solve, you're like an old dog with a new bone. You just stay focused on it and keep gnawing at it until it's gone."

Joe grinned at her. "I like to think it's determination and commitment. Do you need more coffee?"

"Yeah. I made some a few minutes ago. It should be ready."

Joe went to the kitchen, poured two cups, and brought them back to the office.

He handed Candy one of the cups and said, "So now I'm just some old dog."

Candy smiled as she took a sip of the coffee. "I need to get that GPS tracker back from Angelo's car before someone finds it. It may tell us more about who we are dealing with."

"Yes, you're right, but I'm not sure how we're going to do that without drawing attention."

Joe sipped his coffee as he watched the security monitors. He was about to say something when he looked at Candy, shook his head and grinned as he watched her head bob up and down, then slowly drop as she fell asleep in the chair. He thought about barking like a dog, but decided not to, she needed her sleep.

Chapter 11
Bodega Bay, California

Jeffery opened his eyes and tried to reach for the ringing phone, but Libby was already answering it.

"Hello," she said. "Yes, he's here, just a second." She handed Jeffery the phone. "Max needs to talk to you."

"Max?" he said as he watched Libby lie back down. "OK. Pick me up in twenty minutes."

He reached over Libby to put the phone back, then put his arms around her and said, "I'm sorry, this is not how I wanted to spend our first morning together, but I have to go. The sheriff called and asked us to provide security for a witness in a trial that's starting today. I'll probably be gone all day."

"That's OK. You can tell me about it tonight."

"I know the farmhouse is nicer," he hesitated, "but would you like to stay with me again tonight?"

She smiled. "Yes. I would like that."

He kissed her. "I'm sorry, but I have to get ready."

"I know, go."

As she watched Jeffery get dressed, she pulled herself up, put another pillow behind her back and sat up in bed. She smiled and said, "If anyone had ever told me that I would spend the night with a biker, I would have said that they were crazy."

"Well, now you have a story that you can tell everyone about the wild night you spent with an outlaw biker. You might want to leave out the part about staying up half the night doing your laundry."

"Yeah," she laughed, "it might be something I can tell my grand-kids some day."

Jeffery smiled. "I might be a member of a biker club, but I'm still not used to being called a biker."

She watched him finish getting dressed. "You better be safe today."

"The only thing that will happen today, will be the teasing I'll get."

"What kind of teasing?"

"You spending the night with me."

They looked at each other when they heard a knock at the front door.

"I have to go. I'll see you tonight. OK?"

"OK."

She sat in bed, listening, as Jeffery opened the door and she heard both Brad and Dennis speak loudly, "Good morning, Stud."

She lay back in bed, pulled Jeffery's pillow next to her, and hugged it.

~ ~ ~

Courthouse, Santa Rosa, California

Jane Taylor, the witness, was an attractive 28 year old female, with long blond hair, wearing a gray skirt with a white blouse. She was a strong-willed woman. She believed in the law, and that it was her duty to testify, and show that she was not scared, even with the threats that had been made against her in the past few weeks. At first, she had refused the security. She told the sheriff that this was not a third world country, that the threats were just to scare her, and that it would be a waste of taxpayers' money, but he insisted. So she sat beside Brad in the back seat, on the passenger side, behind Dennis, who was scanning the road and giving last minute orders to her and his men. She listened to him and didn't argue, but she didn't feel this was really necessary.

Dennis and Brad were wearing dark blue sport coats over white dress shirts and dark jeans, their standard dress code for a protection detail. The Kevlar vests and the shoulder holsters that carried their Glocks under the sport coats made them look 15 pounds heavier. Jeffery, the driver, had a Kevlar vest over his tee-shirt and a belt holster.

Jeffery drove the black GMC Yukon into the parking lot beside the courthouse, noticed a local TV news truck parked in one of the spaces and said, "Looks like a news crew is here." He circled the parking lot, and stopped in the driveway, putting the passenger side of the SUV parallel to the courthouse building. It was a straight shot for them to get out and walk the 150 feet to the side door.

They saw the courthouse door open and a family walked out. A woman carrying a small child and a man holding the hand of a four year old boy walked toward them. "Let's wait for them to pass," said Dennis. When they reached the front of the SUV they turned right into the parking lot.

"Wait here until we get inside," Dennis said as he hopped out. He looked around and then opened the back door for Jane and Brad. They started walking to the courthouse with Dennis leading and Brad following Jane. Jeffery stayed in the SUV scanning the parking lot, keeping an eye on the family as they walked away and remembering the family he had lost.

Suddenly, two men walked out in front of the family from between parked cars, and quickly headed toward the courthouse. Jeffery felt uneasy when he saw them moving in such a hurry. As the men passed behind the family, one pulled a MAC-10 machine pistol from under his jacket. Jeffery watched the men and started to pull out his Glock. Then he saw the father reach down and lift the young boy into his arms. They were right behind the two armed men who were still moving to the courthouse. Jeffery could not shoot. The other man pulled his MAC-10 out and started to point it at Dennis, Brad, and Jane. Jeffery tapped out SOS on the horn and Brad stopped and turned around to look. Two bullets struck Brad in the chest, and he fell back hitting Jane as he went down. Dennis pulled his gun out as he spun around to get in front of Jane. One of the men aimed his MAC-10 at Jeffery and gave the SUV a quick spray of bullets. Jeffery dropped down and pieces of window glass started to cover him. Dennis pushed Jane behind a large flower pot, then got off a couple of rounds as he ducked behind the same pot. Jeffery raised his head to see where the two men were. They had stopped in the parking lot in front of him when Dennis had started to return fire. Jeffery saw the family running away, but they were still in his line of fire. Both men were firing at Dennis and Jane and the large flower pot was starting to crumble. Jeffery sat up, pulled the transmission into low gear and floored it. He aimed the SUV at the two men as they continued shooting. One man quickly turned to the SUV and sprayed it with another round as Jeffery laid back down. Time slowed as Jeffery waited for the inevitable sound of metal against flesh but it never came. Both men were now firing at the SUV, masking the sound of the sudden collision. Jeffery felt the SUV rock just moments after the gunfire stopped. He stopped the SUV, got out and pulled his pistol, then ran to the back of the SUV. One man was obviously dead, his body distorted and twisted. The other man sat up and cursed as he looked at his crushed leg. Suddenly he raised his head and locked eyes with Jeffery.

The man's hand was moving to his gun and Jeffery yelled, "Don't do it! I'll shoot!"

The man grabbed his gun, and started to aim. Jeffery yelled, "NO!" as he pulled the trigger, and watched as the man fell back onto the pavement. With blood covering his left side, Jeffery stood there, his gun still pointed at the man, watching the blood puddle underneath the man's body, unaware of his own injury and of the news crew filming everything from several hundred feet away.

~ ~ ~

Bodega Bay, California

Kate knocked on the open door of David's office.

David looked up from the papers on his desk and said, "Hi, Kitten, come on in."

Kate sat down in front of the desk and said, "Things have sure changed since I left. When did you start doing security for the County Sheriff Department?"

"I've known Sheriff Sanchez a long time. I met Miguel when he was a Deputy. He pulled me over one day for speeding and after he wrote the ticket we started talking and I found out that he was in the army and in Vietnam at the same time that I was. Over the years we became friends and we watch out for each other."

"Watch out for each other," Kate snickered.

"Yeah, we do. I hear things when the boys and I are sitting around at the bars and men's clubs. Sometimes I pass that information on to him. It keeps the real bad people off the street, and makes him look good. For that he looks the other way at my moonshine dealing, as long as I don't sell any in this county."

"You don't sell to anyone local?"

"No, I try to keep everything very low profile. That's why we only sell to bars during big events like motorcycle rallies."

"But what about the security work?"

"You know the economy has been bad for several years now, so Miguel convinced the county government that it would be cheaper to farm out some of the security work instead of hiring more deputies. And we did him a big favor a few years ago so he gives us some security jobs. Most of the work is like this job, transporting, and guarding low risk witnesses. We guard the witnesses at a safe house, then we transport them back and forth to the courthouse until the trial is over. We almost never have any trouble."

"Who's the witness?"

"A woman that witnessed a shooting at a local pharmacy. A local gang was trying to extort money and drugs out of the owner. The owner refused and two men shot him."

"That's awful, was the owner killed?"

"No, I understand it was touch and go, but he pulled through."

"Good," said Kate. "But just what kind of favor did you do for the Sheriff?"

"His 15 year old daughter ran away from home and got involved with a drug dealer in Lake County. Miguel asked me to see if we could find her. We did, several times, and each time he picked her up and took her home, and then she would run away again. Well, one night the boys and I broke into the dealer's house, and tied him and the girl up. We made them think that we were a rival drug gang trying to steal his drugs. Well, a rival gang wouldn't let the man live. So we made it look like we shot and killed him."

"Oh, wow. How did you do that?"

"Dennis took the girl into the next room to question her about the location of their drugs, but really it was so she could hear, but not see, what was happening to her boyfriend. Max used a Taser on the man until he passed out, and then he and Brad made noises like they were beating him up. After what sounded like a real beating, Max poured fake blood over him while Brad fired a gun loaded with blanks. After they heard the gunshots, Dennis took the girl back to the room to see her boyfriend. We told her that he was dead but we wanted to party with her before we killed her. Then I told Dennis to take her to the van and drive her to the warehouse while we cut up and dispose of the body. He took her outside, and forced her into the back of the van. He drove a few blocks and stopped near a convenience store with a pay phone outside. He moved to the back of the van and sat down beside her then pulled out his gun and waved it in her face and said, 'I'm going to let you escape, but you better never tell anyone what happened. If you do we'll find you and I might not be able to save you again. There's a store just up the street that has a phone you can use, so call someone to pick you up, and never come back here.' Then he cut her free, opened the back door and pushed her out, and drove quickly away."

"That must have been some performance," said Kate. "But what did you do with the guy?"

"We put him in the van and drove him to a beach south of San Francisco. While he was still passed out we wrote a message on his arms saying, 'don't come back or we'll cut your dick off.' We also drew a line around his dick with a message saying 'cut here.'"

Kate started laughing. "You're bad," she said. "What happened to the girl?"

"She went home, and Miguel has told me that she has been a good kid."

Max ran into the office. "Boss, turn on your TV. There was some trouble at the courthouse, you need to see this."

David stood up and turned the TV on and saw the video of Jeffery shooting one of the men. David's cell phone started to ring. He looked at the caller ID and saw it was the sheriff.

"Miguel, what the hell is going on?"

He sat back down as he watched a repeat of the video and listened to Miguel at the same time. When he ended the phone call he said, "Jeffery and Brad are in the hospital. I need to go. And Max, we need to get them out of here."

Kate said, "Was that Jeffery shooting that man?"

"Yes, and Jeffery was shot in the arm. Brad took two in the chest. They both had their vests on and they are going to be OK." He paused, then said, "Kate, Miguel said that this is turning into a media circus and that the news crews may be heading here. I cannot hide you and your friends here with the media outside. I have to move you."

Kate just stared at him and nodded her head.

David turned to Max and said, "Get the RV and take Kate and her friends up to Crescent City and stay there. I'll call you when I find out more."

"Roger that, Boss." Max ran through the living room and headed out the door.

Kate followed David into the living room and saw the confused expressions on both Randy and Libby.

"What's going on?" asked Randy.

"Jeffery and Brad were shot at the courthouse," answered David. "They're both going to be OK. But I need to leave and I need to get you out of here before the news media arrives."

"I need to see Jeffery," said Libby. She looked at David as a tear rolled down her face. "I need to see him."

David put his arm around her and wiped the tear from her face. "Libby, I promise you Jeffery will be OK, and I'm sure he would want you to be safe. I need you to go with your friends. OK?"

She looked up and nodded her head.

Kate put her arm around Libby's shoulders as David walked away. "Libby, we need to go now," she said. "Randy, would you get our things and meet us outside?"

"Sure," said Randy.

The RV pulled up to the back door and Kate and Libby got in. As soon as Randy was in, Max drove away from the house, turning north when he reached Hwy. 1.

Kate saw Max staring in the rear view mirror and asked, "What do you see?"

"Two news trucks just pulled onto the road going to the farm house."

Libby turned her head and looked at Kate. Kate forced a smile, then put her arm around Libby's shoulder again and gave her a little hug.

Randy sat across from the girls and watched Kate consoling Libby. When Kate looked over at him, he said softly, "Kate, I'm sorry."

Kate gave him a half smile and said, "I know, Randy."

They all sat in silence as Max drove.

~ ~ ~

Bodega Bay, California

Max turned the TV on to watch the afternoon news. Sheriff Sanchez had set up a news conference that was being broadcast live. Libby and Kate sat on the sofa and Randy and Max took the chairs across from them. They watched as Sheriff Sanchez walked in, then Dennis, followed by Jeffery, with his left arm in a sling.

Sheriff Sanchez walked up to the podium and spoke first. "I want to start by saying that I am very proud of the courage that these men showed us today by risking their lives so that a witness could testify. I believe this community is safer because of the actions of these people who are willing to take a stand against crime in this country, and I want to thank them for being a part of this community. I'll turn it over to Jeffery and Dennis now."

A reporter asked, "Jeffery, what's it like to be a hero?"

"I had to." Jeffery paused for a second. "No one should rejoice in the taking of human life. Today I had to kill two men to stop them from killing a witness and everyone else around her. I am glad that I stopped them. But I regret that I had to kill them to do that."

Dennis reached over to Jeffery and gave him a pat on the back.

Another reporter asked, "Dennis, do you think Jeffery's a hero?"

"Yes, he saved us today. All I did was get the witness behind a flower pot and stay with her."

Jeffery looked at Dennis, then said, "Most of the gunfire was aimed at Dennis, the witness, and Brad, who is still in the hospital. The return fire that Dennis gave, made both men stop in the parking lot, and gave me the chance to hit them with the SUV."

"Jeffery, you had a gun," said a third reporter, "why didn't you use that instead of hitting them with the SUV?"

"There was a family in the parking lot, behind the two men. They would have been in my line of fire. I couldn't chance hitting them."

Dennis looked at Jeffery and said, "You did good."

The same reporter asked, "Jeffery, what are you going to do now."

"Well, I have a new girlfriend, I would love to just spend some time with her."

"What's her name?" asked the woman.

Jeffery paused as he and Dennis looked at each other, then Dennis said, "OK, folks, I think that's enough. It's been a long day for all of us." Dennis looked at the Sheriff and nodded his head.

Sheriff Sanchez came back to the podium and said, "I want to thank everyone for coming today."

A reporter then started a commentary as they replayed the video taken outside the courthouse. As the video ended the reporter said, "In this reporter's opinion, Jeffery Hodges is a hero, and now the world knows his name, because this video just went viral on the internet."

Libby held her hand over her mouth and started crying. "We just met and I almost lost him."

Max and Randy glanced uncomfortably at each other as Libby sobbed on Kate's shoulder.

Chapter 12
Las Vegas, Nevada

"Claudette, the computers just found something," said Antoine.

"What have you got?"

"Do you remember we could not find anything on Kate Dodson's uncle, David Dodson?"

"Yeah, did you find something?"

"Have you watched the news today?"

"No. Why?"

"Well there's a sheriff that uses a motorcycle club for security work. Members of that motorcycle club were involved in a shootout in the parking lot behind a courthouse this morning. According to the news article that the computers found, the president of that club is David Dodson. There is no property listed for David Dodson, but there is property listed for the motorcycle club. That is why we were not able to find him. Now, I think a bikers' clubhouse would be a great place to hide out."

Claudette thought for a few seconds, then said, "Yes, I think you might be right. Get me everything you have on that motorcycle club and I will send it to Angelo."

~ ~ ~

Las Vegas, Nevada

BAM! Candy jumped when Joe slammed his hand against the desk top.

"Joe, you have to calm down," said Candy, "Libby is a big girl and can take care of herself. With what happened they probably had to go on the run again. If something had happened to her, it would be on the news."

"Yes, I know, I would just like to hear something. I sent her three emails and haven't heard anything back."

Candy left the office, then came back with a cold beer. She put it on the desk in front of him and said, "You haven't been outside in several days. Take a break, go outside and drink that, I'll stay here and watch the security system and check the emails." Joe gave her a disapproving scowl and started to say something, but Candy cut him off and said, "Get your ass outside or I'll push you out the door myself." Candy and Joe locked eyes for a moment. "Now!" Candy commanded.

Joe put the beer in his lap, rolled his wheelchair back from the desk, and said, "YES, Dear!" Then he turned and headed for the back door.

"That's better," said Candy, grinning, as she watched him leave.

~ ~ ~

Bodega Bay, California

David put down his phone. "Dennis, come into the office, I need to talk to you."

Dennis came in and sat down. "What's going on, David?"

"The sheriff just called and said that a detective from the Las Vegas Police Department just called him and asked if he had seen Kate, Libby, or Randy. He was watching the news and heard my name, and realized that I was Kate's uncle."

"Shit, what a day," said Dennis. "If the Vegas Police think Kate might be here, then the people that are looking for her will think the same thing."

"Yeah, that's right. Kate is my family and I will do everything I can to protect her. Even go to jail for harboring criminals. The thing is, I can't ask anyone else to do that."

"David, Kate was like a daughter to Malana and me, too; one that we couldn't have. You know that Malana is the one that got her through her teenage years and taught her how to be a confident woman."

David smiled. "I know, I remember. Kate loved staying with Malana when you and I would go off to the bike rallies."

"David, I'm not going to turn my back on Kate now. She needs us both. Besides Malana would come back from the grave and haunt me if I didn't help Kate."

"Thank you," said David. "Tonight, after the news people leave, we need to lock the clubhouse up and move to the safe room under the lab."

"Yes, it's better fortified, easier to defend, and well stocked. Should you call Max and let him know what's going on?"

"I don't think I can chance calling him. Someone in one of those news vans might have equipment to listen in on our cell phones. If Max doesn't hear from us, I can only trust that he will follow procedure."

"OK," said Dennis, "I'll start getting everything ready."

~ ~ ~

RV Park, Crescent City, California

Max got up from his seat at the table beside Kate. He turned his cell phone on as he sat down in the driver's seat.

Libby and Randy were on the other side of the table with their backs to the front of the RV. When they noticed Kate's expression change, Randy asked, "Is something wrong?" as he looked over his shoulder at Max.

"I don't know," answered Kate.

After five minutes Max turned his phone off and took the battery out. He turned the seat around to face everyone. "I need to talk to all of you," he said. "I have not had any communications with the farmhouse. In a situation like this I am not allowed to call them. We have a procedure. I turn my phone on at 0800 hours for five minutes, then turn it back off, take the battery out, and immediately leave the area. Since I have not heard from them that means that we are totally on our own. If you have not taken the battery out of your phone, please do it now. We have food, water, and $20,000 cash in a safe. So we can hide out on the road for a long time. I'm sorry about this, but the only way I can keep you safe is to keep moving around. Do you have any questions?"

Everyone shook their heads.

"Now I need you to get the inside ready for travel while I go outside and take care of the tanks. OK?"

Kate said, "OK, Max."

"Max, is there anything I can do to help you?" asked Randy. "Right now I feel totally useless."

"Sure, let me look to be sure no one is around, then you can come outside and empty the tanks with me."

"You know, after being inside for weeks, that sounds like fun."

Kate and Libby started laughing.

When the men were outside, Kate asked, "Libby, how are you

holding up?"

"I don't know anymore, Kate, with all the crap that we have been through these past weeks. Then I meet someone that I really like and he gets shot, and now I can't see him because we're on the run again. I'm starting to just feel numb."

"You really like Jeffery, don't you?"

"Yes, I do. I haven't been with a lot of guys because I have never felt that comfortable around most of them. I know that Jeffery and I just met, and it sounds funny, but with Jeffery, I feel like I can just be myself. I feel like I can trust him. And Kate, I'm scared that I'm about to lose him, and I don't know what to do."

"I can tell that he feels the same way when I see you together."

They started getting everything secured for travel, and Kate said, "I once felt like I had lost everything. It was when my mother died and I had to go live with my Uncle David. Dennis's wife, Malana, could see how depressed I was, and she took me under her wing. She had a dog named Buttons and one day she took Buttons and me to a nursing home. She took Buttons around to all the rooms to visit. Then we came to a room where the patient was a girl about my age. She was in a wheelchair, every part of her body was twisted, and she had very little control of her arms and legs. Buttons walked straight to the girl and put her front legs in the girl's lap Then she laid her head in the girl's lap and waited. That girl lifted her arm and rubbed Button's head, and she smiled. Neither one made a sound, but they were communicating. Anyway, when we left there, we went to a park for a picnic, and Malana told me that she had been good friends with the girl's parents, and the girl, Phyllis, had spent time in her home and played with Buttons. Then there was the car accident, the parents were killed, and Phyllis suffered brain damage. Life is not fair to anyone, Malana told me, everyone eventually dies. So when life kicks us down, all we can do is pick ourselves up, and do the best we can with what we have. Later that day we stopped at a store and she bought two stuffed dogs that looked like Buttons. We went back to see Phyllis, and Malana gave one of the dogs to her and one to me."

Kate paused and took a deep breath. "About a year later Phyllis died. When she was buried they put the stuffed dog beside her in the casket."

"Do you still have your dog?"

"Yes," said Kate, as she wiped a tear from her face. "I have never told anyone else that story. But the point I'm trying to make is that seeing that girl made me appreciate my life, and taught me that we have to be strong, for ourselves, and for the people we love. I'm not going to stand here and say that everything is going to be OK. I don't know that. But what I am saying is that we can work through whatever life gives us and we should live every day we have to the fullest."

Kate gave Libby a hug and then they both reached for tissues to wipe their eyes and Kate said, "Let's get this finished. OK?"

"OK."

~ ~ ~

Bodega Bay, California

David sat on the side of his cot and looked at Dennis, who was watching the security monitors. "See anything?" he asked.

"Yeah, another news van. It looks like they finished doing a report in front of the house and are leaving now," said Dennis.

"I'll be glad when they stop," said David.

"Me, too."

David looked over at Jeffery, sleeping on one of the other cots, and said, "That pain pill he took last night really put him out."

"You want me to get him up."

"No, I don't think there's much we can do but wait."

"Yeah. And I don't like it."

David poured a cup of coffee and said, "Get some sleep, I'll watch things." Then he sat down in front of the monitors and said to himself, "0815 hours, it's going to be a long day."

~ ~ ~

Jeffery rolled over onto his injured arm, then quickly rolled back over and said, "Damn! That hurt!"

David and Dennis looked up from their supper.

"We were starting to get worried about you," said Dennis.

Jeffery looked at them eating and said, "Yeah, I can see that it's affecting your appetite. Why don't you bring me some of that."

"Why don't you get your little ass off that cot, bring it over here and get it yourself."

"Is that any way to talk to a wounded hero?" said Jeffery.

Dennis reached into a box and pulled out a can of Spam, then threw it at the wall above Jeffery. It bounced off and landed on his lap.

"Hey, watch it!" yelled Jeffery. "I don't want my dick hurt too. Hell, I just started having sex again."

David and Dennis started laughing, then Dennis said, "That boy is going to be hell to live with now."

David saw some movement on the security monitor. He turned his head for a better look and said, "Two SUVs just stopped on the street at the driveway. Boys, I think we may have trouble."

~ ~ ~

Hospital, Santa Rosa, California

Visiting hours were over at St. Peter's Memorial Hospital-Santa Rosa and the nurses were getting their patients ready for the night. It looked like it would be a quiet night. Then three Hispanic men stepped off the elevator on the second floor.

One of the men, the leader, a well-built, middle-aged man turned to the two young men following him and said, "One of you stay here. When you see me coming back press the elevator button and hold it."

One of the young men stayed behind, leaning against the wall about 15 feet from the elevator door, watching the other two men walking to the nurses' desk.

The leader asked the nurses' assistant, "What room is Brad Jarell in?"

She looked up and said, "I'm sorry, visiting hours are over."

The two men looked at each other, then the leader pulled out his pistol and pointed it at the assistant.

She raised her hands into the air and said in a loud voice, "Room 214." Then with one hand pointed down the hall.

The head nurse was sitting at a desk behind a partition. When she heard the assistant say the room number, she stood up and saw the leader pointing his gun at the assistant. She heard him order the second man to get a wheelchair, then get Brad.

She quickly sat down, dialed the hospital information desk, and speaking softly said, "Two men, with a gun, at the east wing second floor nurses' station, tell Bill to come quickly."

The second man took a wheelchair and ran to room 214. As he entered the room he said, "Mr. Jarell, I'm here to discharge you from the hospital."

"I haven't signed any discharge papers," said Brad. "I think you have the wrong......"

He stopped talking when the man pulled out a gun and pointed it at his head and said, "Get in the chair, now."

After Brad sat in the chair, the young man said, "Don't do anything stupid, old man." Then he hit Brad on the back of his head with the butt of the pistol. He pushed Brad out of the room, and down the hall. As he passed the nurses' station he yelled, "I have him!" to the man still pointing a gun at the nurses' assistant.

Bill Braden, a retired police officer from the San Francisco Police Department, was the only security working tonight. He was talking to the volunteer worker at the information desk in the west wing lobby when the call came in. Bill said to the volunteer, "Call 911, and tell them what you told me. I'm headed over there."

Deputy Tom Gaillard was in the emergency room trying to get a statement from a young woman who had just arrived from an accident on Hwy. 101.

"1421, are you at the hospital?" asked the police dispatcher over the portable radio.

Tom reached up to his shoulder and pressed the PTT button on the speaker mike that was attached to his portable radio and said, "Roger that."

"We just got a call that two armed men are at the second floor nurses' station east wing. Can you handle that?"

"Yes, request backup."

"OK, 1421."

Tom left his clipboard at the emergency room nurses' station, then ran out the emergency room door to his police car and took out the shotgun. He saw Bill running to the west entrance of the center wing. He caught up to Bill as he was pulling out his keys to unlock the door.

Bill turned around and looked at Tom then said, "You ready?"

"Let's do this," said Tom.

Bill gave Tom a quick nod and opened the door to let him go in first.

The elevator door was standing open as they got to the east wing. They ran in and pushed the second floor button. As the doors closed Bill said, "You got here fast."

"I was in the emergency room taking a statement."

"Glad you're here."

Tom, a young man of 24, looked around at the mirrored surface of the elevator walls. He could see the nervousness in his own face. He started going over his training, a mental checklist. Then he remembered what his training officer told him was the most important thing to do in a stressful situation, to breathe. He looked down at the shotgun, turned on the laser sighting system, then pulled back and forth on the forend, that chambered one of the 12 gage double-aught buckshot shells. The elevator stopped and the door opened.

Tom saw a chrome garbage container standing on the far side of the hall, across from the elevator door. He could make out the reflection of a figure walking toward the elevator with his arms sticking out like he was holding a gun.

Bill was stepping out of the elevator when Tom grabbed his arm and said, "Stop."

Tom motioned for Bill to get behind him then yelled, "POLICE! Put the gun down!"

He pointed the shotgun at the garbage container, aiming the laser beam at the reflection of the man who was still walking toward the elevator. The young Hispanic man saw the narrow beam of reflected light move across his hand, then his arm, before landing on his chest. The man stopped, then turned his head and scanned the hallway.

Tom yelled again, "Put the gun down!"

The man nervously started pointing the gun at different locations in the hallway, trying to see where the laser beam was coming from.

Tom noticed that the man had stopped coming toward them, and he said to himself, "NOW." Tom walked out of the elevator, with the gun raised and pointed the 20 inch barrel at the young man's head.

The man turned his head and looked at Tom, then jerked his gun around, just as Tom pulled the trigger. The young man's head exploded, then his body fell back sliding down the wall, landing on the floor.

The loud blast reverberated through the hallway, causing Brad to jump in the wheelchair. As he became conscious, he could see one man in front of him while another man was pushing him. The hallway suddenly became dead quiet to Tom as the blast momentarily caused him to become deaf. Tom pulled back and forth on the forend, ejecting the spent shell and chambering a new one. He looked at the leader, standing fifteen feet away, in front of Brad. The man was focused on Tom, yelling something at him that he was unable to hear. Tom was starting to regain his hearing as he saw the leader aiming his gun at him. Tom quickly stepped further into the hallway as a bullet struck the edge of the elevator door.

Bill stood there wondering, can I still do this. He had not fired his gun since he retired, 7 years ago. He swallowed hard and stepped into the hallway, just as Tom fired the shotgun again. Bill saw the leader fall back landing on Brad, then sliding to the floor.

When the leader fell, the wheelchair rolled back and bumped the man pushing it, causing him to miss his shot at Tom. Then he crouched behind Brad, took aim, and pulled the trigger.

Bill decided he didn't have a clear shot, Brad was between him and the shooter. But then Brad, drugged on pain pills, and still dazed from the blow to his head, reached over and grabbed the man's arm. Bill saw the man hit Brad several times from behind before he got free of Brad's grip.

The angry, frustrated young man stood up, stepped back, pointed his gun at the back of Brad's head and pulled the trigger. As Brad slowly slumped down in the wheelchair, the man locked his eyes onto the pistol in Bill's hand.

Bill took careful aim and pulled the trigger three times, not missing a single shot, then he watched the man fall. He kept his gun pointed at him as he ran up and kicked the dead man's gun away. He looked at Brad, he was dead. He checked the other man lying in front of Brad, dead. Then he turned back toward the elevators and he saw Tom lying in a pool of blood from a neck wound.

As Bill ran to Tom's side, he yelled, "I NEED HELP, I NEED HELP, GET A DOCTOR NOW!"

The head nurse could see Bill kneeling over Tom when she stood up from behind the counter. "Call the emergency room!" she ordered the assistant. "Tell them to send a code team, STAT! Then call 911!"

She rushed down the hallway to Bill's side calling as she did, "I NEED HELP DOWN HERE." Frightened nurses, still shaking, rushed to her aid.

One young nurse, unaware of the sounds of crash carts and footsteps running down the hall, sat curled up in a corner of a patient's room, frozen, paralyzed from fear, eyes affixed on the holes in the wall where moments earlier stray bullets had passed just inches from her head.

~ ~ ~

Bodega Bay, California

David looked at Jeffery. "Are you able to work the security system with one arm?" he asked.

Jeffery took a seat in front of the monitors, tapped on two of the keys on the keyboard, grabbed the joy stick and turned one of the adjustable cameras to the two cars that had stopped at the driveway. He pressed a key on the controller and zoomed in for a closer look.

"I got this," Jeffery said, "but can someone get me a soda?"

Dennis took a can out of the small refrigerator, opened it, and placed it on the table. "Here you go, Stud."

Jeffery cracked a big smile, looked up at Dennis and gave him a quick nod. "Thanks, man," he said and quickly looked back at the monitors.

They watched six men get out of the SUVs and start walking to the club house.

"They don't look like police," said Dennis.

"Yeah, they're not police," said David. "Jeffery, don't do anything but monitor and record their movements. I don't want to confront them unless they come here to the lab."

Jeffery said, "OK," then turned his head to one of the other monitors and said, "I thought I saw some movement outside the lab. I'm going to keep recording the clubhouse, but I want to look around outside the lab." He pulled up each of the cameras that surrounded the lab and stopped when he saw a man squatting next to the building, watching the other men enter the clubhouse. "Who is that?"

"Can you zoom in on him?" asked David.

"No, not with this camera."

They watched the man pull something out of his pocket and put it to his ear.

"Did he just call someone?" asked Jeffery.

"That's what it looked like," said David.

"I bet he's police," said Dennis, "and he just called for backup."

The man stood up and started moving toward the house.

David said, "That dumbass is going to get himself and whoever he called killed."

"What do you want to do?" asked Dennis.

"I can't let him get hurt," said David. "Let's stop this. Jeffery, it's time to try out your homemade stun grenades. Get ready to drop them. Dennis, get the mace guns, tie wraps, and the shotguns. I'll get the utility vehicle ready."

Jeffery watched the monitors as David and Dennis left the lab and drove down the driveway.

Hector Rodriguez stopped and turned, gun in hand, when he heard the utility vehicle coming toward him.

The vehicle stopped and David looked at Hector and said, "This is my place. Who are you?"

"Police," Hector said, and showed them his ID.

"Then you better hop on or you'll miss all the fun," said David.

Hector just stood there looking at them.

"If you don't get on I'm just going to leave your ass here."

Hector hopped into the backseat and David drove toward the clubhouse. They stopped at the side of the house, then got out and leaned their backs against the house.

David handed Hector his shotgun and asked, "Can you handle this?"

"Yes," he said, as he holstered his pistol and took the shotgun.

"Dennis, take point and spray anyone that's still awake," said David. "I'll tie them up." He looked at Hector and said, "You watch our back."

"You're going in there with just mace guns and a couple of shotguns?" asked Hector.

David just smiled, then grabbed his radio and said, "Jeffery, what's their location?"

"One in each bedroom, two in the office, I don't see the other one."

"Drop all of the grenades now."

"Cover your ears," David told Hector, as he and Dennis covered theirs.

Jeffery pressed the computer key that opened the small trap doors in the ceiling of several rooms, releasing all the stun grenades simultaneously. Their half second fuses allowed them to fall halfway to the floor before exploding in midair.

Hector covered his ears just in time to muffle the sounds of the multiple explosions, but he saw the flashes of light, and saw the broken glass coming from the windows.

"Are you coming?" David shouted at Hector as he ran to the front door.

As David got to the front door, the deafening sounds from the smoke detectors echoed through the house. Dennis was already heading into the office, moving through the thin cloud of smoke caused by the spent explosive used in the stun grenades. "Two in the office," Dennis yelled, trying to be heard over the smoke detectors. He sprayed each man with mace and removed their guns, then continued to the first bedroom. "One, first bedroom." Each man moved quickly, trying to concentrate on what they were doing, but the noise, the yelling, the strong odor from the smoke that made their eyes sting and water, gave David and Dennis momentary flashbacks to their time in Vietnam.

David tied up the two men in the office, then ran out and into the first bedroom.

Hector ran in with the gun raised, looking into each of the rooms. He opened the door of the hall bathroom and saw a young man standing with one hand in the air and the other trying to hold up his pants. "I found the last guy," he yelled.

David and Dennis finished tying the other men up and walked back to the bathroom where Hector was pointing the gun at the very frightened young Hispanic man. David stood next to Hector and looked into the bathroom. "Turn and face the wall, put your hands on the wall," he ordered.

The young man looked at David and begged, "Please don't shoot me!"

Dennis looked over David's shoulder as the man let go of his pants and let them fall to his feet. He turned to the wall and put both hands up.

David looked at the toilet behind the man and said, "Good job officer, I think you literally scared the shit out of him."

David tied the young man's hands behind him. "You sick, is that why you're in here?"

The young man bowed his head. "Stomach cramps, I had to go."

David looked at the young man's face; he was just a scared kid, about 14. "Is this your first job?"

The kid shut his eyes and his mouth and turned his head away from David. Hector and Dennis followed as David led the kid, pants still around his ankles, into the living room.

A sheriff's deputy was standing at the front door with his gun pointed. He watched as they entered the room. "What the hell is going on here?"

Hector walked out from behind David and answered, "Officer, everything is under control, I'm Detective Hector Rodriguez of the Las Vegas Police Department. I'm going to take out my ID and show you. OK?"

"What are you doing here and what the hell happened?"

"I came here to talk to David Dodson about his niece, Kate Dodson, and her friends. When I got here I saw these men breaking into the clubhouse, that's when I called 911."

"Wow! What a night, the hospital, now this."

"What happened at the hospital?" asked David.

"I don't know the details. I think the sheriff put a news blackout on it. All I know is two 911 calls came in, the last one reporting shots fired with multiple victims."

David and Dennis looked at each other, then David said, "I need to call the sheriff." He reached for his phone. "Damn," he said. "I left my phone in the safe room."

Hector handed him his phone. "Use mine."

David dialed the number. "Sheriff, this is David Dodson, is Brad OK?"

"No, I'm so sorry David, they killed him."

"What happened?"

"About a half hour ago, three men tried to take Brad out of the hospital. A security guard and a deputy stopped them. The three men are dead, Brad is dead, and my deputy is dead."

"Oh, God," said David. "Sheriff, six men broke into the clubhouse a few minutes ago. We captured them with the help of a Las Vegas detective."

"You captured them alive," the sheriff said, "with a Vegas detective?" He paused. "David, I have a dead deputy, you have a dead friend. Is this retaliation for the shooting at the courthouse, or is there something else going on?"

David paused and looked at the half naked kid, then said, "Sheriff, I'm going to talk to these men and find out."

"Let me talk to my deputy."

David handed the phone to the deputy. "The sheriff wants a word."

"Yes. Yes, sir. I understand. I'll give him any help I can."

The deputy handed the phone back to Hector and said, "Detective, will you please follow me outside. I need to ask you some questions for my report." He turned to David and said, "We'll be outside. If you need any help, let me know."

"Thank you, Deputy," said David.

"What the hell is going on here?" yelled Hector.

David turned and got in Hector's face, "A sheriff's deputy and my friend, Brad Jarell, were killed tonight by friends of these men. I'm going to talk to them, and find out who is responsible. You need to go outside RIGHT NOW!"

The deputy grabbed Hector's arm. "Sir, please come outside."

Hector unwillingly followed the deputy out. "I don't believe this," he said.

David grabbed his radio and said, "Jeffery, record video and audio in the living room."

"Roger that."

Dennis put his arm around the kid's neck to hold him up straight. He had a large size and weight advantage over the kid, but he still had trouble holding him as fear overtook the young man.

David walked over to the half naked kid and took his lock blade knife out of its holster and opened the knife in front of the kid's terrified face. He looked straight into the kid's eyes, grabbed him by the balls and squeezed.

David loosened his grip for a few seconds, waiting for the kid to stop screaming. Then he took the knife and placed it under the kid's sack. "I'm going to ask you some questions. Understand?"

"Y y y y you can't d d do this!" the kid stuttered, his voice an octave higher. "I, it, it's against the law!"

"Do I look like I care about the law? I'm a biker. Your friends killed a biker, and a good friend of mine."

Hector and the deputy turned to look at the now ominous looking farmhouse as the kid's hair-raising screams filled the night air. Hector said, "This is not right." He started to walk toward the house.

The deputy stepped in front of him. "I'm the one that trained the deputy that died tonight. He was a good officer. I got to know him very well. My wife goes to the same church as his parents. If these men have information about who killed him, then I want to know it and I will not let anyone get in the way of getting that information. Do you understand, sir?"

Hector looked at the house as the kid let out another scream. He looked back at the deputy, then said, "Yeah, I understand."

The kid was crying and his legs were getting rubbery giving Dennis more weight to hold up as David yelled again, "Who do you work for?"

"Cortez," he stuttered softly.

"Say it again. Louder!" ordered David.

The kid shouted, "Cortez, Hernando Cortez."

One of the men who was tied up in the office yelled, "Shut up you fool! You will get us all killed!"

David walked into his master bedroom and went straight to the bathroom closet. He reached into the laundry hamper and found two pair of the smelliest used boot socks he could find. He walked quickly to the office, where only one of the two men continued yelling. The men looked up at him as he tied the toe ends of a pair of socks together.

The quiet man asked, "What are you going to do?"

David looked at the man, then tied the other pair the same way. David then leaned down putting one knee into the back of the one that was yelling all the time. He put all his weight on that knee until the man started screaming in pain. David quickly put the knotted end of one pair of socks in the man's mouth and tied the other ends together behind his head. He then grabbed a heavy desk lamp from the desk and hit the man twice on the head with the lamp's base. David looked at the other man, the quiet one, as the man tucked his head low, like he was trying to hide and not make eye contact. David threw the other pair of socks next to the man's face.

The man softly said, "Please, I won't say anything."

David got up, walked to the window, pulled out his pistol, and pointed it at the ground. He pulled the trigger twice.

Hector and the deputy looked at each other.

The house became as quiet as a grave yard as David walked back to the living room where Dennis was still holding the kid. "They won't interrupt anyone ever again," said David. "Now, I want to know why you're here?"

The kid's face had gone white, and his legs were buckling. "To find Kate Dodson, Libby Harrison, and Randy Hunter and to find the information they got from the bank."

Dennis was having trouble holding the kid up, so David got a chair and put it in the middle of the room. "Let him sit down."

"Now," said David, "why did you try to take my man from the hospital?"

"To use him for leverage to get the stolen bank files back."

Dennis and David looked at each other as David asked, "Who told you where we were?"

"Cortez has people in the Vegas Police Department and he has his own computer people."

Outside, Hector looked at the deputy and said, "It's very quiet in there, should we check on them?"

"I will," said the deputy. "You wait."

David saw the deputy look in the door and motioned him to enter. "Call the detective in too," he said.

When the deputy and detective were in the room, David resumed his questioning, "You told me that Cortez has people in the Vegas Police Department. Who?"

"I don't know their names, I did hear them call one of them 'Captain'."

David looked at the detective then back at the kid and asked, "What else do you know about him?"

"He has something to do with the Detective Bureau."

Hector, stunned, dropped his head and ran his hand through his hair.

"Who else does he have on his payroll."

"DEA, Border Patrol, a group of computer people, and some bankers in Vegas."

~ ~ ~

David and Hector continued questioning the kid for another hour, until Sheriff Miguel Sanchez stepped inside the house and asked, "What have you learned?"

"A lot," David answered. "Now that I know who we're dealing with, I need time to create a plan." He paused a moment then said in a lower voice, "Sheriff, you know I have to take this bastard out."

"If you're going after their boss," said Sheriff Sanchez, "then just tell me what I can do to help you."

"I need you to tell the news media that all six men were killed tonight and that my niece, Kate, and her friends, Libby Harrison, and Randy Hunter were also killed. That should get Cortez to stop looking for them."

"OK. What do you want me to do with these men?"

"I need you to hide them until this is over. I can't let Cortez find out that Kate and her friends are alive. Do you think you can do that?"

"I think it would be better if you keep them here. If I have them transported, too many people will be involved and someone may see them."

"I don't have the manpower to guard them," said David.

"I know a lot of retired deputies, I think I can find the manpower. I just can't pay them anything without people asking a lot of questions."

"Sheriff, you find me the men who can keep quiet about who they're guarding, and I'll pay them in cash."

"OK, that problem solved. What next?"

"What are you talking about?" demanded Hector. "Starting a war against a drug lord, in another country? We need to turn these men over to the Feds. Let Homeland Security, DEA and the State Department deal with this."

David got right in Hector's face again, "The FEDS," he said, his voice dripping distrust and resentment. "My brother was an Army Ranger. He served in the 1989 Panama War, Operation Just Cause. His team was sent on a mission that went very bad. The FEDS claim that he and a buddy killed their own team and stole a large shipment of drugs. The FEDS framed them and put out warrants for their arrest, and they have been running ever since. My brother can't prove that they were set up, so they can't come home." David paused, took a breath, calmed himself down, and took a step back. "I don't want the FEDS to know anything about this because it'll get fucked up and get my brother's only daughter killed. And if you don't like what I'm going to do, then get out now." David stepped back and took a moment to study Hector, then he stepped into Hector's space again and said in a low, slow, hostile tone, "And you better not say a damn word to anyone about this, because if something happens to Kate, I will hunt your ass down."

Hector waited for a moment before saying, "I'm sorry about your brother. But do you really think you can get to Cortez?"

"I may not be able to kill him, but if I can't I will make him feel like I kicked him in the nuts." David paused, then asked, "Are you in?"

"David, you're asking the sheriff and me to put our jobs on the line so you can go after a drug lord."

"Detective, you make decisions every day that puts your job on the line."

"I know this Cortez is a drug lord, but you're still talking about murdering him," Hector said.

"This country kills leaders of terror organizations all the time. Just look around and see what he has done tonight. I think he is just another terrorist that needs to be put down. Besides no police department will be involved in what I do because none of you will know anything about it. Your hands will be clean. You and the sheriff will have full deniability."

"What are you going to do with these men when this is over, kill them?"

"I will hand them back over to the sheriff. He can tell everyone that he hid them to protect them after he interrogated them."

David thought for a second then said, "You know if we don't take out Cortez, he will regroup and come after us again, more innocent people will be killed. If I can make Cortez think that his men killed Kate and her friends, then that should give us time. What I'm asking for is time to make a plan to take him out. Besides, while you're waiting on me, you can investigate your police department and find the dirty cops. Who knows, maybe you and the sheriff can lock up the entire drug ring."

Hector stared at David, then cracked a grin and said, "OK, I'm in. But I still need to talk to Kate and her friends when this is over."

The sheriff said, "David, we need the medical examiner in on this. I'll talk to him and explain what we are doing. He probably will have no trouble with it, but I know he likes to drink, so a few bottles of your best stuff might help persuade him."

"Tell him, as soon as I run my next batch, I'll get it to him."

"I don't think I want to know what you're talking about," said Hector.

"The news media will be here soon," said Sheriff Sanchez. "Do you have a place to hide prisoners?"

"Yes," said David, "I can hide them in the basement of my maintenance building. Can you have your men block the road coming to the clubhouse until I get them moved?" He paused for a moment. "And can you tell the media that you're investigating this as retaliation for what happened yesterday? That might get Cortez to put his guard down."

"Sure," he said as he turned to give his deputy orders.

When Sheriff Sanchez turned back, he saw David surveying the damage to his clubhouse with a lost look in his eyes as the reality of the night's events slowly crept in. "David," he said, "I'm sorry about Brad. I know he was a good man."

"Thank you, I'm sorry about your deputy, too."

Suddenly the sheriff turned to Hector and asked, "Why did you come here? Did your department send you?"

"No, I took some personal leave to come and see Mr. Dodson myself. I have trouble trusting what people say on the phone, and I can always get more from a face-to-face conversation."

The sheriff said, "How did that work out for you this time?"

"I did get a lot more than I bargained for," Hector said. Then he looked at David and said, "Mr. Dodson, what can I do to help?"

"You can go back to Vegas and tell everyone that you saw the bodies. That should get everyone to stop looking for Kate and her friends." David paused. "There is something else you can do. Do you know a Joe Morgan?"

"Yes, Libby Harrison worked for him."

"Tell him that Kate, Libby, and Randy are OK. But make sure he knows not to tell anyone and that I will need his help, too."

~ ~ ~

RV Park, Crescent City, California

Libby gently closed the door behind her as she entered the front of the RV. Max woke up, then looked at his watch. 6:14 AM.

"Sorry," said Libby, "I thought you might be up already."

"That's OK," said Max. "I need to get up anyway. I guess you're having trouble sleeping?"

"Yeah, I thought I would go ahead and get up and get some coffee and I wanted to listen to the TV and see if there was any more news about what happened yesterday."

Libby started the coffee, then turned around to see Max pull his pants up and secure them.

She saw a variety of tattoos on his back and shoulders. "It must have hurt a lot to get that much ink."

He turned around as he pulled his tee-shirt over his head. "Yeah, it did."

She sat down at the table. "Max, I want to say thank you for looking out for us. I don't know what we would do if you guys weren't helping."

"I'm glad that we can help," he said. He sat down and looked across the table at Libby. "I know it's been hard on all of you, and I know David and Dennis will come up with something that will get all of you out of this. But it may take some time."

"I hope so, right now I wish we could be back at the farmhouse."

Max smiled. "I have never seen Jeffery take as big an interest in anyone as he has with you. Believe me, I want to get you back there, too."

She smiled back at him and said, "Thanks for saying that."

Max picked up the remote and turned on the TV. "Let's see if there's anything on the news. Are you ready for that coffee?"

"Yeah, thanks."

He stood up to get two cups when a reporter on the TV said, "We have unconfirmed reports coming out of Sonoma County California that a group of men attacked a patient at a Santa Rosa Hospital, and another group of men attacked a motorcycle clubhouse in Bodega Bay. Some are speculating that these attacks were retaliation for the deaths of two men at the county courthouse the day before. The sheriff has scheduled a news conference at 8:00 AM that we will air live. Now here is the weather in your area."

Libby stood up and looked at Max.

He looked back at her and said, "Libby, I don't know what to think. Get Kate and Randy up."

She went back to the bedroom. "Something's happened," she said. "You two need to get up."

Kate came through the door first. "What's happened?" she asked.

"We don't know the details yet," said Max. "Some men tried to attack a patient at a Santa Rosa hospital and another group of men attacked the clubhouse."

Randy walked into the room. "Someone attacked the clubhouse?"

"Yes," said Libby.

"Did they say if anyone was hurt?" asked Kate.

"They didn't give any details," said Max. "They said there would be a news conference at eight."

Libby sat back down at the table, became very quiet, and stared at the steam coming from the coffee cup in front of her. A single tear rolled down her cheek. Randy sat down beside her and put his arm around her.

Libby softly asked, "Randy, why did we do this?"

"We thought that we could do some good."

Kate reached out and softly grabbed Max's hand and said in a low voice, "Would you turn your phone on, just in case they're trying to get word to us."

"I can't, Kate, it may be more dangerous now than before."

~ ~ ~

Kate and Max quickly finished cleaning up after breakfast. Just as the news conference started, Max turned his phone on.

Sheriff Sanchez started by saying, "Last night at 8:00 pm, our community suffered two deadly attacks. The first was at St. Peter's Memorial Hospital, resulting in the death of Deputy Tom Gaillard and a patient named Brad Jarell. All three of the attackers were also killed. If you remember, Brad Jarell was one of the men who was shot protecting a witness during the attack at the courthouse. Deputy Tom Gillard gave his life trying to protect Brad Jarell. The second attack happened at the same time when six men attacked a motorcycle club in Bodega Bay. Brad Jarell was a member of that club. Three guests of the club were killed, Kate Dodson, and two of her friends. We cannot give out their names until we notify the next of kin. The six attackers were also killed. We believe that these attacks were retaliation for the death of the two men that tried to kill the witness at the courthouse. This is a sad day for our community, but I want to reassure the people of Sonoma County that this department will not rest until the bastards that are responsible are brought to justice. Thank You."

Libby and Randy looked at each other, not saying a word.

"Max," said Kate, "what do you think is going on?"

Everyone jumped when Max's phone announced that it had just received a text message.

A tear rolled down Libby's face as Max read the message out loud, "Brad was killed at the hospital. Everyone OK at the clubhouse. Do not come back." He looked up at Kate and said, "This is from David."

Max stood up and started pacing the floor, his rage was building and suddenly he kicked one of the RVs kitchen cabinet doors and tore it off its hinges. Everyone was quiet, not knowing what to say, what to do. Randy noticed Libby's tears, and put his arms around her. Kate watched them until she could no longer see through her own tears. Max opened the door of the RV, and quickly walked outside and sat on top of a nearby picnic table, staring at some young kids chasing ducks at a nearby pond. Kate watched him for a few minutes through the door, then she wiped the tears from her face, walked outside, and sat on top of the table beside him. They didn't speak; they just stared at the kids playing by the pond, tears slowly running down both their faces.

Chapter 13
Las Vegas, Nevada

Antoine knocked on the open door of Claudette's office.

She noticed his expression and the papers he was holding, and asked, "What's wrong?"

He handed her the printouts and said, "Angelo's men found the people that we were looking for and killed them last night. Claudette, they also killed a cop."

She read the news article. "I'm sure it was Cortez who gave the order."

He stared at her for a second and said, "I'm sure he did." He paused, then said, "When I signed on for this, I thought it would be exciting putting together a computer network system for a drug cartel. I didn't realize that part of my job would be to search for people that would be murdered."

"Antoine, it would not be good to let anyone else know how you feel. Remember those people stole files from the bank."

He gave her a hard look and said, "Yeah, they stole computer files. Please, tell me what kind of files are worth killing so many people, including a cop? No one has ever told me!"

Claudette lowered her head, looked at her desk then answered softly, "I don't know what the files contain either. I guess I was too scared to ask."

A quietness slowly washed through the room, as neither one moved nor said a word, as if they were giving the dead a moment of silence.

Then Antoine looked up and said, "When we were searching for them, it felt like it was just a big computer game. Until now, I didn't realize what the stakes were. I guess I should have known that there would be pain from the burns you get when you go to bed with the devil."

"Please don't say anything to anyone else. OK?"

"Sure."

She watched her brother leave her office, then she reached for the desk phone. She wanted to call Angelo, but she paused. She laid her hand on the desk and stared at the phone as she thought about the news article she had just read. She loved Angelo, he couldn't be responsible for this; he couldn't have given the orders to have all these people killed. She picked up her smart phone and smiled at the photo of Angelo wearing only an apron. But something kept gnawing at her, and her smile faded as darkness seemed to surround her, and she wondered - did she really know him; was she sleeping with the devil?

~ ~ ~

Las Vegas, Nevada

"Joe, I'm not going to stop gathering information, just because Libby is gone. I want to nail these bastards, and you know she wouldn't want us to stop."

"I know that Candy. What I'm saying is that I need to take a break for a few days. Just to get my head clear."

Candy looked at the security camera. "That damn kid is back!"

"I wonder how much longer they will keep the surveillance up now," said Joe.

As they were watching the kid, a car turned in and stopped in front of Joe's apartment. The kid tried to move out of sight, but they could still see him near the driveway, keeping an eye on the apartment. Detective Hector Rodriguez stepped out of the car.

Hector rang the doorbell, just as Joe spoke over the intercom, "I don't want to speak to you, Detective."

"Sir, I have some information for you."

"Thank you, Detective, but I already know about Libby."

"Sir, I need to talk to you."

"Detective, I don't feel like talking to you. So please leave."

Hector stood closer to the intercom and said, "I have a message from David Dodson."

Joe and Candy looked at each other, then Joe said, "What is it?"

"It would be best not to say it out here."

Joe pressed the button to open the door. "Come on back to my office."

Hector walked back to where Joe and Candy were waiting. "Good afternoon, Mr. Morgan, can I speak with you alone?"

"Detective, I don't feel like it's a very good afternoon. And she and Libby have worked with me a long time, so please, just tell me the message."

"Mr. Dodson wants you to know that Libby, Kate, and Randy are alive."

Joe and Candy stared at the detective. Then Joe said, "The news said that they were killed at the clubhouse."

"I was there when the clubhouse was attacked. The truth is no one died there."

Candy asked, "What about the hospital?"

"The deputy and the club member were killed there."

"Where is Libby?" asked Joe.

"I don't know where Mr. Dodson is hiding them. I didn't see any of them there that night. There is something else. He said that no one can know that they are alive. He also said that he is working up a plan and may need your help with it."

"Wow," said Joe, as he looked at Candy, "that's good news."

Hector continued, "I helped question one of the men that attacked the clubhouse and found out that there are some dirty cops on the force here in Vegas. One is in charge of my bureau. If I can, I would like to help you. So please let me know if there is anything I can do."

"Detective," said Joe, "I would love your help. But you need to know that this place is under surveillance and if you were to come here very often, they might get suspicious of you."

"So what do I do?"

"Do you have a PC laptop?" Joe asked.

"Yes, I don't use it much, just some occasional genealogy work."

"The first thing you will have to do is get into your PC's BIOS setting and change the boot up sequence to use the USB port before the hard drive." Joe got a new USB flash drive out of a cabinet, held it out to show Hector, and said, "I'm going to put a live Linux operating system on this. What you do is plug this into one of the USB ports, then turn the computer on. It will boot up using the Linux operating system on the USB drive instead of the operating system that's on the internal hard drive of the computer. That will keep the computer's hard drive from being used. That means there will be no digital footprints on the computer's hard drive and if someone looks at the hard drive, they will not be able to tell what you have been doing."

"Can I still use the computer's hard drive if that USB drive is not plugged in?"

"Yes, it will work just like it did before you changed the BIOS. The

USB flash drive will also contain all the information that we have collected and a special email program that I created that automatically encrypts the text before it sends it to a remailer server. Before you leave, I'll show you how to set up your WIFI, and how to view all the information. Please, only use this USB system when reading the information and to send or receive emails from me. You can look at the information anywhere, but don't use the email at your home or work. Someone may be monitoring you. There are a lot of free WIFI hot spots in the city, like fast food restaurants, book stores, coffee houses, doctors' offices, and hotels, so you have a lot of choices. You may even want to change them up from time to time. If I send you more files, then make sure to keep them on the USB drive, not the internal hard drive."

"Is all this security necessary?"

"Yes," Joe said. "They have some good people and they could easily read your unencrypted emails. And people have died because of this information." Joe paused a moment. "Now let's create some new email accounts."

After Joe finished the USB drive, he handed it to Hector and said, "Please keep it safe. Hide it when you're not using it."

Hector nodded.

~ ~ ~

Bodega Bay, California

David sat down at his desk and turned on the TV. Tom Gaillard's funeral procession was being aired live from a news helicopter flying over. He watched as the hearse stopped at the grave site and the pallbearers took the casket out.

Dennis walked into the office and said, "The glaziers are through replacing the broken windows." He then turned to watch the TV.

The images of the ceremony switched to the TV crew on the ground as the last rites were given at the graveside.

Soon the camera switched to the seven men of the Honor Guard firing party, as their commander gave the order, "DRESS RIGHT DRESS."

David and Dennis watched as the firing party shot their three volleys.

The commander then shouted, "PRESENT ARMS."

Their eyes were glued to the screen as the flag was folded and presented to the family. The camera slowly zoomed in on the distant bugler as he started to play the mournful sounds of "Taps." Dennis looked at David and watched him wipe a tear from his face. Dennis knew that David would take this personally, as if he were somehow responsible. Too many times he had seen his friend, Army Ranger David Dodson, lose a piece of himself as he buried the men he lost.

They continued to watch the end of the ceremony as the family slowly made their way back to the vehicles. Then the camera zoomed in on a member of the Honor Guard who started collecting the shell casings and putting them in a white glove to be given to the family later.

As the service ended and David turned off the TV, Dennis said, "Boss, we need to get ready for Brad's service."

Chapter 14
Bodega Bay, California

David and Dennis walked to the front of the funeral home and saw Brad's motorcycle parked next to the front door. His leather vest was draped across the seat, with an American flag doo-rag lying on top. They went inside to see Jeffery arranging a table at the front of the room.

He had just propped up an LP record next to the urn that contained Brad's ashes when David said, "Jeffery, thank you. You did a good job getting everything ready."

Dennis said, "Yeah, putting Brad's bike outside was a good touch."

"Thanks, but the staff here did a lot of this."

They stood close to the table, and talked to several of the visitors who had started to come in. Bikers, policemen, and neighbors stopped by to pay their last respects. As David was talking to some bikers, he noticed a well dressed, but unfamiliar, couple walk to the table and pick up the LP record.

He walked over. "Did you know Brad?" he asked.

The man looked up from the record and said, "Yes, I'm Travis Colten and this is my wife, Sharon. Brad and I made this record."

David smiled. "So, you two were in the band together. I'm glad you're here."

"I haven't spoken to Brad in a long time," said Travis, "ever since we had a fight about his drug use."

"He told me about that."

Travis put the record down. "Did he get cleaned up?" he asked.

"Yeah, it took him a few years, but he did."

"I would liked to have seen him. Damn, I wish he would have looked me up."

"I know he was very sorry about how you two ended," said David, "but he didn't think you would want to see him again."

Travis looked at Sharon and said, "Damn, that boy was stubborn."

"Yeah, he was," said David.

Travis fell silent for a few seconds and then added, "I owe Brad a lot. I bought a vineyard with the money I made from that album." He looked at David. "I don't know what you're going to do with his ashes, but if you decide to spread them, I would like to take some up in my plane, so we can spread them over our vineyard."

David smiled. "I think he would appreciate that. I need to get away from the clubhouse for a while. How about tomorrow?"

"Tomorrow afternoon will work for me."

They shook hands and Travis and Sharon sat down for the service.

~ ~ ~

After Brad's service, while two retired deputies guarded the prisoners in the basement of the lab, friends gathered at the clubhouse to have drinks, tell stories about Brad, and talk about how he had died. David wandered through the crowd, sipping his beer, listening to memories. Through the layers of cigarette smoke that filled the room, he could see the urn sitting on a table in the middle of the room. He sat down and stared at it. He was barely aware of bits of conversations floating by, until he heard, "I'd like to blow up the bastard that did this while he sleeps," and images of Cortez's house blowing up filled his head, playing over and over. Unaware of time passing, he sat there lost in the vision, unconsciously sipping his beer. Then a feeling of deja vu came over him as Nathan's remark about flying down to Mexico and blowing him up came forward from the back of his mind. He felt someone touch his shoulder and the images faded as he slowly became aware of the people around him.

"You ready for another cold one, Boss?" asked Jeffery.

David took the beer and stared at the cold, wet object in his hands. He suddenly stood up, slowly raised his bottle in the direction of the urn, then slightly tilted the bottle and held it there. The room fell silent one person at a time as each one noticed him standing, giving a last salute to a fallen comrade. And one by one they stood and silently repeated the same gesture.

Soon all the guests left the clubhouse, leaving David, Dennis, and Jeffery alone with the urn that contained Brad's ashes. The house was very quiet as David softly said, "Guys, let's get some sleep."

A cool Pacific breeze met them as they left out the back door of the clubhouse and walked the gravel road up the hill to the utility building. They walked quietly through the moonless night, each man deep in his own thoughts. Each step they took into the cool empty darkness seemed to engulf them, pulling them into depression.

Suddenly a shooting star appeared and they stopped and watched as the cosmic object passed through the earth's atmosphere giving up its energy in one last show in the night sky. It took some of their depression with it when it disappeared and the night didn't seem quite as dark as they continued their walk up the driveway.

~ ~ ~

Colten Vineyards, west of Glen Ellen, California

The afternoon sun slowly melted away some of the stress of the past week as they drove to Colten Vineyards, just west of Glen Ellen. David and Dennis led the way riding their Harleys, as Jeffery followed in the truck, carrying Brad's ashes. Jeffery was glad to get away from the clubhouse today and driving though the California wine country was what everyone needed.

As they drove into the driveway, Sharon walked out of the two story house to meet them. "Hi," she said, "Travis is getting the plane ready at the hanger. Just follow the driveway."

"Thank you, ma'am," replied David.

Hundreds of well-cared-for grape vines hung from long trellises that lined the narrow driveway guiding them through the vineyard to a runway and a Cirrus SR22 airplane standing in front of a metal hanger. Travis was busy attaching a tube to the right side wing tip of the plane as a young boy played with a RC controlled airplane nearby.

Travis looked up from his work. "Glad you made it," he said, as he watched the three men walk up to the plane.

"That's a nice plane," Dennis said.

"Thanks."

Dennis pointed to the tube and asked, "Is that how you release the ashes?"

"Yes, I designed and made this using a tube, a butterfly valve in the front, and a latched cover in the back. The butterfly valve is controlled using a servo motor. That gives me some control as to how fast the ashes are released. I just release the latch on the back then slowly open the valve."

"You must do this a lot," said David.

"Yeah, you would be surprised how often I have taken people up to let them release a loved one."

Travis tightened the last bolt. "OK, I'm ready whenever you are."

Jeffery got Brad's ashes from the truck and met the other men in the hanger where Travis had a tray and a small note pad laying on a work bench.

Travis asked, "How much of him can I have?"

"Brad loved Yosemite National Park," said David. "I thought we might spread most of his ashes there."

"From the air or on the ground?" asked Travis.

"On the ground. I thought we would wait awhile, then ask friends to join us."

"I would love to be there," said Travis.

"I'll let you know when."

"Thanks."

Travis picked up the note pad and tore off a sheet. "Something I like to do is let people write one last note to their loved one. I put the note in with the ashes to be released at the same time. If anyone would like to......"

Each of the men tore off a sheet, then took a pen and started writing.

After Travis completed his note, he noticed that everyone else was looking at him, waiting for him to finish. *Men of few words*, he thought, and a sad smile touched his lips when he thought of a bit of a song, *Grief is a bottomless pit, no words can comfort, none can pull me out.*

Travis opened the urn, got a small scoop and put two scoopfuls in the tray. Then he folded the notes and placed them in the tray.

They walked to the plane and Travis secured the tray inside the tube. "Is everyone ready?" he asked.

They climbed into the plane and secured their seat belts. Travis started the motor and released the brakes, and the plane started to slowly move. Jeffery noticed the young boy had moved next to the hanger, and started waving at them while holding his toy airplane. Jeffery asked, "Is that your son?"

"Yes," Travis said as they taxied the short distance to the runway. He completed the engine run-up then turned onto the runway, slightly increased the throttle, and began to align the plane with the runway. When the plane was straight, he smoothly pushed the throttle to full power. Seconds later the plane pulled away from the ground and they climbed to 3000 feet before leveling out. David, Dennis, and Jeffery watched as Travis did some slight banking maneuvers to head back to the vineyard. As they got close, Travis backed off the throttle and deployed the flaps. The plane dropped to about 300 feet above the ground. On their approach Travis said, "David, get ready to push the release button."

When they reached the edge of the vineyard, Travis said, "Now."

They all watched Brad's ashes and the paper notes fly out the tube. David noticed Sharon was standing in the backyard watching them fly by. They climbed back to 3000 feet and Travis flew them around the area before landing back at his vineyard.

After they got out of the plane David said, "Thank you, Travis. I think Brad would approve."

"Thanks for letting me."

David noticed another plane at the back of the hanger. "Does that plane fly?"

"With a little work it can. Why, you want to buy it?"

"Is it for sale?"

"Maybe, I bought it two years ago from a friend. He had to stop flying because he had a heart attack."

"What kind of plane is it?"

"The wing style is a canard, the model is Long-EZ. It's the kind John Denver died in."

David asked, "Can we look at it?"

"Sure, let's pull it out so you can get a better look at it."

Dennis walked up to David and quietly asked, "Boss, what are you thinking?"

"I'm thinking about flying that down to Mexico, and bombing the man that killed Brad."

Dennis stared at David. "Boss, we don't have anyone that can fly it."

"Yes, we do, and he is motivated."

David asked Travis several more questions as he looked over the plane, and Dennis could see that a plan was taking shape in David's mind.

"What would it take to make this plane into a bomber?" asked David.

Travis smiled until he saw the expression on David's face, then he asked, "Are you serious?"

"As a heart attack."

Travis stared at him for a second then said, "You're going after the people responsible for killing Brad and the deputy."

David just nodded.

"It's not that easy to drop a bomb on something," said Travis. "There's a lot of math involved." Just then his son's RC airplane landed a few feet away and Travis watched it roll by. "But with today's technology, it's a lot easier."

"How?" asked David.

"Well, what I would do is make a GPS guided bomb."

"I don't know anyone that can make a guidance system."

Travis said, "I can do most of that." He pointed to the RC airplane, "My son and I put that together. I would use a lot of the same parts."

"What would you need?"

"Servos, GPS receiver, and a micro computer, and you can buy all that from a robot store, online."

"And you can put that together?"

"All but one very important part. I cannot program a micro computer."

Jeffery spoke up, "Libby can."

"OK, where are you going to get the explosives?" asked Travis.

David pointed to Jeffery. "He has a chemical engineering degree from MIT. I bet he could put something together."

Travis looked at Jeffery and said, "MIT?"

Jeffery nodded. "My college roommate and I would try to outdo each other by making small bombs."

Travis then turned to Dennis. "I guess you have a degree in mechanical engineering?"

"I'm still in class, I'm attending the University of Hard Knocks."

Travis laughed. "You people are starting to make me believe we could do this, and that scares me. But," he turned to David, "and I'm sorry, but I can't do anything that's going to put my family in danger."

"I understand. But the people that we're going after aren't going away. If anything, it's going to get worse. The drug cartels aren't just sending drugs into this country. They're kidnapping people in the U.S. and taking them to Mexico and holding them for ransom. They try to kill witnesses in front of courthouses. They're coming into our neighborhood hospitals, and killing police and friends."

"Yes, I know. But I have to talk to my wife before I commit to something like this."

"OK."

"Sharon and I would like for you to stay and have dinner tonight. We'd like to hear more about what Brad was like before he died."

"Did she know Brad?"

"Yes, she and Brad were a couple when Brad and I still had the band together. They were very close until he got into the hard drugs. She couldn't handle him after that, so she left him, and I think she feels bad about not being able to help him."

"Sure, we can stay, thanks."

They walked around the plane again and Travis listened as David and Dennis talked about what they would have to do to the plane to support carrying a bomb underneath. Dennis came up with a removable pneumatic rack system that would drop down enough to clear the rear propeller, and once the bomb was released the rack system could be retracted so the plane could land.

"Can I make a suggestion?" asked Travis.

David looked at him. "Sure."

"Instead of using one big bomb, use, say, four smaller ones. Making them smaller would be easier to make and handle. You can line them in a horizontal row giving better aerodynamics to the plane and better ground clearance. Also, making one bomb is like putting all your eggs in one basket. If it fails, you have lost everything. Think of it as comparing a shotgun and a rifle. It's a lot easier to hit what you're shooting at with a shotgun than a rifle. Controlling each bomb with its own GPS receiver would also allow you to program one or two to land in one room and the others to land in another part of a house."

"Boss, that's not a bad idea," said Dennis.

Travis's phone started to ring and he answered. "OK, we'll be right there." He ended the call and said, "Sharon said dinner's ready."

~ ~ ~

During and after dinner as the wine flowed and the bottles emptied, the laughs got louder as the boys told tales of adventure, and misadventure, that they had shared with Brad.

David said, "Dennis, tell them about when Brad and Max went camping in Yosemite National Park."

"Yeah, that's a good one." Dennis laughed. "It started when Brad and Max met a couple of girls who tended bar in Santa Rosa. And they thought it would be a good idea to take them camping in the back-country of Yosemite."

"Not a good idea," laughed David.

"Well, they had to hike to the campsite, of course. And I don't think the girls got the hike part when they heard back-country. So they weren't too happy, and then to top it off, there was an afternoon storm and they got soaked through."

"Oh my," said Sharon.

"They finally get to the campsite and set up the two tents. They managed to start a fire, and stick some tree limbs next to it for a makeshift clothesline. So the girls go in the tents to take their wet clothes off and hand them out to the guys to hang up. The guys hand each girl some food and a bottle of wine and then they just shed their clothes right there by the fire, hang them up and go to join their girls. So they're in their tents, drinking a little wine, having a little snack, and getting to know each other. Things are looking up." Dennis starts laughing. "But then they start hearing noises outside. And Brad's girl starts freakin' out. And Brad sticks his head out of the tent and there's a bear, or as he told it, 'A BIG HUGE FREAKING ENORMOUS BROWN BEAR!!!'"

"I can just hear him!" laughed Sharon.

"Well, these genius boys had left the backpacks, with most of the food still in them, on the ground outside. And the bear wanted a snack."

Travis laughed, "Well, they did have more important things on their minds."

Sharon playfully punched his arm. "Yeah, you would have done the same."

"By this time," continued Dennis, "Max has stuck his head out too, and they're both yelling their fool heads off trying to scare the bear away, but it just ignores them and keeps tearing up the backpacks. And both the girls are screaming, wanting their tough biker men to do something. So Brad steps out of his tent, nothing on, and picks up a log and throws it at the bear. The bear turns around and, according to Brad, growls and charges at him. Now Max swears that the bear just laughed at him."

Travis and Sharon cracked up at that.

"But either way, Brad runs buck naked into the woods and hides behind a tree. And the bear just keeps doing his thing." He paused and took a drink of his wine. "So now Max is going to be the hero. He steps out of his tent, nothing on, and yells some more. Well, the bear was getting a little irritated by now, so it turned around and yelled back. Which sent Max running to hide behind the tree with Brad. So now, we've got our two brave men cowering behind a tree, and each girl alone in a tent, while the bear just tosses things around."

"Brad should have tried singing to it," said Travis.

"I don't guess he thought of that," laughed David.

"Well, I guess by now the girls had figured out that their tough guys weren't any match for a bear and they might as well quit freaking out. From their hidey hole, Brad saw his girl peek out a slit in the door flap. She watched the bear until it's back was turned toward her, then she darted out, picked something up off the ground, and ran to the other girl's tent. And in a few minutes, Max and Brad saw both girls come out of the tent, both naked, and they start jumping up and down and yelling. The bear has had enough of these crazy people and it starts toward the girls. Brad and Max still want to be heroes, so they step out from behind the tree, but before they get anywhere, Brad's girl shoots the bear with her pepper spray." Dennis picked up his wine again. "The bear is blinded, growling, thrashing, running round and round the campsite. The boys step back behind their tree and the girls hide behind a boulder. Finally the bear's blind movements take him out of the campsite and the girls stand up and holler, 'You can come out now, we'll keep you safe.'"

They all howled with laughter at that, the wine making the laughter contagious, and Travis refilled the glasses while there was a break in the story.

Dennis wiped his eyes and took a deep breath so he could talk again. "Well, the bear's blind rage had made a big mess; their clothes were knocked into the fire, everything in the backpacks was shredded, the tents were too damaged to use. The blankets inside the tents were ragged, but not completely destroyed. So the girls pulled the blankets out while the boys got the fire built back up. And they wrapped up in the blankets and sat in front of the fire the rest of the night. The next morning they found a knife on the ground and cut holes in the center of the blankets to make ponchos for the girls. And the boys made some for themselves from what was left of the tents. Just picture, if you can, the sight they made hiking out, wearing raggedy ponchos and barefoot."

Sharon laughed so hard that a tear rolled down her face. "I can imagine the looks they got!" she managed to say. She picked up a napkin and dried her eyes. She took Travis's hand, looked at the boys and said, "I want to thank you for having dinner with us and telling us your stories about Brad." She held up her wine glass and said, "To Brad."

They raised their glasses and repeated, "To Brad."

"I would like to make a toast to our hosts for providing us with such a delicious meal," said David. He held up his glass in front of Travis and Sharon and said, "To new friends."

"To new friends," everyone said.

"You know that any meal will be good," said Sharon, "if you include friends and a bottle of wine."

A quiet, calm feeling of sorrow seemed to pass into the room as everyone's thoughts turned to Brad and the deputy.

Travis softly took Sharon's hand and said, "If you put on a pot of coffee, I'll clean up. OK?"

David got up to help clear the table and motioned Dennis and Jeffery to do the same. They finished the clean up and sat back at the table as the coffee finished brewing, and Sharon poured them all a cup.

Travis looked at David and said, "OK, David."

David said, "Sharon, we need your help in taking down the drug lord that killed Brad."

"Aren't the police doing that? Besides what can I do?"

"The U.S. police can't touch him in Mexico," answered David. "The Mexican police will not touch him."

"When you say take him down, you mean kill him?"

"Yes."

Sharon looked at Travis. "You knew that they were going to do this?"

"I talked to him just a few hours ago," said David, "and he said that he wouldn't do anything without your support."

With a slight disapproving scowl, she said, "We run a winery, David, what do you think we can do?"

"To start with, you can sell me your unused airplane."

"That can't be all."

"I need Travis to help build a GPS guidance system."

She gave Travis a puzzled look. "What do you know about building a guidance system?"

"They use a lot of the same parts as Travis Junior's remote controlled plane."

She looked back to David. "If we help you," she said, "will that put my family in danger?"

"Only if they find out. That is why I must ask you never to tell anyone about our plan. I realize that you don't know us, and you're not sure that you can even trust us, but I assure you that I will not do anything that I think will put you and your family in danger."

"How long have you been working on this plan?"

"I have been thinking about what to do since we rescued my niece and her friends in Vegas. It just seemed to come together a few hours ago, when I saw your other plane."

"Your niece, the one that was killed at the clubhouse?"

"Yes, but she and her friends aren't dead. I have a man hiding them. He's moving them around in an RV."

Sharon said, "David, before I can give you my support, I need to know what we're getting into. I need to know everything. Understand?"

"OK, but only because we need your help. And I can't emphasize enough that this information has to remain a secret, even from the police, or more people will get killed. If the man responsible for killing Brad finds out you know anything, then your family will be in danger."

Brad's death had stirred up a lot of emotions. Sharon glanced at Travis, and saw the hurt, the sorrow, that now haunted her normally proud and confidant husband. She knew Travis felt like they had deserted Brad when he needed them most, because she felt that way too. As they squeezed each others' hands, she could sense that he really wanted to help, but she also knew it would be her call. She looked at David, paused a moment, and said, "I understand, but I still want to know everything before I give you my OK."

David slowly nodded his head. "You may need to put on some more coffee. It's going to take a while."

~ ~ ~

Sharon poured another round of coffee as David finished his story.

She looked at Travis and asked, "Do you still want to help?"

"Yes. More than ever."

She looked at David. "I cannot believe I'm going to say this. You have my support." She raised her coffee cup. "To new friends and adventures."

David raised his. "Thank you. To new friends and adventures."

"What do we do next?" she asked.

"Dennis can come back tomorrow," said David. "And Travis and Dennis can start designing and get any needed parts ordered. Jeffery can get started at his lab and order what he needs. I still have a lot of planning to do."

Travis looked at Jeffery and asked, "You have a lab at the clubhouse?"

"I have a very nice lab and a comfortable place to live in a maintenance building behind the clubhouse," answered Jeffery.

"I would like to see it someday."

David said, "Until this is all over, it may not be good for us to be seen together, especially at the clubhouse. Someone may still be watching us."

"OK," said Travis.

"Dennis, you should stay here tonight," said Sharon, "so you and Travis can get an early start."

"Thank you. I can sleep at the hanger; it looks a lot better than a lot of places I have slept."

"There is a sofa in the office and a full bathroom there, but tonight, please stay in our house."

"OK, thanks."

Sharon turned to David and said, "The people that are driving around in the RV, I don't see why they can't stay out at the hanger, too. It's very secluded and private. I think they would be safe there, and it has a nice view of our vineyard. I would offer to let them stay in the house, but sometimes we have unexpected guests stop by."

"I'll let them know. Thank you."

Jeffery said, "That's great, I would love to have them close by."

Dennis smiled. "Down, Stud," he said. "You may still not be able to see her for a while."

"See who?" Sharon asked.

"Libby," said Jeffery. "We were just starting to get to know each other before I got shot at the courthouse, and she had to leave."

"We'll watch out for them, don't worry."

"Thanks," said Jeffery.

"It's getting late," said David, "and Jeffery and I need to get back to the clubhouse. Oh, one other thing, I don't think anyone should make any contact with us from this location. I'll come up with a way for us to communicate."

Travis, Sharon, and Dennis walked out to the porch to watch David and Jeffery leave.

As soon as their tail lights were gone, Travis, standing behind Sharon, put his arms around her, held her tight and said, "And now the adventure begins."

She put her hands on his. "Yes, I hope we aren't going to regret it."

Dennis, standing beside them, overheard what she said. He kept looking down the road, staring into the darkness and thinking, David hasn't planned anything like this since he left the Army. He swallowed hard and nervously said to himself, *Yeah, I hope we aren't going to regret it.*

Chapter 15
RV Park, California

Time in the RV had crawled since they had heard about Brad's death. The first moments after hearing, tears had run down Max's rough face as he sat outside on the picnic table with Kate, but he had pulled himself together as he heard Libby inside the RV having a breakdown, crying and blaming herself. He had gone inside, to Randy's relief, and put his arms around her and held her tight, trying to comfort her, even while having his own breakdown. With each hour that had passed since then, Max got more quiet and more isolated as they waited anxiously to hear from David.

Kate and Libby cleared the breakfast table in silence until Max turned his phone back on for the 8 AM call. Then Kate whispered to Libby, "God, I wish someone would call us. I don't know what Max is going to do if he doesn't hear something soon."

"Yeah, he's taking it hard. My meltdown didn't help either."

I guess even tough guys can't hide their feelings all the time, thought Kate.

The phone rang to indicate a text message. Max quickly read the message then turned it off.

Kate asked, "Max, what'd it say?"

"It's from David. It said MC."

"What does that mean, motorcycle club?"

"No, it means that David left me a message in a men's club in Petaluma."

"Where is Petaluma?" asked Libby.

"South of Santa Rosa. Libby, please don't get your hopes up. I know it's close to home but this doesn't mean we can go home yet."

"I know, Max. Thank you."

~ ~ ~

Las Vegas, Nevada

As they drove by the bank and saw the demonstrators protesting, Candy said, "Your friend at Occupy Vegas doesn't kid around. I bet there are 300 people here this morning."

Joe smiled and said, "It didn't take that much convincing when I told him how many homes this bank foreclosed on."

Joe stopped the van on a side street behind the bank.

Candy flipped down the van's sun visor and checked her makeup and hair in the attached mirror. She smiled at her reflection, the conservative style wig and makeup was very different from the street hooker role she played the last time they were here. She stepped out of the van and paused by the door to check her outfit by her reflection in the window. Dark pants suit, white top, and flats, very business-like she thought. She slung her purse over her shoulder, gave Joe a smile as she closed the door and started walking back to the bank.

As she reached the protest lines, a girl put a two way radio to her lips, and said, "Get ready." Another girl joined her and they walked beside Candy to the front of the bank.

Candy could see two security guards standing outside the bank, checking everyone that entered. The girls talked and pointed their fingers at Candy and tried to hand her some leaflets. Candy walked a little faster. The girls stayed with her until they were in front of Angelo's car. The two girls ran in front of her, making her stop. They stood between the security guards at the front door and Candy, with Angelo's car behind her.

The girl put the two way radio to her lips, and said, "Now."

Suddenly, the crowd of protesters jumped, startled by loud booms coming from two corners of the parking lot. Water balloons, launched from air cannons, started landing and exploding next to the security guards. The crowd roared with cheers and laughter as the guards turned and ran into the bank, where they watched from behind the glass doors until several balloons crashed into the doors making it difficult to see outside.

Candy and the two girls ran between Angelo's car and another car. Candy lay on the ground and the two girls squatted, blocking the security guards view. Candy found the GPS tracker that Randy had placed on Angelo's car weeks before and she placed it into her purse as several balloons broke on top of the car, throwing water over them.

When Candy gave the thumbs up, the girl with the radio signaled to stop the assault of balloons. The two girls ran back to the protest line as the security guards slowly came out of the building.

Candy stood there in her wet, almost transparent shirt, her jacket open. The guards stared at her a little too long, then one finally asked, "Ma'am, are you OK?"

"I was going to start a business account with you," she said, as she jerked her jacket closed, "but this bank seems to have some problems. Tell your boss that I don't think I will ever be back to this bank again."

She turned and walked back to Joe's van. She smiled at Joe as she got in and said, "Got it."

Joe put the van in drive, pulled out onto the street and said, "Candy, I had no doubt, because girl, you're good!"

~ ~ ~

Joe plugged the GPS tracker, retrieved from Angelo's car, into his computer and studied the information.

Candy looked over his shoulder and said, "I looked over today's surveillance recordings and didn't see anything of the kid on the bike. Maybe they stopped watching us. What did you find on the tracker so far?"

"Mr. Diego went home, the bank, the airport, a small office building, and a warehouse. I was about to start background searches on the office building and the warehouse. I hope we'll have something soon."

"Do you want me to go and take a closer look at them?"

"No, not right now. I'm going to send the address of the warehouse and office building to Detective Rodriguez. I want to see if what he finds matches what we can find."

"It doesn't sound like you trust him completely."

"On paper he looks like a good cop. But we are dealing with life and death. And he needs to earn my trust."

"Why did you give him all the information if you weren't sure about him?"

Joe thought for a second. "I guess I want to trust him, and I think it would be a good idea to have a copy of this information in the hands of law enforcement in case something happens to us."

Chapter 16
Petaluma, California

It was late, about 11:45 PM, when they pulled off of U.S. Highway 101. The simple neon sign on a pole in front of the building read, "Petaluma Men's Club," with a small sign underneath that read, "Truck parking in the rear."

There was only one light pole in the parking lot near the rear entrance door and Max wasted no time pulling the RV between two of the big rigs at the back of the lot and shutting everything down.

As he walked to the side door of the RV he said, "Girls, I know you want to come in with me, but it might be best you stay here."

Kate said, "I used to work at places like this. I think I could handle myself in there."

Max stopped, turned around and said, "Yeah, but not in a place like this. It's not as nice as most of the clubs in Vegas. If you two were to come in there, it would be like dangling two prime rib steaks in front of a pack of hungry wolves, they would start fighting and tearing each other apart just to see who got to you first."

He smiled at Kate, then winked, and said, "I won't be long."

"Did he just compare us to prime rib?" asked Libby.

Kate laughed, "Yes, but I think he's paying us a compliment."

Kate sat in the passenger seat and watched out the front as Max walked across the parking lot to the back door of the club. As he reached the back door, a couple came out and walked toward the RV. Kate looked back and saw Randy asleep on the sofa and Libby, lost in her thoughts, staring out a side window.

"Libby." Kate motioned her to come up front.

She sat down in the driver's seat. "What's going on?" she asked.

"Check out these two."

Libby said, "Now that's a short dress."

They watched as the man opened the door of the truck that was parked next door. The petite young girl climbed in and slid across the driver's seat, then into the back of the sleeper cab.

Kate looked at Libby and said, "That dress didn't leave anything to the imagination."

They watched as the large man climbed into the cab behind her.

"God, how much do you think he weighs?" asked Libby.

"Has to be over 275."

"That poor girl," she said.

Kate smiled. "She's going to look like a pancake when he's through with her."

They started laughing as the truck started to shake.

Randy raised his head and asked, "What's going on?"

"Nothing, Dear," said Kate, "go back to sleep."

Kate and Libby just looked at each other and laughed again as the truck next door kept shaking.

The fifteen minutes of shaking seemed like an hour, and Kate and Libby jumped when the door of the truck's cab banged open and the girl tried to get out. The man was dragging her back inside and she bit his hand. He let go and she fell several feet. He started climbing out. She managed to get to her feet and tried to run back to the club, but the man caught her and Kate and Libby had a front row seat as he backhanded her face and knocked her back to the ground.

"Kate, what do we do?" said Libby.

"Turn on the headlights."

Libby looked at the dash and yelled, "Where?"

Kate pointed to a switch and said, "Try that one."

As the headlights came on, the man raised his hand in front of his face, shielding his eyes. The girl got to her feet and started running to the club. He watched her go, but didn't chase her. Instead, he looked back at the RV.

Max walked out of the back door to see the girl running straight at him. He sidestepped as she passed by, jerked the door open, and entered the building without slowing down. He looked at the row of trucks trying to see the RV, then realized the headlights were coming from the RV.

"Oh shit, what now?" he said as he started to run.

Kate and Libby watched the man start moving back to his truck, then he turned toward the RV. Kate ran to the door, reaching it just as the man opened it.

Kate yelled, "Randy! Get your ass up!"

He raised his head and said, "Are we there yet?"

Libby yelled, "Kate what can I do?"

"Find Max's gun!"

The man stood on the doorstep and turned his large body to try to enter the RV. Kate raised her leg and tried to kick the man in the nuts, but he grabbed her leg and yanked it, causing her to lose her balance and fall.

Randy, still half asleep, raised his head again and said, "Who's at the door?"

The man stepped back down from the RV and quickly dragged Kate out the door by her legs. She looked up and saw a wide, cocky smile that came closer when he bent over and grabbed her blouse. He started pulling her off the ground and she grabbed at his large hands trying to free herself, as the man's grotesque smile inched closer. Suddenly she saw a blur out of the corner of her eye as Max ran between the truck and the RV and tried to tackle the man.

Max fell to the ground after he ran into the man, but he managed to knock the man off balance enough that he fell to one knee and he dropped Kate back on the ground.

She was amazed to see how fast the large man stood back up. He grabbed Max and shoved him face-first into the RV. Blood gushed from Max's nose. Then he reversed the motion and pushed Max's back hard into the truck. He held Max up and pulled his fist back, preparing to hit him. But he stopped and smiled when he saw Max's eyes lose focus, and he casually let him fall to the ground.

Kate stared at Max for a long moment then slowly brought her eyes up to see the man staring at her with a grin that made her skin crawl.

Suddenly, the man arched his back and started yelling. He turned around, shaking, mouth open, still yelling, his face contorted with excruciating pain. His dark eyes locked on Kate. Seconds later his stare went blank, he dropped to his knees, and he fell, his head landing in Kate's lap.

Kate looked at her torn blouse, at the man's head in her lap, and then at Max, as he tried to lift his head off the ground. She jumped when Libby yelled, "WOW, I HAVE TO GET ME ONE OF THESE!" And when she looked up, she saw Libby standing in the door of the RV, grinning, holding a Taser pistol.

"Libby," said Max, "if you can get me inside I'll buy you one."

"Crap, he's drooling on me," said Kate as she grabbed a handful of the man's oily hair and lifted his head from her lap.

Randy poked his head around Libby and looked at Kate lying on the ground and said, "What the hell is going on? Kate, what are you doing with him?"

Libby helped Max back into the RV as Randy helped Kate get out from under the man.

Max said, "Libby, put me in the passenger seat, I think you're going to have to drive now."

"I can't drive this thing!"

Max raised his voice. "Sit your little butt down, you're going to drive!"

She got in the driver's seat and turned the key.

He saw her hand shaking when she reached for the key and he lowered his voice. "It's no different from driving a car, just bigger," he said, calmly. "You'll do fine. The only thing different is the brakes." He pointed. "Press that in, it will release the brakes."

The air hissed as she released the air brakes, and Max said, "Now drive us the hell out of here before someone calls the cops!"

"What happened out there?" said Randy.

Libby looked around at him, sitting on the sofa, looking confused, watching Kate change her clothes and she shook her head. *Man, Randy, you're almost useless*, she thought. Then she gently pressed the accelerator and the RV crept slowly out of the parking lot and onto the street.

Max, drowsy and holding a handkerchief to his bloody nose, looked up and said, "Make a left at the next light. Then turn right and get onto 101 north. We need to get some distance from here, so Lib, you need to drive faster than 20 miles per hour."

Libby kept a death grip on the steering wheel as she made the turns and followed the signs back to 101. She pressed the accelerator harder to make it up the entrance ramp to merge onto the highway. Traffic was light and soon she reached the posted speed limit and pulled over into the center lane.

She drove silently, nervously scanning the road, jumping each time a car or truck passed. Until today she had never driven anything bigger than her mother's car, but with a great deal of luck, somehow she had managed to keep the RV from hitting anything. She wiped the sweat from her brow and thought, *Thank God*. When there was a break in traffic, she asked, "Where are we going?"

When she didn't get an answer, she glanced at Max. His head was down, swaying back and forth from the movement of the RV. She looked back to the road and saw a sign saying *Santa Rosa three miles*.

She was having trouble seeing the traffic coming up beside her because the rear-view mirrors were not adjusted correctly for her. She yelled, "Hey! I need some help."

Randy and Kate walked up to the front, looked around the large seat and saw Libby sitting in the driver's seat and Max passed out in the passenger's seat.

He said, "I didn't know that you could drive an RV."

"This is my first time and I can't see anything in these mirrors, I need you to help me see."

"Do you know where you're going?"

"No. All Max said was to get on 101 north, and get some distance. Randy, we're almost in Santa Rosa."

He noticed the strain in her voice and said, "OK, you're doing great, just stay in the center lane until we get through the city, then we can find a truck stop or parking lot to stop at. Then we can work out what to do next."

Libby said, "Check Max's pockets and see if he has a letter or something from David."

"I'll do that when we stop," Randy said.

Libby saw a road sign that read *Brad's Truck Stop next exit.*

"Randy, I'm going to turn at the next exit. Help me look for Brad's Truck Stop."

"OK, Brad's Truck Stop, maybe that's a lucky omen." he said.

"Yeah."

She turned down the exit and saw the truck stop located next to the ramp. She slowly pulled into the parking lot, then drove to the back lot and parked next to some noisy refrigeration trucks.

Hurriedly, Libby got up from the seat and headed to the back of the RV and said, "I have to pee. Randy, search Max and find that letter."

"Yes, ma'am," Randy said as she ran by him.

As Randy started looking for the letter, Max jerked, then woke up.

He looked at Randy. "Where are we?"

"In a truck stop near Santa Rosa." He paused, "Max you look like shit."

Max pulled a letter out of his vest pocket and handed it to Randy.

"See what it says. Someone help me to the sofa. I don't think I'm going to be much good for a while."

Kate and Randy helped him to the sofa. Kate grabbed some wet paper towels and started to clean the blood from his face.

As Kate touched his nose, Max yelled, "Oh shit! Stop! I think it's broke."

"Do we need to take you to the hospital?"

"No, they might ask too many questions. I'll just lay down here. I need some ice, and to prop up my head. Other than that, I'll be fine."

Kate wrapped some ice in a cloth towel. She sat at one end of the sofa and made Max lay down putting his head on her lap.

Max placed the ice on his face next to his nose and moaned, "Ow..ow..ow."

Kate looked down at Max and ran her hand though his hair and said, "Thanks, Max."

He opened his eyes, smiled and winked at her, then closed his eyes again.

~ ~ ~

Colten Vineyards, west of Glen Ellen, California

A crash jerked Sharon out of a deep sleep. "Wake up!" She shook Travis. "I heard something outside."

"What, what time is it?"

"It's 5:00 am."

She looked out the window. "There's an RV in front of the house."

Travis sat up. "Our guests have arrived."

Sharon turned to the bedroom door as Dennis started knocking. "I heard something," he said. "Are you OK?"

She put on a robe and opened the door to Dennis holding a gun pointed at the floor. "An RV just pulled in front of the house," she said.

"OK, I'll go down and check it out."

Kate and Max came out of the RV first, then Randy and Libby.

As they started walking to the front door Libby said, "I thought you were going to tell me if I was going to hit something."

Randy replied, "Libby, I thought you could see the mail box. I don't think you need to drive the RV anymore."

"I was doing fine until I hit the mailbox."

"Libby, you almost ran that older couple off the road."

"What couple?"

"When you passed the couple pulling that small white travel trailer."

"You said I was clear."

"I said almost clear."

Libby paused for a second. "I know I have seen that trailer somewhere before," she said.

Max glanced at Kate and said, "God, they sound like they're married."

As they reached the front porch they heard a voice say, "Do you think you can make a little more noise so the neighbors can hear you, too?"

They looked up to see Dennis leaning against a porch column.

Sharon and Travis stepped out onto the porch when Dennis said, "Max, what happened to you?"

He peered at Dennis over his taped up nose. "I got in a fight with a 300 pound trucker."

"More like 275 and you didn't even hit him," said Kate.

Max looked at Kate. "I'm telling this story," he said. "Let me exaggerate a little."

"Now who sounds like they're married?" said Libby.

Sharon said, "Please come in. I'll make some coffee and breakfast."

As they entered the house Libby said, "I'm sorry I ran over your mailbox."

"You were driving?" asked Dennis.

"Yeah, Max was asleep on Kate's lap all night."

"Dennis, we need to move the RV to the hangar," said Travis. "You drive the RV and I'll follow you in the utility cart. And Max, you go on inside and get cleaned up. We'll get this."

"Thanks," said Max.

Dennis put his hand on Max's shoulder, looked at him and said in a soft voice, "I'm glad you're back. Are you OK?"

Dennis could see the hurt in Max's eyes as he said, "Yeah, I'll be OK, but I'm going to miss the hell out of him." Then Max and Dennis gave each other a hug.

"I know man, I'm going to miss him too," said Dennis.

The sight of these two bikers holding each other, comforting each other, caused Travis to pause and reflect on how much Brad had touched their lives, and suddenly a deep sorrow overwhelmed him as he watched the two men wipe their eyes when they separated.

Then Max turned and walked into the house, and Dennis walked to the RV, neither man saying another word.

Using the early morning light to guide his way, Dennis drove the RV up the driveway to the hangar. Travis headed to the large garage that stood next to his house. He walked though his yard, leaving footprints in the dew-laden grass. A sudden cool breeze nipped at him, and he turned his head and stared out at the vineyard where two days before they had spread the ashes of his old friend and music partner, and he softly whispered, "Brad, I'm glad you found some good friends."

~ ~ ~

Las Vegas, Nevada

A tall man with a medium build and salt and pepper hair picked up his coffee. "Thanks," he said to the girl at the counter. He casually walked to a table and said, "I guess policemen can always find the best coffee house. Right, detective?"

Hector Rodriguez looked up from his laptop to see Captain Coleman smiling back at him.

"Hello, Captain, would you like to sit down?" he asked, as he closed the computer.

"No, thank you. I didn't mean to interrupt your work."

"That's OK, I was just catching up on some emails before I came into the office."

"I just wanted to tell you that I just read your report about what happened in Bodega Bay. I bet they were glad you were there."

"Yes, they were."

"Well, good job, Detective. I'll see you when you get in the office."

The captain started to turn around when Hector said, "Captain, I thought I would do some follow-up on the money that the bank said Kate Dodson stole."

The captain looked back at Hector, took a few seconds to think, then said, "OK, but if you don't find something soon, we should turn it over to the Financial Crimes Bureau."

"Thanks, Captain."

Hector sipped his coffee and watched as Captain Coleman walked away. He looked around, then raised the display, turned the computer back on, and read Joe's email again.

~ ~ ~

Las Vegas, Nevada

"Candy, I have a problem that I need your help with," said Joe.

"What's going on?"

"We need to put some kind of surveillance on the warehouse and the office building."

"Joe, you know I'm good, but even I cannot watch two places at once. Maybe Detective Rodriguez can help with that."

"He said the best he could do would be to drive by occasionally. He can't ask the police department to do it because he would have to explain why to his captain. No, somehow we need to put some cameras near the buildings."

"Are you thinking of monitoring the two buildings from here?"

"I wish, but that would cost too much and take too much time to set up. All we need right now are photos of people coming and going. I was thinking of small, self contained, still cameras located around the buildings that we can swap out every few days."

"So you need some place to put them?"

"Yes, the problem is Detective Rodriquez said both buildings have a lot of surveillance cameras surrounding them. So we cannot get too close without tipping them off."

"What if we put up a road construction site near the buildings?"

Joe smiled and said, "I don't think anyone would believe me if I showed up wearing a hard hat, carrying a shovel, sitting in a wheelchair."

"No, but I can put up some of those orange and white drums around some storm drains near the buildings. Make it look like the city is going to do some repair work there. We would only need to put up a couple at each site."

Joe said, "Yeah, that might work. If they're near the entrance, we can get photos of the cars' license plates and maybe photos of the people driving. I could use cameras that are sound activated. The sound of a car driving by should activate them, and we could probably put two cameras at different angles on each drum." He thought a minute. "OK, I can order the cameras and have them here overnight, but where can we get the drums to mount the cameras on?"

Candy said, "There's a construction site down the street. The city just completed the work on the storm drain and there are several drums stacked on the side of the street waiting to be picked up. I could get some tonight."

Joe smiled and said, "I bet the city won't mind if we borrow them for a few weeks."

"I need to make the van look like a city maintenance vehicle," said Candy, "so I'll need to photograph some city vehicles. That will give us some license plate numbers and vehicle markings to copy and put on the van."

Joe said, "I think the city lists road construction sites online, I'll go and find you one."

~ ~ ~

Finally, some luck, Candy thought when she saw that the storm drain was just 15 feet from the driveway of the warehouse. She pulled the van to a stop then noticed the security guard step out of the guard shack to watch her. Candy wanted the guard to get a good look at her, so she got out of the van, walked around the front to the passenger side, then to the back of the van. She opened the back door and took out one of the drums and placed it on the ground next to the storm drain. She looked up to see the security guard, a 30 year old, muscular, black man, standing 5 feet away, staring at her.

"Can I ask what you're doing here?"

She smiled and said, "Hi, Sugar, I'm dropping off two Channelizer Drums for the construction crew."

"What kind of construction?"

"The city's street maintenance is going to repair the storm drains along this street."

"Is that who you work for?"

She smiled and said, "Yeah, Sugar, would you like to see my work order?"

"Yes, please."

She walked to the passenger door and opened it, stepped up on the first step, then lay over the passenger seat, reaching into the center of the van to look through some papers. She waited several seconds allowing the man to have a good look.

Candy stepped down and handed the man some papers.

As he looked them over, Candy put her hand on the man's arm, smiled and said, "Sugar, the last time someone interfered with my work, my supervisor called the police. It almost got ugly."

She hoped that mentioning the police would scare him enough to leave her alone.

He smiled as he handed the papers back. "There's not a problem. I just have to check."

"I understand. You must be guarding something important." She could feel his eyes watching her every movement as she put the papers back in the van.

"I'm stuck out here all the time," he said. "I have no idea what they do inside."

Candy knew that if his supervisors were to ask questions about what she was doing here, he could reassure them that she had a legitimate reason and they might not call city hall to check her out. She wanted to be sure to make this man like her.

She smiled, moved in close, brushed her breasts against his arm and said softly, "I like a man that takes pride in his work." Then she turned and walked to the back of the van.

As she reached for the handle on the drum, she heard the guard say, "Let me help you with this one." He took the drum and put it on the ground beside the first.

The guard, smiling and talking to Candy, had his back to the guard shack when a car pulled into the driveway. He turned when the driver gave his horn a quick tap. "Crap, it's the boss. I have to go."

She said, "Thank you, Sugar," as she watched him run back to the guard house.

Candy placed the cameras inside the battery housing that Joe had modified for them. Then she installed the battery for the flashing light that sat on top of the battery housing. As she moved the drums into position, she watched the guard talking to the driver, sure that the driver was asking about her. She closed the back doors of the van and walked to the driver's side and got in. As she started the motor, she watched the security gate open. She put the van's transmission in drive and pressed the accelerator. As the van slowly moved forward, Angelo's car also moved forward, past the guard shack, into the parking lot of the warehouse. She waved at the guard as she passed and he waved back.

~ ~ ~

Colten Vineyards, west of Glen Ellen, California

David pulled into the driveway, passed the house, and headed to the hangar. He looked over at Jeffery and said, "Jeffery, I know you want to spend time with Libby, but you'll just have a few minutes while we unload the supplies."

"Yeah, I'll take that few minutes. Thanks," Jeffery said as David stopped the truck outside the hangar.

Dennis, Max, and Travis were standing at a work bench, going over some drawings of the bomb rack, as David and Jeffery entered the hangar bay.

Jeffery looked at Max and asked, "What happened to you?"

"Never mind that, Stud. You have a very pissed-off girl wanting to see you." Max pointed to the door of the hangar office. "Libby's in there."

Jeffery smiled at Max, walked to the door and opened it. He stood at the door looking at Libby. "I understand that you're a little annoyed with me."

Libby smiled. "Yes, I told you to be careful!" she said as she stood up from the desk, ran to the door, and put her arms around him. "Are you OK?"

"Yes, it still hurts, but I'm OK." He put his good arm around her and gave her a hug. "Girl, I have missed you."

Randy closed the laptop, stood up from the sofa, and said, "Jeffery, I'm glad you're OK." He walked out of the office and closed the door.

Jeffery held her close and repeatedly kissed her. Then he reluctantly pulled back enough to say, "I can only stay for a few minutes. We purchased the metal and tools to make the bomb rack this morning. After we leave we're going to stop at a chemical supply company to get what I need to make the bombs."

"When can I see you again?"

"I don't know. I'm going to be very busy for the next several days."

"Do you think I could stay with you there?"

"No, it's too dangerous for you, Libby. They may be watching us. We have prisoners in the basement, and I'm going to be making explosives for the bombs in my lab. I need you to stay here where I know that you're safe, OK?"

She nodded her head as a tear rolled down her cheek.

He wiped the tear from her face and kissed her.

The door opened and David looked in. "Jeffery, we need to go, they're almost through unloading the equipment."

Jeffery turned his head to David and nodded.

Libby and Jeffery followed David out to the pickup. "David, I'm sorry I caused all this," said Libby. "Especially Brad."

David stopped and turned to her. "Libby, you're not the one that started this, but with your help, we're going to finish it."

"I'll do whatever I can."

Jeffery and Libby kissed goodbye. "Stay safe," she said.

"Come on, Stud," said David, "we need to go."

Libby waved as they drove off.

She didn't see Dennis and Max walk up beside her until Dennis said, "Oh, young love."

"Ain't it sweet," said Max.

Libby smiled. "Don't you old farts have something to do?"

Dennis laughed and said, "Yes, ma'am."

"Well, hurry up! Stud and I have a lot of catching up to do when this is over!"

~ ~ ~

Santa Rosa, California

The young salesclerk answered the phone as David and Jeffery walked up to the counter.

"Santa Rosa Chemical, this is Gary, can I help you?" he said into the phone.

Jeffery walked over and started looking at the display rack containing chemical handling accessories.

David watched Jeffery browse the rack then asked, "Do you miss working in this?"

"Yeah, sometimes," said Jeffery, "but working for you has been a lot more interesting."

"How's that?"

Jeffery laughed. "Well, I've never been shot before."

When the clerk finished talking on the phone, they walked back to the counter and David noticed the salesclerk staring at Jeffery.

"Can I help you?" asked the clerk.

Jeffery asked, "Do you sell nitromethane and aluminum powder?"

The clerk looked at Jeffery for a second then said, "Let me get the boss. I'll be right back."

As the clerk left, Jeffery said, "David, he knows what I'm doing."

"Let's just wait and see."

They heard the clerk open a door and say, "Dad, there's some people out here that you need to talk to. They want to purchase nitromethane and aluminum powder."

An overweight, 55 year old man with black hair came out of the office. As they approached the counter, the clerk, still looking closely at Jeffery, suddenly said, "I saw you on the internet. You're the guy that killed those two at the courthouse, aren't you?"

The older man looked at Jeffery and asked, "Is that true?"

Jeffery wiggled the fingers sticking out of the sling and said, "Yeah. Is there a problem?"

"Sir, I'm very honored to have you here. That was a hell of a thing you did."

"Thank you. I appreciate that."

"Come back to my office, let's talk." He led the way into his office, then reached out to shake their hands. "I'm Alec Cooper, the president of Santa Rosa Chemical." David and Jeffery introduced themselves. "Have a seat," Alec said.

"Is there going to be a problem getting what we need?" asked Jeffery.

"No, no problem, but if you were to put ammonium nitrate with the chemicals you asked about, you would have a nice simple fertilizer bomb. I hope you two aren't going to do something you might regret. I would hate to see you in trouble."

"Sir, I'm just here to get some supplies for my lab," said Jeffery.

"What kind of lab do you have?"

Jeffery smiled. "I have a degree in chemical engineering. It's not a meth lab and if you want to see it, I can show it to you."

"I might someday."

"Well, you're welcome to come by," said David.

"Thank you," Alec said as he stared at each man. "I need to know something and I need straight and honest answers and I assure you whatever we say in this room will never leave this room. I need to know if you're going after the people that killed your man and the deputy."

Jeffery asked, "Why do you need to know?"

"Because I want to help."

Jeffery asked again, "Why?"

Alec put his elbows on the edge of his desk and leaned closer. "My oldest son died two years ago of a cocaine overdose. I searched for a year trying to find his dealer. I was so obsessed that my wife left me, and I almost lost my company."

"I'm sorry," said Jeffery.

"I never did find his dealer and probably never will. But if I can help you, then it'll help me, because I need to feel like I did something."

"I understand how you feel," said David, "so, yes, we're going after them and that better not leave this room."

"If you want to help," said Jeffery, "then sell us what we need."

Alec said, "It would be better not to sell you those supplies."

"What do you mean?" asked David.

"If I sold you those chemicals, there would be a record that could be traced back to you and me. You and I would go to jail, and I would lose my company. I still have one son. I can't do anything that would jeopardize his future."

"OK, what do you suggest?" asked David.

"I'll give you what you need. I'll just have to do some creative bookkeeping to make it all disappear and the fact that no money changes hands between us will make it difficult to follow."

David smiled and said, "I can live with that."

"But I'm curious," Alec said to Jeffery, "why are you screwing around with an ANNM fertilizer bomb. That's not even considered high explosive. I would think someone with your knowledge could make a high explosive device."

"I would love to make something like RDX," said Jeffery, "but my lab isn't big enough to make the amount we need. Besides right now I only have one arm."

"If you could get a large enough lab with the proper equipment, and the chemicals, would you like to make something with a lot more kick."

"Hell, yeah."

David asked, "Can we get 200 pounds in a week?"

"No," said Jeffery, "but we would only need about 40 pounds to have the same effect. With the proper equipment we should be able to make that in a week. And if we can make more, so much the better."

"With the economy like it is, my warehouse is half empty," said Alec. "I have plenty of room for a lab. And my brother owns the fertilizer plant down the road. He just updated a small production research lab and I bet he still has the equipment that was replaced. Let me make some phone calls."

As Alec made his calls, David turned to Jeffery and whispered, "Are you sure about this?"

"Yeah, RDX is a very high explosive. My roommate and I made some in college. It's not that hard to make with the proper equipment, and it's safer to handle than ANNM. Besides, we can always fall back and make the ANNM if we need to."

"OK, Stud."

Alec ended the call, looked up from the phone, and said, "My brother wants to talk to you, if it's OK."

"Sure," said David.

"Good. He should be here in a few minutes. Would you like to look at the warehouse while we wait for him?"

"Yes, I would," Jeffery said.

David stood back and watched as Jeffery and Alec talked about what needed to be done in the warehouse.

~ ~ ~

A tall, slim, well dressed man in his late 50's stepped up next to David and asked, "Are you Alec's new friends?"

David shook the man's hand and said, "I guess so. I'm David Dodson."

"Jack Cooper. Alec's brother."

David could see the man trying to get a read on him, trying to see if he was some crazed biker out for revenge, or maybe someone that really wanted to try to do something.

Jack said, "I understand that you're going after some local drug dealers."

"Yes."

"OK, let me be sure I understand this. You're going after a local drug ring with two hundred pounds of explosives. Something that would force Homeland Security and the ATF to investigate. I would think a simple drive by shooting would accomplish the same thing and not bring in the FEDS. So using that logic, you're not very bright, or you're not telling me everything."

As David and Jack's eyes locked, David felt uneasy, and very perturbed at himself for getting caught in a lie.

Jack said, "Mr. Dodson, I've been a successful businessman for a long time, simple logic is my first tool to analyze any problem."

David took a long slow breath. "Mr. Cooper, your logic seems to serve you well. The truth is, I'm going to Mexico to find and take out the drug lord that killed my friend and the deputy, and stop him from killing anyone else."

Jack's intense stare meant that he was analyzing the new information and after a long pause he spoke in a slow drawn-out voice, "Damn, boy, you dream big and I like that."

"This hasn't been a dream, it's been more like a damn nightmare."

Jack turned and watched his brother and Jeffery talking. "My brother was in a very bad place two years ago. I know he wants some revenge for what happened to my nephew, but I don't want him to get his hopes up on a harebrained scheme and get in some kind of trouble. I don't think he could handle it. So I want to hear your plan."

David smiled and said, "I just got Alec to agree not to talk about this, and now it seems I have to tell everyone."

"One person cannot do a large project alone," said Jack. "A real leader always knows what his limitations are and when to ask for help. Let's go into Alec's office and talk."

As Jack sat down, David began, "I have several groups of people working on this project, and for security reasons I keep them separate and unknown to each other. I can't tell you who the other people are. I also can't tell you all the fine details of the mission. What I can tell you is an overall view of my plans. Will that be OK with you?"

"Sure. Tell me what you can, then I'll decide if I can help you."

"I have an Air Force pilot. I have an airplane. I have people making a bomb rack for the plane and the bomb casing. I have people building a GPS guidance system for the bombs. I'm hoping you and your brother can help with making something called RDX high explosives. When I have everything ready I intend to trailer the plane and the bombs to Mexico. The pilot will fly over the bastard's villa, drop the bombs, and, I hope, kill him. We then trailer the plane back home and everyone lives happily ever after."

Jack smiled and said, "That doesn't sound completely like a fairytale. It sounds like you have done a lot of work already."

"Yes, and everyone helping me has been touched in some way by what has happened the past week. I hardly have to ask for help. It's like this project has taken on a life of its own and everything suddenly seems to be falling into place."

"You have people making a GPS guidance system?"

"Yes," David said.

"My brother said that the man with you is a chemical engineer."

"Yes. A degree from MIT."

Jack stared at David and said, "How did a MIT chemical engineer become a biker?"

"The simple story is, he tried to do the right thing while working for a pharmaceutical company, and he ended up losing everything. I met him in a bar when he was hitting bottom and I took him in. That has proved to be one of the best moves I ever made."

"Have you ever pulled off something like this before?"

"Similar, yes. Most of my club members were Special Forces. I served in Vietnam with a member of my club. Another was in Iraq, the first Gulf War. Jeffery is the exception, he has no military background."

"OK," said Jack, "I have one other question. Do you make or sell drugs?"

David watched the expression on Jack's face as he answered, "Yes, but not the kind you're thinking about. My club makes moonshine, and we sell it all across the west coast and the central states to biker bars during motorcycle rallies. That's how we make most of our money."

Jack's expression softened as he studied David for a second, then he smiled and said, "Sometimes my father would drive to Bodega Bay to get some shine."

David smiled back and said, "Probably from my father."

Just then Alec and Jeffery walked into the office and Alec asked his brother, "What do you think?"

Jack paused, looking around the room at each man. "Let's make some explosives."

A big grin came across Alec's face until Jack said, "But Alec, you can't put the lab here. It would put Gary and your employees in too much danger. I'm sorry. Besides, it's too open here, someone might see it and think you're making meth and call the police."

"Where then?" asked Alec.

"That old warehouse on the back lot of the plant. It's an old metal building but it's still in good shape and I think the utilities are still on. I'll have my technicians check it out this afternoon. If it looks OK, I'll have them put the lab equipment together in the morning." He looked at Jeffery and said, "If everything looks OK, can you be at the plant in the morning to supervise?"

A surprised Jeffery smiled and said, "Yeah, sure. You know I only have one good arm?"

"Yes, I know. But I don't think that will be a problem, because a lot of my employees were very upset about what happened to the deputy and your friend. I'm sure I can find some people to help you."

"Thanks," said Jeffery.

David shook Jack's hand. "I appreciate your help," he said, "I can understand why you want to keep your brother out of trouble."

"These drug lords and cartels have too much power," said Jack. "I think it's time one got taken down a notch." He grinned. "And I like to see men dream big and succeed. Call me if you need anything else."

"Thanks," said David, "I would, but I don't think we should contact each other until all this is behind us. I'm afraid they may still be watching the clubhouse and I wouldn't want anyone to find out that you're helping me."

"If that's the case, Jeffery should come and stay with me until the explosives are made."

David looked at Jeffery and said, "That sounds like a good idea."

"I do need to stay near the lab," Jeffery said.

"David, during World War Two there was a secret project called *The Manhattan Project*," said Jack. "I think you should give this project a name, something like, *The Sonoma Project*."

David laughed. "I might do that."

Chapter 17
Colten Vineyards, west of Glen Ellen, California

Travis said, "Libby, I just looked at the specifications of the GPS and it may not work like I first thought. Commercial GPS receivers aren't designed to work at the speed the bomb is going to fall at."

"I know it will be dropping very fast," said Libby. "I calculate that at 8000 feet it will only take about 30 seconds to hit the ground."

Dennis saw Libby and Travis looking over the bomb drawing and asked, "Is there a problem?"

"I think we need to slow the bomb down so the GPS will work reliably," said Travis.

"How are we going to do that?" asked Dennis.

"A small parachute would be the easiest thing to do, something like a drogue parachute."

"How small?" asked Libby.

"Well, about two to three feet in diameter should slow it down enough for the GPS to work, and that will give your guidance system more time to control it."

"That doesn't sound very big," questioned Dennis.

"The wind might affect a large parachute," answered Travis, "and you don't want it to drop so slow that there isn't enough air going over the fins to have any control. I think a canopy about two or three feet in diameter should slow it down enough and a center spill hole will make the descent more stable." He drew it out on a note pad with Dennis and Libby watching and then he added, "Libby, you will have to program it to deploy after the bomb leaves the plane or it might get tangled up in the plane's prop. I would give it about a 5 second delay."

Dennis said, "Sounds good, but where do we get one?"

"It can't be that hard to make," said Travis. "I have seen them used in amateur rockets, so I bet I can find some plans on the Internet. Sharon has a sewing machine. I can get her to help me make something. Let me go to the house and see what I can find online."

~ ~ ~

Bodega Bay, California

A morning blanket of fog engulfed David as he walked out the front door of Jeffery's living room and started walking down the driveway toward the clubhouse. The cars on the coastal highway sounded close today and he smiled as the sound of the fog horn welcomed him to a new day. He came to a sudden stop when he heard a car engine crank near the driveway. He looked in the direction he thought it was coming from, but the fog was too thick to see anything. Then he heard the tires rolling over the rocks that were scattered on the narrow road as the car moved slowly past the driveway, headed to the coast. A narrow break in the fog gave him a quick glimpse of a dark car stopping as it reached the highway, but it was too far to see the make of the car or who was driving. David stood frozen, listening, as the cool moist air lightly touched his exposed skin. The fog horn spoke again, but David was not smiling now.

He entered the clubhouse with his pistol drawn and searched each room twice to convince himself that no one else was there. Then he walked out to the garage to check his bike. He checked the fluids and cranked it up. He let the engine idle for several minutes to warm up, then scanned the gauges, reassuring himself that everything was OK before turning it back off. Then he grabbed a clean rag and started wiping off the week long accumulation of dust. Finally, he walked back into the house, got clothes from his closet and changed, and walked to the front window where he stared toward the bay watching the sun burning away the last of the morning fog.

David returned to the garage and pushed the button to open the big garage door. He sat on his bike and waited for the whining electric garage door motor to complete its job before he restarted his bike. An uneasy feeling swept over him as he slipped the transmission into gear. He released the clutch, and slowly eased his way down the driveway to the Bay Hwy. and past the bay, keeping one eye on his rear-view mirror, expecting to see a dark car tailing him. Soon, he was moving down the Bodega Hwy, and had to increase his speed to keep up with the heavy commuter traffic. Miles passed until he had to stop at a light soon after reaching the Santa Rosa city limits. Again, he scanned the cars around him, looking for the black car and the reason for the uneasy feeling.

Moments later a red Mini Cooper S Convertible pulled up on his right side, driven by an attractive middle aged woman. David gave her a quick glance, then heard the engine rev up on the little car. He turned again to see the woman staring at him, and he gave his throttle a quick twist. She grinned as she turned her head back to the light, just as it turned green. David was surprised by how fast the Mini Cooper took off from a dead stop. He took off after her, smoothly shifting through each gear as he quickly pulled closer to the woman in the red car. He was almost up to her bumper when the next light turned red and he had to back off. She pulled to a stop at the light, and waited until David was beside her. They smiled at each other, then she turned right and waved at David as she drove off. He thought about following her, talking to her, asking her out for drinks, and maybe taking their little flirtatious street race to another level. But his smile slowly dissolved as the uneasy feeling found its way back, making him remember to stay focused and to take care of business first. He continued watching the woman in the little red car move further and further away, and didn't notice the light turning green until someone behind him tapped their horn. David took off straight ahead, and waved at the car behind him, but his mind was still on the woman in the Mini Copper, wishing he could thank her for the distraction.

~ ~ ~

Santa Rosa, California

David pulled into a McDonald's restaurant, parked the bike, went inside and ordered a coffee. He sat down at a corner booth so he could watch the other customers, and pulled out his smart phone and connected to the restaurant's WiFi. He read all the emails and sent a reply saying that everything was starting to come together and thanking everyone for their help.

A sudden sensation of being watched came over him, and when he finished the email, he closed that app, but kept staring at his phone as he pressed the camera shortcut. Being careful and trying not to draw attention, he very slowly panned the phone around the room, zooming in on different people to see if anyone was watching him. A neatly dressed man with short hair, about 30 years old, with the obvious bulge of a gun under his jacket, was sitting across the room. David got up, walked across the room, and stopped at the trash container. He gave the man a quick glance as he threw his cup away. The man never looked up. David walked to his bike, and pretended to check something on the bike as he watched the man get into the passenger seat of a dark car. He pulled out onto the street and a few seconds later, the dark car did the same.

The car followed David as he made his way closer to the center of town. David stopped and parked on the street in front of an old Mom-and-Pop store.

He walked into the store, and the old salesclerk said, "Hello, David. It's been a long time. Is there something I can get you?"

He gave the salesclerk a 20 dollar bill and said, "No, Paul, I know what I want. I'm going to get a water gun and a small funnel and go out the back if that's OK."

"Why out the back?"

David smiled. "I'm going to play a trick on someone. You can keep the change."

"Thank you, David. You have a good day."

David walked around the side of the building to the street. He could see the dark car parked a couple of parking places from his bike. He quietly walked up from behind, then quickly opened the back door, hopped into the back seat and put the water gun to the back of the passenger's head.

"Let me have your guns, one at a time, passenger first. NOW!," ordered David.

He pulled the clip out of each gun and placed the guns on the floor of the back seat. "OK, boys, I want your ID and your wallets now."

He pulled the drivers license out of each wallet, then took a photo of each license with his cell phone. He read out loud the name and address on each license.

Next he opened the badge holder and said, "Wow, the FBI. Please tell me, why is the fumbling bureau of idiots following me?"

The two men just looked at each other. The driver was clearly agitated, but held his anger in as he spoke in a slow and calm voice, "Mr. Dodson, you need to put the gun down before you get into any more trouble."

David shoved the gun harder into the passenger's head and said,

"Sure, as soon as you answer my question."

The passenger said, "OK, we're here to see if your brother came back because of his daughter's death."

"So, you bastards are still looking for him. Take the keys to the car and throw them outside, then handcuff yourself to the steering wheel."

David got out and walked to the passenger window.

"My brother is not here. Boys, don't follow me anymore. I don't want you to get hurt."

David aimed the gun at the driver's crotch and pulled the trigger several times and quickly switched his aim to the passenger and again pulled the trigger several times. Each man jumped as the liquid struck him.

The driver was so enraged that his face turned red, and he looked like he was about to explode. He yelled at David, "You son of a bitch, you just assaulted federal officers!"

David pulled out his phone and took a photo of them as they stared back at him. He smiled and said, "Thank you, another photo for my wall of shame." Then he got on his bike, cranked it up, and drove off without even looking back at the two men.

The passenger said, "A FUCKING WATER GUN!"

The driver sniffed the air, then looked at the passenger and said, "That's not water, it's PISS!"

~ ~ ~

Colten Vineyards, west of Glen Ellen, California

"WAY TO GO, GUYS!" yelled Travis as he, Libby, and Randy leaned over a workbench intently watching the rudders on their first GPS guidance system. Dennis and Max walked over to the workbench to watch as the rudders leaned right, then left, and back again.

"What's going on?" asked Max.

"Right now Libby's computer is simulating a GPS receiver," answered Randy. "It's sending different GPS coordinates out the USB port, to the GPS input of the micro controller board. The controller board reads the data and decides if it's off course. If it thinks a correction is necessary, it calculates how much and in what direction. Then it sends the new data to the servo controller board that makes the servos move the rudders in the proper direction."

Max looked from Randy to Dennis and back, then looked back at the rudders moving back and forth, and asked, "Is it working correctly?"

Libby looked up at Max, and said, "Yes, our prototype seems to be working very well. I want to continue testing the software this afternoon. If everything still looks OK, tonight we can put everything into one of the bomb casings for testing tomorrow."

"For testing?" asked Dennis. "You mean it will be ready to drop from the plane?"

Libby grinned and said, "Yes."

Then they looked back at the rudders, silently watching their smooth movement as they danced along with the changing display of each new GPS coordinate being sent by Libby's computer.

~ ~ ~

The local weather forecast called for clear skies, light NW winds, with a high of 88. The temperature was 78 now, but to a nervous Travis it seemed much warmer. As he drove from the house to the hangar, he went over a mental checklist, looking for anything that he might have missed, anything that would cause a problem or possibly a fatal crash.

The large hangar door was already up as he arrived and he pulled to a stop just inside. Libby, Dennis, and Max were standing next to the bomb, talking. He got out, walked toward them, stopped, then smiled at Libby, bowed, and with a hand gesture to the utility cart, said, "Your chariot awaits, fair maiden."

Libby laughed, turned to pick up her laptop and GPS receiver and said, "When this is over, I'm going to have Jeffery come here for lessons from this man."

Dennis and Max started laughing. "Sorry, Libby," said Max. "Remember he has been around us for a while now, it may be too late."

Still smiling, she turned her head and stuck her tongue out at Max.

Travis drove the cart to a location in the center of his property that was farthest from any buildings. They parked next to the red flag that Travis had already placed between the end of the runway and a row of grape vines.

He got out and held the GPS up high with his right hand. She plugged the GPS receiver into the laptop and a smile spread across her face as they waited for the GPS to lock onto as many satellites as it could.

"What are you smiling about?" he asked.

"You look like the Statue of Liberty," she said, and they both started laughing.

Libby got her reading and saved the data and Travis climbed back in the utility cart and started back to the hangar. "I'm a little scared," she suddenly said. "I've never done anything like this before and I can't imagine what you feel like having to fly that plane this morning."

He stopped the cart, and for a few moments stared down the runway to the hangar. Then he turned to look at Libby and said, "I would be lying if I said I wasn't scared too." He paused for another moment. "When David told me his plan, I really wasn't sure if we could do something like this. But over the past few days, watching all of you work so hard, I believe now that we have a very good chance of making this happen."

She smiled. "Thanks, it's good to hear someone say that." He smiled back and pressed the accelerator. A few seconds passed when she added, "I want to thank you for doing all this. We couldn't have done any of this without your help."

"Brad was my friend, too and I owed him a lot."

They were soon back at the hangar and Libby plugged her laptop into the bomb's micro controller and loaded the GPS coordinates. Travis walked around the airplane, checking the engine, tires, and rudder, while Dennis and Max jacked up the test bomb to the rack and secured it to the bomb rack release system.

After they crawled out from under the plane, Libby asked, "OK, are we ready? Does anyone have any questions?"

"Why can't the bomb be dropped higher than 8000 feet?" Dennis asked.

Travis said, "The higher the altitude the lower the temperature, especially at night, and that will affect the electronics."

"And at 8000 feet," said Libby, "the control system has less than 50 seconds to work before the bomb hits the ground. So Travis, remember the less horizontal speed the better. You're going to have to slow the plane down to just above stall speed before you release and you'll need to be very, very close to the target's GPS coordinates."

"I can do that."

Randy asked, "Libby, are you doing any data logging to look at later?"

"Yeah. I'm storing it on a flash drive. I just hope it will survive the crash."

Dennis, Max, and Travis pushed the Long-EZ plane out of the hangar. Travis got into the plane, started the engine, and quickly waved to everyone as he taxied the short distance to the runway. Everyone silently watched as Travis took off. They all walked to the end of the hangar to watch the target, the red flag at the end of the runway.

Travis flew north until he reached 8000 feet above sea level. He leveled off, then banked the plane left to turn around. When the plane's cockpit GPS system displayed that he was 2 miles from the target, he backed off the throttle, and lowered the bomb rack. He adjusted the trim; keeping everything level. A wave of anxiety started to move through him as he waited for the last few seconds to pass. Those seconds seemed to take forever. The temperature inside the cockpit was cool, but his hands were starting to sweat as he placed his left hand on the bomb release lever. He made slight adjustments with his feet to the rudder while watching the GPS. He pulled the release lever, and the sudden loss of the 50 pound bomb caused the plane to jerk up, almost causing him to panic. Long seconds passed as he scanned the instruments and listened for any unusual sounds and when he was sure that the bomb had missed the rear propeller, and everything was normal, he remembered to breathe again.

Travis looked back over his shoulder and said, "God, I hope that doesn't hit my house."

The size and the speed that the bomb was dropping made it very difficult to see. Everyone on the ground watched, unable to see anything until the last 2000 feet. And then only because of the 2 foot drogue parachute that was being dragged behind it. They all jumped when they heard the 50 pound test bomb hit the ground at over 300 MPH.

Travis circled the runway, dropping in altitude, and with each pass looked to see if there was a hole in the roof of his house. As he made his landing approach, he took a quick look at the flag near the end of the runway and saw a hole in the ground about 55 feet away from it.

"Not too bad," he said.

He landed, taxied next to the hangar, turned the engine off, and opened the canopy. "I'm not sure, but I think it hit about 55 feet away," he yelled as he climbed out.

"I need to get that flash drive to see what course it took as it dropped," said Libby.

Max grabbed some shovels and hopped onto the utility cart with Dennis, Travis, and Libby.

As they drove down the runway, Travis smiled at Libby and said, "I think it did very well for our first test."

"Yes, but we have to get it closer."

Dennis and Max started digging as soon as they arrived. When they had enough dug out, they opened the back of the test bomb to access the control board and found the flash drive still connected. Dennis reached in, flipped the master power switch off, and watched the LED power indicator slowly dim until it went out completely. He then disconnected the flash drive and handed it to Libby.

Then Dennis asked Travis, "Do you want us to dig it all the way out now?"

"No, right now let's get Libby back to her computer so she can analyze her data. We can come back later with the tractor and pull it out."

Libby plugged the flash drive into her computer as soon as they got back to the hangar. Moments later, a graph of the bomb's flight path displayed on her screen.

"Travis, look at this," Libby said as she pointed to the screen. "You released it right on target, but the path looks like it overshot. It spent all its time trying to get back to the target coordinates, but didn't have time to make it. I think next time you need to release it several seconds before you reach the target coordinates, that would let it glide into the target coordinates. What do you think?"

Travis studied the screen, "How much lead time should I give it?"

"Let me study the flight path and we can talk about it later."

"Libby, when can we have another ready to test?" asked Dennis.

"If everyone can help, we should have 3 or 4 ready after lunch."

~ ~ ~

Colten Vineyards, west of Glen Ellen, California

Libby ran her test software on each of the test bombs. As she completed the test on the last one, she was so tired that the dancing movements of the rudders was hypnotizing and her mind began wandering back to the night she and Jeffery had spent together, holding, touching, and loving each other. With all that had happened, that night seemed so long ago. It almost felt like it was just a dream. But she knew it wasn't, because she could still see the look in his eyes, and feel the heat of each kiss and his tender touch on her breasts and hips and thighs. She wished he was here, now, holding her tight, telling her that everything was going to be OK, that they would soon be free of the drug lord who wanted to kill her.

"Is everything OK, Lib?" asked Kate.

Libby turned to look at Kate and said, "Oh, yeah, they all seem to be working fine. I was just daydreaming."

Kate put her arm around Libby's shoulders. "You're going to see him soon."

Libby laughed. "Am I that obvious?"

"Well, yeah," said Kate, laughing, too.

Libby moved away from Kate as she turned off the power to the bomb guidance system and unplugged her computer.

"How did you learn to do this, anyway?" asked Kate.

"I was in junior high. Back then the school just had one PC computer in each classroom and that was just for the teacher to use. I was very shy then, didn't have friends. But one day my science teacher saw me looking at the computer. We started talking and she asked me if I wanted to come by after school and learn to use it. Of course I said yes. She showed me how to use some of the programs on it. After about a week, she could tell I was hooked. One day she told me that the computer came with a programming language called Basic. She handed me a book on how to program in Basic and let me take it home. I read that book from cover to cover over the weekend. The next Monday she let me write my first program. After that I knew I had to have one of my own. Christmas was very close, so I asked my parents if they would help me buy one. I used all the money that I had saved and they gave me the rest. I kept learning other programming languages and in high school I was on the Internet all the time. The Internet was still very new then and it was mostly boys. They didn't treat girls very well, so I pretended to be a boy. I made online friends and found out that companies would hire programmers online. I managed to get several programming jobs, and I never had to meet the bosses or interact with other people. They didn't know I was a girl and still in high school."

Kate laughed and said, "That's cool. But how did they pay you?"

"I had them make the checks out to my father. He would go to the bank, cash them, and put the money into my savings account." She smiled then and said, "During my senior year I purchased a used Vespa scooter. I paid cash for it and I was so proud of that scooter, I drove it everywhere."

"I bet you were at the top of the class in school."

Libby grinned. "Well, I was in science."

"OK, smarty," Kate teased. "Do you think you would have liked going to college?"

"I'm not sure. I do know I could have gotten scholarships to pay for college, but my father died and I felt like I needed to stay home and help my mom."

"Are they ready?" asked Dennis as he and Travis joined them.

"They're all yours," said Libby.

"How soon before the target coordinates should I release this time?" Travis asked.

"On this test, I'm going to set the release coordinates on your cockpit GPS system to about four seconds before target coordinates. Then on the next test, eight seconds. I hope we can fine tune everything with the last two test drops."

"Does that mean we could be through testing today?" asked Dennis.

"We could," said Libby, holding up her crossed fingers.

"Dennis, do we have the GPS coordinates of the real target in Mexico?" asked Travis.

"No, not yet."

"How are we going to get that?"

"I guess I'll have to go down there and get it."

"How?" asked Libby. "Just walk up to the building with a GPS receiver? It will be guarded, won't it?"

"Yeah, I'm sure it will be," said Dennis. "David and I are going to use a laser range finder system to calculate the coordinates."

"You have to be able to see the target to do that, right?" said Travis.

"Yeah. That's right. Why?"

"I may have a way to do it without putting anyone in danger," said

Travis. "Several companies are now making remote control UAVs."

"What's that?" asked Libby.

"Unmanned Aerial Vehicles. I'm thinking Quadcopters, they're like helicopters, but a lot easier to use. You control them using a RC controller, like the one my son uses for his airplane. Some companies have installed video cameras on them so you can guide them while looking at a computer monitor."

"So you don't have to be in view of the target," said Libby. "You fly the UAV to the target using the onboard video camera, take a GPS reading, then fly it back."

Travis smiled. "That's right."

Dennis said, "I don't think David or I would know how to operate one."

"I can," said Travis.

"That would put you in too much danger. I can't ask you to do that," said Dennis.

"I think it would be less dangerous to use the UAV than to get close enough to use a range finder," said Travis, "and it would allow us to use the same GPS receiver that we're using on the bombs, which should give us even more accuracy."

"Do you think your wife would let you do something like this?" asked Dennis.

"If I explain exactly what I'm doing. I think she will agree."

"Let me talk to David. OK?"

"OK," said Travis, "but I'm going to talk to Sharon about it tonight and order what we need."

Dennis nodded. "OK," he said. He turned then and saw Max and Randy talking by the hangar doors. "Max," he yelled, "we could use some help over here," and he pointed to the bomb lying on the bench.

Dennis and Max secured the test bomb to the rack. Then Travis started the engine, taxied to the runway and flew off for the second test.

"What do you think of Travis's idea of using a UAV?" Dennis asked Libby as they watched the flag.

"I don't want anyone else to get hurt, so I think it would be a lot safer to try that first. If that doesn't work, then use the range finder."

Dennis thought for a few seconds then said, "Yeah, I agree."

~ ~ ~

Las Vegas, Nevada

Staring at his computer at the photos from the surveillance cameras hidden in the barrels, Joe said, "I like your new boyfriend."

Candy said, "Who?" as she looked over Joe's shoulder. "You mean the tall good looking guy at the warehouse. Yeah, he would do in a pinch."

Joe laughed. "Yeah, I bet he would."

"He's nice. He comes out to talk each time I stop to replace the battery and swap cameras."

"OK, just don't let him catch on to what you're really doing."

"I'm careful. I give him a good view of my butt, so he stays distracted."

Joe laughed. "Girl, I really hate that you have to work your butt off."

She laughed, too. "Anything for you, Joe."

Joe then carefully studied each photo, cataloging each into a database with the date, the time, and any other information that seemed important.

When he was through, he asked Candy to look at several of them. "Four or five times every evening, these unmarked trucks leave, and come back." he said.

"Do you think that's how they're delivering the drugs?" Candy asked.

"Yeah. I think I'll tell Rodriguez, he needs to follow them to see what they're doing."

~ ~ ~

Detective Rodriquez needed his caffeine fix, and he felt he deserved it after a long stressful day. The aroma of the coffee was enticing, begging him to indulge himself and take a sip. But he knew it was too hot to drink so he sat it down next to his computer and started reading Joe's emails. After reading the last message, he looked at his watch and said, "Shit!" when he realized he only had 10 minutes to get to the warehouse. He grabbed his laptop and left the coffee shop, leaving behind his needed caffeine fix, knowing that it would get cold before he ever got to drink it.

The last truck was pulling out of the driveway when he reached the warehouse. He knew that a one man tail would be difficult to pull off without being noticed, but he stayed as close as he could. He lost the truck when he was stopped by a traffic light and when he got the green, he drove slowly, looking down each side street. He was about to give up when he saw it. A man was handing out backpacks to three kids on bikes. Rodriquez watched the kids attach smart phones to their handlebars, then ride off in different directions. The truck driver got back into the truck and drove off. Rodriquez followed a little closer, trying not to lose the truck again. The next time it stopped, four kids on bikes rode up and stopped directly behind the truck. Again, the driver got out and handed each kid a backpack, and again each kid put the pack on his back, attached the smart phone to the handlebars, and rode off.

The driver got back into the truck and drove off again. This time Rodriquez pulled a video camera out of a bag and checked to be sure it was working. He followed the truck and saw the same thing repeated. This time he was ready, and recorded everything. He followed the truck to the next stop, but instead of staying behind, he drove past the truck and parked half a block in front of it. He waited and watched as one of the kids rode his bike past him. The kid stopped just 100 feet away and handed someone in a car a small package. The kid reached over to the handlebar and touched the smart phone, then rode off to another car further down the road, and did the same thing.

"Damn, they're using kids to deliver the drugs," Rodriquez said as he watched the truck drive past him. This time he decided not to follow. He felt he was already pushing his luck. He sat in the car and played back the recording. He decided to go to his apartment and copy the recording to the computer flash drive that Joe gave him. He wanted to have everything ready to send a copy of the video to Joe first thing in the morning.

~ ~ ~

Colten Vineyards, west of Glen Ellen, California

"I don't like it," said Sharon.

"If I don't, it will put more people in danger. And risk everything that we have done so far," said Travis.

Sharon stared at Travis as she tried to calm down and then asked, "There's no other way to do this?"

"It's the safest and most accurate way to get the information we need."

"Sharon, I understand your concern," said Dennis. "And I promise you that I will protect him as best as I can. But I cannot guarantee anything and if you say no, then David and I will find another way."

"And Libby thinks this will work?" asked Sharon. "That this is the best way of getting the information you need?"

"Yes," said Travis.

The boys noticed that Sharon's mood had changed. She seemed more anxious, scared, and she tried to cover it up when she asked in a voice that hinted of anger, "Speaking of Libby, when am I going to get my mailbox fixed?"

"I'm sorry about the mailbox, I have been a little busy."

Dennis added, "The plane is done, so Max and I can replace the mailbox. First thing in the morning, I'll go to the hardware store and buy the best one they have."

"Thanks, but just replace it with the same thing. That road is narrow and it has to be replaced often."

She paused for a long breath, then asked Travis, "When will you leave for Mexico?"

"In a few days. I have some equipment to order first."

"How long will you be gone?"

"It should take 3 days," answered Travis. "One to fly down. One to do the job, and one to fly back. If there's bad weather it may take longer."

"Are you going to fly our plane?"

"No, commercial will be faster. And if we do this at night, we can sleep on the way back."

"When I said that we should help, I never realized that you would run off to Mexico and turn into James Bond." She put her arms around Travis. "You better stay away from all those young senoritas."

Travis laughed. "You know that you're the only Bond girl for me." He pulled her close and kissed her.

She looked over at Dennis and said, "Dennis, you better bring him back safe, understand?"

"Yes, ma'am."

~ ~ ~

Las Vegas, Nevada

"Have you found any of the money yet?" asked Captain Coleman.

Rodriguez looked up from his desk and said, "What money?"

"The money that Kate Dodson stole from the bank. Isn't that what you're working on?"

"Yes. Yes, I'm sorry, I haven't found anything yet."

"Well, it's time to turn it over to financial crimes. They may be better equipped to see what she did with it."

"Yes, sir. I'll get my notes together and take it to them now," said Rodriguez.

"Good. What other cases are you working on?"

"I thought I would look at the car bombing on I-15. It's still an open case."

"That's the Lara Manning case, right?"

"Yes, she and her family were killed."

"I already have someone working on that one."

"Who?"

"Don't worry about that. I want you to work with the new guys, John and Glen. They have several open cases that need some fresh eyes."

"Yes, sir," said Rodriguez.

"Go ahead and take the files over to financial crimes. When you get back, talk to them to see where they're at on their cases."

"Yes, sir," said Rodriquez. He started gathering the files and putting them into a folder.

The captain walked away, motioning from his doorway for John Lawson and Glen Carter to come to his office.

Still moving files around, Rodriquez watched the captain close his door when the two men entered. He turned to the detective at the desk next to him and softly asked, "Have you noticed that the captain always closes his door when he's talking to those two? Do you know what's going on?"

The detective just shrugged his shoulders and went back to his own paperwork.

Rodriguez stared at the closed door again, then stood up, grabbed the folder, turned, and walked out of the room, knowing that something wasn't right.

~ ~ ~

Las Vegas, Nevada

Candy was in the kitchen pouring coffee when she heard Joe say, "Crap!"

"What's wrong?" she asked, as she handed him his cup.

"Rodriguez just sent me an email. His captain just assigned him to work with two other detectives. It's going to limit what he will be able to do for us. Also, he thinks the captain may be on to him, and he's suspicious of these detectives, too."

"What are we going to do?"

"I don't know yet. Wait and see what happens, I guess."

"Have you heard from Libby lately?" asked Candy.

"Not since the email I told you about a few days ago when she said that things are coming together. Whatever that means."

"I know you're worried about her. But she's not going to give us any details. The less we know about what they're doing, the safer they are."

He took a sip of coffee. "Yeah."

~ ~ ~

Puerto Vallarta, Mexico

Travis and Dennis walked out of the Puerto Vallarta International Airport into the stifling hot and humid Mexican air. Travis saw a man standing by a van holding a sign with their hotel's name and they walked over and loaded their bags in the back.

Two men in their mid-twenties approached the van. As the driver loaded their bags, they introduced themselves as Bobby and Mike. Dennis noticed one of them take the other's hand and gently squeeze it.

Tired from the long flight and the heat, Dennis entered the van first and sat in the back row. Travis sat beside him and Bobby and Mike sat in the middle seats. The driver gave a running commentary on the restaurants, places to visit, and the history of the area, pointing some of them out as they passed. But the old van's air conditioner was barely better than nothing, like one ice cube in a big pot of hot water, and the drive to the hotel seemed to be taking forever.

Travis was looking at a map of the area on his smart phone. The day before, he had preloaded GPS way-points showing the approximate location of the Cortez Villa and the location of their hotel. He watched the display as they moved closer to the red dot marking the location of the villa and he looked up and pointed it out to Dennis as they drove by the large ornate gate blocking the driveway.

"Who lives there?" asked Bobby.

"All I know," said the driver, "is that about a year ago a very rich businessman finished building a large home, a mansion, up there that overlooks the ocean. He's only there on the weekends and it's heavily guarded when he's there."

A minute later the driver turned into the hotel's driveway and stopped in front of the lobby. This part of the hotel was small with ten rooms all facing the ocean. The lobby was located at the north side of the building with a small outdoor bar near a small rocky hill that spilled into the ocean. The south part of the property had ten bungalows, eight of them by the beach, two on top of a thirty foot hill that overlooked the ocean. The hill's rocky face protruded twenty-five feet into the ocean forming a private beach area for the hotel. This hill also kept the beach on the south side private for Cortez and his guests to enjoy.

"I'm expecting a package, has it arrived?" Travis asked the clerk at the front desk.

"No, sir," answered the clerk. "We haven't had any packages delivered. Most of the time packages arrive before noon, so it will probably come in tomorrow."

"OK, I'll check back then."

The clerk handed Travis two keys, one for the bungalow and one for a golf cart that was parked outside. Then he picked up a map of the hotel and marked the route to their bungalow on the hill.

"Could I have another set of keys, please?" asked Travis.

"Of course, sir," answered the clerk as he handed him the keys.

Travis and Dennis loaded their bags onto the back of the cart and drove away.

"We didn't get our package?" asked Dennis.

"No, he said tomorrow, but it should arrive before noon."

"That's OK, we can do a little scouting in the morning. Right now, I want to drop off the bags, then get something to eat."

"That sounds good to me, too."

Travis opened the door as Dennis grabbed the bags.

Dennis saw Travis standing just inside the door looking around and asked, "Is something wrong?"

"Yeah, only one bed."

"Wow, how romantic."

Travis looked at Dennis. "You OK with this?"

Dennis smiled. "Sure, it's a big bed, but where are you going to sleep?"

"I think I'll call the desk and ask for a cot."

"No, wait," said Dennis. "This is a great location. We want to keep a very low profile and I don't want to make any waves with the staff. We can manage with this for a few nights."

They left the bags, locked the door, and walked back to the cart.

Travis saw Bobby and Mike unloading their cart at the bungalow next door and said, "We have neighbors."

"They'll be too focused on each other to pay any attention to us," said Dennis.

"Yeah, I think you're right," said Travis, as he started the cart to drive to the bar for drinks and dinner.

~ ~ ~

Hotel, north of Cortez villa

Dennis and Travis relaxed at a table at the open air bar, drinking beers, listening to the soft Spanish guitar playing through the speakers, and enjoying the ocean breeze and the changing colors of the clouds as the sun sank into the ocean.

Travis broke the mood when he slurred, "Did you know that the oldest winery in the Americas is here in Mexico?"

"I did not know that," Dennis said. He grinned as he realized that they were both a little wasted from the combination of the long exhausting day, the lack of a good meal, and the beers.

Inspired by his intoxication, Travis rambled on about the history of wine making until the waiter brought their fish tacos, Spanish rice, black beans, and more beer. With the sight of the food and the aroma filling the air around them, both men forgot the history lesson and grabbed their forks, wasting no time making the food vanish.

Halfway through their meal a man sitting a few tables away with a woman slammed his fist on the table and yelled, "Bitch! Don't tell me I can't call them fagots. Let's get out of here."

Travis and Dennis stopped eating and gave each other a quick glance. They heard a chair scraping across the tile floor and looked at the muscular, white man, six feet tall with short blond hair, leaning on his chair for support.

The heavily intoxicated man staggered toward the exit, yelling "Let's go!" to the woman still sitting at the table.

The woman stood up and said as she walked by, "I'm sorry, guys, he's been drinking all day."

The man turned around to her. "Come on! Don't be talking to those fags!"

Travis glanced at Dennis and noticed the muscles in his arms and neck flexing and he saw his hand slowly squeeze into a fist, forming a death grip around the fork he was still holding as he watched the man stagger to the exit.

"Dennis, let it go," said Travis. "We're here to do a job and keep a low profile."

Dennis continued watching as the man and woman made their way to the exit. Just then Bobby and Mike walked in and stopped when the man got in front of them and said, "Look, some more of them!" Stunned, Bobby and Mike watched as the man, helped by the woman, turned back to the exit and staggered out.

~ ~ ~

Dennis was suddenly wide awake when his alarm went off at 05:00 AM. He quickly turned it off and waited as Travis turned over and went back to sleep. Then he slipped out of bed and put on pants, a long sleeved shirt, and boots. He got his binoculars and a flashlight out of his bag, and slipped outside, quietly closing the door.

He walked around the south side of the bungalows. He could see the outline of jungle growth at the foot of the hills in the early morning light and he walked toward it. He searched the heavy growth looking for a recent path that might lead around, or over, the hill to the beach on the other side. He stopped near a boulder where the foliage was only waist high. He turned on the flashlight and carefully walked into the jungle.

The morning sun could not penetrate the trees' canopy, so the flashlight was his only light source and the built in compass his only means of direction. The old path seemed to hug the inland side of the rocky hill, so he felt comfortable with only the occasional look at the compass. The sounds of the surf breaking ashore grew louder as he made his way around to the south side of the hill. He stopped short of the beach to listen, and to watch for any guards that might be posted nearby. After a minute he stuck out his head to do a quick look down the beach. He then scanned the beach and the tree line again using the binoculars. Dennis felt the beach was deserted, but his military training said to keep his guard up, especially with no backup. He estimated the beach was 400 yards long and averaged 75 feet wide with scattered rock formations that a guard, or he, could hide behind. He started walking to the south end of the beach, making mental notes of places to hide and good locations to set up the equipment when he and Travis returned the next night. He noticed that he was able to see more detail in the growth of the jungle. He looked at his watch, 06:00 AM. The sun was higher. That made him easier to see. Just 100 yards away was the golf cart path that led to the top of the hill where Cortez's villa overlooked the ocean. Dennis wanted to go further but decided it was too risky. With the binoculars he made one last scan of the beach and cart path, and he saw the security camera looking down the cart path to the beach, and him.

"Oh shit, a security camera," Dennis mumbled to himself as he slowly walked closer to the tree line to hide in the dark shade.

He hoped the camera was just monitoring the cart path and a small area of the beach. But he couldn't take the chance that someone had seen him so he turned and started back, staying as close to the tree line as possible, hiding in the shade. Halfway back he noticed that everything was getting brighter. Now he was concerned that someone might see him come out of the jungle near the bungalows. Comfortable that he was out of view of the Cortez security camera, he picked up his pace. He stopped when he reached the hill at the north end of the beach. He turned around and watched the beach for several seconds, catching his breath, and making sure that no one was coming after him.

Still breathing hard he said to himself, "Damn, I'm too old for this."

He quickly followed the path back around the foot of the hill. As he came out of the jungle he noticed that lights were on in some bungalows. He took a quick look at his watch, 07:00 AM. He walked up the hill to their bungalow. The light was on and he could see Travis sitting at the desk looking at his computer.

Travis turned to the door when he heard it open. "How did it go?" he asked.

"A slight problem. There's a camera looking down the beach from the south side. We'll have to stay closer to the tree line and get no closer than 150 yards from the building."

"I can work with that," said Travis.

~ ~ ~

"Let's get some lunch and see if our package is in," said Travis.

"OK."

They parked their cart and walked to the front desk and asked if their package had arrived, but the sudden crash of a chair being thrown against the wall got everyone's attention. Dennis went quickly into the bar and saw Bobby sitting on the floor looking up at the drunk man from the night before.

Everyone's eyes were on the man towering over Bobby as he yelled, "I'm going to kick the shit out of you, fagot."

Dennis moved quickly and slid his arm around the man's neck from behind. He outweighed Dennis by 20 pounds, and he struggled, knocking over tables and chairs, but all the drinks he'd had that morning slowed his speed and maneuverability. They both fell to the floor, but Dennis kept the pressure on the man's neck and the choke hold slowly started to work until finally his grip on Dennis's arm relaxed and his hands fell to the floor next to his sleeping body.

Dennis looked up as Travis extended his hand. He grabbed it and Travis helped him up.

"Are you OK?" asked Travis.

"Yeah."

The front desk clerk came up to Travis and Dennis, and said, "I called the police. They should be here soon."

Dennis looked at Travis, then he looked at the clerk and said, "I cannot have any record of being here. What can I do to keep my name out of this?"

"I understand," said the clerk, "we have a lot of male couples who want to be very discreet. I'll tell the police something and keep you out of it."

Bobby and Mike were standing nearby. Bobby walked over to Dennis and threw his arms around him giving him a hug. "Thank you," he said.

"Would you like to get even with this guy?" asked Dennis.

"How?"

"Get his phone, take some photographs of you and Mike together with him, and send them to everyone in his contact list. Text everyone that he has found some new friends here."

"I'll help you if you want to do that," said the clerk, "but we'll need to hurry."

"Where's the woman he was with?" asked Travis.

"She left this morning, with a black eye."

"Damn, I hate mean drunks," said Dennis.

Travis and Dennis picked the man up and put him in a chair beside Bobby and Mike. The clerk took the man's phone and started taking photos.

Travis said, "We're going to get our package and go. Are you good here?"

"Sure," said the clerk, "and thanks."

They walked out of the bar to the front desk.

Travis took the package from behind the counter. "Got it."

Two policemen walked into the lobby as Travis and Dennis walked by the bar door.

"What the hell!" echoed out of the bar as the man started to come to.

They stopped at the door and watched.

The man was trying to stand up. He managed to get up and was taking a swing at the clerk just as the police entered the bar. They tackled the man, pulled his arms around his back, and put handcuffs on him.

They heard the clerk tell the police that the man had been trying to proposition the male guests and that he was asking him to stop.

Dennis looked at Travis. "Let's go," he said.

As they left the lobby, Travis said, "Man, I thought we were going to keep a low profile."

Dennis smiled. "Sorry, Dear."

Chapter 18
Petaluma, California

Each time David down shifted, a deep rumbling sound bellowed from each muffler, then echoed from the neighboring buildings. He slowly pulled his bike into the mostly empty gravel parking lot of the Petaluma Men's Club. He backed the bike up against the building, took off his helmet, and ran his hands through his hair as the sign in the parking lot came on and started to flicker its neon "Welcome," to guide the other weary patrons. The ride in the cool evening air was a welcome change from the day's heat and the stress of worrying if his plan was going to work. David was always good at making plans, and this one was easily falling into place, a little too easy, and that had him worried. He looked at the sign again and smiled as it stopped flickering. *I need a distraction*, he thought, *and nothing clears the mind better than a long ride, a good drink, and some company. Now for the drink and company, even if the company is just a table dance.*

The bouncer at the front door said, "Hi, David," when he walked past and sat down at one of the tables.

The night was early and there were just a few customers in the building watching the young blond on stage dancing and swinging from a pole.

A smiling, busty, 32 year old redhead placed a drink in front of David and said, "Here you go, Honey. I went ahead and got you your usual."

"Hi, Red, how you been?" asked David.

"About the same. When you have two kids and a lazy old man, it's a pleasure to come to work and get some peace."

David laughed. "Well girl, you still look good and I would love it if you would run away with me."

"Thanks, but I need to stay here and be sure the kids get fed. You let me know when you're ready for a table dance, OK, Honey?"

He picked up his drink, gave her a wink and said, "Sure, Red."

He sipped his drink while watching the girl performing on stage, wondering, *how can she hang from that pole like that.*

Red walked by with a drink for one of the other customers. David smiled as he watched her place the drink on the table, bending over, showing off her Orange County license plate, or trash stamp, as some people call them. He got her attention when she turned around.

"Are you ready, Honey?"

David smiled. "Yeah."

"Would you like a private dance in the back?"

"Sure, Red, why not."

She took him to a small room in the back and shut the door. He paid her, then sat down as she turned on a CD player. She bent over, her eyes following his, then gently slid her hands between David's legs and spread them apart. As she stood up she slowly moved her body between his legs as the music began to play. He watched her pull her top off, letting her long red hair fall, almost covering her breasts. She bent over and placed both of her hands on his shoulders, moving to the music, her breasts just inches from his face. She stood up, picked up his hand and placed it on the zipper of her shorts. He pulled the zipper down and watched as she turned her back to him, bent over and slowly pulled her shorts off.

"Damn, girl, you do look good!" David said, as she pressed her legs against his.

She turned to face David and put her hands on his legs as she lowered herself to a squatting position. She leaned closer, arching her back, and slowly pulled herself up, keeping her body just inches from his.

She had practiced this dance routine for years, having her breasts just inches from the customer's face as the music stopped. She held this position until David looked up into her eyes and said, "Red, you are still the best."

"Thanks, Honey."

David watched as she put her clothes on, and asked, "Has business been slow?"

"Yes, very. We only have about half the customers we had 2 years ago, and the ones that still come, don't buy as many dances."

"I hope things get better."

"Yeah, me too. I don't know how many more years I can keep doing this. There are a lot of younger girls out there looking for work. I think the only reason I'm still here is that I have a good dance routine."

David pulled out another 20 dollar bill and handed it to her.

She smiled and said, "Thanks, David," as she gave him a big hug.

He followed her out to the tables and was about to sit down when he noticed two men sitting in a booth against the wall. He stared at them for a second, then smiled and waved at them.

He walked across the room and stood in front of their booth. "If it isn't the FBI. Are you guys still following me?"

"Yes, we're just doing our job, Mr. Dodson."

"And you're doing a great job. Listen, tonight I just want to have a drink and enjoy the company of these fine ladies. I really don't want to fight with you. OK?"

"Mr. Dodson, we're just trying to find your brother, we're not here to start anything with you."

"Can I sit down so we can talk?"

"Sure."

David sat down. "First, call me David. Now, what are your names again?"

"I'm Ryan Powell and this is Phillip Rawlins."

"I want to apologize for what I did the other day," said David. "With what happened at the clubhouse, I get a little paranoid when I see someone following me. Now about my brother, I haven't seen or talked to Charles in several years. I really don't know where he is."

"We still have to look for him," said Ryan.

"And I understand that, you're just doing your jobs." David looked at them for a second. "Can I buy you a drink?"

Phillip said, "It might be best if we buy our own. Thanks anyway."

"OK. I'll leave you to your jobs now. If you guys have any questions, don't hesitate to ask."

"Thank you," said Ryan.

David got up and walked back across the room and sat down at a table near the stage. He watched as a new girl did her dance.

"David, can I get you another drink?" asked Red.

"No, not right now, thanks."

"What's wrong, Honey, don't you like the new girl?"

"Yeah, she's fine. I've just got some stuff to work out."

"Well, if you need anything, just wave at me," said Red.

David watched her as she turned around and walked to the bar and picked up a tray of drinks for another table. As she left the table she gave David a look. He smiled and kept looking at her. She smiled back and went to the bar again for another tray of drinks. When she delivered those and turned to the bar again he waved at her.

"What do you need, Honey?"

"How would you like to make a little extra money tonight?"

"David, you know I love you, but I'm married."

"A thousand dollars."

She looked at David and said, "I think I better do you right here on the table before you can change your mind."

David laughed. "Can we go to the back room and talk?"

As she shut the door she said in a dubious tone, "I have never brought a customer back here just to talk. What do you have on your mind?"

"The two men I was talking to in the booth, they're FBI and they're following me to try to find my brother. I need something to blackmail them with."

"What do you want me to do?"

"I need you to drug them, and have them pose with you or some of the other girls while I take their photos. And one other thing, if anyone comes in and asks about the photos, I want you and everyone else to say that those two men and I came in together to party and that I paid for the girls, the drinks, everything." He waited for her to say something then he said, "Red, I will give you a thousand dollars if you can help."

She stared at David for a second, thinking, then said, "One thousand won't be enough. I'll have to pay a couple of girls three hundred each, the bartender two hundred, the doorman two hundred. That doesn't leave anything for me, and I want a thousand just to set this up."

"Damn, girl. OK. I have a thousand dollars cash on me right now. You can pay everyone else with that, and I'll have to owe you a thousand."

He reached around her and pulled her close, their faces just inches apart, one hand gently massaging the small of her back. "And I also want a free dance."

Red smiled. "And a free dance, are you sure that's all."

"For now."

"Sit down then."

David sat on the chair and cracked a big grin as he watched Red start the CD player again. She had just taken her top off when the door cracked open about four inches.

She turned around and looked at the door when David said, "Hi, Ryan."

Red gave the man peeping around the door a smile and said, "Honey, you're going to have to wait your turn."

David and Red stared at each other and smiled as Ryan closed the door.

~ ~ ~

Hotel, north of Cortez villa

Dennis's eyes popped open as soon as the alarm on his watch announced it was 03:00 AM. He shook Travis and said, "It's time to get up if you want to play Double-Naught spy with me."

Travis sat up and thought about what Dennis had said, then he looked at him and said, "Are you saying we're more like Jethro Bodine of the Beverly Hillbillies than Ian Fleming's James Bond?"

Dennis laughed. "We're both from California, neither one of us has a British accent, and I like Granny's moonshine better than a martini, shaken or stirred."

Travis slipped into his boots. "Well, shucks, I always wanted to be a Double-Naught spy."

As Dennis laced up his boots, he started running down his mental list of things to do. They had checked and rechecked all the equipment the evening before and everything seemed to work fine. The UAV, remote control, and the computer all fit into two medium bags. There was a half moon shining this morning so there would be plenty of light for the night vision monocular scope. Satisfied, he stood up, looked at Travis, and asked, "OK, Mr. Bond, are you ready to go?"

"Almost."

Dennis handed Travis a nylon knife sleeve that held a plastic knife. "Put that in your boot. I want you to have something to protect yourself."

"What is it?"

"It's called a CIA knife. It's made of a strong nylon composite. It's not designed to cut anything, but you can stab someone with it if you need to."

Travis took it out and quickly looked at it. "OK, I'm ready," he said, as he put the knife into his boot.

They each grabbed a bag and a flashlight and quietly left the bungalow. Travis followed Dennis to the overgrown path that he had taken the morning before. Dennis didn't bother with the compass, he just followed the broken grass and weeds. They made good time and reached the beach about 15 minutes later. Dennis stopped and took out the night vision scope. He scanned the beach for several seconds then said, "Let's move out."

Dennis led the way only to stop and scan the beach and tree line every few minutes. They stopped behind a large rock, about 150 yards from Cortez's villa, and started to set up the equipment. Assembling the UAV and getting the computer and RC controller ready took less than 10 minutes. Dennis looked at his watch, 04:20 AM.

Travis did his final check then said, "I'm ready."

Dennis looked down the beach again. "Go," he said.

Travis picked up the UAV and placed it on the beach between the water and the tree line. He ran back to the controller and gently moved the altitude control. The UAV went straight up and hovered about fifty feet off the beach. He watched the video on the computer monitor as he increased the altitude control. When he could see above the trees, he turned the UAV to get a look at the villa. No lights were on. He increased the altitude to about five hundred feet to be sure he was clear of any unlit communication towers and to reduce the noise that could be heard from the ground.

Dennis kept scanning the beach as Travis guided the UAV to its target.

Travis stopped the UAV at the tree line and did a quick sweep of the area. Nothing was moving. He guided the UAV over the master bedroom area and decreased the altitude to hover about ten feet above the roof. He pressed the aux switch on the controller to take a GPS reading from the external GPS receiver which would transmit the reading to the computer and automatically store the information on his hard drive.

"I've got the coordinates," Travis said softly. "Bringing it back now." He guided the UAV back to their location. Soon the noise of the UAV was above their heads and Travis decreased the altitude to land it back on the beach not far from a pile of dead seaweed that had been washed ashore.

Dennis looked down the beach and saw light moving in their direction. He turned to Travis and grabbed his shoulder just before he walked out to retrieve the UAV. When Travis looked around, Dennis put his finger to his lips and pointed down the beach.

Using the night vision scope, Dennis could tell that the man walking toward them was holding an assault rifle with a light attached to the barrel. As the light got brighter, Dennis took his knife out of his boot and held it out, getting ready to jump the man if necessary.

Suddenly the light was gone. Travis and Dennis looked at each other and froze in place.

The waves washing ashore made hearing difficult, but Dennis could barely make out a new sound, a steady stream of water close by. He looked around the large rock and saw the man urinating, no more than fifty feet away. Just a few feet away from the man's feet was his gun, leaning up against the rock with the flashlight turned off. As Dennis watched, the man zipped his pants, reached into his shirt pocket, took out a cigarette, and lit it. He leaned against the rock and smoked as he looked out at the ocean. When he was done, he flipped the cigarette onto the beach, grabbed his gun and started walking back to the villa.

Travis heard Dennis take a deep breath, and say, "That was too close." Dennis then checked his watch and said, "05:30. The sun will be up soon. Why don't you put everything back into the bags while I keep an eye on our friend patrolling the beach."

Travis asked, "What about the UAV?"

"I can pick it up when we start back. We can disassemble it later."

Travis nodded and quickly packed the bags. "I'm ready," he said.

Dennis put the night vision scope to his eye one last time, and said, "It's clear, let's go." Then he ran out to the UAV and picked it up without stopping. Travis grabbed the bags and followed as they made their way up the beach hugging the rocks and tree line as best they could. They stopped when they reached the south side of the hill and Travis placed the bags on the ground as Dennis handed the UAV to him. He had it apart and in the bag in less than 5 minutes. Dennis looked at his watch, 06:10 AM. The sun was up. They followed the path around the hill back to their hotel, and noticed that lights were coming on in some buildings.

Bobby was standing at the bathroom sink, shaving, when, out of the corner of his eye, he saw people run by. He looked out the window and recognized Travis and Dennis running to their bungalow, and said to himself, "I wonder what kind of games they've been playing tonight?"

~ ~ ~

Santa Rosa, California

The heavy morning traffic on Hwy. 101 woke Ryan up. He was lying back in the driver's seat of his FBI vehicle and he covered his eyes to let them adjust to the bright sunlight of the new day. A noise from the backseat startled him and he sat up and looked back. Phillip was asleep on the back seat with his mouth slightly open, grunting, his cheek twitching slightly. Ryan scanned the parking lot trying to determine their location.

"Phillip, wake up!" yelled Ryan.

"What?" Phillip said as he started to stir. He put his arm over his eyes and said, "Why is it so bright?"

"Because the sun is up, dumb-ass."

Phillip sat up, wiped the drool from his mouth, and squinted out the window. "Where are we?"

"We're sitting in the middle of the parking lot of a 24 hour Wal-Mart."

"What are we doing here?"

"Damn it, I don't know, I can't remember anything of last night."

Ryan looked around the parking lot for a few seconds then said, "I'm going into the store, I got to pee."

"Yeah, me too."

As they walked to the front door, Phillip asked, "What city are we in?"

Ryan looked at Phillip's wrinkled suit and uncombed hair and said, "I don't know!"

~ ~ ~

Colten Vineyards, west of Glen Ellen, California

"How did I miss that?" said Kate.

Everyone looked up from breakfast to see her looking at a laptop. Randy questioned, "What did you find?"

"I saw this yesterday but wasn't sure about it, so I got up early this morning to look at it again. I think the bank president, Mr. Powell, set up a dummy account to trade securities."

Randy said, "OK, why would he do that?"

"The bank has an investment banking research division that is completely separate from the rest of the bank. They handle several local pension funds, advising them to buy or sell securities. What happens is, Mr. Powell will get the report before the pension funds get it. He can make a trade using his dummy account before the pension funds make their trade. When the pension funds trade, they buy or sell in very big blocks of stocks. Most of the time, that can change the price of a stock. If they buy a large quantity of stock, that tends to make the price go up. If they sell, that makes the price go down. Mr. Powell can buy a stock, then wait for the pension funds to buy the same stock. The price then goes up and he can sell it, making him a very nice profit."

Max said, "That sounds like a nice racket."

"Yes, it is," said Kate. "It's called front running, and it's illegal."

Libby said, "So, Mr. Powell, the president of the bank, sets up the holding company that has a gambling website that we think collects drug money and launders it through the bank, and he also has this front running thing. Have we found anything about the bank's large number of foreclosures?"

"Not so far, it looks like they just did a lot of bad loans, just like a lot of other banks," Kate reported.

Kate watched as Libby turned back to the table and picked at her breakfast, not saying a word.

"I need to get this information to Joe. Libby, can you help me after while?"

"Yeah, I need to be doing something."

Max asked, "Libby, have you checked your email this morning? Dennis and Travis may have sent you the coordinates."

~ ~ ~

Beatty, Nevada

The midday sun filled the cockpit as Travis banked the plane to start his approach to runway 34 of Beatty airport in Nevada. Beatty airport is between several restricted areas. On the west is a MOA, military operations area, that has restricted air space above Death Valley National Park. On the east is a restricted military air and land area, where several atomic bombs were tested and also the famous

Area 51. After landing, he turned right at the end of the runway to the apron, where only a few planes were tied down. As he stopped and shut the motor off, he saw a tall middle-aged man kiss a woman and child, then he watched as the woman and child got into their car and drove down Airport Road to Highway 95. Travis was standing by the plane as the man approached him carrying a small duffel bag.

The bright desert sun reflected off the man's short hair, highlighting a few spots of gray. He reached out his hand to shake. "Hello," he said. "I'm Nathan Connor, I think you're here for me."

Travis grabbed Nathan's hand and said, "Yes, Travis Colten."

"I like your plane. It looks like a small jet fighter."

For a moment Travis thought he was on a military base as he watched Nathan, wearing a green jump suit, walk around the plane doing a preflight inspection.

Travis said, "I have never flown a military jet so I don't know how they compare, but this little thing is a lot of fun to fly, and it's the plane that we have modified to fly the mission."

"This is the plane. What's to keep the bombs from hitting the prop in the rear."

"David's men designed a bomb rack that can be lowered and retracted that gives the bombs clearance from the prop. I know that it works, because I flew and released the test bombs."

"You made the test runs." Nathan looked at Travis and said, "That took a lot of guts."

"Everything looked sound or I wouldn't have tried it. I do have to admit, the first test flight was very unnerving."

"I bet. I know that any kind of test flight can be dangerous."

Travis said, "Yeah, my wife wasn't too thrilled about me doing that, but I was the only one that could do it."

"Your wife knows about what we're doing?" asked Nathan.

"Yeah, we're using my home as a building and testing area, there was no way I could have done this without her support."

"Right now my wife isn't very thrilled with me. I just sent her and my son off to be with family for a week. I told her that there were threats made against military families at the base and that she needed to go and stay with her family until I call her."

"Does she know anything about what we are doing?"

"No, and I don't want her to know what I'm about to do. She lived through enough of that when I flew missions in Iraq during the first Gulf War."

"What did you tell her about having to meet me here?"

"I said that I was going to a secret facility for training, and would not be able to talk to her for several days."

"Well, Nathan, it is a secret, you didn't lie about that. And we probably do need to be going, so hop in the front. You need to get as much flight time as possible."

Nathan smiled. "So I get to fly it back?"

"Yeah, and I'll fill you in about what I know about the mission."

The wheels of the plane left the runway, and Nathan banked right and headed north by northwest on a heading of 310 degrees. As they talked about the plane's characteristics, Travis could tell from Nathan's voice that he was enjoying being at the controls. Then Travis did something he seldom got to do, relax and enjoy the view. He sat back and watched the snow capped Sierra Nevada mountains going by. Then, alone with his thoughts, he realized that his part of this project was about to end, that this would be the last time he was going to be in this plane.

Chapter 19
Santa Rosa, California

The Thursday morning sun was starting to show itself and promised to make for a very warm day. David pulled the truck and trailer to the back lot of Jack's fertilizer plant, where he saw Jeffery waiting with Jack and Alec Cooper at the open door of a loading bay. They carefully loaded and secured the four containers of explosives to the trailer wall, behind David's motorcycle.

David closed the doors of the trailer, then as he locked them he asked, "How much were you able to make?"

Jeffery grinned and said, "With all the help, I was able to make 200 pounds."

As David reached for the door handle of the truck, Jack said, "David, I hope you boys have a very good weekend."

David laughed and said, "Thanks to you, I think we'll have a blast."

Jack smiled, looked at Jeffery and said, "Don't forget, if you ever get tired of working for David, give me a call."

"Thanks, Jack, I'll keep that in mind."

"Are you trying to steal my man?" David asked as he got in the truck.

Jack said, "You have a very talented guy there."

David waved at Jack and Alec, then started the truck and slowly pulled out onto the street. "You might want to give Jack's offer some consideration," he said to Jeffery.

"I thought about it last night, but I think I can make more money working for you."

"Yeah, but you might not get shot working for him."

Jeffery laughed. "Yeah, that is something to think about."

~ ~ ~

Colten Vineyards, west of Glen Ellen, California

Everyone could sense the anxiety in the air knowing that the mission was almost ready to be carried out. In the hanger office, Dennis, Max and Nathan were going over the mission details as Kate and Travis listened. Libby, always worried that she might miss something. She felt compelled to do one last check before they secured the guidance system into the bomb casing. At a bench against the back wall, Randy and Libby worked quietly as a soft buzz from the overhead lights filled the hanger bay. Holding a voltmeter, Randy stood next to Libby, calling out the reading in a reassuring voice as she carefully placed the voltmeter probes to the terminals of each battery pack that would be used in the bombs' guidance system. Suddenly, they both heard the sound of a vehicle stopping outside the hanger and Libby turned her head to Randy and saw a smile creep across his face.

"Go see if that's him. I'll finish up here."

Without saying a word, she quickly walked across the hanger floor and opened the door to see Jeffery standing a few feet away. She ran into his arms, looked up into his eyes and said, "Hi."

Jeffery put his arm around her and kissed her as David walked by and entered the hanger. He saw the bombs lying on the table and walked over to give them a close examination.

Randy saw a little smile grow on David's face, then Randy asked, "What do you think?"

"They look good, Randy." The office door opened, and David turned his head to see everyone coming out of the office to greet him.

Nathan shook David's hand and said, "Man, I am amazed at what your people have pulled off here. I think this has a good chance of really working."

Libby and Jeffery walked back in as David said, "Yes, I believe we can pull this off. Even with the FBI following me."

"The FBI has been following you?" said Libby. "You know someone put a tracker on Kate's car. Have you looked to see if they have put a tracker on your vehicles?"

"Damn! I didn't think about that." He turned and headed to the trailer, and the others followed.

Nathan walked beside David with the others straggling along behind. "David, why is the FBI following you? Do they suspect something?" asked Nathan.

"I don't think so," said David, "but let's wait for the others and I'll tell you all at once." They waited outside the trailer for everyone to catch up. "If you didn't hear," David said to the group, "Nathan just asked if the FBI suspects something. I don't believe they know what we're doing. What they're trying to do is locate my brother, Charles, Kate's father. They thought he might come back when he heard our story that Kate was dead. For those of you who don't know his story, here's the short version. He was Army Special Forces and about 15 years ago during the Panama war, he and his team were sent on a secret mission and things went sideways, most of his team were killed. The government said there was no mission and blamed the entire thing on Charles. They made it look like the entire operation was Charles's idea and they put out arrest warrants for him and the only other surviving team member." He paused for a second. "Now, let's get to work." He turned back to the trailer, opened the door, and walked in with Dennis following.

"Don't bring the bike outside," called Libby. "If there is a tracker on it, it probably isn't working inside the metal trailer."

David stood next to the door and flipped on the trailer's 12 volt light system. They walked past the four containers of explosives that were secured to the side of the wall, and squatted down beside the bike. David held a small flashlight as Dennis pulled the cover from around the battery and fuse block area and noticed a suspicious wire connected to a fuse tap on the fuse block.

Dennis said, "I have never seen this before."

"Dammit, me neither. A few days ago I thought someone had managed to get inside the clubhouse. I bet they only got into the garage and installed it then," said David.

They followed the wire to a small box located behind a bundle of wires in the center of the frame.

"Do you want me to pull it?" asked Dennis.

"No, I don't want them to know that we found it. Let me go outside and talk to our experts first."

David and Dennis went outside and told the others what they found.

Libby said, "If it's attached to the battery, it's probably the kind that has a built in radio or cell phone that sends your location to them."

David said, "I don't want the FBI to know that we found the device and I don't want them to know where I am right now. Jeffery and I need to get back to the clubhouse, so how can we temporarily disable the device until we get back there?"

"Just disconnect it from the battery," said Randy.

Libby said, "Wait, that might not work. It may have a battery backup."

"I can drive you and Jeffery back to the clubhouse," said Dennis. "We can unload the bike, then I can drive the truck and trailer back here. While I'm gone the men can start breaking the plane down and getting it ready to load on the trailer when I get back."

"If there's not a tracker on the truck," said David. "Let's go look."

After a thorough search of the truck didn't turn up anything, David said, "OK, let's get the explosives out and get the bombs put together. Then you can take us back."

Before they could start working, they heard a vehicle coming up the driveway and turned to look. Sharon was driving up in a utility cart. She got out holding a digital camera in her hand and approached David. "I would like to take a group photo of everyone in front of the plane, if that's OK."

David smiled and said, "I think that would be nice. I would like a copy to print out and hang in my office."

Sharon snapped several photos of the group. She could not help but notice Jeffery and Libby with their arms around each other.

"Hold on," said David, "you're part of this family, too. Does that thing have a timer so we can all be in the picture?"

"If I can find a good spot to put it down where it will see us," said Sharon.

"I have an idea," said Travis. He pulled a ladder out of the hangar and set it up, then experimented until he found the best step to use.

When they got a couple of shots with everyone, Sharon asked Libby and Jeffery if they would like her to take some photos of them together.

"Sure, if you don't mind," said Libby.

After several minutes, David said, "Sorry, Jeffery, I need you to help get the bombs ready."

As everyone walked back to the bombs, David reached into his vest pocket and pulled out four glass vials and gave them to Jeffery.

"Here," he said. "I put a little of Brad in each of these. I think he would like to be there when they go off."

Jeffery took the vials and agreed, "Yeah, I think he would like that."

Libby and Randy finished putting the guidance systems back into the bombs as Dennis and Max brought the explosives into the hanger. David said, "OK, I want everyone outside as Jeffery and I put this together." Everyone turned to leave except Libby. David stared at her and said, "Libby, I mean it. I want you outside."

She locked eyes with David and said sternly, "David, I'm the one responsible for this mess. I'm not leaving. Besides Jeffery only has one good arm and you may need help."

"Libby, please." said Jeffery.

"NO!"

David waited while everyone else left and then said, "Stud, with her attitude, I think she'll be a real good biker chick."

Libby's and David's eyes were still locked when Libby grinned. "My Vespa and I do OK," she said.

David cracked a grin. "OK then, let's get started."

Jeffery explained that the two wires coming out of the explosives were for the detonator system and needed to go in first then feed into the control area of the bomb.

Under Jeffery's guidance, Libby carefully pulled the detonator wires into the back of the bomb as David slid the explosives into the front. Libby hooked up the wires to the control board as David secured the explosives in place by installing the front cone back on the front of the bomb. For the next thirty minutes, they repeated the process until all four were completely assembled.

"I know that Dennis and Max know how to arm these," said David. "But could you go over it with me?"

"Sure," she said.

Jeffery smiled as he watched her explain the system to David. When she stopped, David said, "You have done an outstanding job on this. Thank you."

"You're welcome, but I hope I never have to make anymore."

"I hope so, too." He then turned to Jeffery and said, "Dennis and I will meet you at the truck and we'll head back to the clubhouse."

As Dennis and David reached the truck, David turned to look for Jeffery and saw him near the hangar holding Libby. "Come on, Stud, we gotta go!" he yelled.

Dennis looked around, too and they saw Jeffery kiss Libby.

"It will only be a few days now," Jeffery said.

She smiled. "I know." Then she reached around and pinched his butt.

"Oh!" Jeffery smiled.

David and Dennis were still laughing at Jeffery as they got into the truck. Dennis said, "What's the matter, Stud, that girl too much for you?"

David, still laughing said, "Yep, biker chick."

~ ~ ~

Bodega Bay, California

Everything seemed dull and flat and gray and shadow-less, as the mid-afternoon sun hid behind a thick overcast sky.

David pulled past the clubhouse and slowed to a stop in front of the maintenance building. "Jeffery, go check on the guards and see if they need anything. I'm going to take my bike out for a ride so the FBI will follow me and not follow Dennis back to the vineyard. I'll be back soon."

"OK."

As Jeffery walked away, David said to Dennis, "In the morning, I'm going to leave about 03:45, a little before you. But with the FBI watching me, I may have trouble at the border. You may have to finish the mission without me."

"Yeah, I understand," said Dennis.

They got out of the truck, walked back to the end of the trailer, opened the door, and pulled out the ramps. David straddled the bike and put the transmission in neutral. While keeping both feet on the floor, and his legs wide, he started to push himself backward out of the trailer. Keeping the front wheel straight and letting gravity do the work, David, his right hand gently squeezing the front brake lever to maintain control, slowly rode the bike down the ramp backwards.

He cranked his bike, and let it idle.

"How long should I wait before I leave?" Dennis shouted over the deep rumble of the exhaust.

"About 10 minutes, then go up the Coastal Hwy. Don't go back the same way we came in," he paused, "I know it'll take longer, but it might be easier for you to see if you're being tailed. I'll go in the opposite direction, down the Coastal Hwy. and into town. I don't think the FBI will follow you, but I don't know for sure. So watch for a tail, OK?"

"Yeah."

David put on his helmet, revved the motor once, then looked back at Dennis and said, "I'm counting on you, old friend. Follow our plan. Even if I'm not there."

Dennis nodded his head as he watched David slip the transmission into first gear and ride off.

~ ~ ~

Las Vegas, Nevada

Claudette looked up from her desk to see Angelo staring back. "You're early," she said. "It's not lunch time yet."

"Yes, I thought I needed to tell you in person."

"Tell me what?"

"Cortez called, he wants to talk to both of us."

"About what?"

"Expanding into other cities."

She hesitated, "I guess he thinks we're ready?"

"Yes, things seem to be going very well now that the California mess is behind us."

"OK, when?"

"He wants us to come down tomorrow and spend the weekend at his villa."

"I have never been in Mexico. Do you think we may have time to play tourist."

"If we can get our business done early enough."

"I need to do some shopping," she said.

Angelo smiled. "I thought you might. Come on, I'll take you."

"Have you made the travel arrangements?" she asked.

"Yes, we leave in the morning."

~ ~ ~

Colten Vineyards, west of Glen Ellen, California

The afternoon's gray overcast sky was replaced with a beautiful evening sunset tinting everything with a soft red glow. Travis opened the large hangar doors as Dennis pulled the trailer in front. Everyone had been busy disassembling the plane and getting it ready to load into the trailer when he got back. Soon the trailer was loaded and the doors were closed and locked.

Travis said, "Sharon wants everyone to come down to the house this evening and have supper. I know that you're going to leave early in the morning, so we'll try not to keep you up late."

Dennis said, "Thanks, I'm looking forward to it."

"Would she like some help?" Kate asked.

Libby said, "I would like to help, too."

"I think she would enjoy the company," responded Travis.

Randy stood outside and watched as Travis drove the girls down the driveway. He went back into the hangar bay and found it empty, but the lights were on in the office so he opened the door. He took a seat inside and listened to the end of a story that Dennis was telling about himself and David on one of their missions in Vietnam. Time seemed to rush by as Dennis, Max and Nathan took turns, none holding anything back. Randy, fascinated by these men, sat quietly, soaking in real stories of war, some funny, most horrific, and nothing like the computer games that Libby and he sometimes played.

Chapter 20
Bodega Bay, California

David grabbed the envelope from the office desk and put it in his vest pocket, then he looked at his watch, 03:45 AM. He walked to the garage and flipped the light on, then for a second, just stood there and looked at his bike. He grabbed a rag, and gently started to remove the dust and grime of the road from his beautiful machine. With each pass of the rag, he thought of how the old cavalrymen would brush and clean their horses. He assumed that all warriors wanted their mounts to look good when they rode off to battle. David threw the rag on a nearby workbench, opened the garage door, mounted and started his steed, and slowly rode down the driveway.

The cold morning air nipped at his neck and chest and he stopped at the end of the driveway and pulled up the zipper on his leather jacket. The air was surprisingly clear near the bay as he passed through town, going south on the Coastal Hwy. David enjoyed the bay. It was a place to be alone for a few hours. The slow pace helped him relax, think, and work out most problems. He liked to watch the boats come and go, and the families playing at the waters' edge when the weather was good.

He smiled as he saw the lights of the fishing boats reflecting off the water as they moved out to sea to net the catch of the day. As he reached the end of Bodega Bay, David raised his hand and waved at the boats, knowing that no one would be able to see this lone biker traveling at night on an almost deserted road.

Coastal Hwy. turned east, away from the coast and David slowed as he followed the winding road toward Santa Rosa. He knew this road was dangerous at night, but not as dangerous as driving to Mexico, launching an airplane with four GPS guided bombs, and killing a drug lord. As the road leveled and the curves straightened out, David began to increase the throttle of the powerful motor on his mechanical steed carrying him to do battle. He held himself up in a proud and upright position, much like the cavalrymen of long ago.

~ ~ ~

Colten Vineyards, west of Glen Ellen, California

Travis gently got out of bed and walked to the bedroom window when he heard the truck and trailer pass by the house. Sharon watched him pull the drapes back and stare out the window as the red brake lights reflected off his face.

She got up and put her arm around him and they both watched the truck and trailer pull out of the driveway and disappear down the road.

"You wanted to go with them, didn't you?"

He closed the drapes and put his arms around her. "Yeah, a little."

She looked up at him and said, "I'm very proud of you."

He smiled. "That's good to hear."

"Are you ready to go back to bed?" she asked.

"I might as well stay up; I don't think I can sleep."

"I'll make us some coffee," she said, then gave him a gentle hug and a kiss on the cheek.

~ ~ ~

San Francisco, California

"Answer your phone!" she said.

"What?" said Phillip Rawlins.

"Answer your phone!" she said again.

Phillip picked up his FBI issued cell phone, pushed a button and said, "Yes."

"Sorry to wake you partner. David Dodson is on the move," said Ryan.

Phillip looked at the clock and said, "It's 04:00 am. Where would he be going at this time of night?"

"I don't know, but it must be important. Can you be ready in 30?"

He said, "Yeah," and ended the call. He looked at his wife. "Sorry, I have to go."

She rolled over without speaking, turning her back to him.

He watched her lying in bed as he got ready. This job was putting a real strain on their marriage and he did not know how many more of these late night stakeouts she was going to put up with. He wanted to kiss her goodbye, but decided it best to just leave. She seemed to always want to start a fight just before he left for work. Right now he just couldn't handle another.

He saw the headlights shining into his home when Ryan pulled into the driveway. He walked out to the car and took his normal position in the passenger seat. He looked up at the window of the bedroom that he and his wife shared. Not long ago he would have seen her standing there waving him goodbye. But not tonight.

Ryan said, "Pull up the tracker app on your phone and see where he is."

Phillip looked at the map with the red dot indicating the location of David Dodson. "He's on the 101, heading south at 60 MPH, just north of Petaluma," he said.

"I wonder where he's going?"

Phillip stared out the window. "He's probably just going back to the men's club to get his rocks off with that redhead."

Ryan looked over to Phillip and said, "Are you OK, Partner?"

"Yeah," he said, still staring out the window of the car, but thinking of his empty bedroom window.

~ ~ ~

California

The sun was starting to peek over the Sierra Nevada mountains when David turned south onto Interstate 5. The traffic was light and he was making good time, but he knew that LA and San Diego on a Friday afternoon would be slow going. He reached up to his vest pocket to make sure the envelope was still there. He caught himself constantly looking in the rear view mirror to see if anyone was following. He never saw anyone but he knew they were near. Early afternoon traffic in LA was just what he expected, fast, then slow, then stop, move slowly, and stop again. As he cleared the center of town the traffic moved faster and faster until he was traveling at, or above, the posted speed limit with fewer interruptions.

Mid-afternoon traffic on Interstate 5 between LA and San Diego was heavy and after such a long day, he had to fight the urge to get off the interstate and take a slow easy relaxing ride by the shoreline. His butt hurt, and he found himself constantly moving around on the seat to keep blood circulating. To a biker, that seemed a small price to pay.

Long lines of cars filled each lane at the border crossing. The stop and go traffic gave him time to watch the border agents' routines, to get a sense of what was normal. Numerous cameras were located in each lane, and he assumed that by now they knew who he was. As he got closer to the border agents' booth he saw four armed agents walk out of a building nearby. They divided up, two of them walked to the booth and waited while two made their way behind David. The four men surrounded David as he pulled up to the booth.

One of the men pointed to a parking area and said, "Sir, I have to ask you to park over there, then come with us."

David looked at the agent and nodded his head.

The four agents escorted David to a small room with a table, four chairs and two cameras in the corners of the room.

"How long will it take before the FBI agents, Ryan and Phillip, get here," asked David.

The agent looked at him and said, "I don't know." Then he closed and locked the door as he left.

David sat down, leaned back, put his feet on the table, closed his eyes, took a deep breath and started to relax.

~ ~ ~

California-Mexico border

"Where's David Dodson?" asked Ryan as he walked to the Customs Border Patrol front desk holding up his badge.

"In the back," said the agent manning the front desk. "I'll get someone to take you."

Soon a short heavyset man walked up to Ryan and Phillip, "You the FBI agents that asked us to hold David Dodson?"

"Yes, can you take us to him?"

"Sure. Follow me."

The border agent asked, "What has this guy done?"

Ryan said, "We just need to talk to him."

"Did you have any trouble with him?" asked Phillip.

"No, I wish everyone was as cooperative as him. I think he has been napping ever since we put him in a room. We did a quick search of him and the bike and didn't find anything unusual except an envelope with your names on it. We can tear the bike apart if you want us to."

"An envelope. What's in it?"

"We didn't open it. It was marked Classified Information FBI only, and listed your names and badge numbers."

Ryan said as they reached the door, "OK, bring me his stuff."

"Sure, I'll be right back."

"Hello, David," Ryan said, as he and Phillip entered the room.

David smiled and said, "Hey, boys, are you going to Mexico, too? Hell, if I had known that, we could have rode together and saved gas."

Ryan just stood there and smiled.

David took his feet off the table and said, "Sorry about that, did you know that in some cultures it's a sign of disrespect to show someone the bottom of your feet. I learned that from one of the cable TV shows."

The smile vanished from Ryan's face as he looked at David and said, "David, cut the shit. Why are you going to Mexico?"

"Boys, I just need a vacation. Do you realize the stress of running a motorcycle club? The constant boozing, fighting, and all the girls at the men's clubs. Believe me, it can take a lot out of a man."

The border agent knocked on the door before he entered and handed a bag with David's belongings to Phillip. Ryan continued to ask David questions as Phillip opened the bag and looked inside. David grinned at Phillip as he took the envelope out of the bag.

Ryan yelled, "Look at me when I am talking to you!"

David slowly turned back to Ryan and said in a soft voice, "Yes, sir, Agent Powell."

Phillip held the unopened envelope in his hand and asked, "What is this? Another one of your tricks?"

With a hard, cold face, David said, "No, sir, Agent Rawlins, I don't play tricks. This is very serious."

Ryan said, "What the hell are you pulling now?"

David watched as Phillip opened the envelope and looked inside. Phillip pulled out one of the chairs and sat across from David.

He pulled the photos out of the envelope and looked at each and every one. "What are you going to do with these?" he asked.

"I'm not going to do anything with them."

"Is someone else going to do something with these?" asked Phillip.

"What time is it, Agent Rawlins?" asked David.

As Ryan started to look at the photos, Phillip leaned back in his chair and stared at David.

Ryan said, "Photos from the men's club. Do you think you can blackmail us with these? Everyone can tell that they have been staged."

"Agent Powell, I'm not asking for anything!"

"I don't believe you," said Ryan. "You're up to something and I want to know what it is."

David waited for a few seconds then said, "Agent Powell, you do not have anything I want or need, and I'm not asking you for ANYTHING! Understand, Agent Powell?"

Phillip stood up, "Ryan, I need to talk to you outside."

Ryan looked at Phillip, "What the hell for? He doesn't have anything on us."

Phillip opened the door, "I NEED TO TALK TO YOU OUTSIDE, NOW!" He looked at David as Ryan walked out the door and into the hall.

David said, "Tick, Tock."

Ryan looked at Phillip and said, "What are you doing? We can charge him with blackmail."

"How? He has made it very clear that he doesn't want anything from us," said Phillip.

Ryan said, "This is bullshit."

Phillip and Ryan stared at each other for several seconds. Then Phillip said, "If these photos get out, there will be an investigation and our careers will be put on hold until the investigation is over. Yes, we will be cleared, but our careers will be over and when my wife sees these photos, my marriage will be over, too."

Ryan said, "What do you want to do, cut him free?"

"Hell, Ryan, he's going to go free anyway. We can't hold him because he hasn't done or said anything that we can hold him on."

"But he drugged us at the strip club, and what about assaulting us with a gun?"

Phillip said, "Look at the photos, it looks to me like we were putting away several drinks, and the gun was a water pistol. Do you really want to try to arrest him on that? And how are you going to explain how he got the upper hand on us, took our guns, and handcuffed us to the steering wheel using a water gun. We'll be laughed out of the bureau."

Ryan turned his head, looked down the hall and stared for several seconds without saying a word.

Ryan turned back to Phillip, "Why is he interested in the time?"

"I can only guess that if we don't let him free by a certain time the photos will probably be sent to the news media, or FBI office, or something like that."

"Shit. He's going to screw us again."

Phillip said, "Let's cut him loose. OK?"

"Yeah."

Phillip and Ryan walked back into the room and Ryan said, "We're going to let you go."

David stood up and nodded his head.

Phillip held out the envelope of photos to David and said, "Are we good?"

David stared at the photos and said, "Those are yours, keep them. I don't want them." Then he looked at Phillip and said, "We're good. Thanks."

David got his stuff from the bag and headed to the door.

He stopped and looked at the agents and in a soft voice said, "Boys, when this is over, I would like for us to sit down and have a drink together."

Ryan and Phillip looked at each other as David turned around and followed the border agent out to his bike.

"What did he mean, when this is over?" said Ryan.

"I don't know, and I'm not sure I want to know."

~ ~ ~

California-Mexico border

Dennis, Max, and Nathan cleared the U.S. side of the border, and then pulled into a border inspection station on the Mexican side. The border agent asked Dennis to step out and open the trailer.

The agent looked inside the trailer, examined the plane, and asked, "What is your business in Mexico?"

Dennis said, "We have been hired to do some aerial photography and video work for a travel agency."

"Where?"

"Cabo San Lucas area."

The agent said, "Why bring this plane? We have planes here."

Dennis pointed to the bomb rack, "This one has a specially

designed camera rack that we can install underneath the plane. It allows us to mount the cameras outside the plane, but gives us control from inside the plane. Also, this plane has the prop in the rear; that lets us point the camera at the front and not have the prop interfere with the camera view."

The agent noticed the crates and tool boxes secured in the front of the trailer, "What is in the crates?"

"Spare airplane parts, camera mounting equipment and camera control cables," Dennis said.

When everyone had loaded the trailer the afternoon before, Dennis had made sure that the crates would be in an area that would be difficult to get to without taking the plane and wings out. The bombs were in the bottom of the crates with a wood panel separating the plane parts, the pipes, and cables lying on top.

The agent did one last look around then said, "OK, you can go."

Dennis smiled and thanked the agent as he locked the trailer. He turned to walk to the truck when the agent said, "Sir."

Dennis stopped, put his smile back on, turned back around and said, "Yes."

The agent walked up to him and said, "Take many good photos, please. We can use the tourist money."

Dennis's smile became bigger as he put out his hand to shake, then said, "We always do." As the agent turned to walk away, Dennis got back into the truck. Max handed Dennis a music CD by the Kingston Trio.

Dennis put it into the CD player then repeatedly pressed a button to find the song he wanted as Max said to Nathan, "Whenever we come down to Mexico he likes to play this song." Dennis turned the volume up as the song 'Tijuana Jail' started to play. Dennis started to sing and soon Max joined him. Nathan, embarrassed, slowly started sinking deep into his seat, pulling the brim of his baseball cap over his face, appearing to be taking a siesta. Dennis looked out the side window for any traffic that might be coming. He saw the border agent, standing twenty feet away staring at him.

He smiled, waved at him and yelled, "Muchas gracias," then drove off.

The agent watched for a moment, then turned, walked away, and said softly to himself, "Muy loco."

Chapter 21
Cortez villa, north of Puerto Vallarta, Mexico

"What a place," said Claudette as the driver drove around the fountain in the center of the large circular driveway and pulled to a stop in front of the villa. The wind blew her hair into her eyes as she stepped out of the SUV. She walked a few feet, stopped, and stared at the sunset over the ocean.

Angelo came around the vehicle and admired the view of Claudette holding her hair back, as the cool ocean breeze gently blew her dress around her long sexy legs, the sunset giving her skin a soft pink glow. The only thing he could think about was how beautiful she looked.

He stood behind her and put his arms around her waist, bent over and kissed her neck, then softly said, "That sunset is almost as beautiful as you."

She turned to him, raised her hand to his face and guided his lips to hers. They softly kissed as he held her close.

"I hate to leave this moment," Angelo whispered, "but we should go in."

When they started toward the front door, Claudette noticed a young girl looking down at them from a second floor balcony.

"Does Cortez have any children?" asked Claudette.

"No, why?" asked Angelo.

"I just saw a girl looking at us from the balcony."

"She's probably one of his companions."

"Companions?"

He gave her a wink and said, "Yes, he keeps several with him all the time."

"Angelo, she looked very young."

The housekeeper met them at the door and told the driver which room to take their luggage to. Then she said to Angelo, "He's already here, they're on the patio."

Angelo and Claudette joined the group. Claudette saw the young girl and two others lying on chaise lounges in bikinis. She saw the young one staring at Angelo and she saw him give her a smile and a little nod.

Cortez stood up to greet them. He smiled, put his arms around

Claudette, and kissed her on the cheek, then said, "So, this is Claudette."

Claudette said, "It's nice to meet you."

Cortez turned, still holding one arm around her waist and said, "Please, come and sit with me." He looked at Angelo and said, "Angelo, I am so jealous, you never told me she was so beautiful." Then he turned to the three girls and said, "Girls, get our guests some refreshments."

Claudette, Angelo, and Cortez sat at a small round table.

One of the girls handed Claudette a drink, then said, "If you need anything, just ask."

Mayra smiled at Angelo as she handed him his drink, "Do you need anything else?"

Claudette watched Angelo as he smiled at Mayra and said in a soft voice, "Thank you, Mayra, I'm OK right now."

No doubt about it, Claudette thought, *they know each other. They know each other very well, their body language shouts it. Could be just friends, close friends.* She watched him as Mayra turned around and walked back to her chair. *But these girls aren't here to be friends, are they? No, they're lovers.* She managed to smile at Angelo when he turned his gaze back to hers.

He could see in her eyes that she knew. He kept his eyes locked on hers until Cortez asked, "Claudette, how's your drink?"

She turned to see Cortez smiling at her, not a friendly smile, but a self-satisfied smile lacking any warmth. She looked into his cold eyes. He seemed to be looking deep inside her, but not the flirtatious, lustful, way she was accustomed to from men. That had never bothered her. But the way Cortez was looking was unnerving. It was like he was trying to examine her down to the smallest detail, trying to see what made her tick, trying to see into her soul.

She said, "The drink's great, thank you," realizing after she said it that she had not even tasted it yet.

She studied Cortez as they talked, knowing that he was still studying her as much as she was him. She listened to his words, but paid more attention to his actions and his eyes. She watched the way he treated the three girls that waited on them, and could see that he had no feeling for them at all. He would toss them away as easily as tossing an empty hamburger wrapper.

She watched Mayra, too; the way she looked at Angelo and she thought, *she's so young, she looks hurt, and a little depressed. I think she might have a little crush on Angelo.* As she looked at Cortez again, a cold wind suddenly blew over her shoulder. It felt like an invisible force tapping on her shoulder, trying to get her attention, then whispering in her ear, "Be careful! This man is evil!"

~ ~ ~

Las Vegas, Nevada

It had been a long week and Detective Hector Rodriguez was glad it was Friday afternoon. The stress of trying to do two police investigations at the same time was taking its toll. His partners, Detectives John Lawson and Glen Carter, could probably tell his mind was not fully into their case. He sensed that they, too, were keeping something from him, but he didn't want to say anything that might upset his ability to work on the investigation with Joe Morgan.

He drove by the warehouse, just to see if anything was happening. As he got there four trucks pulled out in front of him, heading in the same direction he was going. This time he stayed further back because he already had a general idea where they would go. A traffic light stopped him and he watched as the last truck moved further away. The long stressful week, the Friday evening traffic, and the sight of the last truck pulling away caused Hector's anxiety level to rise. He took deep breaths as he reached into his bag and pulled out the video camera, and didn't notice the black SUV Suburban with heavily tinted windows that pulled up beside him. The light changed and Hector accelerated, slowing to look down each side street. When he saw one of the trucks parked near a street corner, he stopped and picked up his camera. Before he could press the record button, a man with a limp walked up to his passenger door and tapped on the window with an automatic pistol. Hector looked up and saw the gun. The man motioned for him to unlock the door. He glanced quickly at the door and found the button. His heart sank as he heard the mechanical sound of the door unlocking, then he heard the driver side door being jerked open and he looked around just in time to see a stun gun moving toward his neck.

~ ~ ~

Las Vegas, Nevada

Candy saw the security guard standing in the doorway of the security building smiling at her as she parked Joe's Public Works van next to the barrels on the street, close to the warehouse driveway.

"When are they going to start working on the drain system?" yelled the security guard.

Candy waved at him and said, "I don't know, but I'll keep coming out to replace batteries as long as they tell me to. What's the matter, honey, you're not getting tired of checking me out, are you?"

His smile broadened as he started walking out to the street. As he got closer he said, "No, not at all."

She was about to open the battery case when a black SUV Suburban, with heavily tinted windows, pulled up beside the security building of the warehouse. The guard started walking back to the building when the back window rolled down.

A man stuck his head out of the window and said, "Hurry up!"

"Yes, sir," said the guard as he moved a little faster.

Candy watched the man sit back, then she saw a familiar face, leaning forward, and staring at her from the center of the back seat. She stood there, almost paralyzed, as she watched the Suburban pass through the gate, and drive up to the warehouse. She replaced the battery, then grabbed the camera and replaced it with a fresh one.

She waved to the security guard as she drove by the driveway of the warehouse, then she grabbed her phone, dialed, and said, "Joe, I just saw them take Detective Rodriguez into the warehouse. I think he's in trouble."

~ ~ ~

Candy burst into the apartment. "Joe! What are we going to do!"

"Give me the camera," said Joe.

He looked at the photos. "Shit, it's him. We're going to have to tell someone with the police department."

"Joe, how do we know who to trust?"

"I don't know."

Candy said, "What if Detective Rodriguez tells them about us?"

Joe looked at the deep concern on her face and said, "I guess the safest place to be now is at the police station. Let me get all the photos copied and put into the safe, then we'll go."

~ ~ ~

Las Vegas, Nevada

As soon as he came to, Hector knew he was in serious trouble. These men did not bother to hide their identity, or hide the location of the warehouse as they drove him here. They didn't care if he knew and that was always a bad sign. Marcos's grip on his arm felt like a vice grip, painful at first, but now it was numbing. Marcos threw him to the floor in one of the empty offices at the back of the warehouse, and Carlos limped in, the leg brace he had to wear since being shot in Randy's apartment slowing him down. Hector watched as Carlos looked through his bag.

"Get Antoine, bring him here. Tell him I have a laptop I want him to search," Carlos ordered the driver.

Marcos stood by Carlos and watched him examine the contents of Hector's bag.

Carlos looked at Marcos and said, "Ask Detective Rodriguez what his password is to this laptop."

Marcos walked over to Hector, grabbed him with both hands and picked him up, then pushed him hard into the office wall, breaking the drywall behind him. Hector was stunned by the quickness of Marcos's actions and just looked at him with his mouth open. Marcos held him up with one arm, then slapped him twice with his free hand. Hector looked dumbfounded as he looked into Marcos's soulless eyes. Blood began to run from Hector's nose and lip as Marcos slapped him twice again. Hector raised his bound hands in an attempt to break Marcos's grip, but it proved impossible. One of his eyes was completely swollen shut and he only had a narrow opening left in the other. Each strike of Marcos's slaps was like a normal man's fist, inflicting pain, and causing Hector to momentarily lose consciousness.

"Stop," demanded Carlos. "I need him to stay conscious until we see what's inside his computer."

Marcos let him go and watched as he slid down the wall. Hector, now sitting quietly on the floor with his head gently bobbing around, fought to stay awake. Marcos placed his foot against the side of Hector's face and pushed him to the floor.

The door opened and Antoine Godard walked in. He came to a sudden stop when he saw Hector lying bloody on the floor. "Is he dead?" he asked.

Carlos said, "Don't worry about him. How did you get here so fast?"

"I was in the warehouse server room finishing up a software update."

Carlos handed him Hector's computer and said, "I need you to get past the password on this computer and let me know what is on it. Sit at the desk and don't leave until you have it. Understand?"

Antoine watched Carlos and Marcos walk out of the room and close the door. He heard it lock. He walked over to the table and noticed Hector's badge lying open. "Oh my god, you're a cop," he said, as he picked it up and read the ID. He looked down at Hector, as Hector turned his bloody face to try to see who was in the room.

Antoine forced himself to turn away from Hector and do as he was told. He sat down and turned on the computer. He watched what was displayed as it booted, then stopped the boot up when the BIOS setting function key appeared. He scanned through the menu and found the boot sequence setting, and stared at the menu when he saw that the boot up sequence had the USB port already selected to boot first. *Someone is using a flash drive to boot from*, he said to himself. He took a flash drive out of his pocket and put it into one of the USB ports, and rebooted. The computer rebooted using the Linux operating system located on the USB flash drive. He wasted no time in viewing the contents after doing a software mount of the hard drive. Nothing important was on the hard drive; in fact it looked like the Windows operating system had not been used in a long time. He sat back in the chair and stared at the computer, then at the contents on the table, no flash drive. He reached over to Hector's bag and started to feel around, looking for anything that didn't seem right. Something hard, about the size of a flash drive was hiding in the lining at the bottom of the bag. He moved it around until he noticed a small cut at the corner of the bag. Out came the drive as he pushed it to the corner. He held it up and said, "There you are."

Antoine heard Hector moan, but wouldn't look at him, knowing it was best for him to ignore the poor man. He replaced his flash drive with the one he found and started to examine its contents. He could not believe what Hector had. There were photos of the warehouse and the office building where he and Claudette worked, emails and files from the bank, notes about the murder of Lara Manning, emails from Libby Harrison after she was supposed to be dead, and notes from the interrogation of the men who attacked the clubhouse. Hector moaned again, and Antoine looked down at his bloody face on the blood splattered floor.

Antoine felt like a condemned man. He knew that Carlos and his buddy Marcos would probably kill Hector, and he knew that if he didn't do what they said and keep his mouth shut, they would kill him, too.

Hector moaned. Antoine assumed that he was unconscious, he hadn't moved or tried to speak. He looked at Hector and said softly, "If you know so much about us, why haven't you arrested us?" He listened, knowing he wouldn't get an answer, but he listened. *I wish I could call Claudette*, he thought, *but she's in Mexico with Angelo, and her phone is lying on top of her desk.* "Crap!" he said.

Antoine almost leaped out of his seat, startled by the sudden noise of the office door flying open.

"How much longer?" demanded an obviously annoyed Carlos focusing his dark, unforgiving eyes on Antoine.

Antoine hesitated, not knowing what to say. He stared down at the laptop, and realizing he needed more time to think, he looked at Carlos and said in a timid voice, "It's, it's going to take several more hours."

Carlos stood there, a disapproving scowl on his face. "You have one hour," he said. "We're going to eat. You work. And watch him."

"OK," said Antoine nervously.

Carlos closed the door and turned the key. The sound of the deadbolt sliding into the steel door frame made Antoine feel more than ever like he was in prison, on death row, in the cell next to a man with only hours to live. A wave of anxiety and dread swept over him and suddenly he found it difficult to breath.

Antoine put his elbows on the desk, laid his face in the palms of his hands, "CRAP! CRAP! What am I going to do?"

~ ~ ~

Las Vegas, Nevada

The phones were ringing off the wall at police headquarters as Joe and Candy entered the building. It was a typical Friday night, the phones never stop ringing and the line at the desk never ends. The officers on the street take care of one call after another, sometimes not even getting to eat. When Joe and Candy tried to move to the front of the line, those waiting started yelling at them.

The officer at the front desk, holding a phone to his ear, looked up at Joe and said, "I'm sorry, you're going to have to wait in line like everyone else." Then he turned his attention back to the phone.

Joe and Candy stepped to the side. They watched the officers running around answering phones and talking to people for a couple of seconds. Then Joe looked at Candy, took a deep breath, and yelled, "YOU HAVE A POLICE DETECTIVE THAT HAS BEEN KIDNAPPED AND WE KNOW WHERE HE IS."

The Captain stuck his head out of his office when he heard the yelling. The people near Joe and Candy stopped talking. The officer at the front desk lowered his phone. Joe started yelling again, "YOU HAVE A POLICE DETECTIVE THAT HAS BEEN KIDNAPPED AND WE KNOW WHERE HE IS."

All eyes were on Joe and Candy now and the only thing you could hear were the phones ringing.

The Captain walked up to Joe and said, "You have information about one of our detectives being kidnapped?"

"Yes, sir, I do," said Joe.

The Captain looked at them both and said, "This better not be a joke." He turned and started toward his office. "Follow me."

Joe and Candy followed him into his office. He shut the door, sat at his desk, and asked, "OK, what detective do you think has been kidnapped?"

Joe said, "Detective Hector Rodriguez."

"What makes you think he was kidnapped?"

Candy said, "I saw him being driven into a warehouse that we have under surveillance."

"What do you mean, have under surveillance? What kind of bullshit are you pulling on me?"

Joe looked at the Captain and said, "This is someone's life we are dealing with, and I don't bullshit about that. Please call someone that can do something about this."

The Captain stared at Joe for a few seconds then reached for his phone, dialed a number and said, "Chief, this is the Captain at the front desk. There's a couple in my office saying that a Detective Hector Rodriguez has been kidnapped and taken to some warehouse."

The Captain slowly lowered the phone, "He will be right down."

Joe said, "Thank you, Captain."

After several minutes the Night Duty Chief walked into the office and introduced himself and said, "I understand you think Detective Hector Rodriguez has been kidnapped, is that correct?"

Joe pulled the flash drive out of his pocket and held it up. "Yes, we have photos of him being driven into a warehouse where drugs are being sold from."

"How did you get this?"

"We have been helping him build a case against these people."

"He works for the Police Department. Why would he need your help?"

Joe looked at the two officers and said, "Because we believe several high ranking officers are working with these people. We suspect his captain and the two men that he was assigned to work with."

"That's very serious. Can you prove that?"

"Detective Rodriguez heard this from some prisoners that attacked the motorcycle clubhouse in Bodega Bay, California several weeks ago."

The Night Duty Chief said, "Shit." He reached for his phone, dialed, then said, "We have a problem, Detective Hector Rodriguez has been kidnapped. Meet me in my office in ten minutes." He dialed another number, "Dispatch supervisor, call in everyone in the Tactical Unit. I need them in their office in one hour."

He looked at Joe and Candy and said, "Follow me."

The Chief's phone rang as they entered his office.

"Hello. Yes sir, Captain, call in all of your men and get them ready."

Joe watched as the Chief dialed another number, "Sheriff, it looks like one of our detectives has been kidnapped and is being held in a warehouse. Yes, sir, I am putting it together now. Thank you."

The door opened and Captain Coleman, Detective John Lawson, and Detective Glen Carter walked in.

Coleman asked, "Sir, what do we know?"

The Chief said, "Mr. Morgan says that he and Rodriguez have been working together on a drug case."

"Our drug case?"

"It sounds like it. According to Mr. Morgan, Rodriguez interviewed prisoners that attacked the motorcycle clubhouse in Bodega Bay several weeks ago. They mentioned you."

"I thought they were all killed."

Joe looked at Captain Coleman and said, "You're Rodriguez's Captain? The man the prisoners said worked for them?"

The Chief said, "Mr. Morgan, Captain Coleman is head of a task force that has been working on this drug operation. About a year ago a big drug organization contacted the Captain and offered to put him on their payroll. He and the DEA agents, John Lawson and Glen Carter have been trying to get inside their organization ever since."

Captain Coleman asked, "How do you know Rodriguez?"

Joe said, "That's a long story that I will be glad to tell after you get Rodriguez out of that warehouse."

Coleman smiled at Joe and said, "The Chief is on the phone working on that right now. Can you give me some information as we wait."

"I'll give you the Cliff Notes now. After you get Rodriguez out, I'll give you everything I know."

The officers listened intently as Joe explained everything, amazed at the amount of information that just dropped into their laps.

John asked, "And you can back this up?"

Joe reached into his pocket and pulled out the flash drive. "Everything is on this and it's yours as soon as you get back."

The Chief suddenly hung up the phone, looked at Joe and Candy and said, "You two stay in my office until this is over." Then he looked at the other men and said, "Let's go get our man."

Chapter 22

Cortez villa, north of Puerto Vallarta, Mexico

Knowing Claudette was upset, Angelo watched her all evening. She was polite during their evening meal and later during drinks on the patio she would occasionally give him a little smile. She laughed as she listened to Cortez tell stories of his and Angelo's childhood, but she said few words to either of them.

Claudette could sense that Mayra felt uneasy. She stayed very quiet and would divert her eyes and slightly bow her head each time Claudette looked her way, trying not to draw attention to herself. Unable to help herself, Claudette studied Mayra as the evening turned into late night and then she could see the child hiding underneath all the makeup and the exposed skin. And she could see her loneliness as the older girls ignored her. And she almost felt sorry for her.

Claudette and Angelo walked to their room in silence. When Angelo reached for the doorknob he looked at Claudette and said, "I'm sorry." She gave him a half smile as he opened the door.

They entered the room and Angelo said, "Please, don't be mad at me."

She pulled off her sandals, slipped out of her dress, walked over to him, put her arms around his neck, and said, "Angelo, we're not married, nor engaged, and I'm not mad at you. I am disappointed."

Angelo pulled her to him then whispered in her ear, "I need to talk to you in the shower. They may be listening to us."

She pulled her head back and looked at him for a few seconds, then said, "I love you, too." She finished getting undressed and said, "I'm going to take a shower, do you want to join me?"

He smiled. "Yes."

Claudette started the shower and entered, not waiting for Angelo to undress. She turned on the shower and the water quickly emerged from the large shower head mounted high on the wall. She stepped into the stream and turned her back to let the warm gentle water massage her slender shoulders and lift the tension from her muscles. She closed her eyes and stood still allowing the moisture to roll down her back, to her hips, to her legs, and finally to her feet where the water and tension quietly slipped away from her body. He entered the shower and silently stood by watching her. He desperately wanted to hold her, touch her, but he was scared that she might resist. He wondered if he was about to lose her, and he didn't know what to say or what to do. She looked at him over her shoulder, then she stepped back to where her soft skin was pressed against his. Angelo wasted no time and cradled her in his arms, holding her tight, then gently kissed her shoulder. She put her hand against his face. He bent down and kissed her, softly, passionately.

As their lips separated, he said, "I love you, and I don't want to lose you."

She softly smiled and said, "I love you, too."

He held her for several minutes before Claudette slowly turned around and asked, "Does Cortez have the rooms bugged?"

"I think so. I know he has cameras all around the inside and outside of the house. So I wouldn't put it past him to record what happens in the bedrooms."

A few moments passed and he could feel her body quickly growing tense again. He had never seen her upset and wasn't sure what to expect. She looked up to him and Angelo knew he must have imagined the glowing red fire that seemed to be burning in her eyes as she angrily said, "A rich U.S. banker having sex with a poor underage Mexican girl. Blackmail, right?"

Taken aback by her powerful harsh voice and the sudden display of anger, Angelo paused, closed his eyes, nodded, and softly said, "Yes, that's what I believe."

"Why did you let yourself get in that position?"

"Cortez said that she was mine for the weekend."

Claudette said, "You could have said, 'No, thanks.'"

"Cortez has a very bad and quick temper. It's not a good idea to refuse his hospitality. So I didn't say no to him. After Cortez left Mayra and me together, I told her that I was involved with you, and didn't think I should be with her. She said that Cortez would get very upset at her if she didn't please me."

"And you believed her?"

"She was very convincing and unless she is a very good actor, I believe her. When you talk to her you can tell that she's from a farming community and I know that most small farmers in this country don't make very much money. I believe she is doing what she has to do to survive and help her family. The next day she was telling me about her father, who was murdered, and how her mother became sick, and how Cortez paid most of the medical bills, and she also mentioned her sisters, who she is trying to help support. I know that Cortez is just the kind of person to use someone like her, he can be a real bastard."

Angelo pushed the wet hair from her face, then asked, "Do you believe me?"

He could tell that she was starting to relax again. He held her tight, not willing to let her go. She said nothing for several moments, just stared at the streams of water falling down the shower wall, then slowly she turned her head to look at Angelo. When their eyes locked, Angelo could still see the red in her eyes, not from anger but from disappointment. She sounded hurt as she softly said, "I believe that's what happened. I don't know if I believe Mayra's story." Her voice suddenly hardened as she continued, "but, from what I saw in Cortez's eyes today, I do believe he used her to get something to blackmail you with."

"What did you see in his eyes?"

"I sensed that he was testing me, that he wanted to see how long it would take for me to figure out that you and Mayra were lovers and how I would react. I think he is a very subtle, manipulating bastard and he scares me."

Angelo asked, "Are we good?"

She softly smiled at him and said, "I'll let you buy me something nice tomorrow."

He laughed. "Oh, just remember that I didn't really want to be with her."

"Yeah, a young, attractive, and motivated girl. Don't even try to tell me you didn't enjoy her."

~ ~ ~

Las Vegas, Nevada

Half an hour later Antoine was still looking at the contents of the flash drive. His mind wasn't really on the drive, it was torn between saving Hector or not. He tried to work it out logically, like he would with his computers, but people aren't ones and zeros, there were too many gray areas to consider. He got so flustered that he picked up his smart phone and looked at it, wondering, *is there an app for this.* He knew that whatever he decided, a prison cell would be involved, either now or later.

He jumped when he heard Hector say in a low mumble, "Help me." Antoine looked at him for a few seconds, then nervously turned his attention back to the computer. A stream of sweat rolled down his face and he wondered if something had happened to the air conditioner.

"Help me, please," said Hector.

"I can't, if I help you they will kill me and my sister."

"Just hide me," Hector paused, "until the police come."

Stunned, Antoine looked at him and said, "What makes you think that the police are coming."

"One of my partners saw me come in here," Hector said slowly.

Antoine just stared at him, "The police are coming here?"

"Yes."

"How long before they're here."

"I don't know, I've been a little out of it if you haven't noticed," he managed to say.

Antoine stood up, quickly walked to the door and tried to open it. He knew it was locked, he had heard Carlos lock it earlier, but he wanted to be sure his ears weren't playing tricks on him.

"It's locked," said Antoine. He turned his head to see Hector's head drop for several seconds. When Hector opened his eyes again, Antoine asked, "Are you awake?"

"Yeah."

"I'm sorry, I don't know how I can help you."

"If the door is locked," said Hector, "then try to knock out a wall." He paused, then spoke again. "It's just drywall.... It's not that hard to break."

Antoine looked above Hector to where the drywall was broken from Marcos throwing Hector against it. He pushed it and watched as it gave.

Hector said, "Kick it first to break it. Then tear it out with your hands. Find the studs first. You'll hurt your foot if you kick one."

"If I help you, can you protect me and my sister?" asked Antoine.

"I'll do everything that I can."

Antoine said, "I still don't know. I don't want these guys coming after me."

"Look, your fingerprints are on everything," said Hector. "When the police dust for prints, they will know you were here talking to me. That's not going to look good for you and you won't do well in prison."

Antoine leaned back on the desk, shut his eyes and said, "Shit, I'm so fucked."

"Get me to safety. When the police get here, I will help you."

Antoine looked at the broken drywall again, "OK."

He kicked the wall and a small break appeared. He kicked several more times and a large piece of wall broke away.

Hector said, "See if you can pull it to you and break the rest off."

Soon he had a hole that he and Hector could crawl through. Antoine went through first to see if the door in the next room would open.

"It's open," said Antoine as he came back and helped Hector up. "Let's get out of here."

He helped Hector get through the wall, then helped him up and out the door. Hector's balance was unstable and they moved slowly. "We can't go outside or to the front part of the warehouse because there are cameras everywhere," Antoine said as they moved down the hallway. "But they don't bother watching the utility room where all the electrical and water enter the building."

They made it down the hallway to the utility room at the end of the back office area. It was a small, hallway-like room with shelves of cleaning supplies lining the walls. "There's a room at the back of this room," said Antoine, "where the telephone and internet enter. It's tiny, but it has a heavy steel door and I have the only key, we'll hide there."

He got Hector in the room and said, "I'll be right back. I need to get my computer so we can watch the security cameras." He locked Hector in the room as he left.

He ran to the server room, found his computer, and started back to the utility room when he saw Carlos and Marcos enter the side door. He hid around a corner and waited until he heard one of the office doors open and close. He peeked around the corner, then ran back to the utility room.

Antoine unlocked the telephone room and handed Hector the computer. He went back into the utility room, leaving the door open just enough for him to slip back through. He slid an almost empty shelf in front of the door leaving just enough room to slip by the side. He quickly filled every inch of shelf space with large boxes and packages of paper products. Besides himself, the cleaning crew were the only ones who ever came back here, and they had already left for the day. So he hoped that this would hide the door, as long as no one took the time to look closely. Then he slid past the shelf, closed the door and quickly locked it.

Hector asked, "Did we leave my computer in that office?"

"Yes, I'm sorry but it's too late to try and get it. Carlos and Marcos are back and they will start looking for us very soon."

Antoine turned his computer on. "I have a WIFI router in the server room that I use when I am working here. I hope I can connect to it from here. If I can, we can watch the security cameras and see what is going on." He moved the computer around in the cramped room, but could not connect.

The room was hot and sweat was pouring off his face. He sat down, looked at Hector, and said, "I can't get into the network, we're blind."

~ ~ ~

Carlos unlocked the office and entered with Marcos following. He stopped so abruptly that Marcos ran into him.

"Sorry, Boss," said Marcos. Then he saw the empty room. He walked around Carlos to the hole in the wall, looked through it, and said, "That must be how they got out."

"Wow, you think?" said Carlos as he walked to the desk and phoned the security office.

Marcos gave Carlos's back a dirty look as he listened to him give orders.

"Get everyone looking, and don't let them out of this building," said Carlos to the person on the phone.

"What do you want me to do?" asked Marcos, when Carlos hung up the phone.

Carlos turned around and faced Marcos. "Well, I think it would be very helpful," he started softly... "IF YOU WOULD FIND THEM!" he yelled. "PLEASE!"

Carlos walked over to the computer, grabbed the mouse and started searching each folder. Like Antoine, he was amazed at what Hector had. He was especially dumbfounded by the interrogations of their men at the motorcycle clubhouse.

About thirty minutes later, Marcos walked back into the room and said, "We can't find them and we've searched everywhere twice."

Carlos looked up from the computer. "Tell the driver to get the Suburban ready, we're leaving."

"What about the detective?"

"The police know about this place. Give the order to burn it down, destroy everything, nothing left, especially the detective. Then meet me at the car."

Carlos picked up the bag and put Hector's computer and flash drive in it. As he limped to his office to open the safe, he heard Marcos shouting the order to BURN IT DOWN! DESTROY EVERYTHING! He took all the cash out of the safe and added it to the bag, then limped to the Suburban where Marcos and the driver were waiting. As they drove off, they saw two of their men carrying five gallon containers of gasoline inside.

The security guard opened the gate as they pulled up. "Lock it down," Carlos ordered. "Don't let anyone in."

As the Suburban passed through, the guard pulled the gate together and secured it with a heavy chain. He activated the tire spikes and watched as they rose out of the driveway.

Halfway down the street the driver said, "Boss, look, I think it's police."

They saw several vehicles coming toward them without their headlights on. As they passed they could see the Las Vegas Police Department emblem. Carlos and Marcos turned to watch the vehicles as they approached the driveway of the warehouse. The area was suddenly lit up by the headlights and flashing police lights as they stopped at the guardhouse.

The driver yelled, "Boss, I think they have the road blocked."

Carlos and Marcos turned around to see flashing lights coming toward them. Carlos yelled, "Pull into one of the other warehouses. Park behind it."

The driver made a quick turn at the next driveway and headed to the back of the warehouse. Just before he turned the corner to go behind the building, Carlos saw a police car turning into the driveway.

Carlos said to the driver, "Damn! A cop is behind us. We're getting out, I want you to keep going." Carlos and Marcos jumped out of the

Suburban, then Carlos pointed a gun at the driver and said, "Drive and don't stop. Remember I will kill your family if you stop or get caught."

Carlos and Marcos hid behind a dumpster as the driver crashed through a short chain link fence that separated the back of the lot from a residential neighborhood. The car chasing them came around the building just as the Suburban bounced over a drainage ditch and out a driveway into the street.

The police car skidded to a stop when the officer realized that his car could not make it over the ditch, and he watched the Suburban moving away.

As the flashing lights reflected off the buildings, lighting up a large area, Carlos and Marcos ducked down even lower, but with their guns out, ready for a shootout.

But the officer never saw them. He called in the description of the Suburban as he turned his car around and drove back out to the street.

Carlos and Marcos stayed where they were, still and quiet, listening to the police cars as they drove up and down the neighborhood streets searching for the Suburban that got away.

~ ~ ~

Several police tactical vehicles were parked in the street in front of the guardhouse. The chief drove his car as close to the driveway as possible, then got out and made his way to the guardhouse.

He stopped as he saw the captain of the tactical unit point to the fence beside the driveway and yell at two men, "You two take your vehicles and knock down that fence."

The large, all-black, 4-wheel drive SUV's had black heavy duty bumpers, grill guards, and large all traction tires giving each vehicle an ominous Mad Max look as they started to back up. The chief watched as the two men pulled their vehicles back to the other side of the street. Each driver started to race the large block V8 engine, then the vehicles moved, quickly, deliberately, at the tall barbwire topped fences that surrounded the warehouse. As the tires of the SUV hit the curb, each vehicle seemed to leave the ground and lunge at the fence. They hit the support poles of the tall fence almost at the same time. The poles were no match for the heavy SUVs, the fence easily surrendered, and each vehicle passed over it without straining. Both vehicles stopped as soon as they cleared the fence.

The captain looked with pride at his tactical team, all in black helmets, black boots, black tactical cargo pants, long sleeve black tee shirts, and bullet proof vests that carried a pistol and extra clips for the assault rifles. He pointed at the broken fence and yelled, "GO!"

Courage and confidence radiated from the team of men and women moving forward in lines behind the two SUVs. Each movement deliberate and second nature from the physical and mental training it took to be a part of this unit.

As they approached the warehouse doors, heavy automatic gunfire erupted. The battle had begun.

The captain listened to his radio as the tactical team lieutenant reported from inside, and he repeated the information to the chief. "They're doing a sweep now. Two down so far. Everyone else gave up without a fight. But they haven't found our man yet and they're telling me that there's fire, and gasoline cans, looks like they were going to burn the place down."

The chief picked up his radio. "Dispatch, have the fire department send a pumper and an ambulance. Have them stand by at the end of the street at my location."

As the chief and captain anxiously waited, they started seeing the flames. And the team inside reported that the fire was growing, the smoke was becoming too thick, they were having trouble breathing and couldn't see. They needed to pull out.

Suddenly, the captain yelled, "Chief, they think they found him. Two men were hiding in a back room. The smoke chased them out. My men think one may be Detective Rodriguez, but they're not sure. His face is badly beaten up."

The chief smiled, took a deep breath and let it out. "Good work, Captain."

Chapter 23
Cortez villa, north of Puerto Vallarta, Mexico

A cool morning breeze blew across the patio as Cortez and Mayra sat together talking. Mayra got up and sat in a chair nearby when she saw Claudette and Angelo coming out.

"I hope you slept well," said Cortez as Claudette and Angelo walked out onto the patio.

"Yes, the room is very nice, and I slept like a baby," said Claudette. "I hope you did as well."

Cortez laughed and said, "I always sleep well when I stay here. Come, sit with me. Mayra, get us some coffee."

Mayra poured three cups of coffee, then brought the tray to Claudette first.

Claudette took a cup, then smiled at Mayra and said, "Thank you, Mayra. You look very pretty today."

Stunned, Mayra paused for several seconds. Everyone was looking at her and she started to blush. She was unaccustomed to women giving her compliments about her appearance. Most of the compliments she heard were from the men that Cortez told her to entertain, and those were about her ability to role play a sexy young school girl, a role that she didn't have to work very hard at.

Mayra smiled, and said, "Thank you. So do you."

After Angelo and Cortez took their coffee, Mayra glanced at Claudette, who was still smiling at her. Her smile was soft and friendly, not the forced, cold smiles of other women, or the lustful smiles of the men she had to entertain. Claudette's smile was caring, like the smile her mother gave her when she was a child, a smile she desperately missed and ached to see again.

She thought about her childhood friends, wondering what they were doing, what they were learning in school, and wondering what they would think of her if they saw her now. She didn't have friends in this life, with this job. To the other girls here, she was a threat, competition for Cortez's attention. And they were so different; they wanted to be here, to party, to be seen with Cortez. She just wanted to pay back her debt to Cortez, even if it meant a friendless, lonely life, and entertaining men was the only way she had to do that. When she had left her family to be one of Cortez's companions, she had quickly learned what was expected of her and she had realized that her young age was the most important part of her job. Soon she wouldn't have that and she knew that she had to find other, unique, ways to keep men interested.

Mayra sat down and watched as Claudette talked to Cortez and Angelo. She saw how the men looked at her, they seemed to be mesmerized by her. She wished she had someone like Claudette to teach her how to dress, how to act, how to be a lady, and have that kind of life. She continued to watch the way Cortez and Angelo looked at Claudette as they flirted with her, and she wondered if someday a man would treat her like that.

Claudette sipped at her coffee and waited until there was a lull in the conversation, then said to Cortez, "Angelo said that you want to expand into other cities."

"Yes, I have operations in LA, San Diego, and some of the smaller cities in southern California, but they're handling the lower income customers. What I want is to expand to the upper income clients like you did in Las Vegas."

"OK, what time frame are you looking at?"

Cortez said, "I was thinking that since you already have the software written that it wouldn't take very long. Maybe six weeks to do LA and San Diego."

Claudette took several seconds to think before she said, "I need more than six weeks just to set up one system in one warehouse, and that is if I push everyone hard. One system probably would handle San Diego. LA is so spread out that it might take two or more systems and warehouses just to handle that city."

"Are you sure it takes so long to do each city?"

"Yes, it will take over one week just on the delivery of all the equipment that we'll have to order. The mapping of the delivery points will take the longest time, because we have to be sure that there are no police or business security cameras aimed at the delivery points. Then there's the training of the drivers and the packers."

"Can't you hire more technical people?"

"I feel it would pose a security risk if we hired a lot of temporary technicians to do the installation. I strongly recommend that we take a little more time with each system, and use the people we already have. Once the system is installed and the bugs are worked out, then we hire one or two technicians at each system."

Claudette could see the frustration growing in Cortez's face.

He was surprised when she reached over and took his hand. She said, "It does take some time to put a system together. I worked 12 to 14 hours a day on the Vegas system and when I slept, it was in a room at the office. That system took us a year, and yes, most of that was developing the software." She leaned forward a little more to let Cortez see down her blouse. "Please, it will take me more time to do it right."

Cortez smiled and said, "You would make a good negotiator. OK, as soon as you can, start with San Diego. When that's done, start central LA. After that I will have you come and be my guest for the weekend. We can talk about how long it will take to expand to the other cities."

She smiled and said, "Thank you."

"Angelo told me he wants to take you into town when our business is finished," said Cortez. "I'll tell my driver you're ready."

"I need to go back to the room and get my purse," said Claudette.

"I'll meet you out front, OK?" said Angelo.

Mayra watched as Cortez and Angelo walked out the front door and Claudette walked up the stairs to their room. She ran up the stairs and caught Claudette as she was coming out of the bedroom.

"Can I help you, Mayra?"

She paused for a second before she said, "I just wanted to thank you again for what you said to me. No other woman, except my mother, has ever told me that I was pretty."

Claudette smiled at her and said, "Mayra, you are very pretty, and soon you will be a beautiful woman."

Claudette noticed that Mayra held herself up a little straighter and smiled.

They walked together down the hallway and when they reached the top of the stairs Mayra said, "I have never seen anyone get what they wanted from Cortez before."

Claudette laughed. "I thought you would have realized by now."

"Realized what?"

Claudette stopped, then turned to Mayra, and with as serious an expression and mysterious a voice as she could create, softly said, "It's a secret that only we women know. That when a man sees a woman's breasts he seldom thinks with his brain."

Mayra looked at her, not sure what to say. Suddenly, Claudette started laughing and a second later so did Mayra. They continued to walk down the stairs and laughed again each time they looked at each other.

When they reached the foyer Claudette turned to Mayra and softly said, "I just wish that it worked all the time, but with most men, it really only distracts them for a short period of time."

Mayra still laughing said, "That's good to know."

"If there's time in the morning," said Claudette, "I would love for us to talk. If that's OK with you."

Mayra said with a big grin, "I would love that, thank you."

"Well, the boys are waiting for me, and I better not keep them much longer or Angelo might change his mind about taking me into town."

Mayra said, "Bye," and watched Claudette cross the foyer to the front door. A breeze pushed its way through the door, lifting Claudette's skirt, and she held it down with one hand as she looked back at Mayra and gave her a quick wave.

~ ~ ~

Puerto Vallarta, Mexico

Claudette and Angelo spent the day playing tourist around Puerto Vallarta. They explored historic sites and walked through the open markets.

As they walked around one of the old historic Spanish churches Claudette said, "I think Cortez wants me to come back and spend a weekend, and he didn't mention you joining me. Is that what you understood?"

"Yes, I got that, too."

She said, "I don't trust him, and I don't know what to do if he asks me to come back alone."

"I don't know what to tell you. I know he can be a real mean bastard when he doesn't get his way."

She stopped, turned to him, and said, "Yes. And that scares me. What would he do if I turned his invitation down? What would he do if I turned his advances down?"

Angelo put his arms around her, held her tight and whispered in her ear, "Maybe he has a young school boy that he wants to give you. A reward for doing a good job."

She smiled. "I don't want a shy young school boy trying to fumble his way around me." She put her hand on his hip and gave him a gentle squeeze. "I prefer a man who knows what he is doing, someone that can make me feel sexy, that can arouse me, and keep me aroused." She kissed him and said, "Someone like you."

He held her tight, kissed her again and said, "I love you."

"I love you, too."

As they continued on their walk around the church, Angelo thought about what he would do if Cortez asked her to come back without him. His mind started to run wild, wild with anger and jealousy, with thoughts and feelings he'd never had before, and he didn't like having them now. He was scared. He loved her. He wanted to protect her. He was scared for her. And he didn't know how to protect her. *We're in too deep*, he thought, *I don't know how to get her out.*

His thoughts were making him crazy. His life was out of control. He seemed to be constantly fighting with himself. His plans, his feelings, and his life seemed to be at odds. Too many things were happening that he could not contain and control; the files being stolen from his laptop, the killings ordered by Cortez, his feelings for Claudette. His plan had been to make his fortune in ten to fifteen years, then break his ties with Cortez and leave that life behind. Then fall in love and start a family. Falling for Claudette now wasn't part of the plan, but he wouldn't change it, she was part of him now. He couldn't see a future without her. He looked at his beautiful Claudette and wondered if anyone's life ever turns out the way they plan, and a quote he'd heard somewhere popped in his mind, *Life is what happens while you're busy making other plans.* For now all they could do was wait and see where this would take them.

She looked at him and noticed the long face, and asked, "Are you OK?"

He smiled at her and said, "Yes." He took her hand, and gave it a gentle squeeze and continued to hold her hand, not ever wanting to let go of her.

Late in the afternoon Claudette found a nice jewelry store and tried on a simple but nice necklace and earring set that went with the outfit she was wearing.

"What do you think?" she asked Angelo.

"I think you're the best looking thing in this store."

She smiled and said, "Thank you, and I know you mean that. Now what does this look like on me?"

He smiled. "I do like it, and it looks very nice on you."

"I like it, too. Now I think you should find something nice for Mayra."

Angelo gave her a puzzled look. "What? You think I should buy Mayra something?"

"I don't think she has any nice jewelry, and a girl on the verge of womanhood should have at least one nice necklace and pair of earrings. It'll be a nice gesture, a special memento of your weekend together. And I think she needs some kindness in her life."

Stunned, he stared at her, mouth slightly open and a questioning look on his face, "Are you sure about this? I would think most women would be jealous."

She turned to face him and as his eyes looked deep into hers he could see that her emotional wound was still there, but she slid her soft hand into his and took a slow breath, gathering her thoughts, then slowly said, "I am, but I realized something this morning. That if I were in her shoes, I would be doing the same thing." She gave his hand a gentle squeeze, forced a grin and said, "Besides, I want to see Cortez's face when you give it to her."

Angelo smiled at her and softly said, "You keep surprising me; I think that's why I love you." He bent down and gave her a very soft kiss. "Will you help me pick something out?"

~ ~ ~

Saturday afternoon, La Paz Mexico

David rode up to the pumps at a gas station on the south side of La Paz Mexico. He filled his tank, then moved the bike to a spot in front of the station's small store and parked. He noticed people watching him, wondering about the gringo biker sitting sideways on the bike while eating a can of tuna and sipping a cold soda, and he greeted them with a nod. When he finished eating, he went inside the store. He stopped momentarily and breathed deeply, trying to absorb as much of the cool air conditioning as he could, then he waved at the cashier as he walked to the men's room in the back.

As he returned to the front of the store, he looked out the window and saw two men standing next to his bike, eyes scanning the parking lot. He walked out, smiled, and said, "It's about time you showed up." He scanned the row of gas pumps, saw Dennis filling the truck, and gave him a quick wave.

"You been waiting for us long?" asked Max.

"Not really."

Nathan asked quietly, "How did it go at the border?"

"Not that bad. They did hold me for a while until the FBI boys showed up and talked to me." He smiled and continued, "I told them I was coming down here for R&R and they let me go."

"I assume you disabled their tracker," said Max.

"Yeah, not long after I crossed the border."

Dennis walked up, looked at Max and Nathan and said, "Why don't you two go in and get us some supplies."

"OK." said Max.

Dennis and David watched as the two entered the store. Dennis said, "Glad you made it. Everything OK?"

"Yeah, and you?"

"I don't think Nathan likes my music, but other than that, we're good."

David laughed. "He just don't know what's good, does he?"

They continued to talk until Nathan came out and handed Dennis one of the two cold sodas in his hand.

"Nathan," David said, "San Jose Del Cabo will be our next and last stop before your flight. You need to be thinking about what supplies you need to take with you so we can pick them up there."

"OK."

Max walked out with a drink and three sacks of junk food. David smiled at Nathan and joked, "Be careful, these guys might feed you so much that you won't be able to get that plane off the ground."

Nathan grinned. "Yeah, I can see that might be a problem."

"Well, I hate to break this party up, but we still have several miles to go," said David as he hopped onto his bike and cranked it up.

Dennis started walking toward the truck and called, "We're right behind you, Boss." Max and Nathan followed Dennis to the truck. As Nathan opened the back door he noticed that everyone at the gas station was watching David pull out.

~ ~ ~

Saturday 10:00 PM, La Fortuna, Mexico

The drive to the southern tip of the Baja California Peninsula was long and tiring and hard on the nerves. Dennis was the oldest of the group and the drive was taking its toll on him the most. He wanted to prove to himself that he could still handle military-type operations. He was in good shape, just not a young man anymore. He drove all he could, asking Max to drive occasionally so he could take short naps, but only when he had to; when he couldn't even hide the fatigue in his voice.

As they neared their destination they all got more anxious and Dennis reached over and turned off the stereo. The sudden silence let them hear the sound of the tires on the road saying,"Hush, be quiet, it's time."

As Dennis and Max quietly watched the taillight of David's bike, Nathan got ready. His part of the mission was about to start and he had to stay sharp and alert, so he needed to expel the energy-depleting anxiety that he was feeling. He closed his eyes, slowed his breathing, relaxed his muscles, and focused his mind on a mental check list he used before each flight. Moments later he let his mind go blank. Slowly he felt his energy increase as he drew electricity from an invisible force in the night air.

There was a break in the trees and David pulled off the road into it. The truck followed and pulled far enough in that they wouldn't be seen from the road. David walked back to the road and waited behind a tree, watching to see if anyone was following. When he was satisfied there was no tail, they pulled back onto the road and continued until they found the dirt road that would take them to the dirt runway where they would launch the air attack. And if all went as planned, they would catch Cortez asleep in his bed.

"How does David know about this place?" asked Nathan.

"He has some good sources," said Dennis.

Nathan smiled. "Not going to say, are you?"

"I can't. Let's just say that David knows a lot of people in a lot of places and he prefers not to tell too much so people can have deniability. Most of the time, I don't know how he finds out things. But 99 percent of the time, it's very accurate."

"Did he do intelligence work when he was a Ranger?"

"Yes."

Nathan looked out the side window as they pulled off the road and drove to the far end of the runway. There was enough moonlight for him to see that this was mostly a well maintained runway, and he could feel that the ride was smoother than the road had been. That gave him hope that the plane would not shake itself apart on takeoff. When they reached the end of the runway, they turned right into a small grove of trees that shielded them from the road.

Nathan got out into the hot, muggy, night air and looked around. This place appeared to have been made with security in mind. During the day this runway was probably used by crop dusters, but at night it could easily be used for smuggling drugs. *How many drug planes have flown out of this field*, he wondered. His thoughts were broken when he heard Max unlock the back of the trailer. He walked over, grabbed one of the doors and secured it. Time was crucial for the success of their mission. Then he thought, *how ironic that tonight this airfield, normally used to transport drugs into the United States, would be used to launch a covert air strike to assassinate a drug lord.*

David walked up to Nathan and asked, "What do you think?"

"I'm sorry, what?" he asked, as he was pulled back to reality.

"I was wondering what you thought about the airfield."

"Oh, I think it will be fine. The truck rode smooth while we were driving down it. But it has much larger tires than the plane."

"You still think the larger tires you installed on the plane will work OK?"

"They have to, David," Nathan said, "we all have a lot riding on this."

"Yes, but I don't want anyone else getting killed."

"Well, we'll find out in a few minutes," Nathan said with a solemn expression.

David nodded. "Everyone, I'm going back to the road now, man your radios." He got on his bike and rode back to the other end of the runway where he parked behind some short bushes. He walked out to the road and looked up and down, then picked up his portable radio and said, "All clear to begin."

Max got out the battery operated LED work lights and mounted them on a stand, then placed them on the far side of the trailer. Nathan, Dennis, and Max pulled the plane out of the trailer, pushed it to the far side of the trailer, and assembled it. Then Dennis and Max opened the crates that held the four bombs. They performed the final assembly and secured them to the bomb rack. The plane was ready by 11:15 PM, after only one pause, when a single car drove by on the old country back road.

Dennis radioed to David that they were ready and David gave them the all clear. Nathan started the plane's motor and did his preflight checks while Dennis and Max drove to the other end of the runway. They turned the truck to face the plane and parked with the headlights aimed down the center of the runway.

Suddenly David said into his radio, "Hold position and lights off. Hold position and lights off."

Dennis turned the truck's motor off and killed the headlights. Nathan killed the plane's motor, then turned off the lights of the instrument panel. Then they all waited, wondering what was going on.

As he waited, Nathan looked up at the sky and was amazed how bright the stars were. He started to make out constellations that he had learned as a young Boy Scout and wished he had thought to bring a star map to pass the time on the flight. Then his thoughts went to his son, *he's growing up so fast, and I'm missing it. And my wife, I miss my wife. Can we ever get back to the way we were? How did I get myself into this mess? How could I have been so stupid, thinking that young, beautiful girl was really interested in me. Why wasn't I suspicious when she sought me out like that? Then the phone call, that damn phone call, saying they had a recording of my afternoon with the hooker, including me killing her.* "Enough!" he told himself. "Relax, clear your mind. This is one of the most important missions of my life. I better keep my mind on it." He shut his eyes and took several deep breaths. When he opened his eyes he saw the Milky Way peeping over the tree tops smiling at him. He smiled back and he took it as a good sign.

David stuck his head out from behind a tree and carefully observed an old truck slowly weaving back and forth as it made its way down the road toward him. A strange noise was coming from the vehicle and David thought the truck had some mechanical trouble. As the truck came closer, he could hear the radio. Its volume was turned up as loud as it could go, and the driver, who was drunk, was trying to sing along, his volume wide open, too. David shook his head and smiled as the truck went past and continued down the road and out of sight.

"All clear, we have a go. All clear, we have a go," said David.

Nathan turned on the instrument panel lights, started the motor, and waited. The motor didn't take long to warm back up and when it was ready Nathan said, "I'm ready for takeoff."

Dennis started the truck, turned on the headlights, and spoke into the radio, "You have a go."

Nathan maneuvered the plane to the runway and turned it toward the truck. Without runway lights, it was impossible to see the runway at this time of night from a moving plane. All he could do was aim for the truck's headlights and pray that there were no obstacles in his way. He increased the engine throttle and the plane began to shake while accelerating down the dirt runway, and he whispered, "Please, Lord, don't let those bombs fall off."

Dennis and Max sat in the truck and watched the plane as it approached closer and closer, not realizing that Nathan would need the entire runway to get enough speed to take off. When they saw that Nathan was going to be cutting it close and that they had no time to escape a possible collision, their eyes grew larger, every muscle tightened, and their butt cheeks seemed to grab at the fabric of the truck's seats. Just in time, the plane lifted off the ground and flew over their heads. As the roar of the straining engine faded away, Dennis and Max started breathing again and slowly relaxed. Then they grinned at each other. Four, fifty pound, homemade bombs had just passed over their heads, moving at about eighty mph, and they couldn't stop grinning. "Man, that was a rush!" said Max.

David watched as the plane gained altitude then made its turn east, to the Gulf of California. He put his portable radio to his lips, "Good luck," he called.

"Roger that," was all Nathan said as he leveled off at 600 feet with the coast line of La Fortuna, Mexico passing underneath the plane. He looked at his GPS and noted that the time was 11:30 PM and his first way-point was 45 minutes away. At the way-point he would change his course to the southeast and stay 125 miles from the coast of Mexico while staying parallel with it. At that distance, and flying at only 600 feet above the water, he knew that no land based radar would pick him up. His only concern would be air based radar or military naval ships, but with this small sleek-lined fiberglass plane, he didn't think that would be a problem.

Chapter 24
Sunday 12:45 AM, Cortez villa, north of Puerto Vallarta, Mexico

Warm air slowly moved through the bedroom, circulated by the ceiling fan above the large bed that Mayra and Cortez shared. She lay still and listened to his soft snoring. She was biting her knuckle to keep from making any noise as tears fell from her eyes. She couldn't let him hear her cry. He had fallen asleep with his chest pressed against her back and his large arm around her soft naked body. When she was a child, not that long ago, she found comfort in being held by her mother or father during a bad thunderstorm or after she had a bad dream. But tonight, his arm felt like the jaws of a large steel trap that she could not free herself from. She mustn't let him hear her cry. After he was through with her tonight, he had informed her that next weekend he was going to bring her sister, too. He would leave the younger girl at home for now, but he wanted the two oldest. *I came here so my sisters could have a normal life*, she thought, *so they wouldn't have to do this. What can I do? What are my options? I can't let him hear me cry. No options, none. I hate him! I hate him! I hate him!* She felt sick, almost gagging at the disgusting smell of his sweat that lingered on the sheets, the pillows, and her. *Can't let him hear me cry.*

She jumped at a sudden pounding on the bedroom door, but Cortez was exhausted and didn't wake up.

"Cortez, it's important, I need to talk to you," yelled his lieutenant, Raul, still beating on the bedroom door.

Mayra got up, wiped the tears from her face and opened the door. "He just fell asleep."

For a moment the stunned lieutenant stared at her body, then said, "I need to get him up. We have trouble in Las Vegas." He ran to the side of the bed and yelled, "Cortez, I need to talk to you."

Cortez raised his head. "What the hell is so damn important?"

"I just got a call from Carlos. He said that the police raided the warehouse and Claudette's office. But that is not the worst of it. He captured a police detective and found information about our entire operation on his computer. He said that no one was killed at the motorcycle club in Bodega Bay, and that all our men were caught and are telling everything about our operations in Southern California. He also said that it looks like Claudette's brother, Antoine, is helping the police."

Cortez sat on the side of the bed, staring at his feet as he tried to wake up and process the information. Mayra and the lieutenant stood next to the bed watching as Cortez slowly started to put on his clothes.

"When did all this happen?" asked Cortez.

"Carlos said that he and Marcos have been hiding from the police all day. He said that the warehouse was hit very early Saturday morning and the office was hit about noon. The TV news reports show Claudette's brother taking the police into the office building." Raul waited for an order, but none came. "Cortez, what do you want Carlos to do?"

Cortez stared at him for a second, then said, "Tell him to put a contract on Claudette's brother, Antoine, then I want him to find and personally kill Kate Dodson, her friends, and anyone that they think was helping her. And especially everyone at that damn motorcycle club." He paused, then asked, "Are Angelo and Claudette in their room?"

"No, sir, they have not come back yet."

Cortez said, "If they know about this, they would be smart to not come back."

"What do you want me to do with them if they come back?"

"Take them to my office and hold them. I have something I want to tell Angelo. Then, I will kill them."

A cold chill entered Mayra's naked body, a painful chill, a chill that was cutting inside her. She heard Cortez and Raul continue talking, but she didn't hear them. The only thing she could hear was the voice in her mind, his voice, the voice of Cortez repeating the phrase, "I will kill them. I will kill them." She watched Cortez and the lieutenant leave the bedroom. Fear gripped her as she stood next to the bed, shaking. She began to feel sick again and she sat on the side of the bed and crossed her arms around her stomach. His voice came back, louder, repeating the phrase, "I will kill them. I will kill them." She ran to the bathroom to vomit, her body retching, making it just in time. Then she laid on the cold bathroom floor, shaking, crying, still listening to his voice in her mind, but now he was screaming, "I WILL KILL THEM! I WILL KILL THEM!"

~ ~ ~

Sunday 01:00 AM, Gulf of California

Nathan had made his turn and now headed southeast, parallel with the Mexican coast. He was in the center of the Gulf of California, 500 feet above the water. All he could see below him were the occasional lights from fishing boats. But above him the Milky Way's smile was still there keeping him company. He scanned the plane's instrument panel and found nothing wrong. At his next way-point he would turn west and head to the coast, taking him just north of Lo De Marcos, Mexico.

~ ~ ~

Sunday 01:50 AM, Cortez villa, north of Puerto Vallarta, Mexico

The guard opened the gate as the driver pulled the Suburban into the driveway. Angelo put his arm around Claudette and held her close.

She smiled at him and asked, "What time is it?"

He checked his watch. "It's 1:50, way past my bedtime."

She laughed. "I didn't mean to keep you up so late. I guess we shouldn't have stayed so long listening to the band at that club. It's been a long time since I have done that."

"Did you have a nice day?" he asked, running his fingers along the sides of the new necklace caressing her skin.

She looked up and said, "Yes, thank you," as she put her hand on his leg.

The driver parked the Suburban near the front door. Angelo got out, then helped Claudette. As he turned to thank the driver and to apologize for keeping him up so late, he noticed that he put the keys in the console on the ceiling.

A cold breeze wrapped its arms around Claudette, like it was trying to hold her in place, to keep her still, to keep her from going inside. She hugged herself and looked around, unable to see anything except what was near the lights by the front door. Suddenly a soft voice whispered in her ear, "Don't go inside. He is evil." She jumped and quickly turned around looking for the voice, for a person, but no one was there, only darkness and the cool ocean breeze.

Angelo noticed the goose-bumps on her skin and that she had her arms wrapped around herself. He took his jacket off and put it around her.

Claudette saw the lights on in the office and asked, "Does he stay up like this often?"

"I don't think so, but I don't know for sure," said Angelo.

Two guards opened the front door as they reached the villa. Raul waited in the foyer for them to enter.

The cool breeze blew in the open door and grabbed Claudette's ankles. She turned her head and watched the guards close the doors, and the cool breeze around her ankles slowly let go.

Claudette and Angelo sensed something was wrong from the expressionless way Raul stood, and said, "Cortez has something important he wants to discuss with you, he's in his office."

Claudette and Angelo followed him into the office. A very different looking Cortez was sitting at the desk, staring at them, holding a large drink in his hand. He looked tired, about ten years older, his clothes were wrinkled and his hair uncombed.

"Glad you're back, have a seat," said Cortez, with a drunken gesture of his hand to the chairs in front of his desk.

As they sat down, Angelo asked, "Are you OK?" Then he noticed the guards standing behind them.

Raul walked over to Cortez and stood behind him. Cortez answered, "No, it looks like my entire operation has been destroyed."

"Cortez, what happened?" asked Claudette.

He looked at her for several seconds, then leaned over his desk and said, "Your brother."

Claudette closed her eyes and dropped her head into her hands as the energy left her body, then she heard Cortez yell, "YOUR FUCKING BROTHER!"

A quiet fell over the room as Cortez stared at Claudette and Angelo.

Angelo asked in a very soft voice, "How bad is it?"

"Everything is gone, or will be by the end of today. The warehouse was raided very early yesterday morning. My men saw Antoine take the police inside Claudette's office building on the evening news. And I found out that no one was killed at the motorcycle club. They captured my men and now know everything about my California operation."

"They know about the bank, too?" asked Angelo.

Cortez smiled. "Yes, the police have everything that Kate Dodson and her friends got from the bank." He paused, then laughed as he said, "That's right, Angelo, you have lost everything, too."

Angelo stood up and leaned over the desk. "Cortez, let me try to fix......," was all that he said before the guard hit him over the head with the butt of his gun.

Claudette's eyes flew open at the sound and she saw Angelo on the floor, reaching for the back of his head. She started to reach down to help him, but the other guard grabbed her hair and pulled her back into the chair. Her breathing stopped as panic paralyzed her body. Seconds, that seemed like hours, passed as she stared into Cortez's eyes. She had never seen eyes like his before - this dark, this cold, this evil.

"Please," she stammered in a whisper, "what can I do to fix this?"

"Nothing."

"Please!" she sobbed.

Cortez smiled and said in a drunken stupor, "Claudette, my dear, I would take you to my bed right now and enjoy every part of you if I wasn't so drunk and exhausted from spending the evening with Mayra. You remember Mayra, don't you? The pretty little girl that served us coffee this morning. The pretty little under-aged whore that spent the weekend here alone with your Angelo. I wish there was time to show you the videos of their weekend. You would be proud of him, that man has stamina like I have never seen before. It was like he never wanted to let her go. You know, maybe it wasn't just stamina, maybe he was just more energized by having a very pretty young whore that knew how to keep him going. Well, either way, Mayra seemed to be pleased." He laughed, then continued, "I overheard her tell the other girls that he was the best lover she had ever had and I was a little hurt by that."

"Cortez, let Angelo and me try to fix this, please," she pleaded.

"I'm sorry, Claudette, I must make an example of you. Your brother talked and I must show my men what happens when anyone FUCKS WITH ME!"

Cortez stood up, pointed to Angelo and said, "Tie him to the chair."

As the guard picked up Angelo and secured him to the chair, Cortez looked at Raul and said, "Get the girls and take them to the plane, tell the pilot to get it ready. When we're through here, we're going to leave, and we may not be able to come back."

Raul hesitated, and Cortez saw him leer at Claudette as he asked, "What are you going to do with her?"

"You have been the most loyal of all my men," said Cortez. "When you've taken care of the girls and talked to the pilot you can take her to her room and do whatever you want to her. My friend, Angelo, and I will watch you as we talk." He paused, then said, "Don't kill her, I want to do that."

"Tie her hands behind her back and leave her," Raul ordered the guard behind her chair. "Then come help me get the girls up and ready."

When they stepped out of the office, Raul said, "Go, start getting them up while I call the pilot." When he finished the call, he went upstairs. The guard hadn't gotten to Mayra yet, so Raul went into Cortez's bedroom and found her curled up and naked on the bathroom floor. "Get up and clean yourself up or we will leave you here."

She turned her head and looked at him through red, swollen eyes, and started retching again.

He left her on the floor and went into the hallway where the guard was waiting with the half asleep, half dressed girls. They could all hear Mayra through the open door. "Leave that little bitch," Raul said, "I don't want to listen to that on the plane."

The guard herded the girls out to the plane.

~ ~ ~

A weak Mayra slowly pulled herself up on her hands and knees and crawled into the shower. She lay on the shower floor letting the warm water run over her. As her queasiness began to subside, she began to think about her options again. Cortez's empire was beginning to unravel and she didn't know what her place would be, for all she knew she could end up as a common street whore. She stood up as her strength started to return and she turned down the hot water to let the cold revive her, and thought, *maybe I can escape and find a job in the city. But I don't have any experience, I couldn't make much money.* She turned the water off and stood there, cold and wet, and thought about her parents' farm. She wished she was there with her mother holding her, comforting her, telling her everything would be OK. *But no,* she thought, *I can't go back there, Cortez would find me. And I have to think about my sisters, he already wants one. If I try to hide from him, he'll just go get them both.* She dried herself off, walked into the bedroom, and sat on the edge of the bed, staring at the floor, feeling lonely, sad, and depressed. She thought of Claudette and Angelo, how nice they were to her. *I hope they heard the news, I hope they're hiding.*

Suddenly she heard Cortez shouting and she knew; *Claudette and Angelo didn't know, they came back.* She shut her eyes, but this time no tears fell. She was cold, trembling, and hearing his voice repeating, "I will kill them. I will kill them."

~ ~ ~

Sunday 03:00 AM

The ocean was calm tonight, a light wind was blowing from the west, and the lights from the fishing boats and cruise liners were easily visible moving slowly across the water. This was business as usual on most nights, but tonight was not usual. Tonight the ocean had a visitor, and this visitor had business with a man in the villa at the top of the hill. Deadly business.

The 10 horsepower outboard motor had no trouble pushing the small black Zodiac boat close enough to shore to let it be carried the rest of the way by the ocean waves and guided by a single paddle. The lone gunman got out and pulled it up the beach, and hid it behind some large rocks. He picked up his suppressor equipped AR-15 automatic rifle, turned on the night scope, squatted to one knee and made a quick scan of the beach. He gathered and checked the rest of his gear, then started running to the south end of the beach, where Cortez's villa overlooked the ocean.

~ ~ ~

Gulf of California

Nathan unwrapped a piece of hard candy, and placed it in his mouth. He was having a hard time staying awake as he sat alone at the controls of the plane. Though he didn't have to drive to the airstrip, the ride down was not very restful. He hadn't been on a long mission in several years, and he was starting to feel the strain of it. He knew his age was catching up to him. He slowly sucked on the candy as he looked out the cockpit at the night sky still smiling at him and wondered what people would think if he ever mentioned this friendly face that watched over him tonight. He looked at the GPS; his next way-point would be here in a few minutes. At that time he would turn west and head to the coast, taking him just north of Lo De Marcos, Mexico.

He looked at the clock and said out loud, "ONE HOUR TO GO!"

~ ~ ~

Cortez villa, north of Puerto Vallarta, Mexico

Angelo's head hurt; a small knot was forming where the guard had hit him with the butt of the gun.

Cortez sat across the desk staring at Angelo and Claudette over a half empty bottle of tequila. Each time Claudette started to cry, Angelo would try to get free, jerking, pulling, and stretching his body until he would turn red and finally give up, frustrated. And each time, Cortez would laugh and pour himself another drink.

They had taped Angelo's mouth, so he was unable to express his hatred, his rage, his deep desire to kill Cortez, except with his eyes. Eyes that screamed, "I will kill you if you hurt Claudette!"

"I really don't understand why my father liked you so much," said Cortez, derisively. "Look at you, you're always trying to protect someone; you're so weak, so damn pathetic, just another highly educated person who works for me. If you had only taken half of the anger that you feel right now, you could have really made something out of yourself; had some real power; but, no, you couldn't do that. Now look at you."

Raul walked back into the office and said, "Mayra is sick, she's in your bathroom vomiting. I didn't think you would want her on the plane getting sick, so I left her there."

"That's fine, leave her," said Cortez.

He got up and walked around his desk, reached down and pulled Claudette's head back by her hair. He bent down to where their faces were inches apart. The sickening alcoholic stench of his breath made Claudette nauseous as he spoke, "I really wanted to see what you were like in bed, now I'll never know." He moved in closer to kiss her but she turned away, crying.

He turned to Raul and said, "Take her."

Claudette turned her head and looked at Angelo, knowing it would be their last time together. A tear ran down his cheek when he saw the sorrow in her face, the loss of all hope. Her soft eyes stayed focused on his, saying what they both felt, *I love you*. Too soon the lieutenant pulled her up from the chair and led her by her arm toward the office door. Angelo tried to stand up, tried to go after her, tried to save her. He struggled against the bindings, fighting them, even with his wrists bleeding, he continued fighting them.

Cortez turned the computer monitor on his desk around and moved it closer to Angelo, then said, "My friend don't worry, he will be very gentle with her, at least for the first few minutes."

Claudette started to sob louder as she was being led up the stairs. Her body was weak, she was swaying and having trouble climbing each step.

At the top of the stairs Raul yelled, "Stop that damn noise."

Stunned, with her lip bleeding, she lay on the floor looking up at him, surprised by how fast and how hard he had slapped her.

He yelled again, "Stop that damn crying!"

The noise shook Mayra from her thoughts, and from the voice inside her mind. She turned her head and stared at the closed bedroom door. She wanted to go look into the hallway, but she was scared and unsure that she really wanted to know. Without making a conscious decision, she turned off the bedroom lights, quietly cracked open the door a few inches, and found herself peeking around the edge of the door. She started trembling when she saw Claudette on the floor; her blouse soaked from tears and spotted with blood from the cut on her lip.

She saw Raul pull Claudette up to her feet and lead her down the hall toward her room. As they came closer to her door, she moved behind it, out of sight, and she held her breath. She heard him say in a low vulgar voice, "I have never had a classy whore like you before." Then she peeked through the crack between the door and the wall and watched Raul leading Claudette to her room, much like a butcher leading an animal to slaughter. Mayra bit her bottom lip when she saw the man smile as he grabbed a handful of Claudette's hair, opened the door, and pushed her into the room.

He didn't bother to close the door, why should he, he knew he had an audience anyway. He knew that Cortez would make Angelo watch. Cortez wanted Angelo to suffer, to know that he had lost everything important in his life. He pushed Claudette face down on the bed and held her there while he got his knife out of his pocket. He held the knife in front of her face and pressed the button. He wanted her to see the blade pop out of the handle. He jerked her skirt up and her body tensed as he slowly moved the blade up one leg and down the other. He raised her hands up far enough to get the knife under the ropes and he cut her hands loose. Then he got up, put a chair in the middle of the room and sat down.

She rolled over and looked at him, afraid of what was going to happen now.

"Stand up and take your clothes off. I want to watch," he said as he repeatedly pressed the button on the knife, letting the blade pop out then pop back into its handle.

She sat on the side of the bed and started to take her blouse off.

He yelled, "Stand up, I TOLD YOU TO STAND UP!"

She obeyed, and finished taking off her blouse.

He leaned back comfortably in the chair, then crossed his legs, and spoke again with that low vulgar voice, "Now the rest."

Claudette stood erect, jaw clinched, and stared straight ahead, not looking at the man who was making her get undressed. It was an act, an act of defiance, maybe her last act of defiance, and she felt it was the only act she had left. A single tear appeared in her eye, and it slowly ran down her face, stopping midway, holding on to her cheek, not wanting to fall, as if it refused to fall, as if it was a last act of defiance toward him, too.

Raul didn't even notice that Claudette wasn't looking at him as he unbuttoned his shirt. His eyes were trained only on Claudette's legs as she unfastened her skirt and let it fall to the floor. He smiled as he watched her take her bra and panties off and toss them on the floor.

Raul's smile grew as he said, "Now, slowly turn around. I'm sure Cortez wants Angelo to have one last good look at you before I begin."

~ ~ ~

"Leave the room," Cortez ordered his guards. "Close the door and don't interrupt us. And be sure everything is ready to leave."

He stood behind Angelo and looked at the monitor as Claudette's skirt fell. "I see why you like her. She is very attractive."

Angelo looked up at the monitor as she was taking her bra off, then bowed his head and looked at his feet again.

Cortez pulled the tape from Angelo's mouth and said, "Angelo, did you ever wonder who your benefactor was?"

In a soft voice Angelo responded, "What do you mean benefactor? I never had a benefactor."

Cortez started laughing, "Damn, you didn't realize that someone was helping you your entire life?"

Angelo turned his head to look at Cortez and said, "What do you mean?"

"Did you think that your grandmother made enough money to live in that nice home in the U.S.? Where did you think that college grant came from? DO YOU REALLY THINK THAT YOU EARNED EVERYTHING THAT YOU HAVE?"

"What are you talking about?" said Angelo.

"After my father died, I found papers in his office where he set aside money in a bank account for your grandmother and for your college education."

"Why would he do that?" Angelo asked. "I remember him as a very nice man. I remember playing games with him. But why would he do that?"

"Yeah, I remember that, too. The reason is, because he was your father, too."

Angelo stared at Cortez, but he was seeing his father, their father. He was remembering the man who was his mother's boss, and the way that nice man had treated his mother. He was remembering the way his mother had looked at her boss. Even as a young child he knew this man was special, but he didn't understand why until now. Angelo suddenly realized that if this was true, Cortez was his half brother, and not knowing what to say, he just looked back at his feet.

Cortez sat on the edge of the desk in front of Angelo. He grabbed Angelo's hair and pulled his head up so he could see his eyes. "That's right, your mother was my father's WHORE!"

They stared at each other until Cortez released Angelo's hair and his head dropped back down.

Cortez grabbed the bottle from the desk and poured another drink. He looked at Angelo and said, "It didn't take that long before my mother realized who your father was. She never said a word to my father about it, but he could tell that she knew. Everyone knew. My mother tried to do everything she could to get you, your mother, and your grandmother off the ranch and away from my father. Everything she did, my father would stop. My mother started talking to me about how my father was going to move us off the ranch and move you and your mother into our house. She even said that you would get my room."

"Cortez, I never knew any of this," said Angelo.

"I know, you were too busy PLAYING WITH MY FATHER!"

Cortez paused, took another drink, then said, "I was beginning to see how differently my father treated you and realized that my mother was right. It would be only a matter of time."

Angelo looked up and saw Claudette on the monitor. She was standing in front of the man, naked, and turning around.

He quickly turned his eyes to Cortez. "That's when you changed, wasn't it? When we were very young you and I played together, but suddenly you changed. You started fighting me all the time and you never let up on me. You were several years older and bigger than me. I never had a chance fighting you."

Cortez smiled and said, "Yes, I hated you and your mother. My mother was getting so upset about you being around that she started talking about killing you and your mother. She would talk to me about how easy it could be done, that your mother loved to take walks near the river. She even said that's where your mother would meet my father and they would plan how they were going to get rid of us."

Suddenly, a part of Angelo's memory was being pushed up from deep inside his mind. He started to recall the day his mother died. It was just pieces, small fragments of images and words from that very dark day in a young boy's life, a day that took years for the young boy to bury. Now it was being pulled up, to be relived. Angelo never knew who killed his mother; that information had been kept from him. His grandmother would never talk about that day. But, Cortez must want him to know, must see it as another way to torture him before he died. *Your life passes before your eyes when you're dying,* Angelo thought. *This could not be what that means, not this, not like this.*

Angelo took a deep breath, to prepare for what was coming. "Did your mother kill her?"

Cortez grabbed Angelo's hair and pulled his head back. He wanted to see Angelo's face, his expression, his anguish when he yelled it. "No, Angelo, I did! I KILLED HER!"

A hot, trembling anger grew quickly through Angelo, taking his breath away, and he jerked his head from side to side to get Cortez's hands away from him as he relived that dark day, seeing the images, rehearing the words that were spoken and he couldn't breathe. Now he had a new vision to process, a vision of a young Cortez taking a knife and stabbing his mother, over and over. And he could see Cortez's mother looking on approvingly. He rocked back and forth, gasping for air, suffocating, as this new image played over and over, burning, burning, burning into his memory. He had to get away from Cortez, he couldn't share the same air as this man, he couldn't breathe. Then the sight of Cortez sitting on the edge of his desk, smiling, enjoying his pain, forced Angelo to slow his breathing, calm himself down, and push the anger to a place deep inside.

~ ~ ~

Mayra sat back down on the bed and stared nervously at the door, wondering what to do. She liked Claudette and Angelo and wanted them to get out, run away, and live their lives together. *Claudette is being raped right now,* she thought, *and who knows what Cortez is doing to Angelo. If only I could find a way to help them escape.* She got dressed and as she finished putting on her shoes, she noticed the nightstand. She reached over and pulled the drawer out. Cortez's chrome plated 45 automatic pistol was still there. She picked it up. Just last week Cortez had shown the girls how to use it. She had been scared of it at first. The startling recoil, it's deafening blast, all of it was intimidating. But after she shot it several times, she knew basically how to handle it. She even hit the corner of the target once. She released the magazine and pulled it out. Seeing that the magazine was full of hollow point rounds, she pushed it back in. She grabbed the top of the gun, pulled back the slide, released it, chambering a round. She looked at the safety, flipped it off, then back on. The gun was ready, but she wasn't sure if she was. She stared nervously at the gun, which seemed to get heavier the longer she held it. Then she heard Cortez yelling, "No, Angelo, I did! I KILLED HER!" The words lingered, echoing off the walls of the villa, I KILLED HER, I KILLED HER, I KILLED HER! As visions of Claudette lying dead filled her mind, Mayra marched down the hall to the bedroom, not knowing what she would do when she got there, not even aware she still held the pistol in her hand.

~ ~ ~

Angelo turned his eyes to the monitor and saw Raul take handcuffs out of the nightstand and cuff Claudette to the bed.

"If you hated me that much, why did you agree to my plan to turn your drug operation into a high tech operation?" asked Angelo.

"I was intrigued that you would even talk to me, much less present a plan that would make me look like a legitimate businessman. I had to see if you were for real, that's why I had my men, Carlos and Marcos, with you all the time, to be sure that you didn't screw me."

"I did everything that I said I would do, I even helped put together a plan to tap into the U.S. Drone system. I made you a lot of money and I can do it again, you don't need to kill us."

"Yes, I loved what you did with the drone system. Except you were too weak when it came to killing that hooker."

"She didn't have to die," said Angelo.

"I wanted to be sure we had that Air Force Commander by the balls, killing her was the only way to do that."

"Please, let me try to fix this."

"Angelo, the U.S. police now know my entire operation. They will have a warrant out for me. That means that the Mexican army will start looking for me to extradite me to the U.S. Do you realize that I'll have to start hiding out in the mountains? I have lost everything because of you and your plan."

Angelo started jerking, jumping, and pulling at every rope that held him in that chair.

Cortez watched in amusement then pointed to the monitor and said, "I want you to watch what he is going to do to Claudette. I want you to know that after he is through with her, I am going to walk up there and kill her. I want you to know what it's like to lose everything, your house, car, and the woman that you love."

Cortez was drunk and unstable, so he sat on the side of the desk beside the monitor watching Angelo take in the torture and rape of his love, his Claudette. Cortez wasn't watching the full high definition view of what was happening in the bedroom. At the moment he didn't care about watching her, he only wanted to see Angelo broken. He wanted to look into Angelo's eyes as Raul humiliated and tortured her. Then when Raul is done, Angelo will watch her die.

Cortez smiled as he thought, *And after I put my gun to Claudette's head, and put a bullet through her brain, I think that Angelo will ask me to kill him, too; to end his pain. And what else can I do? Isn't that what brothers are for?*

~ ~ ~

Mayra walked into the bedroom and saw Claudette, lying on the bed, handcuffs gripping her wrists and holding her arms stretched out above her head. Her head was turned to Mayra, and her eyes were open, but there was a blank stare in them, an empty stare, the stare of death. She stood in shock, watching Raul lying on her, thrusting his body, grunting with each thrust, staring at the movement of Claudette's breasts with each thrust. Mayra's hand tightened around the handle of the pistol as she watched, horrified and sickened at what she saw and what she heard. Mayra's hand turned white and started to shake as she continued to watch and listen. Cortez's voice came back to her again, saying I KILLED HER, I KILLED HER. The next thing she saw was the back of Raul's head, as she stood over him. His stare was still on Claudette's breasts, enjoying his moment of power. Mayra changed her grip on the pistol, then raised it as high as she could and hit Raul on the back of his head with the butt of the gun. Raul's body stopped, but his stare was still on Claudette's breasts. Mayra raised the pistol and hit Raul again. This time his head seemed to wobble back and forth. Mayra raised the pistol and hit him a third time. This time Raul fell unconscious, still lying on Claudette. Mayra stood there, biting her lips, shaking, as she began to realize what she had done.

A tear trickled down Mayra's cheek as she looked at Claudette's blank stare, and in a trembling voice she said, "I'm sorry." Then she took a quick step back, her eyes grew large, and the blood drained from her face as Claudette slowly turned her head.

~ ~ ~

Something made Angelo look back at the monitor. He was stunned to see Mayra hitting Raul on the head. He looked at Cortez still sitting on the side of the desk. He had to distract Cortez, keep him from looking at the monitor. *Maybe I could talk to him,* he thought, *plead with him, but that might only encourage him, and bring him around to look at the monitor. No. I have to do something to the monitor. Destroy it.* He drew every bit of his strength and made one last effort to set himself free. The ropes around his legs gave, allowing him to stand. He knew he did not have time to get his hands free, so he made a run at Cortez, bringing his shoulder into Cortez's midsection, and taking them both over the desk, making sure that everything on top of the desk fell to the floor with them.

~ ~ ~

Mayra stood there looking at Claudette, handcuffed to the bed and squirming as she tried to get Raul off. She forced herself to move, and she helped to roll Raul off onto the floor. "I thought you were dead," she said as she turned to the nightstand to get the handcuff keys.

"So did I," said Claudette.

"We have to hurry," said Mayra while unlocking the cuffs. "They might be watching us right now."

As Claudette got up from the bed, Raul started to move. She looked at the pistol in Mayra's hand and said, "Let me have that."

Mayra said, "Don't shoot him, everyone will hear it."

Claudette hit Raul just as he was rolling over. Then she hit him again and again.

Mayra reached over and put a hand on Claudette's shoulder. "That's enough, Claudette, we need to go."

When she stopped and turned her head, Mayra saw eyes that were very different from the dead eyes of moments ago, now they were filled with anger. She turned back to Raul's bloody face, raised the gun again and hit him one more time, then took a deep breath and stared at the unconscious body of her rapist. "Now it's enough," she said.

Mayra took the pistol back and Claudette picked up her clothes. As she put them on, she stared at the bed, the bed where she was supposed to take her final breaths.

"Hurry!" Mayra said. "We need to go!"

Claudette slipped into her shoes and they both ran out of the bedroom and down the hall.

~ ~ ~

Sunday 03:50 AM, Lo De Marcos, Mexico

Nathan started increasing his altitude just before he reached the way-point of Lo De Marcos. He turned south to fly over Mexico Highway 200, then flipped on the remote power switch for the controller and GPS systems on the bombs to allow the GPS receivers enough time to find as many satellites as possible. The plane was flying at 3000 feet and climbing as he checked the plane's GPS. He was scanning the instrument panel more often the closer he got. Everything still looked good. He looked out and saw a few lights in some of the buildings. He was unable to see any detail on the ground, but was sure he was on course for the next way-point, one mile east of Cortez's villa.

~ ~ ~

Cortez villa, north of Puerto Vallarta, Mexico

The soothing sounds of the surf washing ashore were interrupted when the bullet reached the housing for the security camera that overlooked the beach. The bullet created a small hole in the front window, passed through the fragile camera inside and tore its way out the back. No one was nearby to see it; no one was nearby to hear it. The sound of the explosion faded quickly as the surf took back the night. The gunman picked himself up and collected his rifle from the rock that he had used to steady it while he made the 100 yard shot. He knew he had to hurry to cross the beach and get up the cart path to the top of the cliff. He had to find a suitable location before the fireworks began.

Chapter 25
Cortez villa, north of Puerto Vallarta, Mexico

Angelo stared at Cortez as he lay next to him, laughing.

Cortez said, "Damn, brother, you surprised me. One last desperate act to save yourself and your woman. I should have seen that coming."

Cortez pulled himself up, then took his fist and hit Angelo as hard as he could in the face. As Angelo was getting his senses back, Cortez hit him again and then again. Angelo, unable to defend himself, just lay there bleeding.

Cortez stood up and looked at his office. "You fucking bastard!" he yelled.

He kicked Angelo several times in the side, breaking his ribs.

Cortez picked up the broken computer monitor and placed it back on the desk. "Damn, Angelo, the monitor is broke, you're going to miss the best part."

Angelo opened his eyes and tried to smile, but could not remember why he felt the need. His head was spinning and his body hurt, but he still tried to smile.

Cortez saw Mayra open the door and look in. He said, "Get down to the plane, we're going to be leaving soon."

She walked in holding his 45 automatic. The gun looked like a large canon in her small hands as she raised it and pointed it at Cortez.

She could see the anger building in his eyes, "Put that down you little bitch, or I'll...." was all he said. He stopped talking when he saw Claudette walk in.

He and Claudette stared at each other as she walked past the desk to help Angelo off the floor.

Cortez looked back to Mayra and softly said, "Mayra, remember, I paid for your mother's hospital bills."

"Yes, and I think I have paid you back many nights over. By the way, I don't want you near my sisters. If you come near me or my family again, I will hunt you down like a mad dog."

"Mayra, I have treated you very good. There's no need for this."

Claudette finished untying Angelo. "Shut up you bastard!" she said. "Mayra remember, he will kill you the first chance he gets."

Mayra said, "Get on the floor, put your hands behind you."

Cortez didn't say a word; he got down and let Claudette tie his hands and feet.

Mayra and Claudette helped Angelo stand up and walk to the door. He was unstable and slow, but they managed. They moved slowly through the foyer to the front door, and Mayra looked outside for the guards. She motioned to Claudette and Angelo, and they went out. Mayra opened the back door of the same Suburban that Claudette and Angelo had spent the day in, and helped Angelo lie down in the back seat. Claudette got in the driver's seat and she suddenly realized the keys were not there.

"DAMMIT, I don't know where the keys are."

Mayra got into the passenger seat and laid the pistol in her lap. She said, "They usually just leave them in the ignition."

~ ~ ~

Sunday 03:58 AM

One mile east of the Cortez villa, 7500 feet and still climbing, Nathan turned west. At this altitude and having the plane's full side profile visible to the radar at Puerto Vallarta International Airport, he was a target for the Mexican authorities. Drug smugglers flew their planes out of the mountains just east of his position, and he knew the air traffic controllers had to report any suspicious planes that did not follow normal flight paths. Nathan and David knew this was a risk, a risk Nathan decided he needed to take. The next way-point, Cortez villa.

~ ~ ~

Cortez villa, north of Puerto Vallarta, Mexico

The adrenaline from his growing fury was sobering Cortez up fast as he struggled with the ropes, trying to set himself free.

Raul, hands holding his aching head together, stumbled into Cortez's office and found his boss tied up on the floor. "Sorry, Boss," he said, as he cut Cortez free, "someone hit me from behind."

A steady stream of dark blood flowed down Raul's face as he watched Cortez angrily throw the ropes across the room.

"Probably that little bitch, Mayra." Cortez stood up, walked over to his desk, took another 45 automatic pistol from a drawer, and said, "Come with me. It's time to kill them all."

~ ~ ~

Sunday 03:59 AM
One half mile east of Cortez's villa, 8000 feet high

Nathan slowed the plane down, leveled it out, then lowered the bomb rack. He put his hands on the release lever as he watched the GPS display move closer and closer to its last way-point.

Chapter 26
Cortez villa, north of Puerto Vallarta, Mexico

Mayra heard Angelo say something but was unable to make it out. She leaned over the seat to listen.

He pointed to the console on the ceiling and said, "Sunglasses."

Claudette watched Mayra open the sunglasses compartment and pull the keys out.

"Thank God," Claudette said when she had the keys in her hand. She started the Suburban and began pulling away. Suddenly, the rear view mirror exploded. Shards of glass flew everywhere and bullet holes with spiderweb-like cracks appeared at the top of the front and back windshields. "Get down!" she screamed. She slid down as low as she could and still see over the dash as she looked for the way around the circle and onto the driveway. When she found it she floored the accelerator, quickly increasing their distance from Cortez. But the frightening, sporadic sound of lead was still pounding against the steel body of the Suburban and could easily be heard over the roar of the engine, and in the side mirror she could see the dark shadowy figure of Cortez running after them, hand raised, flashes of light coming from his gun.

~ ~ ~

Sunday 04:00 AM

Nathan released the bombs. As they cleared the plane, the small parachutes opened on all but one. That one fell much faster than the rest and the GPS receiver lost the signal and the controller was unable to guide it.

He raised the bomb rack, increased his speed, then pushed the control stick forward to drop his altitude as fast as possible. He looked out the canopy, trying to see the villa. It was too dark to see and he turned back to the front. "Good night, bastard," he said as he waited for the shock wave from the blast to hit.

~ ~ ~

Cortez stopped running just thirty feet from the villa's door, but kept firing at the Suburban as it moved away. "Get a vehicle! They can't get past the gate," he yelled at Raul.

Raul ran to one of the vehicles, started it and pulled up to where Cortez was standing.

The ground shook as the bomb with the failed parachute landed on the ground on the east side of the villa, blowing a large hole in the side of the building. Cortez put his hand on the Suburban to steady himself and looked back to see smoke rising over the roof of the villa.

The gunman saw the flash of light just before he reached the crest of the cliff.

Mayra, trembling, dropped down on the front seat, and yelled, "NOW WHAT ARE THEY SHOOTING AT US WITH?"

Seconds later, the other bombs crashed through the roof of the villa, on their way to Cortez's bedroom, where he was supposed to be sleeping.

The sudden force of a hundred and fifty pounds of high explosives caused the southwest area of the villa to be nearly leveled, debris flying as far as the ocean. Cortez saw his front doors fly by just ten feet from where he was standing just before the concussion from the explosion knocked him off his feet, slamming him into the vehicle, and covering him with smoke and debris.

The gunman jumped behind a nearby rock as the debris started hitting the ground close by.

~ ~ ~

Claudette stopped the vehicle.

Mayra said, "What happened?" as she turned her head and stared in disbelief at the smoke slowly moving around what was left of the villa. Then she turned back and saw Claudette bent over the steering column.

"Claudette, Claudette!" she yelled.

"I think you're going to have to drive now," Claudette said. "I think I have been shot."

Mayra carefully slid Claudette over to the passenger seat, then ran around to the driver's side and got in. She was scared. She saw a lot of blood around Claudette's shoulder, and she had never driven anything but the golf carts.

She slowly drove to the gate and yelled at the guard, "Open the gate, these people are hurt."

"What happened?" asked the guard.

"The villa blew up. Open the gate, I need to get these people to a hospital!" said Mayra.

The guard studied Mayra, the sweat on her face, Claudette's blood on her hands and clothes. He quickly looked back toward the destroyed villa, now visible only by the small flickering fires surrounding it.

"Hurry!" Mayra yelled, "Cortez doesn't want these people to die."

"OK!" he yelled as he quickly released the locks and opened the gates manually.

Mayra slowly moved the vehicle past the gate and headed to Puerto Vallarta.

~ ~ ~

Nathan watched the altimeter as he fell through 1500 feet on his descent. He backed off the control stick, and leveled out at 500 feet. He pushed the throttle to 100% as he tried to get as much distance as possible from what was left of the villa.

~ ~ ~

Clouds of dark smoke lingered and floated around what was left of the villa. A shaken Raul tried to peer out the cracked windows of the still running Suburban. The light from the headlights was being reflected back into the passenger area and he was unable to see past the hood. The amount of reflected light changed as the smoke passed by the headlights. He turned the motor off, headlights still burning, and sat there staring at the dark smoke creeping into the vehicle from the ventilation system. It floated above the passenger seat and grew in size as each second passed, then it started moving, slowly at first, traveling around inside the vehicle. The moving and constantly changing light gave the dark smoke an eerie lifelike appearance and it seemed to move with purpose, with intelligence, and it started to move toward Raul. Almost in panic, Raul pushed and pushed at the door. The debris lying next to the vehicle finally surrendered to his constant pushing and shoving. He got out and with his hand touching the side of the vehicle, walked around to find Cortez lying on the ground next to the vehicle with tile from the roof lying on top of him.

"Cortez, Cortez!" he yelled while shaking his shoulder.

Cortez could barely hear from the ringing in his ears, but he slowly moved his hand, and turned his head to Raul, and said, "What happened?"

"Cortez, are you OK?" asked Raul loudly.

Before Cortez could speak, another voice said, "He won't be for long."

Raul stood up, turned toward the voice, and could just make out the outline of a man standing ten feet in front of him. The dark smoke slowly passed around and between the two men as they stood staring at each other, then he asked, "Who are you?"

Cortez barely heard three muffled shots and watched Raul slowly fall at his feet, dead, from the tightly grouped bullet holes in the center of his chest. Dazed and bewildered, Cortez watched as the dark smoke quickly engulfed his lieutenant and longtime friend.

The gunman walked into Cortez's line of sight, bent down on one knee, and said, "So you're Cortez."

Still dazed and unsure of what had happened, Cortez said, "Who the fuck are you?"

"I'm Charles Dodson."

"Is that supposed to mean something to me?"

Charles smiled and said, "It might. I'm Kate Dodson's father." Then he pulled a 7 inch blade Ka-bar knife from its sheath.

As Charles put the point of the blade under Cortez's chin, a panicked Cortez grabbed Charles's arm. Cortez pushed as hard as he could against Charles's arm, but the blade gradually penetrated his skin. Soon, the blade was two inches deep, just past his tongue, and slowly headed for his brain. Cortez tried to push harder and tilted his head back as far as he could, but he was too weak, the blade of the knife kept moving, and now it was at the bottom of his brain. Cortez started to see visions of black smoky, shapeless, forms, quickly floating past his head. Sometimes they would stop in front of his face, stare at him, then quickly dart off.

Cortez slowly moved his eyes to look at Charles and tried to say something. Blood and saliva dripped down his jaws as he tried to speak, but the sounds from his mouth were nothing more than a gurgling noise instead of real words. Cortez and Charles stared at each other, eyes locked as they both seemed to peer deep into each other's soul.

Suddenly, Cortez felt his body starting to thrash and shake as the blade slowly entered his brain. The last thing he saw were the dark forms as they suddenly stopped and hovered in front of him, then they quickly entered his body. Cortez's grip on Charles's arm relaxed as the point of the blade reached the top of his skull. Charles twisted the knife handle, and slowly pulled the blade out. Cortez lay dead, looking up at Charles with blood slowly dripping from his lips and his chin, and his face locked in an expression of terror.

Chapter 27
Sunday 04:10 AM

A sudden jolt as the vehicle strayed off the road jerked Angelo awake. A soft painful moan escaped his lips as the Suburban rocked back onto the road, then settled back into its normal movements. He opened his eyes, listened, and tried to remember the things that had happened before he passed out. Cortez, the beating, his rescue, yes, the rescue. He moved his hand to his side where the pain was intense. Cortez must have broken some ribs.

There was a moan from the front seat. "I'm sorry Claudette," said Mayra, "are you OK?"

It was clear to Angelo from the strain in her voice that something was wrong. He pushed himself up from the seat and stared around the vehicle trying to clear his head. As the fog in his mind slowly evaporated, he noticed that Mayra was driving instead of Claudette. "What's wrong?" he asked. "How long was I out?"

Mayra yelled, "Claudette's been shot in the shoulder. I'm trying to get both of you to the hospital."

It took Angelo a few seconds to comprehend Mayra's words, then he said, "How long has it been since she was shot."

"I don't know, about ten minutes."

"Hi, Babe," said Claudette, her voice weak, "I'm glad you're OK."

"Thank God, you're alive," said Angelo. "How bad is it?"

"I can't see it, I just know it hurts like hell."

"Do you have a bandage on it?"

"No," Mayra said, "we were in a hurry to get out of there, and I didn't know if they were going to follow us after the villa blew up."

"You blew up the villa?"

"No, it just blew up as Cortez was shooting at us."

"I don't understand, but you can tell me about it later. We need to stop the bleeding. We need to put some kind of bandage on her shoulder," said Angelo. "Claudette, I need you to put the seat back and lay down, I'll try to bandage you as we're moving."

Angelo fought through the pain in his side and helped Claudette with the seat. "Mayra, I need some light, I'm going to have to turn on the overhead light. That's going to make it harder for you to see, so try to be extra careful."

Angelo tore her blouse open to examine her wounds. "I think the bullet went into the back of your shoulder then across and out right above your breast. Girl, you're going to have a scar, so you better be thinking of a story to tell our kids."

"Kids? How many are you thinking?" Claudette asked, as Angelo took his shirt off and tore it into strips.

"How many would you like?" he asked, as he wrapped her wounds.

"Ask me when we get back home, OK?"

"I'm sorry, Claudette, but we won't be able to go home."

"Why?"

"The police know about us, they will arrest us if we go back to the U.S."

"What are we going to do?"

"I know someone we can live with; she has a place overlooking the ocean. After we're better, we'll decide what to do."

Claudette, very weak and barely intelligible, said "Another one of your lovers?"

Mayra glanced around at them, wondering if she had heard Claudette right, and if Claudette was looking at her when she said it.

Angelo laughed. "Well, she was one of my first loves, and I must admit, I still have very strong feelings for her."

He bent over and gently kissed Claudette on the forehead. "Try to get some rest," he said as he covered her with his jacket and turned the light off. "Is she going to be OK?" asked Mayra.

"The bullet must have missed the major arteries or she wouldn't be alive. When we get to my friend's house, I'll call a local doctor that I can trust."

"You mean we're not going to the hospital."

"We can't, if we go there, we'll have to explain how she was shot, they'll call the police, and we'll be arrested. I don't think she would make it in a Mexican jail."

"OK. Am I headed in the right direction?" asked Mayra.

"You're headed to Puerto Vallarta, right?"

"Yes."

"Then we're good. Her place is about thirty minutes south of Puerto Vallarta."

His side and face hurt from the beating Cortez gave him, but that seemed insignificant compared to Claudette's ordeal - first in the bedroom, and then taking a bullet while saving their lives. He ran his hand gently down her cheek, stroking her soft skin. "Hang in there, girl," he whispered.

"Mayra, are you sure nobody followed us?" he asked.

"I don't think so."

He turned and stared out the back window. Nobody was staying behind them. The few cars on the road quickly passed them. "Mayra, why are you driving so slow?"

"This is the first time I've ever driven on a highway," she said nervously.

~ ~ ~

Sunday 09:00 AM, Gulf of California

Nathan yawned as he scanned the instrument panel. It had been a long night. The lack of sleep from the drive down, the long flight to the target, and the stress from the bombing had left him exhausted. Earlier, as the glow of the morning sun began to spill over the horizon, Nathan's eyes began to shut and his head began to slowly bobble. As soon as his chin reached his chest he quickly jerked his head up. His mind was foggy and he wasn't sure what had happened, but he knew he had to fight the feeling of panic that was beginning to enter his body. The shot of adrenaline from the scare began clearing his mind, but it took several seconds before he realized he was flying the plane. Thankfully the rest of the flight was uneventful and when he was about a half hour out he radioed David.

David, Dennis, and Max arrived at the runway about 9:50am and got the truck and trailer in position at the far end. When Nathan landed they disassembled the plane and were ready to go in 45 minutes.

Nathan got into the back seat of the truck and said, "I'm exhausted, guys. Please don't wake me until we get to the border." He lay down, put his hat over his face and minutes later started snoring.

Dennis glanced at Nathan as foghorn-like noises filled the truck and said, "These fly-boys sure have it easy!"

~ ~ ~

Santa Rosa, California

"Why are we here on a Sunday morning?" questioned Phillip Rawlins. "My wife had a fit when I told her I had to go to work."

"All I know is the Sheriff asked for us personally. He said he had something to give us. Something to do with David Dodson," said Ryan.

"Are we ever going to be through with that guy?" snarled Phillip.

The Sheriff met the two FBI agents at the front desk and asked them to follow him to a conference room. As they walked down the hall, they saw that everyone in the building was watching them.

Phillip said under his breath, "Is something wrong? Why is everyone looking at us like that?"

"I don't know and I don't like it. It gives me the creeps. It's like we're in a Hitchcock movie." replied Ryan.

The Sheriff opened the door, grinned, then said, "Come on in, gentlemen."

They followed him into the room and found 6 handcuffed men being guarded by two deputies. "What is this?" demanded Ryan.

"It's the men that you, David Dodson and his men, and the detective from Las Vegas, captured at the clubhouse, the night that my deputy and Brad Jarell were killed."

"What are you talking about?" asked Ryan.

"David Dodson asked me to include you two in my report. The interrogations of these men provided detailed information on one of the largest drug rings in California and Nevada."

Ryan said, "Sheriff, I'm surprised that you would be part of one of Mr. Dodson's jokes."

"Son, this is no damn joke. We have had men guarding them since all this started."

The Sheriff walked over to a box sitting on the conference table, put his hand on the box and said, "Here's the information you will need to bring yourselves up to speed. If you're interested in taking some credit for this bust then have a seat and start reading. If not, turn around and leave now."

For a moment the two FBI agents stared at each other, then turned their stare to the box. Phillip asked, "Why is Mr. Dodson doing this?"

"I think he feels bad about what he did to you two."

"Sheriff, why did Mr. Dodson go to Mexico?" asked Ryan.

"I think he just needed a vacation."

A deputy knocked on the door, entered, and spoke softly to the Sheriff.

The Sheriff started to laugh and said, "Tell the rest of the department. They need some good news." As the deputy left the room to spread the word, the sheriff leaned over putting both hands on the table. He quickly raised one hand and slapped the table. All eyes were now on him. He turned his head and stared at each of the 6 handcuffed men for a moment before he spoke in a slow clear voice, "Cortez is dead. Someone blew up his villa this morning."

The prisoners sat in stunned silence for several seconds, then suddenly started laughing and clapping.

Ryan asked, "Why are they so happy?"

"Because now," said the sheriff, turning to face Ryan, "they, and their families, might not get killed for talking to us."

"DAMN!" said Ryan, as a grin took over his face. "David Dodson on vacation, RIGHT!!!"

~ ~ ~

11:00 PM, Las Vegas, Nevada

Candy pulled the van into the apartment driveway and Joe said, "Let me out in front of the apartment, I'll make us some coffee while you park the van."

"No coffee for me, I've had enough of that. I think that's all policemen drink. All I want to do is get a shower, then sleep for a week."

Joe laughed. "Yeah, after staying at police headquarters all weekend, that does sound better."

Joe got out of the van and entered the apartment as Candy drove away. He went straight to the refrigerator and pulled out a cold beer. Then he parked himself in front of the computer desk and started to read his emails. He tagged several to delete just by looking at the subject line. Then movement on one of the security monitors caught his attention and he looked closer. There was the kid sitting on his bicycle in the driveway. He sat back in his chair and watched. There was something different this time, the kid seemed more nervous, more jumpy, than normal. Then he saw Candy coming in. She stopped in the open doorway when she noticed the kid watching her. Joe did a quick scan with the other cameras and saw a backpack leaning against the back door. Then he saw Candy turn and take two steps toward the kid as he reached into his pocket, pulled out a phone, and dialed.

Joe quickly backed his chair up, turned to the door and yelled, "CANDY, RUN!"

She had taken a few more steps when the explosion ripped the back of the apartment apart, blowing debris out the front windows and front door. She was knocked to the ground with enough momentum to push her across the asphalt, scrapping her arms, legs, and face. Her ears began ringing, and she was unable to hear the sounds of the debris falling around her. Instinctively she covered her head with her arms as she curled up on the ground. Moments later her body started to regain its senses. Her head hurt, and blood trickled down her face. She opened her eyes to find a slightly out of focus world as she peered around the arm that still covered her head. When she was able to make out some small detail, she realized that she was facing the street. Her attention moved to a blurry object that slowly crossed to the middle of the driveway and stopped. Her vision was clearing, and she knew something was there but was unable to make out exactly what it was. Slowly she moved her arm and put out her hand toward the object, only to see a young boy slowly ride off on a bicycle.

Every muscle in her body screamed as she painfully pushed herself up on her elbow to see what was left of the apartment building.

"Joe," she said softly, waiting, listening to hear his voice. "Joe," she said louder, again waiting, listening. "JOE! JOE!" she screamed.

Chapter 28

The early morning rain had washed away the stress, the fears, and the anxiety at Colten Vineyard. Kate and Libby breathed in the scent of wet dirt in the clear, warm morning air as they walked.

"You two seem to be better. Did you forgive him?" asked Libby.

Kate smiled. "Yeah, I can't stay mad at Randy for long."

"Kate, I hope you can forgive me someday."

Kate put an arm around Libby's shoulder as they walked by the hangar. "I don't blame you, or Joe, or Randy for what happened. I know that you were just trying to expose the bank. You thought that they were doing something criminal. And you were right, just not what you expected."

Randy yelled from the RV door, "Hey, you two might want to see this."

The news conference had already started by the time they got back to the RV. The Sonoma County Sheriff, two FBI agents, and one DEA agent were standing at the podium. The sheriff announced the capture of six men who provided information that led to the shutdown of one of the largest drug operations in California and Nevada history. Then the FBI agent took over and announced the arrest of Jerry Powell, a Las Vegas bank president, who was charged with several crimes, ranging from money laundering to illegal equity trading.

Kate started laughing. "See Libby, you did good."

"Yeah, but it cost Brad and the deputy their lives."

Kate put an arm around her again and held her tight.

~ ~ ~

Monday 01:00 PM

Jeffery drove up in one of the small trucks and parked in front of the RV.

Libby burst out of the RV. "I hope you're here for me," she said, as she threw her arms around him.

He kissed her. "I guess you heard the news conference this

morning?"

"Yes," she replied.

Jeffery noticed Randy and Kate standing in the door of the RV and waved. They waved back, then Kate turned to Randy and said, "Let's give them some privacy."

Jeffery and Libby started wandering away from the RV as Kate and Randy went inside. "I don't know if it's safe yet," Jeffery said. "The rest of the guys should be back tomorrow afternoon. I can pick you up then."

"Yes, but if we were to leave right now, we could be alone for 24 hours."

He smiled. "Well, I can see that I'm going to have a lot of trouble saying no to you."

She looked back at him with a big smile.

"OK," he surrendered. "But I don't know if I can handle you for 24 hours. My arm is a lot better but I don't know about 24 hours."

She kissed him, then smiled and said, "You're not going to be on top all the time."

~ ~ ~

Hotel, south of Puerto Vallarta, Mexico

"She needs to stay in bed. She's lost a lot of blood, and she has a fever. And give her these," said the doctor, handing Angelo the pain medication. "They'll help with the pain and help her sleep."

Claudette, sweating and uncomfortable, and weak from loss of blood, faded in and out of consciousness. At times she would throw the cover off her body, to cool off, to feel the freedom of nothing touching her, nothing holding her down. The moving air from the ceiling fan was a blessing, and the sound of it spinning around and around, chasing itself, like a dog chasing its tail would lull her back to sleep. But in her sleep the haunting images of that night would replay in her mind like a horror video in an endless loop. And she would jerk awake in a cold sweat, scared and shaking. Then the pain from moving her shoulder would hit her again.

She woke a few days later as a gentle hand placed a cool washcloth on her forehead. She opened her eyes and saw an older woman sitting on the side of the bed.

The woman smiled at her and said, "Hello, Claudette, how are you feeling this afternoon?"

"I don't know, where am I?" she asked.

The woman cradled Claudette's hand in hers, and said, "You're safe now, don't worry about that. You just lay there and rest, I'll come back later and put new bandages on your wounds, and if you think you can eat, I'll bring you some soup."

She looked at the woman and asked, "Is Angelo OK?" but before the woman could answer, the medication kicked back in, her eyes slowly shut, and she fell back asleep.

The woman gently pushed Claudette's hair out of her face and continued to sit on the side of the bed watching her sleep and thinking about her own daughter.

~ ~ ~

Monday 10:30 PM, Bodega Bay, California

Two sixty watt light bulbs emitted their illuminating energy from the ceiling fixture in the living room. No one was in this room to see its affect as it traveled, searching for objects to reflect from. The bedroom door stood partially open, allowing a small amount of this energy to quietly sneak in and peek at the two exhausted lovers lying on the bed, holding each other, still glowing from their day of exploring each other's bodies. Libby smiled as she laid her head on Jeffery's arm and watched his eyes slowly close, then open, then slowly close again. She ran her fingers gently through his hair as he slept, his injured arm laying over her, still holding her close.

Libby slid gently out of bed and took a quick shower. As she walked back into the bedroom, she laughed quietly to herself as her stomach began to growl loudly. They had stayed in each other's arms practically the whole time since they had arrived at his place at the clubhouse. They didn't want to let go of each other, not even to eat.

She opened his closet and found her favorite shirt of his, the black button down that she wore when they spent their first night together, washing her clothes. She left the bedroom leaving the door partially open, walked through the living room and into the open kitchen. The subdued light that reflected from the living room into the kitchen was enough that she didn't bother to turn the kitchen light on. She made a peanut butter and jelly sandwich and took it and her laptop to the sofa so she could check her email as she ate. She had not heard from Joe today; not that unusual, but she wanted to know if he had heard anything new about the bank. Then a slight noise near the front door distracted her. She almost ignored it, but something told her to look at the security monitor.

She stared at the monitor, stunned, as she saw the two men that had attacked her and Randy at his Las Vegas apartment. Carlos was picking the lock as Marcos stood near, ready to run in and secure the area. She stood up and dropped her laptop, then ran to the kitchen table to get her backpack. She took out the Taser that Max had given her, then dropped down to the floor behind the kitchen table and chairs. She held the Taser tightly in her hand as she listened to Carlos picking the lock, not knowing if there was time to warn Jeffery before they entered.

The door opened and the thirty second delay warning went off on the alarm control panel. She bent down low, hugging the table and chairs, and saw Marcos run in, quickly look around the kitchen and living area, then head straight to the bedroom. Carlos limped into the living area and stopped. She heard noises from the bedroom and could only imagine what the big man, Marcos, was doing to her Jeffery, but she could picture Jeffery putting up a good fight, slamming his face against the big man's fist. She was scared, and worried, but the Taser could only shoot one shot at a range of fifteen feet, without reloading.

The noise from the bedroom was distracting and seconds seemed like hours as she waited biting her lips. Shadows from the table blanketed her small body, concealing her from view. She held her breath as Carlos slowly walked into the kitchen and stopped at the table, across from her, the tips of his highly polished boots pointing at her, trying to give her location away.

Carlos turned around when a sudden crash came from the bedroom. When he did, Libby, unable to stand by anymore, stood up, aimed, and fired, sending thousands of volts through his body. He shook, muscles twitching in pain as the pulsing energy passed through him. Thirty seconds later his eyes rolled to the back of his head and he fell to the floor.

Libby waited until she was sure he was unconscious, then took out a new cartridge from her backpack, and replaced the one in her Taser. She quickly picked up Carlos's gun and put it in the refrigerator, behind the milk, where no man ever looks, then she ran to the bedroom where Jeffery was lying unconscious on the floor.

Marcos saw her enter and he turned and started coming toward her.

"How's your balls after I used them for soccer practice?" she taunted him.

His face turned red with anger as he remembered the last time they met. "You little bitch!" he growled.

She waited until he was five feet away; she wanted to be sure she did not miss this man. Then she raised the Taser and shot him in the chest. He stopped just a foot from her, started to shake, and then dropped to his knees. With his face twisted in pain, and fighting the muscle spasms, he looked at her and reached out and grabbed her leg.

When the gun stopped thirty seconds later, his eyes had gone blank and his hand had dropped from her leg, but he still wasn't unconscious. She yelled, "All I wanted was to spend time with my boyfriend, and you FUCKED THAT UP!" Then she reached down and pressed the two permanently mounted probes on the end of the Taser against his neck, and turned it back on. His head jerked back and within seconds he had toppled over like a giant sequoia struck down by lightning.

After he was down, she became aware of a loud noise. Angry, scared, and confused, she looked around the room for the source. Finally, she realized that the alarm had gone off and all she wanted to do was sit on the floor and cry.

But they won't stay unconscious for long, she thought, as she fought off the wave of anxiety. *I need to do something. What should I do? Do I tie these men up? Do I check on Jeffery?*

She took a deep breath. "OK," she said out loud, "I don't have any more cartridges for the Taser, I better get their guns." She took another deep breath. "I hope the police get here fast."

She searched the big man and found his gun. *I don't like the idea of shooting someone*, she thought, *but, if I have to....*

Adrenaline made her senses more aware of what was around her. *This is nothing like the video games that Randy and I would play after a long day of coding*, she thought as she ran back to the kitchen with the gun in hand, *this is not fun at all*. She stopped in her tracks. Carlos was not on the floor. She instantly raised the gun and pointed it around the room as her eyes scanned every location where someone could hide. She went around the table and looked into the shadows that had hidden her earlier. "Crap!" she said. There were only shadows staring back at her.

The front door was still open. *Maybe he left*, she thought, *he must have left.*

She closed and locked the door, then went to check on Jeffery. He was badly beaten, but still alive and able to talk to her. She picked up the phone, dialed 911, and told the operator that she needed an ambulance. She explained what happened, and gave a description of Carlos. Then she sat on the floor next to Jeffery, keeping a tight grip on the gun.

A tear ran down her face as she gently leaned over and kissed him on the forehead, and said, "I'm sorry, Jeffery."

He slowly raised his bloody head and looked at her through the only eye that he could open, and softly said, "Girl, don't be sorry, you saved my life, and not just tonight."

She wondered what he meant by, 'not just tonight,' but suddenly a noise from the center of the room grabbed her attention. The big man was stirring, regaining consciousness.

He raised his head and saw Libby, sitting eight feet away, staring at him, wearing nothing but Jeffery's shirt, and pointing his own pistol at him.

"My Taser is dead," she said solemnly, "I can't give you anymore behavioral modification treatments." She hesitated, "I'm sorry, maybe that's over your head, I mean shock treatments." Then she raised the gun and pointed it at his head. "Your next treatment will be more invasive, lobotomy maybe."

He pushed himself up to a sitting position, pulled the Taser wires out of his chest, and said, "You didn't kick my balls this time, thank you."

She kept the pistol pointed at him as a little grin appeared on her face. "No, but I did kick your ass."

He stared at her, then slowly he started laughing. "Yes, you did, you're the only woman to ever do that," he said.

"The police will be here soon, don't get up or I will kill you."

He studied her face. "You have never said that to anyone before, have you?"

Libby looked deep into his eyes and with a confidant voice said, "No, but I'm not the same girl that you met before."

He nodded his head. "I can tell," he said.

Chapter 29

The door to Claudette's bedroom squeaked as Mayra slowly opened it and entered with a load of fresh towels. She was walking by the bed when she heard Claudette asking, "Have they got you working?"

Mayra put the towels down on a chair and sat on the side of the bed. "How are you?" she asked.

Claudette's eyes were barely open, but she tried to smile as she answered, "I feel weak and drugged."

"I'm glad you're all right. We were very worried about you."

Claudette reached over and held Mayra's hand. "Mayra, thank you for saving our lives. I know that you must have sacrificed a lot to do that." She saw tears in Mayra's eyes and asked, "What's wrong?"

"Angelo told me that you had figured out that he and I were lovers. You knew that and you were still very nice to me. I want you to know that I'm very sorry."

Claudette squeezed her hand. "There is nothing to be sorry about. We're not married."

Mayra wiped the tears and said, "I think you will be soon. The way he talked to you in the car as he tried to stop the bleeding. I believe that he is very much in love with you."

"I love him, too."

"He is very special," said Mayra. "The weekend that we spent together, he never once treated me like a cheap whore."

Angelo walked to the bedroom door, leaned against the door frame, and asked, "What are you girls talking about?"

Claudette said, "Mayra was just telling me how special she thinks you are, and I agree with her."

"I found the gift that we bought her," said Angelo. "It's still in my jacket. Let me go get it."

Mayra looked at Claudette and said, "When did you buy me something?"

"The day we went out to Puerto Vallarta."

Angelo came back and presented her with a small box that she excitedly opened.

She gasped and put her hand over her mouth. "They're beautiful," she whispered as she stared at the contents of the box. "Thank you." Then she looked up and asked, "But why?"

Claudette smiled and said, "Every girl needs nice jewelry."

She grabbed Claudette's hand and said, "Thank you so much." She stood up and gave Angelo a hug and said, "I'm going to put them on," as she ran to the bathroom.

Angelo sat on the bed next to Claudette. "I guess I'm going to have to buy you another necklace, I can't find the one I bought you."

She smiled at him. "If that's what it costs to get away from Cortez, then it was worth it."

He pulled something out of his pocket and held it up so Claudette could see it. "I did find this for you."

"What is it?"

He smiled at her and said, "It's the bullet that went through your shoulder."

"What are you going to do with that?"

"I thought I might have a necklace made around it."

She started laughing, but stopped and said, "Oh God, stop it, it hurts to laugh."

"When you get better we can talk about it."

"OK, but I think it will take me a while before I can wear that. Right now, all I want to do is forget about that night."

Mayra came back and asked, "How do they look?"

Angelo smiled at her and said, "Mayra, you look beautiful."

"Thank you," she said, beaming.

Claudette took Angelo's hand. "You are special."

"You are, too." He bent over and gave her a soft kiss.

~ ~ ~

Santa Rosa, California

A deputy was sitting outside Jeffery's hospital room carefully eyeing anyone that entered. Jeffery was playfully arguing with Libby saying, "I don't need to stay in the hospital, you can take care of me at home, all you need is to dress up in a nurse outfit, you know, one with a sexy little short skirt."

Libby laughed and said, "If you think that will get you well faster, I'll see what I can do."

Jeffery was having trouble keeping his eyes open now, as the pain medication took hold, and Libby grew quiet. *I wish you felt like going home*, she thought. *I wish we didn't need this deputy guarding us.*

She could hear the deputy outside the door talking to someone about the upcoming football season. *Probably that man I saw mopping,* she thought, *cause that awful disinfectant smells like it's in the room.* Suddenly a chill went up her spine. *What if that man is here to kill us, what if the mopping is just to get near us! He could be a killer, an assassin!*

Then she couldn't hear them anymore. Suddenly she couldn't breathe. She was too frightened to move. *I have to do something. I have to see. Get up. Get up!* She slowly stood up and tiptoed to the door. She still didn't hear anything. She cracked the door open. The deputy was sitting there reading a sports magazine. He looked up at her and nodded his head.

She forced a smile, closed the door, took a deep breath and went back to her chair beside the bed. She watched Jeffery sleep, hypnotized by the slow movement of his chest. *Will this business with Cortez ever end?* she wondered. *Will we ever be able to stop looking over our shoulders? Even in death, he's still tormenting us.* A sadness overcame her and she had to fight back her tears.

A few hours later Jeffery opened his eyes again. Libby was curled up in a chair by a window, staring outside with a sad faraway look. He watched her for several minutes wondering what she was thinking, wondering if she was having second thoughts about being with him. "Lib, it's going to be all right. I'll be out of here soon, thanks to you saving my butt."

She turned her head and took a moment to look at the stitches and bandages on his arms and face, then she smiled and said, "Yeah, and I'm not ever going to let you forget it either."

They both laughed then Jeffery said, "I bet the guys won't either, I can hear David now saying that you really are turning into a biker chick."

They laughed harder, but Jeffery's face showed his pain. "Oh, God," he gasped, "I have to stop laughing, that hurts too much."

Libby softly bit her lips, trying not to laugh again, as she moved closer and took Jeffery's hand into hers. They stared silently at their entwined hands, and the sounds of the busy hospital and the machines in the room faded away as she started to slowly caress the back of his hand and arm. He smiled as he watched her slow gentle movements and thought about how much he enjoyed her touch and he fell into a deep relaxed state.

She brought her eyes up to his and softly asked, "Jeffery, last night in your bedroom, what did you mean when you said that I saved your life, and not just that night?"

Jeffery waited for a second. "Right before I met David," he said, "my life was a mess. I was hitting bottom. He and the guys saved my life. They gave me a purpose and they gave me something that I never got from anywhere else that I worked, friendship. For that, I'll always be grateful. But even with everything they did for me, I still felt that something was missing." He paused and took a deep breath. "Then you walked into the RV and started talking to me and I knew what I was missing. And girl, it was you. And you saved my life."

She took his hand. "No one has ever felt like that about me before," she said, fighting back her tears. She bent over and softly kissed him. As she pulled back, she said, "I love you."

"I love you, too."

She gazed at him lovingly for a moment, then grinned and said, "I guess I need to go shopping soon."

"Why?" he asked, puzzled.

"If I'm going to get you well faster, I guess I need to buy that sexy nurse uniform you mentioned."

He started laughing again, then said, "OH, stop it, that hurts."

She bent down and kissed his hand and gave it a gentle squeeze as she noticed the soft buzzing from the machine that controlled the morphine injection.

"Lib, do me a favor," he said, "don't mention to anyone what I said about the guys. Talking about my feelings like that. It would ruin my bad boy biker image."

She laughed as she watched the morphine take effect. His eyes slowly closed, his grip relaxed, along with the rest of his body, and she knew that he was now in a deep restful sleep. For several moments she stared at their hands, smiling, wondering whether he would even remember their conversation.

Thirty minutes later there was a soft knock on the door, then David walked into Jeffery's room and asked, "How is he doing, Libby?"

"He's not as bad as he looks. The doctor said he might be able to go home in a few days." Then she asked, "Did you just get back?"

"A few hours ago. The sheriff called and told me what happened."

"Don't be mad at Jeffery, I convinced him to take me back to the clubhouse, I guess I should have stayed in the RV with Kate and Randy."

"Libby, don't second guess yourself. The sheriff said that you saved his life so you were where you were supposed to be and you did what you needed to do. I will always be grateful to you for that." He sat down beside her and took her hand. "You should be proud of yourself, I am."

"Thank you," she said, fighting back her tears, "With everything that's happened, I needed to hear that."

"Hi, Boss," said Jeffery, groggily, "you're not trying to steal my girl, are you?"

"Hi, Stud. I'm glad you're going to be OK," said David. Then he grinned. "Libby is quite a woman and if I was a few years younger, I might just try to take her away from you," he winked at her, "but I don't know if I could handle her now."

Unaccustomed to compliments, Libby blushed. "OK, guys, enough of this silliness," she said sternly. But then she grinned and joked, "You can duel over me later."

Libby, still blushing, enjoyed her moment of attention. They had a brief moment of fun, laughing together. But before her blush had even had time to fade completely away, the laughter was gone and she squeezed David's hand. "I'm glad you're back," she said. "Did we really get him? Cortez?"

David nodded. "Yes, yes we did. I have some photos if you want to see them." He pulled out his phone and showed them the photos of Cortez and the villa, noticing that Libby never flinched as she looked at Cortez's corpse.

"Who took these?" asked Libby.

"I'm sorry, it's best that I not tell you. And if anyone ever asks, it might be best to say that you don't know anything about what happened."

She gave David a little grin and nodded her head.

As David was putting his phone away he looked at Libby and said, "I'm very sorry about Joe Morgan."

"What are you talking about?" she asked.

"I thought you knew. Someone blew up Joe's apartment Sunday

night. He's in a coma."

David and Jeffery watched as she closed her eyes, put her hand to her mouth, and shook her head.

"Libby, I'm so sorry, I thought you knew. Detective Rodriguez, from Las Vegas, sent me an email about it. He said that Candy was hurt, too. She has a broken leg," said David.

"No, I didn't know. I hadn't heard from Joe in a few days, so I was sending him an email last night when those men broke in. I never got to finish it."

"I still want all of you to stay at the clubhouse until we're sure this has blown over. But I'm taking Nathan back to Las Vegas tomorrow and I thought you, Kate, and Randy, could go too, so you can get some of your things and put everything else in storage. And while we're there, I'll take you to see Joe. I would like to meet him."

"What about Jeffery? He's going to need a lot of help," said Libby.

"Max is going to stay here. I'll have him watch Jeffery while we're gone."

"Libby, you go and see Joe, I'll be fine," said Jeffery.

~ ~ ~

Thursday 09:00 AM, Creech Air Force Base, north of Las Vegas, Nevada

Commander Nathan Connor disconnected the drone surveillance network tap and put it in his pocket, then walked back to his office, sat down and stared out the window.

"Commander, are you OK?" asked the man knocking at the open door.

"Yes, Captain. What is it?"

The man handed Nathan a large envelope. "Sir, here are the area photos you asked for."

"Thank you, Captain," said Nathan. "Close the door on your way out." He opened the envelope and spread the photos out on the desk. As he looked at them, he realized he was smiling. His smile grew bigger as he examined each photo of the remains of Cortez's villa. He felt a great relief, followed by a longing to see his wife and son. *It's time for a family vacation,* he thought, *a long overdue vacation.* He picked up his phone and called his wife.

Chapter 30
Hotel, south of Puerto Vallarta, Mexico

The lingering aroma of freshly brewed coffee filled the patio as Angelo gazed over his cup at a small catamaran playing in the light ocean wind. As he sipped the hot beverage, he thought about his mother and father. He barely knew them. He could remember the few times that he had seen them together, and it seemed to him now that he could remember seeing their love for each other. And he had felt their love for him. But he had to keep pushing away the thoughts of that horrible day that his mother had died. He couldn't bring himself to accept the fact that Cortez was her murderer and his half brother. Someday he would think about that, process it, and store it away in a deep corner of his memory, but not today. Today he wanted to remember the good things.

Claudette opened the door, slowly walked out onto the patio, and said, "This is a beautiful view."

"Hi." Angelo put his coffee back on the table and turned around to look at her. "I'm glad to see you feel like getting up." He helped her to a chair at the table. "Would you like some coffee?"

"Yes, please." She looked out at the bay. "Where are we?" she asked.

"This is my friend's place," he said.

"Is that the woman that has been nursing me?"

"Yes." Angelo watched her as she looked out at the bay and sipped her coffee. "You're not going to ask me about her?"

"I know you will tell me when you're ready." She took his hand and asked, "Where is Mayra?"

"She wanted to help out. I think she is cleaning some of the bungalows."

"How many bungalows does your friend have?"

"Here, about fifteen. She also owns two more properties with twenty on each. She likes to stay busy, so she manages this one and hires someone else to manage the others."

Claudette said, "Since we're broke, I guess I need to help out as soon as I'm able."

Angelo started laughing. "I can't see you cleaning bathrooms and changing sheets."

She gave Angelo a mean look and said, "I'm going to have to do something."

"Claudette, you're up," said Angelo's friend, as she walked onto the patio. "It's good to see you moving around now."

"Hi," said Claudette, turning slowly to face her. "I want to thank you for helping us, especially knowing how much trouble I have been."

She bent over and gave Claudette a kiss on the forehead and said, "You're no trouble at all."

"Angelo has never told me your name," said Claudette.

The woman looked at Angelo and said, "She took a bullet while saving your life, I think she deserves to know who I am."

"Yes, you're right. Claudette, this is my grandmother, Felicia."

"I'm so pleased to meet you." Claudette smiled. Then she turned to Angelo. "Why did you tell me that she was dead?"

"I told everyone that she was dead. I knew that I had to somehow protect her before I got involved with Cortez. I knew if something went wrong he would come after her. So I made it look like she died in the U.S. Then I bought this place so she could live here and have an income if something happened to me."

Felicia said, "I really hated that he got involved with Cortez; I didn't want him to do it. I thought about taking a switch to him, but I think we both have gotten too old for that."

Claudette started laughing. "You and I must sit down and talk about him some day. I would love to know about his childhood."

Felicia smiled. "Yes, we must do that." Then she looked at Angelo.

Claudette noticed the look and said, "Oh, God, I'm sorry Angelo, I forgot about your mother."

Angelo took her hand, brought it to his lips, and kissed it. "Don't be sorry. I want you to know everything about her."

"I'll go back to the office and let you two talk," said Felicia. "If you need anything just call."

When she was gone, Angelo said, "I'm sorry I lied to you about her."

"You had a very good reason. Don't be sorry for protecting her."

They sat quietly, sipping their coffee, and watching the activities along the beach. Claudette watched two topless young women walk onto the beach and lie down to sunbathe.

"Is this a topless beach?" she asked.

"All the beaches are public, and it's illegal to go topless," said

Angelo. "That said, unless a lot of people complain about it, it's very seldom enforced."

She gestured at the newspaper on the table. "Is there anything about Cortez in there?"

"Yes, it seems everyone was surprised that the body of a drug lord was found next to a destroyed villa that was supposed to be owned by a wealthy businessman from Mexico City." He took a long moment and glanced at her, then continued, "Cortez and Raul didn't die in the blast. The police found them outside, in front of the villa. Cortez died from a knife wound to the throat, and Raul had three bullet holes in his chest."

Claudette said, "Who did that, and why blow up the villa?"

"The police think it was probably a rival drug cartel."

"You don't sound convinced. Who do you think it was?"

"I'm thinking it might be those bikers who were hiding Kate Dodson. They'd have the motivation to protect her and they'd want revenge for the death of their man in the hospital. A lot of bikers are ex-military, and they somehow captured all the men that Cortez sent to the clubhouse. It was no secret that Cortez loved that villa and that he spent every weekend there. I think the bikers interrogated Cortez's men and found out about the villa and when Cortez would most likely be there. They also had enough time to put something like this together."

She stared at the table for several seconds before saying, "Are we safe here?"

He could hear the concern in her voice. He reached up and moved her hair back from her face and said, "I believe we are. That's why I had Mayra drive us here instead of the hospital." He paused a moment, "I know I risked your life in doing that. But it's the only way I knew to keep us safe. I have been very, very careful about my grandmother and this place. I don't think anyone would know to look for us here." He paused another moment. "I think we'll be OK here. I will have to secure some new papers for us."

"We are going to need a lot of money to hide," said Claudette. "What are we going to do?"

"While I worked at the bank, I talked Cortez into letting me hide his money. He paid me a small percentage, and I soon made enough to pay off the loan on this property, and then later to purchase the other properties, and I put a little aside for retirement. All the properties are paying for themselves. We won't be able to live in a big villa, but with your help in choosing the proper investments, we could live a very comfortable life here."

Claudette became very quiet, sipped her coffee and watched as two young men started talking to the two topless girls sunbathing on the beach. "What about my brother?" she asked. "Do you think Antoine is all right? Do you think I will ever be able to see him again?"

"He helped the police, he'll be OK. I'm sure they have him in witness protection. But you won't be able to see him. I'm really sorry."

Claudette became very quiet again and Angelo wondered what she was thinking as she stared silently out at the water. He worried that she was upset about everything that she had lost. He had always known that if things went wrong in the United States that he would lose his house and car, and everything else he had there, and he had made plans to come back to Mexico. But he hadn't known Claudette when he made his plans. Now she would be a fugitive, too. She would never be able to see her brother again. Maybe she would resent him, maybe she would hate him.

"Two," she said.

Angelo gave her a puzzled look.

She turned to look at him and said, "The other day you asked me how many kids I wanted, that's how many I would like to have. At least two kids."

~ ~ ~

Saturday 06:00 PM, Santa Rosa, California

The deputy grabbed his radio and said, "I need an ambulance to the county jail. I have one to transport to the hospital."

"What happened?" asked the sheriff as he ran into the jail cafeteria.

The deputy pointed to two handcuffed men lying on the floor and said, "Those two jumped him, he's not looking very good, that's why I called for the ambulance."

The sheriff looked down and realized that it was Marcos who was bleeding on the floor. "Cuff him right now!" he ordered. "This guy is dangerous!"

Two EMTs were brought into the cafeteria and they secured the prisoner to the stretcher, then rolled him out to the ambulance under the deputy's watchful eye. One of the EMTs and the deputy got into the back of the ambulance with Marcos while the other EMT got into the driver's seat and started driving to the hospital.

Marcos kept his eyes shut, listening to the two men talking over the crying of the siren. Suddenly, he heard the tires screech and the men yelling as they grabbed hold of anything they could to keep from falling.

Marcos opened his eyes and smiled when he heard the back doors of the ambulance open and his long time partner, Carlos, yell, "Toss your gun out and take those damn handcuffs off of him now!"

As Carlos's team kept their guns on the deputy and EMTs, Carlos and Marcos ran back to their car. When they jumped in the back seat and the driver pulled away, the gunmen raced to the second car and followed.

"Thanks, Boss," said Marcos as they sped away. "Now I want to get that woman!"

"What are you talking about?"

"That little bitch, Libby! She kicked my ass twice. I can't let her get away with that!"

"You'll have to let it go!" Carlos said. "We have to get back to Mexico. We're wanted men here."

"I want to get her now! Cortez would understand that!"

"Cortez is dead! We have to regroup, plan."

Marcos looked stunned. "Dead? No!"

"And now, with your escape, Libby will be heavily guarded. It's better to wait."

"DAMN!" Marcos shouted. "Dead? How?"

"I don't know the details."

"Damn!" he shouted again. He stared out the front window, cursing under his breath, as he forced himself to calm down, to think it through. "OK," he said at last, "I'll let her go. For now."

~ ~ ~

One Month Later, Yosemite National Park

Very little water was flowing over the upper and lower Yosemite Falls as David, Dennis, and Max got off their motorcycles and stored their leather jackets. They looked around the visitors' parking lot and saw Kate, Randy, Jeffery, and Libby arrive in one of the club's crew cab trucks. Travis and Sharon Colten were already there and when they saw the others arriving they got out of their car and went to meet them.

"I guess we're all here," David said, as he took the backpack with the container of Brad's ashes off the back of his bike. He put his arm through one of the shoulder straps and said, "Let's go."

Everyone followed David as he walked out of the parking lot and down a path to a meadow between the river and the chapel. When he found a spot he liked he stepped a few feet off the path. Jeffery, Max, and Dennis went with him.

Travis put his arm around Sharon as they watched from the path with Kate, Randy and Libby.

David took the container out of the backpack. "Goodbye, friend," he said, as he emptied it among the tall grasses and wildflowers of the meadow.

Jeffery walked back to Libby and saw a tear fall from her eye. He put his arms around her and held her close, then said, "Let's go for a walk."

Randy and Kate followed them to a wooden footbridge over the river. They leaned on the rail and silently watched the water flow underneath their feet.

Their reverie was broken when suddenly a woman yelled, "Do you know what you're doing?"

A red kayak was floating down the river toward them and the older man and woman in it were trying to steer it away from the legs of the bridge.

"No, Honey," the man answered, "but aren't we having fun!"

The older couple looked up and waved. Just as the kayak started passing under the bridge, the old man saw Libby and Randy standing beside each other, and he raised his hand and gave them a thumbs up.

Libby and Randy looked at each other and said at the same time, "Was that the couple we saw in Vegas pulling that small trailer?"

~ ~ ~

A hundred yards away, a black Suburban with tinted windows was parked on the side of the road. A slim Panamanian man was sitting in the passenger seat, binoculars to his eyes.

"Do you see him?" asked the large, muscular driver as he stared over the steering wheel at the group.

"No, I see his brother and daughter, but not Charles Dodson," said the passenger bitterly. He lowered the binoculars, but continued to stare at the group. "Let's go," he said, "I don't think he's going to show."

David was still standing in the meadow with Travis, Sharon, and his men, talking, when the Suburban spun its large tires in the gravel that lined the side of the road. The tires finally found solid asphalt, and it slowly made its way down the road. David watched as the big vehicle passed by and said in a very low voice that only he could hear, "That looks like trouble."

The End

Thank you for reading my novel, The Sonoma Project, the first in this series. I hope you found this story as entertaining as I did while writing it. I need your help. The only advertising I have is you, so I need you to please rate this book. The easiest way is to go to my website that's listed below, then click on the appropriate retailer.

www.vernonjessup.com

About The Author

My wife and I make our home in Memphis, Tennessee, where I am constantly working at my computer, writing, doing research, computer programming, or just trying to keep up with the new technologies that seem to change the world overnight.

About The Characters

Kate "Kitten" Dodson: Office manager, JP Bank of Nevada
David Dodson: Retired Army Ranger, Kate Dodson's uncle, biker
Charles Dodson: Ex Army Ranger, Kate Dodson's father, wanted by the FBI
Randy Hunter: Programmer, Kate Dodson's boyfriend
Libby Harrison: Programmer, works with Randy Hunter,
Joe Morgan: Disabled Army Veteran, programmer, friend of Libby Harrison
Candy Fletcher: Works with Joe Morgan

Dennis Lawford: Retired Army Ranger, biker, rides with David Dodson
Max Henderson: Ex Army Ranger, biker, rides with David Dodson.
Jeffery Hodges: Graduate MIT chemical engineer, biker, rides with David Dodson
Brad Jarell: Musician and band member with Travis Colten, biker, rides with David Dodson

Hernando Cortez: Mexican drug lord
Angelo Diego: Vice president of JP bank of Nevada, Works for Cortez
Jerry Powell: President of JP Bank of Nevada
Claudette Godard: Programmer, works for Angelo, Antoine's sister
Antoine Godard: Computer engineer, works for Angelo, Claudette's brother
Mayra Garcia: Companion, works for Cortez
Raul Melendez: Cortez's Lieutenant
Fernando Melendez: Works for Cortez, Raul Melendez's brother
Carlos: Works for Cortez
Marcos: Works for Cortez
Felicia: Angelo Diego's grandmother

Nathan Connor: Cmdr. Creech Air Force Base

Travis Colten: Owns a vineyard with wife Sharon Colten, pilot, musician and band member with Brad Jarell

Sharon Colten: Owns a vineyard with husband Travis Colten, friend of Brad Jarell

Miguel Sanchez: Sheriff of Sonoma County, California, friend of David Dodson

Alec Cooper: Pres. Santa Rosa Chemical

Jack Cooper: Pres. of a fertilizer manufacturing plant, Alec Cooper's brother

Hector Rodriguez: Detective, Las Vegas Police Department

Gary Coleman: Capt., Las Vegas Police Department

John Lawson: Detective, Las Vegas Police Department

Glen Carter: Detective, Las Vegas Police Department

Ryan Powell: FBI agent

Philip Rawlins: FBI agent

'Captain' Jack Roberts: Pres. of CJ Global Securities Inc., Miami, Florida

Frank Warwick: Dir. of Intelligence of the DEA Miami Field Division, feeds information to Jack Roberts

Lara Manning: Fired from JP Bank of Nevada

Jane Taylor: The witness

.